HILDA

THE JUGGLE

EMMA MURRAY

Boldwood

First published in Great Britain in 2021 by Boldwood Books Ltd.

Cover Design by Alice Moore Design

Cover Illustration: Everyday People Cartoons

A CIP catalogue record for this book is available from the British Library.

Paperback ISBN 978-1-83889-485-6

Large Print ISBN 978-1-83889-486-3

Ebook ISBN 978-1-83889-487-0

Kindle ISBN 978-1-83889-488-7

Audio CD ISBN 978-1-83889-480-1

MP3 CD ISBN 978-1-83889-481-8

Digital audio download ISBN 978-1-83889-483-2

Boldwood Books Ltd
23 Bowerdean Street
London SW6 3TN
www.boldwoodbooks.com

For my husband, Sam, and our two daughters, Ava and Anya. None of this would have been possible without you.

1

My four-year-old daughter Anna has been at school for two weeks now, and frankly I'm already having second thoughts. For starters, I appear to always be late for pick-up and today is no exception. I grab my raincoat and keys and shut the door behind me. Two seconds later, I let myself back in again. I have forgotten to bring Anna's snack. Last week I forgot her snack and she started screaming at me in the middle of the playground. The mortification was endless. I have lived in fear of a repeat of 'snackgate' ever since. So, I open the 'cupboard of crap', as my husband David likes to call it, and grab a packet of those flavoured cheesy cracker things that flight crew sometimes give you on the plane. I can't even think of them now without feeling airsick.

Shoving the snack into my pocket, I walk out of the door a second time, and head down our street, pausing at the end as usual, antennae poised to scout for any sign of the Organics – another reason I am not exactly enthralled with Anna starting school. The Organics are a group of 'supermums' who only feed their children top-of-the-range organic food and judge other mums (like me) for giving their children total rubbish. They are also anti-screens – TV, iPads (or free babysitters as I like to call them) are out, and they frown upon full-time working mums (why have kids at all if you're not at home with them 24/7?). Top of my list to avoid, of course, is Chief Organic Tania Henderson, hideous administrator of our local Facebook group, Vale Mums, but any one of her entourage of judgemental keyboard warriors is just as bad. Typically, most of the Organics' offspring are now in Anna's class, which makes them much harder to avoid. So far, I am relieved to see that the coast is clear. I shove my hands in the pockets of my light grey raincoat, surprised at the sudden drop in temperature. It's mid-September and probably still around eighteen degrees, but after the scorching summer it seems a lot cooler. My phone pings. Then it pings again... and again. My stomach sinks. Multiple pings can only mean one thing. I reef my phone out of my pocket, hating myself for not having the willpower to ignore the messages.

Caroline (Senior Organic who always wears a complicated ballet bun):
Ooops! Forgot Oscar's school snack and I'm already at the school!! Such a bad mum. (Covered face emoji.)

Tania:
(Crying laughing emoji.) Don't worry, we've all done it! He can share some of Heath's yoghurt raisins instead.

Jane (Full-time working mum who I haven't met yet):
I'm in work but I'm pretty sure our nanny packed some cheesy crackers for Holly if you want to add that to the mix.

Tania:

So nice of you Jane, but I think those crackers might be a bit too salty
for my LO!

And there it is, the classic Organics' judgement.

Jane doesn't reply (understandably, given she has just been
accused of poisoning her child) and I march on, shoving my
phone back in my right pocket, trying not clench the packet of
cheesy crackers in my left pocket too hard for fear they will end
up in tiny pieces. Technically, this is all my fault. I joined the class
WhatsApp group because I reasoned it couldn't be any worse
than the Vale Mums Facebook group, but I was wrong. Now,
instead of raging at the Organics' comments at my leisure on
Facebook, I am instantly bombarded by their WhatsApp texts all
the live-long day.

I'm just about to reach the zebra crossing in front of the
school when I hear a familiar low rumbling noise behind me.
The sound grows louder and my ankles start to twitch. Instinctively, I take a step sideways, and just about miss a collision with
Tania, who sails by, without a word of apology for almost ham-
stringing me, on her adult scooter. She flies across the zebra
crossing in her usual uniform of padded gilet with yoga top and
black designer leggings. This happens almost every day – the
near miss, the no apology. And it's not just Tania who does this
with her lethal death machine – it's her whole gang too. Not a day
goes by when I'm not at risk of having my ankles sawn off by one
of her bloody Organics crew. And it doesn't help that Tania and
her minions have practically taken over the whole class, leaving
nobody for me to talk to.

My best mum friend, Bea once told me that all I needed to do
is find one friend at school: to ask about homework, bitch about
the Organics and slag off the PTA, but I haven't even managed to
do that. Given that Tania has bulldozed her way into the chief

PTA job, you can imagine how desperate I am to slag her off to another class mum, but I haven't found quite the right fit yet. But having no pals at school isn't my only problem. My heart quickens the second the school gates come into sight, and I crane my head to see who's standing outside to greet the parents. My heart rate slows in relief when I spy the assistant head teacher there. At least it's not the head teacher – I can't bear to see him today, or any other day, in fact. Feeling a bit more relieved, I walk into the playground and take my usual spot by the back fence opposite Anna's classroom. Against all odds, the big school clock tells me that I'm ten minutes early, so I lean against the black wire fence, and take out my social crutch, or iPhone as some people call it, to pretend I'm not the Billy-no-mates that I appear to be.

After a couple of minutes of tapping at nothing, I glance up at the clock again. The playground is starting to fill up, and I take a moment to marvel at the uniformity of it all. The eight scooter mums (Organics) huddle together just outside the classroom door, identically dressed in designer gym gear, speaking in hushed voices, no doubt slagging off the full-time working mums for 'neglecting' their children; the nannies and au pairs gather at the other side, feverishly tapping their phones, rarely talking to each other; and the two Charity dads stand in identical power poses in the centre of the playground, swapping cricket, football or rugby scores. I call them the Charity dads because I have over-heard them talking loudly about 'doing something for charity every month'. Which is all very well and good until you hear them constantly bitch about the daily 10,000 steps they are undertaking for 'Steptember'. I glance over in their direction, wondering if they'll be brave enough to go sober for October.

Finally, there's Ambrose, the casually dressed, permanently 'plugged in' trendy guy, who always stands to my left, his head encased in noise-cancelling headphones. Technically Ambrose and I should be friends or at least acknowledge each other now and then. After all, his daughter, Milly is Anna's new best friend, but I have never approached him. His firmly crossed arms and blank stare don't exactly feel like an invitation to socialise. Then again, perhaps it's for the best. Milly might have told her dad that Anna regularly refers to her as 'Milly with the brown face' – something which I have tried to put an end to but it's not as easy as you think trying to explain race relations to a genuinely perplexed four-year-old ('But she *does* have a brown face'). Even so, I would like to meet Milly's mum, but I have never seen her at school, so maybe Milly's mum isn't in the picture, and I'm loathe to open that can of worms.

Time continues to tick by slowly and the autumn chill starts to eat into my bones. As I reach into my pocket to get Anna's snack, I see a familiar petite figure moving lightly towards me and my heart sinks into my boots.

So, here's the thing: although it's true I have no real friends at school, that doesn't mean I am always by myself. Sometimes I am joined by Diana, the impossibly perky mum with her bouncy shiny hair and carefully straightened fringe, from the 'other' reception class. Just before school started a couple of weeks ago she had dropped over a parcel (a new vibrator but she doesn't know that) that had been accidentally left at her house in the next road to ours by the delivery guy. Instead of doing a quick drop and go, she stood on my doorstep chatting aimlessly for a good twenty minutes. Looking back on that first interaction, it was small talk at its worst. No area of mundanity was left uncovered: the weather ('What a hot summer we had – can't believe it's going to be autumn soon' – accompanied by exaggerated shiver); the kids ('What a coincidence that both our children are going to the same school!' – I would soon find out that Diana is the type of person who thinks *everything* is a coincidence); and how she couldn't believe how much time had flown by and that her son Jonty had actually reached school-going age. I found it hard to engage with that last one, because frankly, after dealing with Anna full-time for the last couple of weeks of the summer, I've been living for her to start school.

But the small talk wasn't the worst of it. It was only when I met Diana on the school run on the first day that I found out that she is a diagonal walker. Instead of walking beside me and keeping a suitable distance like most people, Diana bumped her hip against mine before walking diagonally directly into my path, forcing me to come to a sudden halt lest I trip over her intrusive leg. What had begun as a normal routine walk to school had turned into a merry dance of stops and starts punctuated by mumbled apologies (her) and ill-disguised swear words (me). Now, every time I see her on the walk to school, I leg it so I don't have to deal with the constant hip-bumping and excruciating small talk. But here I am trapped against the school fence with nowhere to hide.

'Hi, Saoirse!' she says, bumping her hip with mine, which is eminently frustrating given we are both stationary.

'Hi, Diana,' I reply, taking a deliberate step to the side.

'It's getting colder, isn't it?' she says, her fringe hopping up and down as she shifts her weight from one foot to another, mercifully not moving any closer.

'It is.'

'What have you been up to today?'

I want to say 'masturbating' because it's true (thanks for delivering that parcel, Diana!) but since that goes against all the rules of small talk, I say, 'I did a bit of washing,' (also true).

To my dismay, her face brightens.

'What a coincidence! I did some laundry, too!'

Then a pause.

'Colours or whites?' she says, her little face full of expectation.

'Which one did you do?' I say.

'Whites,' she says, laughing (for no reason). 'What about you?'

'Colours,' I say, just to watch her face fall (it was whites but my nerves won't allow any more than one 'What a coincidence!' per conversation).

Mercifully the school clock finally settles in the right place and the kids start spilling out of their classrooms. Diana rushes off to pick up her child, and before I know it Anna has wrapped herself around my legs, shouting for a snack. I give her too long, tousled brown hair ('No, Mummy! You can't cut it. I'm trying to grow it like Wapunzel!') a kiss and ask her how her day has been.

'Snack!' she says.

I reach into my pocket but her little hand finds the packet before I do, and she rips it open with her teeth and starts shovelling the yellow rounds of fake cheese and salt into her mouth as if she hasn't been fed for months. I'm just about to tell her to slow down when something unexpected happens. A little boy appears beside Anna and makes a grab for her cheesy crackers. Anna hesitates but then gives him a few, which surprises me because Anna is not known for her sharing abilities. The little boy chews thoughtfully, and then smiles at Anna. 'Yummy!' Then he looks me dead in the eye and says, 'I want a playdate with Anna.' Now this wouldn't be such an issue if it wasn't for one teeny tiny problem. You see, the little boy is Heath Henderson. Tania's son. I wouldn't mind but Anna hasn't given him so much as a mention since she started school. How are they on playdate terms? Things are moving too fast. I look at Anna, praying that she tells Heath where to get off. After all, her best 'boy' friend is Harry, Bea's son – she wouldn't dare look at anyone else. But, judging by the adoring look she throws at Heath, her head has been turned.

'Can Heath come to our house, Mummy? Pleaaaase...'

I shake my head in what I hope looks like a regretful manner. Of all the kids she could have taken up with...

Then Heath joins in and now they're both begging me as if their little lives depended on it. Enough.

'Oh, sweetheart, we're a bit busy today,' I say, in the saddest tone I can muster.

I have bugger-all planned for after school, but she doesn't know that.

'Pleaaaase, Mummy,' she says, her big brown eyes filled with desperation.

'Pleaaaase,' Heath echoes.

Time to change tack.

'I'm sure Heath's mummy is busy too,' I say, gesturing towards Tania, who is still gossiping by the classroom door, hoping he'll bugger off to his mum, so I can skedaddle with Anna. But Heath just looks at me and shakes his blonde curls.

'We're not busy,' he says sullenly.

Then the pleading starts again and I start to feel flustered. How the hell am I going to get out of this one? There is no way this playdate is going to happen. Suddenly I notice Tania's eyes start to wander, and then narrow as they settle on Heath and Anna. She crosses the playground quickly and immediately bends down to Heath.

'Oh, there you are, darling. I've been looking for you everywhere.'

This is total bullshit, obviously, given that she's clearly been knee-deep in gossip this whole time.

'What do you have on you?' she says, fussily wiping off the yellow crumbs off his mouth left over from Anna's cheesy crackers.

'Anna gave them to me,' Heath says, happily.

Tania straightens, folds her arms and glares at me.

'I don't usually give Heath that type of snack,' she says, through a frozen smile.

Of course – death by sodium. How could I forget?

'Don't you?' I say breezily. 'He loved it!'

Before she can reply, Heath and Anna join hands and start an ear-splitting chant of 'Playdate *now!*' A look of horror descends over Tania. Like me, she has no desire to encourage any bonding between our two children. She tries everything from 'We're busy' (nope) to 'We have to go and pick up Daisy' (Heath's little sister) but Heath outs her with that one by saying, 'No, we don't – she's at Gran's tonight.'

Tania runs her fingers through her long dirty-blonde hair, grimacing in frustration. Suddenly I have a brainwave.

'Oh, my goodness, I totally forgot!' I say slapping the side of my head as dramatically as possible. I bend down to Anna and whisper, 'You have a playdate with Harry today!'

I make a mental note to text Bea the second we leave school – I have no idea if Harry is around or not.

Anna instantly stops whingeing and a wide smile spreads across her face. Heath starts to sob and then scream.

'Well, come on, let's go!' Anna says, tugging my hand. And off we go, leaving a bereft Heath and a harassed Tania in our wake.

I knew Heath had just been a fly-by-night passing fancy, I think smugly, as we approach the school gate. Harry will always be her true north. I am so lost in my thoughts that I don't notice the head teacher standing there until it's too late. Jesus, why isn't there more than one way out of this bloody school? I take a deep breath and try to walk past him without making eye contact. Then Anna pipes up.

'Bye, Mr Wussell!'

I have no choice but to give him a brief nod. To my annoyance, he is already traffic-light red. I turn away and lead Anna out of school as quickly as I can. Anna is too busy chatting about her fictional playdate with Harry to notice how fast her little legs are going. Honestly, I'm not sure how long I can put up with whole Mr Russell thing for. I mean, I wish he would just get over it. After all, it must be at least ten years since I gave him a blowjob.

2

As soon as we leave the school gates, I text Bea, praying she and Harry are around this afternoon. She sometimes works from home on Wednesdays and I'm pretty sure she said something about 'insult day' happening this week, which is Bea-speak for inset day – a training day for teaching staff which means an extra day off school for kids. I am just hoping Harry is around, otherwise Anna is going to destroy me. Two minutes later, Bea gives me the thumbs-up. I break the good news to Anna who does a little jig in the middle of the street and then demands that we go 'wight now!' So we take the route to Bea's house, Anna skipping the whole way there.

I can't help but do a double take when we get to Bea's street. I'm not the most observant but I'm pretty sure I haven't seen the mustard-yellow Maserati parked in front of her red Fiat Uno before. It looks completely out of place on her narrow street lined with modest, red-brick terraced houses. Instinctively and perhaps unfairly, I glare at the car and mutter the word 'wanker' under my breath as I press the doorbell. Bea opens the door almost instantly with a look of rage in her eyes. Her usually naturally straight, highlighted blonde hair is dishevelled and there are blobs of something cream-coloured on her fitted navy sweater.

'Playdate?' I guess.

She nods grimly.

'He's a little prick,' she hisses in my ear, as she ushers me and Anna into the house.

I throw a doubtful look at Anna. She's not going to be happy that she doesn't have Harry all to herself. Bea catches the look and bends down to Anna. 'Sweetheart, Harry's friend is called Mathias and he's a very bad boy. You tell me if he's being mean to you, okay?'

Anna gives Bea a serious nod and runs off upstairs. She loves being a tattletale.

'What are they doing up there, anyway?' I say, peering up the stairs, worried that I have just sent Anna into battle with no armour to defend herself.

'They're watching a movie,' Bea says. 'Mathias isn't allowed television or any other type of screen in his house so I figured the novelty would shut him up. That and a big bowl of popcorn and four thousand jellies should do the trick.'

'Take a rest and I'll make us a cup of coffee,' I say, linking her arm and steering her into the kitchen.

She flops down on one of the wooden kitchen chairs with a groan and surprises me by telling me that she can't face coffee. To put this into context, Bea normally drinks about five cups of coffee a day – she even takes one into the bath with her (when she's not drinking wine, that is).

I look closely at her; her usually sallow skin is pale and her eyes are a little bloodshot.

'Are you feeling all right?' I say, abandoning the kettle to come and sit next to her.

She takes off her glasses and buries her head in her hands.

'Is the playdate that bad?' I quip, but inwardly I am worried about her. She doesn't look well at all.

'The playdate is horrific,' Bea says, sighing as she raises her head. 'In hindsight, it was a gigantic mistake to suggest that we make our own pizza.'

'From scratch?' I say, horrified.

She gives me a weary nod.

'It was one of my mother's recipes and it looked so simple: a bit of flour, yeast, water... what could possibly go wrong?'

Bea's mum is the famous Arianna Wakefield, the children's cookbook author with the unfeasibly immaculate apron.

'So, I'm guessing the boys got a bit carried away with the dough, then,' I say, spotting a few more drops in her hair.

'Well, Mathias seemed to think it was hilarious to roll the dough into little balls and fire them at me,' she says.

'What did Harry do?'

'He just laughed, the little traitor,' she says, picking angrily at the stains on her jumper as if it's the first time she's noticed. I don't have the heart to tell her she has some bits in her hair too.

'So, after all that, we couldn't make the pizza and I had nothing else in for lunch, so I had to dig into the emergency supplies,' she continues.

The corners of my mouth start to twitch. I'm dying to know what she gave them in the end.

'So, what did you do?'

'I already told you,' she says, sounding puzzled. 'They're having popcorn and jellies!'

I burst out laughing and she gives me a wry smile which soon turns into a grimace.

'Jesus, Bea, what's going on?' I say.

'I don't know!' she says, rubbing her stomach. 'I've been feeling nauseous for the last couple of days. Maybe it's a bug.'

'Oh, that's rotten,' I tell her, getting up to fetch her a glass of water.

Bea has no time for illness so she must be feeling really bad to even mention it to me.

I hand her the water and she smiles her thanks. Then I tell her that I'll take Harry after Mathias leaves if she wants to get some rest, but she shakes her head.

'No, no, I'll be fine. I'll stick Harry in front of some video games when that little bastard goes. He won't bother me,' she says, giving me a wan smile.

'When is that little... Mathias going, anyway?' I say, glancing at my watch.

It's just gone 4.15 p.m. I hope Bea hasn't promised him tea, too. The sooner she gets rid of him the better.

'His dad should be here any minute. You probably saw his obnoxious car outside,' she says, waving in the direction of the front door.

I raise my eyebrows at her.

'Is he?' I say.

'A wanker? Absolutely,' she says, replacing her glasses in one swift movement. 'He lives in Surrey but his parents live in Wood-vale so he's gone off for a quick visit.'

'You'd think he'd want to bring his son to visit his grandparents,' I say, indignantly.

Bea fixes with me with one of her trademark incredulous looks, and says, 'I'm not surprised he doesn't want to bring Mathias anywhere with him!'

Fair point.

She grimaces again and then sighs suddenly. 'Anyway, distract me from my stomach woes. Tell me how you've been.'

So, I tell her all about what happened at school, Anna's

sudden crush on Heath ('What? I won't have it!') and the tedium of trying to make small talk with Diana.

'Did she diagonally walk into you today?' Bea laughs.

'No, but she did give my hip a little bump.'

'And how's our favourite head teacher?' she says, giving me a prod with her elbow.

'Oh, don't,' I groan, putting my head in my hands.

Why did I tell Bea about Mr Russell? She's already had such great mileage out of it.

'Was it an ears-blush or a whole body flush this time?' she giggles.

'Red from top to toe,' I mumble through my fingers.

I raise my head slowly and glare at her.

'Change of subject, please!'

Bea takes another sip of water.

'What's the latest on the motherhood book?'

I shrug. Nothing much. A couple of months ago, I had written a pitch for a book about motherhood. As a ghostwriter, whereby my clients received all the credit, I had always dreamed about writing a book that would be published under my own name. What I didn't consider was that the topic would be motherhood – something that I would never have counted as one of my greatest strengths (or frankly, even a strength at all). Still, during a welcome break in Ireland, and after much soul-searching, I had managed to write the pitch and subsequently earned a publishing contract. Now there's just the small matter of writing the first draft.

I tell Bea that my agent Harriet has negotiated an end of the year deadline for the first draft which should be plenty of time, given I have bugger-all else to do apart from school drop off and pick-up. So, every day, I try to sit down and write – both loving and hating the process simultaneously, but also grateful that the words seem to be flowing at least. Even so, I don't feel I am occupied enough. I have told Harriet that I'm in the market for ghostwriting work, too, but she hasn't been in touch. One thing's for sure, I need something else to do apart from taking Anna to and from school and making inane small talk with Diana. The sheer tediousness of it is getting a bit too hard to bear. I've never mentioned this to Bea but I envy her lifestyle. For starters, she never has to do the school run to Harry's ultra-posh private school in Surrey because Maria, her nanny, does it, and she has a great job that not only pays well but pretty much lets her do whatever she pleases.

An otherworldly scream pierces my thoughts, and my ears.

Anna.

I jump to my feet, telling Bea to stay where she is. When I reach the top of the stairs, Anna is in floods of tears. Full seconds go by as I sit her on my hunched knees and try to calm her down.

'What happened?' I ask, over and over, gently wiping the tears away from her flushed cheeks.

'I hate Mathias,' she says eventually, burying her head in my shoulder.

The rest of the story comes out in great heaves, but it seems as though Mathias has picked up on Anna's struggle with the 'r' sound and used it as weapon.

'He kept asking me to say the word "wabbit" over and over, Mummy, but I *was* saying it!'

The little fucker.

Then something else occurs to me.

'Where was Harry when all this was going on?'

Usually Harry is Anna's protector and vice versa.

'He's doing a poo,' she sniffs sadly.

Aha! That makes sense. Harry would have rushed to her defence if he hadn't been answering nature's call.

Right.

I pick Anna up and carry her into Harry's room where an overly-tall-for-his-age five-year-old sits in red jeans and a long-sleeved green polo shirt, emblazoned with a familiar designer logo – his face one inch from the television screen.

'Mathias,' I say in my best firm voice. 'Anna is very upset because…'

Mathias makes absolutely no sign that he has heard me.

I put Anna gently down on the ground and crouch beside Mathias, but he doesn't flinch.

'Tell him off, Mummy!' Anna cries, clearly desperate for justice to be served.

'I'm trying, Anna!' I say, waving a hand in front of Mathias' glasses, but still nothing. Resisting the urge to give him a good poke in the ribs (that would get his attention), I get to my feet to a protesting Anna and calm her down by promising her an ice cream when we get home. As I am leading her downstairs, there is a knock on the door. I call to Bea that I'll get it and pull open the door. A tall, slim man in an expensive dark navy fitted suit with hair framed like curtains around his high forehead stands on the doorstep, clutching a set of car keys. He doesn't toss the keys in the air at least, but he looks like the type of person who is well capable of it.

He gives me a cursory look up and down, and then asks for Bea. No hello, no nothing. I coolly ask him to whom I am speaking (I actually say the word 'whom') and he gives a little sigh of impatience and tells me that he is Mathias' dad. Giving him the tiniest trace of a nod, I take a step towards the stairs, intending to call up to his devil child, but as soon as I move, the man steps quickly into the hallway and closes the door behind him.

I let out a little 'Oh!' because I'm not sure how to deal with this. I've never had anyone come into our house uninvited, let alone picking up from a playdate. I mean, don't get me wrong – I've had the odd *hoverer* who lingers on the doorstep for a bit while I retrieve the child from whatever corner of the house he or she has managed to destroy (i.e. all of it) but I've never had anyone just walk in, especially a dad. The dads are usually the first ones to cut and run. Just as I'm wondering if this is all normal and if, in fact, I am being a bit sexist, Bea calls out from the kitchen in a voice considerably weaker than her usual strident tones.

'Who's at the door, Saoirse?'

Before I have the chance to reply, Mathias' dad roughly brushes past me and crosses the hallway to the kitchen in several quick strides. It is only then I realise he is wearing a pair of mustard-coloured suede shoes. I bet he's had them dyed to match the colour of his Maserati – the wanker. They probably cost him a fortune.

Anna and I follow him into the kitchen where he is giving Bea far too many 'mwah mwahs'. His back is to me, so I take the opportunity to make a highly unladylike wanking gesture. Bea gives me a wink, then resumes her poker face and politely steps back from his greeting.

'How has Mathias been?' he says, roughly pulling out a chair and man-splaying on it for all he's worth.

Bea folds her arms and tips her glasses to the end of her nose – a sure sign she has no intention of holding back. I lean against the doorway, fully planning to enjoy the show. Anna starts tugging at my hand but I pull out my iPhone and tell her to look at photos of herself (which she loves more than anything on YouTube). There is no way I'm missing this.

'Well, let's see, Jonathan,' Bea begins. 'Firstly, he's had no lunch because he insisted on firing pizza dough all over me;

secondly, he's had nothing to drink because apparently he only drinks Evian and all we have is "stupid" tap water; and finally, he made Harry's best friend, Anna cry because...'

And here she gestures towards me. Mathias' dad twists around in his seat and looks at me as if this is the first time he has seen me.

'Oh, yes, he was making fun of Anna's speech...' I begin, but Anna cuts me off.

'*And* he didn't even say he was sowwy,' she says.

There is a brief silence and then Jonathan gets to his feet. He puts one hand casually on Bea's hip and leans in far too closely. Her mouth sets into a hard line.

'I am sorry about Mathias,' he says, with what he probably thinks is a charming grin. 'He can be a little spirited at times. I keep telling my wife not to spoil him.'

Spirited? Try feral. And while you're at it, try to avoid putting down the mother of your child while blatantly flirting with my best friend.

Bea's mouth twists and I'm waiting for her to, at the very least, give him the verbal equivalent of a knee in the nuts, but then she does something far, far better. Her upper body suddenly gives a great big jerk and she pukes all over his expensive shoes.

I have the giggles all the way back from Bea's house – frankly I don't know what was funnier: Bea puking on the sleazy bastard, the expression of sheer horror on his face, or the spectacle of Mathias and Harry racing in and belly-laughing when they saw the vomit on the floor. I don't think more than two minutes could have passed between Bea dyeing Jonathan's suede shoes a different shade of yellow and him scooping up Mathias and hotfooting it out of the house. Even Bea saw the funny side eventually, and despite the grimness of the clean-up, we failed to catch each other's eye without smiling. I offered to stay longer but she waved me off, proclaiming that she was feeling a lot better now, especially after inadvertently teaching that idiot a lesson.

To my surprise, my husband David opens the front door as I'm rooting around for my keys. He says, 'Hi,' to me in a way that avoids eye contact and bends down to give Anna a kiss but he is too slow.

'iPad!' she growls and races off up the stairs.

I feel my shoulders sag, the joy of the previous event at Bea's house seeping out of my body. Ever since Anna had outed Harry's dad, Ryan – Bea's ex-partner – for kissing me in the park a few weeks ago, things were tense, to say the least, between David and me. Of course, I had explained to him over and over that Ryan had kissed me and not the other way around, and that I obviously had no feelings for Ryan, but he was understandably hurt and confused, and frankly embarrassed, given that Anna had announced it in front of my mum, Bea and Jen, my best friend from Ireland. Bea and I had already sorted it out – after all, she was the one who saw Ryan kiss me that day, but it was painful having to explain what happened to Jen and my mother. Especially my mother, who spent a good hour lecturing me about the dangers of 'temptation', which frankly I could have done without. They have both been warned to never bring up the park incident again. But, of course, the main person suffering the brunt of all this is David. Every day, I regret ever meeting Ryan during my Irish trip last summer (even though he's a dead ringer for the actor Ryan Gosling) and I hate the way that one stupid kiss has driven such a wedge between us. I know it's all very fresh and it will take time to get back on track again but there is no denying that there is an element of frostiness and formality in our relationship that wasn't there before.

I follow David into the kitchen.

'You're home early,' I say.

He nods and goes to the cupboard and grabs a broom.

'How was your day?'

'Busy,' he says, poking at the cobwebs on the kitchen ceiling.

Good talk, I think wryly.

Then he asks me about my day and, despite the tension between us, I am unable to contain myself, and I burst out with the story of what happened at Bea's. It's not long before David is in hysterics and I laugh too but more with the relief that we can still laugh together after everything that has happened. But then, all too quickly, the moment passes and the awkward silence descends again.

I start grabbing a couple of pots to make Anna's tea – a daily combination of pasta and cheese – but then he asks a question that stops me in my tracks.

'Did you see him today at the school gates?' David says, as he pours the pasta into the pot.

Although he says it casually enough, I recognise it as a loaded question.

In hindsight, maybe it was a mistake to tell David about Mr Russell, especially so soon after the Ryan incident. But the second I saw him at the school gates, I feared, knowing my luck, that David would find out anyway. I think the biggest mistake I made was to tell David the more graphic details of the episode hoping he would find the story as funny as I did at the time, but he didn't find it funny at all. Quite the opposite.

'So, let me get this straight,' he had said, after I had confessed that I had seen quite a bit more of Mr Russell than perhaps most women. 'You met him in a club in Shoreditch years ago on a work night out, snogged him, then took him back to your place, where you tried to "make up" for the fact you had no intention of having sex with him by attempting a blowjob.'

'Well, yes,' I had said, nodding.

After all, he seemed nice enough and I didn't want to come across as a tease.

'But when – in your words – it "didn't wake up", he pulled up his jeans and ran out of your place, drowning in embarrassment.'

'While leaving his skid-marked underpants on my bedroom floor,' I reminded him. That was the funny part, the flaccid bit was only to be expected considering how much we'd had to drink.

Then David had gone very silent for a bit.

Finally, he had just said, 'I don't know, Saoirse. First Ryan, now Mr Russell... it's a lot to take in.'

So we have tried to brush it all under the carpet, but there are times, like this one, that David can't help bringing up Mr Russell. I know it's not easy for him, and I am trying to be patient with him, but he's really starting to get on my nerves.

I grab some cheese from the fridge and start grating it furiously. Obviously picking up on my reluctance to get into yet another 'I can't believe you blew the head teacher' argument, David wisely changes the subject back to Bea.

'What do you think is up with Bea?' he says.

I stop the grating just before the skin comes off my hands and tell him I presume it's a stomach bug. 'She's off her coffee and everything,' I say. 'It must be a nasty one.'

He takes the colander out of the drawer below the gas hob, looking thoughtful.

'The last time you went off coffee, you found out you were pregnant,' he muses.

A moment goes by and our eyes meet for the first time since I got home.

Jesus, could Bea be pregnant?

I give David a frantic wave that tells him nothing, and I race out of the kitchen to find my bag, which I have dumped at the bottom of the stairs. As I'm rummaging among the receipts, discarded snacks for Anna, and an empty tube of concealer, I finally manage to find it. I'm just pressing the call button when Anna appears on the stairs in her usual uniform of iPad and headphones.

'I'm hungry,' she says, in the sort of whiny voice that makes me want to stick pins in myself.

'Daddy is getting dinner ready for you now,' I say, hurriedly.

'What?' she says.

I curse those bloody headphones – she probably has the volume up far too high.

'DADDY HAS PASTA FOR YOU IN THE KITCHEN,' I shout, speaking to my daughter in capitals, and not for the first time.

'Oh, GOOD,' she smiles, and skips down the stairs, brushing past me and heading into the kitchen.

I heave a sigh of relief: alone at last.

My finger hovers above the call button, but suddenly I can't do it. I drop the phone to my side. This is ridiculous. So I'm going to call my sick friend to ask her if she's pregnant for no other reason save the fact that she's gone off coffee and puked all over Harry's friend's dad's shoes. What gives me the right to even ask the question? Instead, I drop her a text to see how she is and then walk back into the kitchen to find Anna sitting on a stool at the island still firmly plugged into her iPad, the wires from the head-phones trailing into her bowl of pasta.

'WHERE'S YOUR DAD?' I shout.

She presses the pause button, looks up at me beatifically with her massive brown eyes and says, 'Dunno, Mummy,' through a mouthful of pasta, before resuming her very important YouTube watching. Wondering if we'll ever eat as a family again, I go out into the garden and spot David coming out of the shed with the bigger broom.

'Was the other one not doing the job?' I say.

'No,' he says, thoughtfully. 'This one has a better reach for the cobwebs.'

Right.

'I didn't call Bea in the end,' I tell him as we walk back into the kitchen.

'Probably for the best,' he says. 'Do you think she's pregnant?'

'No,' I say, too quickly, 'Definitely not.' But I'm not sure I'm even convincing myself.

3

The alarm goes off at 7 a.m. and I haul myself out of bed, already lethargic at the thought of the school run. Last night, David had mumbled something about an early meeting, and so it's just me and Anna this morning. I have a quick shower and get dressed in my usual choice of skinny jeans and a loose jumper (in any colour) that's just long enough to cover my undeniably expanding arse. Brushing my hair in front of the bathroom mirror, it always strikes me as peculiar that while Anna doesn't have a school uniform, I appear to have a uniform of my own, wearing the same thing every single day. I walk into Anna's bedroom, tripping over a distressing pile of dolls, 'cuddlies', LEGO, and slime (which has been unsuccessfully banned from our house) and pick my way to Anna's bed where she is buried underneath the quilt, poised to spring out at me. I know this because she does it every morning, and if I don't react authentically she gets really pissed off with me, which only adds endless delays to the whole 'getting ready for school' process.

'Boo!' she says, throwing the quilt off her dramatically.

I clutch my chest in mock horror.

'Jesus, Anna! You frightened the life out to me!' I say, and then reinforce the drama with, 'I thought you were in the bathroom!'

She studies me closely to assess the genuineness of my reactions and then crawls out of bed to give me a hug.

A wave of relief passes through me. I have passed! Next stop RADA.

Then I go to her chest of drawers, which is covered in stickers, including the promotional ones that shops put on clothes (such as 'two for one' and so on) and offer her an array of different tops and leggings to let madam choose which ones she would like to adorn herself with today. After she gets dressed, we wander down the stairs together, Anna chatting away, never once deviating from the daily script.

'What day is it today, Mummy?'

'It's Thursday, sweetheart,' I say.

'And what are we doing today?'

'We're going to school,' I tell her, as I guide her into the kitchen.

Silence as she tries to absorb something that she does every bloody weekday.

'And what are we doing in school?' she says, tugging my hand.

I don't know, Anna. I don't go around all day badgering teachers for a copy of the fucking daily curriculum.

'Maybe drawing?' I say.

'We did dwawing yesterday!' she says, in her best 'Mummy, you're a moron' voice.

I can see how this 'game' is going to end and my nerves can't take it, so I reach for my best tried and true distraction technique.

'TV?' I say brightly, grabbing the remote.

'Only if it's Netflix,' she says happily.

'Do you know, Anna,' I say, as I'm pressing the red button. 'When I was a child growing up in Ireland we only had five channels and that's all we needed!' Which is bullshit, as those five channels were shit but, still, she needs to know that once upon a time there was a world without this much choice.

Anna cocks her head to one side, holds her hand out, and says, 'Wemote.'

I pass it to her and she deftly moves to her own icon and scrolls to one of her favourite episodes of Dora.

After a breakfast of Cheerios and nothing else, she heads to the toilet to pretend to brush her teeth, and I grab her pink padded winter coat, schoolbag and shoes and place them at the foot of the stairs, so she will have no other recourse but to get ready for school. After a few false starts ('I want to bring my lamb cuddly on the walk to school!' and 'No, I've changed my mind, I want to bring Molly dolly!') followed by the inevitable squabble (I take serious issue with Molly dolly, given that she is almost as tall as I am), we finally make it out the door. I walk to the end of the road, holding Anna's hand with my left hand and Molly's with my right – another battle lost. True to form, Anna has lost interest in Molly about twenty seconds after leaving the house.

As we round the corner towards the village, I stop dead. Tania is up ahead, her scooter lying across the path, fingers bashing furiously on her phone, leaving Heath looking sullen as he repeatedly kicks a low wall. I bet she's on the class WhatsApp group. I let go of Anna's hand to reach for my phone but it's not there. I must have left it at home. Good. I can't bear those messages at the best of times, let alone first thing in the morning.

Anna tugs my hand but I'm not moving until Tania clears off. So I bend down on the pretext of giving Anna Molly to hold, but Anna's arms stay firmly by her sides. When I straighten up, I am gratified to see the back of Tania's gilet in the distance. With the coast clear, Anna and I continue our walk to school together, taking a happy tally of dog, cat and fox poo along the way.

Thankfully, drop off is uneventful – my ankles have remained intact, Diana hasn't made an appearance, and there has been no sign of Mr Russell at the school gates (hurrah!) – and I arrive home in relatively even-tempered spirits. I find my phone on the kitchen island and switch it on to find thirty-six WhatsApp messages. I bloody knew it!

Karen (another Organics grim reaper – privately called 'Misery' as she is probably the most negative, miserable person I have ever come across):
Just curious but what age do you think children should have their ears pierced?

Now bearing in mind this is a *school* WhatsApp group I'm wondering what relevance ear-piercing has to bake sales, school clubs, or lice warnings. But judging by the deluge of texts sent in response to her stupid question, I'm the only one who thinks so. Scrolling down through the responses, I see that the only one who seems to have stuck her neck out is Jane, the full-time working mum:

I suppose it's up to the parent really but I know my niece had hers done three weeks after she was born.

Big mistake. Cue the flood of judgement, everything from:

Oh, that's FAR too young – I've told Maisie she has to wait until she is 7!

To:

Not until she is in her late teens.

And:

Never! They will be scarred for life!

That last one is from Tania, if you haven't guessed already. Of course, everyone else now agrees with Tania, including Misery, who was the one who posed the question in the first place.

I sigh. Poor Jane – I don't know why she partakes in these discussions. The fact that she's a full-time working mum means that she will be criticised by the Organics for everything she says, regardless of whether she agrees with them or not. I put my phone down with a clatter and go to the fridge to see what I can prepare for lunch later. This has been my routine since Anna started school: dropping off Anna, coming home, looking at food, writing motherhood book for a bit, idly checking my ghost-writing website mailbox for enquiries (I might as well just have said crackpots and serial killers need only apply), eating lunch (followed by too many biscuits and jellies), watching YouTube videos of cringeworthy reality TV shows while on a sugar high, trying and failing to educate myself on serious political podcasts in a vague attempt to 'learn something', before going back to substance-free reality shows. Then coming down from the sugar high and sinking into a mild depressive state before putting on a happy face and picking up Anna from school.

As I am finishing the 'staring at food' part of my daily schedule, a pinging sound alerts me to an email. I shut the fridge door quickly and grab my phone with the eagerness of a child receiving a letter through the post for the first time. It's from Harriet, my agent, and she wants me to call her ASAP.

I hit the call button straight away. She answers after six rings, even though she's just emailed me.

'Who is this?' she says, exhaling.

She is still the only person I know who vapes and the only person who still insists on calling me 'Searcy.'

'It's Saoirse,' I say, trying not to sound too indignant. After all these years of working together she could at least be bothered enough to list me as a contact on her phone.

'Oh, yes, hi Searcy. I need to talk to you about something,' she says in the manner of someone who is very, very weary even though it's barely 10 a.m.

My heart sinks. Harriet is dour at the best of times, but this doesn't sound like good news. My mind immediately jumps to the motherhood book. The publisher doesn't want the book; they're taking back the advance; the publisher has gone bankrupt...

'Is it to do with the book?' I ask, in a tiny voice.

'What book?' she says, sharply.

'The motherhood book,' I half-screech. What does she mean, 'What book?'

'No, no, nothing to do with that,' she says with more than a hint of impatience.

I blow out a sigh of relief. Deep breaths, Saoirse...

'I've had a call from this guy called Sebastian Fox looking for a ghostwriter,' she breathes.

I perk up. I could definitely do with some ghosting work, not just to break the monotony of the daily routine, but for the extra money. The advance for the motherhood book will probably last another month or so but then that's it – skint again.

'What's the book about?' I say.

'Well, he won't say,' she says grumpily, 'but he seems to be awfully enthusiastic about it.'

She says 'enthusiastic' in the same way as you might say 'disgusting'.

My heart sinks. I've had too many of these enquiries over the last few years to know that an overly enthusiastic client (read 'delusional') are the most difficult ones to work with, mainly because their expectations are unrealistically high. But I decide to ask a few follow-up questions, just in case I'm jumping the gun.

'Did he say that it was going to be bestseller?' I ask.

'Yep,' Harriet sighs.

Strike one.

'Did he say his book was going to change the world?'

'Bingo,' she says dryly.

Strike two.

'Did he say that the ghostwriter should feel so privileged to work with him on such an amazing project that payment would be an insult?'

That last one is my favourite ('But think of what it will do for your writing portfolio!').

But Harriet surprises me by exhaling, 'Actually, no.'

Now I'm intrigued.

'It's all a bit odd, really...' she begins.

It turns out that Sebastian Fox is a former banker (cha-ching!) who claims he has invented something major. He wants a writer to document the journey of creating this new world-changing innovation. Apparently, he is willing to pay a big chunk of cash to the lucky writer who gets to work with him.

'What's he invented, then?' I say.

'Don't know. He won't tell me that either,' Harriet says, clearly annoyed.

Then she tells me I will have to sign a 'cast-iron' confidentiality agreement if I want to work for him, which is fine because I can keep a secret – most of the time.

But there is one more thing I need to know – the most important question of all.

'How much is he paying?'

'No idea,' she sighs. 'Wants the ghost to name the price.'

Jesus – how long is a piece of string?

'Well, what do you think is a fair price?' I say, because frankly as an agent she should know better than me.

'Oh, I'm not involved in this whole thing at all,' she splutters. 'He wants to self-publish. Besides, no publisher would touch this book. He's a complete unknown and most likely a total nutcase.'

'So why are you calling me then?' I say, confused.

'To get him off my back, Searcy! I've been ignoring his emails for weeks and he's really starting to get on my nerves,' she says.

Wow – I'm so flattered.

'So, if you can fit something else in around the motherhood book, then I'll send him over your contact details.'

I do some exhaling of my own before I respond. Sebastian Fox sounds like a typical crackpot but, then again, he sounds like a crackpot with money so really I have nothing to lose.

'Okay, fine,' I say. 'Go ahead and give him my details.'

'Already done,' she says.

Then she hangs up.

I flop down the kitchen stool for a moment and Google Sebastian Fox. He is indeed a banker who seems to have switched banks (and countries) pretty frequently over the last few years. I wonder what could have made him give up his well-paid job to pursue his new innovation. Still, I shouldn't be too quick to judge – I gave up my fancy banking job to pursue my dream of being a writer (and became significantly poorer in the process). I have to admit it – I am intrigued. It's been a while since I interviewed for a ghostwriting job; maybe this is a good thing. With a new skip in my step, I head upstairs to the guest room and work on the motherhood book for a couple of hours, only stopping when I hear my phone ping.

It's Bea.

Puked in the bin on the way to work. (Green puke emoji.)

I quickly type back.

OMG! Are you OK?

I watch the dots until the next text comes in.

I'm at home.

I text back just as quickly.

I'm on my way.

4

Bea has the door on the latch so I push it open and call out to her.

'In here!' a tired voice mumbles.

I take the door to the right and find her in the living room, sitting on the couch with her legs tucked up beneath her, covered up to her nose with a massive fleecy blanket. She looks about fifteen.

'This fucking bug,' she says, wearily. 'It just won't leave me alone.'

I sit down on the couch beside her, not sure how to respond. My mind is still whirring with what David said yesterday. Could she be pregnant? I can't seem to shake the thought.

She wriggles her way out of the blanket and sits up taller. I notice she is wearing the flannel pyjamas her mum gave her last year for Christmas.

I open my mouth and close it again.

'What?' she says, narrowing her eyes.

Before I can control it, I let out a high-pitched nervous giggle.

'Nothing!' I insist.

She leans closer and stares at me until I can't take the pressure any more.

'It's just that... do you think you might be pregnant?' I blurt out.

'Oh, for goodness' sake, Saoirse, of course not!' she says, instantly, flopping back against the couch.

Now I feel like a knob. What is wrong with me? Why can't I mind my own business?

I hold my hands in the air and apologise and she gives me a nod of forgiveness, and then looks a bit thoughtful for a minute.

'I mean, I haven't been on Tinder for a couple of months now, and the last person I was with was Ryan...' her voice trails off.

'And did you and Ryan use anything?' I say.

'Well, I'm on the Pill...' she says, staring into space. 'But Ryan didn't use anything.'

She looks at me for a moment and our eyes lock.

'*Fuck*!' she says, throwing the blanket off and racing into the hallway.

I follow her as quickly as I can.

'Where are you going?' I ask.

'To the chemist to buy a pregnancy test,' she shouts. 'Where the *fuck* is my bag?'

I put my hand on her arm and say as calmly as I can, 'You're still in your pyjamas. I will go and get the test.'

She stares at me for a moment and her shoulders go slack.

'Okay, thanks,' she mumbles as I lead her back to the couch and tuck her in again.

As I pick up my bag again, she looks at me with wide eyes and says, 'This is ridiculous. I'm not pregnant. Besides, I was never sick with Harry.'

'Listen, you have nothing to lose by taking the test. I'm sure it's all fine. I'll be back soon,' I say, pulling on my coat.

My mind races as I walk briskly to the chemist. What if Bea is pregnant? I grab three pregnancy tests off the shelf and march up to the counter to pay. Then I almost pass out at the price of them – I had forgotten how expensive these bloody things are. Just as I am about to shove them into my bag, I hear a familiarly unpleasant voice behind me.

'Expecting good news?'

It's Tania. Great, now it will be all over school before lunchtime that I'm up the duff. I'll have to style it out.

'Yes, actually!' I say brightly. 'Fingers crossed for triplets!'

'Oh, I'll keep everything crossed for you,' she says, giving me one of her fake smiles.

I give her my best smirk and push past her towards the door.

'It will be so nice for Anna to have siblings,' she says to my back. 'It's no fun being an only child.'

It takes every ounce of strength I have not to turn back and punch her in the face. I march through the door, spitting out a new swear word for each step back to Bea's house.

Bea opens the door as soon as I reach the gate.

'Did you get it?' she says with the fervour of someone waiting anxiously for a drug dealer.

'I got a few,' I say, handing her the bag as I take my coat off in the hallway.

'Right!' she says, brandishing all three tests in the air. 'Wish me luck!'

As I watch her head to the upstairs bathroom, I ask her if she needs me to go with her, to which she replies, not unkindly, 'No, thanks. Peeing on a stick is something I can manage on my own.'

I walk back into the living room and stand there for a bit, wringing my hands. The whole thing seems so surreal, Bea could not only be pregnant but pregnant with Ryan's baby. The same Ryan whose lips touched mine in the park a few weeks ago, not long after he had slept with Bea. My stomach does an annoying flip, which I try to ignore – I have absolutely no feelings for Ryan, no matter how jaw-droppingly gorgeous he may be.

Instead, I try to focus on the fact that Harry might have a new brother or sister. But that only reminds me of that bitch Tania Henderson's 'only child' comment. I am so deep in thought thinking about all the ways I could 'accidentally' disrupt Tania Henderson's life (a home-made icy puddle on her scooter route perhaps? Or a fake email from her posh gym revoking her membership?) that I don't hear Bea coming down the stairs or even into the room for that matter.

'Saoirse,' she says, softly.

I jump about a mile in the air and look at her. She is as white as a sheet.

'Well?' I say, although her face tells me everything I need to know.

'I'm pregnant,' she says, slowly.

I walk over and throw my arms around her.

My mind whirls. Bea's pregnant.

Now what?

5

Bea sits silently on the couch, the blanket on the floor, her back ramrod straight as if she is on high alert, waiting for something bad to happen. I sit beside her, casting her furtive glances every now and then, wondering if I should say something or not. Then Bea breaks the silence.

'Stop looking at me, Saoirse!' she says.

I apologise, then she apologises, and we give each other weak smiles and suddenly we're back on safe ground again.

She sighs.

'I just need time to process all this.'

Then she buries her head in her hands.

'How could I have been so stupid? I mean, I'm on the Pill, but I should have made him wear a condom too,' she groans.

Then she lifts her head out of her hands and looks at me.

'I mean, Ryan, of all people! The father of this child! I don't even like him. He's really been getting on my nerves these past few weeks. He's going to be unbearable now when he finds out about this baby.'

'What's he been doing?' I ask, and I am curious because she barely gives Ryan a passing mention at the best of times.

'Oh, he's been on my case about seeing Harry more. He already Skypes him every other day. He even wants me to take Harry to South Africa at Christmas so Harry can meet his parents.'

Then she lets out a huge sigh and leans back on the couch, her mouth tight, her head shaking in incredulity. I don't think I have ever seen Bea floored before. I've seen her angry and tearful but never floored. For a moment, I'm at a bit of a loss too. I want to help her but I don't know what to do. Then suddenly, an idea hits me and I know exactly what to do. Be her.

'Right!' I say, standing up quickly. 'First things first.'

'What are you doing?' she says, frowning.

I ignore her and go straight into the hallway to find my bag. Then I find the number I'm looking for on my contacts list and press the call button. While the inevitable muzak pipes up, I walk into the kitchen to fetch Bea a glass of water before returning to the living room.

'What's happening?' she mouths, as I hand her the glass of water.

But before I can answer her, a human voice comes on the phone. I hold up the same warning finger I give Anna when she looks like she's about to interrupt me.

'Yes, I would like to make an appointment with the doctor as soon as possible... the reason? I think I'm pregnant... 4 p.m. today?'

Now it's my turn to mouth at Bea. 'Is that okay?'

She nods with her lips firmly pressed together – never one to like being bossed around.

Then I give the receptionist Bea's full name and address and hang up triumphant. A same-day doctor's appointment – who knew!

But I'm not finished yet.

'So that's step one,' I say, tapping my foot. 'Step two is lunch.'

Bea winces. 'I can't eat.'

I shake my head at her. 'Yes, you can. You haven't puked since this morning. It is now almost 1 p.m. so you will be well capable of eating something.'

Besides which, I'm starving. I usually eat at midday.

Without saying anything else, I march back into the kitchen to assess the ingredients. Eggs. Good. I scramble enough for the two of us, butter a couple of slices of toast, and cut them into soldiers just for the hell of it. Then I call out to Bea and tell her to come into the kitchen.

She walks in slowly with her arms across her chest, looking like she is ready to fend off the food I have made her, but I take her arm firmly and guide her into the chair. I eat quickly, pretending not to notice that she is pushing her food around the plate with a fork like a child. Then I leave the kitchen to go to the loo. When I come back, the plate is empty. She has eaten everything. Because I'm such a good friend I try to keep my expression neutral. I don't want to gloat.

'Stop looking so smug,' she says, crossly.

I ignore her and fill up the kettle.

Moments later, I feel her hand on my shoulder.

'Thanks, Saoirse,' she says softly.

I wave her away. There's no time for soppiness when I'm in Bea mode.

Looking at my watch I can see I have just enough time for my next task.

'Step three,' I announce.

I go upstairs and run the bath. Bea has clearly cottoned on

and is already at the top of the stairs before I even call for her. 'Okay, okay,' she says, shaking her head, tugging at her pyjamas. 'I'll have the bath!'

While she soaks away, I go downstairs and rummage in my bag for a notebook and pen. Then I stroll back to the kitchen table and spend about half an hour making Bea a list of all the stuff I used to survive on to get me through the morning sickness with Anna. It takes a while to remember everything but I'm pretty pleased with what I have come up with.

Just as I'm finishing up, Bea appears in the kitchen, fully dressed in a loose knitted jumper, a pair of velvety-looking, straight-cut, navy cords and a pink towel tied turban-style around her head.

I'm glad to see some colour back in her cheeks.

I take her through the list, giving her full instructions about what to eat and when to eat it.

'So, you're trying to tell me that I must have a packet of dry crackers by my bedside at all times,' she says, in a voice that holds nothing but scepticism.

'CREAM crackers,' I say. 'AND a glass of water.'

'And these are the first things I must eat as soon as I wake up,' she says.

I nod my head.

'Life savers.'

'I was never sick with Harry,' she repeats.

'Well, then you were very lucky,' I say curtly, reliving unhappy memories of stuffing cream crackers into my mouth, and being ready to kill David for complaining about the crumbs.

I glance at my watch again and give a little start. Anna will be out of school in half an hour and I still have to get back to the house to collect her snack. I ask Bea if she wants me to take Harry after Maria drops him back from school, to give her the freedom she needs to go to the doctor, but she says that Maria is staying until Harry's bedtime tonight. Then I make her promise to call me AS SOON as she's finished with the doctor and she says she will.

As I walk home, I'm glad to be back to myself again.

It's exhausting being Bea.

6

My mind is so full of Bea that I barely remember the walk to school. I don't look for Mr Russell at the school gate and hardly register the furtive glances from Tania and the Organics and the hushed whisperings of the word 'triplets'. I walk towards the back fence in the playground, deep in thought. Three positive pregnancy tests is a pretty clear sign – Bea's doctor's appointment is merely a formality. I mean what is she going to... OUCH!

'Oh, sorry Saoirse! I didn't mean to make you jump!'

It's Diana and she's just walked across me, kicking one of my ankles on the way. I give her my best scowl, but she still doesn't move.

'So, what did you get up to today?' she says, blowing her fringe off her face.

I look at her with unabashed perplexity. Why is she here? WHY isn't she standing outside her own child's classroom boring other mums, rather than hovering around me?

'Nothing much,' I lie.

Only that I was with my best friend who's been knocked up by the bloke who kissed me over the summer, in front of my daughter and his son and how my mind is spinning so much with it all that I can't seem to focus on anything else. The last time I saw Ryan he was angry with me for rejecting him. How will he behave the next time he sees me? He's bound to be around a lot more if he's visiting his new baby…

But Diana continues to look at me like a puppy begging for a treat, and my conscience tells me I need to give her more.

'Erm, I went to the chemist,' I tell her.

Her little face lights up.

'Did you? What did you get?' she asks with the enthusiasm of someone who's been told they've won an all-expenses paid holiday to the Bahamas.

I'm just forming the word 'tampons' when the classroom doors fling open.

'Ooops!' she says, regretfully. 'I must run and pick up Jonty. Hold that thought for tomorrow!'

I shake my head and wave her off, waiting for Anna to find me, but seconds go by and there's no sign of her. Or Milly for that matter. I look to my left but there's an empty space where Ambrose usually stands. It's time to investigate. I walk towards Anna's classroom, passing reluctantly into the Organics' territory. Ignoring the inevitable 'we don't like your type around here' stares, I peep into the classroom only to find Anna sitting on the carpet holding hands with Milly. Their teacher, Miss Bridges, who is roughly twenty years younger than me, stands over them with a grim look on her face. Then Miss Bridges catches sight of me and beckons me in.

'Everything okay?' I say.

But before Miss Bridges can answer, Anna pipes up.

'We're in twouble, Mummy.'

Then she looks at Milly and the pair of them burst into giggles. It takes everything in my power not to join in. Given the stony-faced looks from their teacher, I'm guessing it's something pretty serious, or as serious as it can be for a couple of four-year-olds.

Before Miss Bridges can open her mouth, a woman walks casually into the room. She is dressed in ripped dungarees, covered by a huge, rainbow-coloured, thick-knit cardigan. Her hair is one big mass of shaggy brown that 'could do with a brush' as my mother would say, and she wears a pair of old-school, beaten-up, black biker boots. I'd put her in her early thirties.

Milly lets go of Anna's hand with an exclamation that sounds something that sounds like 'ShoSho!' and throws herself into the woman's arms. The woman smiles at Milly and then looks from Miss Bridges to me.

'I'm Sho, Milly's mum,' she says, in a strong east London accent.

My mouth falls open. Milly's mum! Finally! I must talk to her. Oh, the playdates we will have!

But before I can introduce myself, Miss Bridges cuts in with an icy tone.

'I'm afraid Anna and Milly haven't been very well-behaved today,' she says.

'Oh?' Sho says, glancing at the teacher and then me, in a voice that holds no interest whatsoever. She releases Milly who heads straight back to sit next to Anna and walks over to the middle of the classroom, folding her giant colourful cardigan around her slim frame. As she does so, I spot a tattoo on her hand, of a rose surrounded by a ring of thorns. With a sinking heart, I realise that she is not my type at all – she is way too cool for me. She even has a cool name.

As if sensing her moment has finally come, Miss Bridges gives an important cough and tells us that Anna and Milly had left the playground during playtime and run back into the classroom by themselves. Then she stops, as if to pause for effect, but before she can go on, Sho says, 'And what were they doing in the classroom?'

Miss Bridges gives her head an impatient shake, clearly annoyed to be interrupted.

'They were doing arts and crafts,' she says indignantly.

I catch Sho's eye and we both crack up.

'They had the scissors out without supervision!' the teacher says, but that only makes us laugh harder.

To her credit, Miss Bridges doesn't break form. She glares at us until we calm down.

'I'm not sure what their behaviour shows you, but what it shows *me* is...'

'Initiative!' Sho and I say at exactly the same time.

'Disobedience!' Miss Bridges says, almost shouting now.

Sho cocks her head to one side.

'So, let me get this straight. Two four-year-olds who are under your care managed to get back into their classroom and take out all the arts and crafts stuff totally unsupervised?'

'*With* scissors!' I join in, delighted to add weight to the argument I'm impressed to realise Sho has constructed already.

Miss Bridges opens her mouth and promptly shuts it again. Clearly she hasn't thought of this angle. Sho shakes her head, and scoops up Milly, while I reach down to take Anna by the hand. Without another word, we walk out of the classroom in perfect unison, only to almost stumble straight into Misery, who has clearly been eavesdropping outside the door. The snide comments from her judgemental crew will be coming thick and fast over the next few days. Judging by her reddening cheeks, she knows she's been rumbled.

'Oooh, those two are late out today,' she says, gesturing at

Milly and Anna, as if she doesn't know that they've just been bollocked by the teacher.

'They got in trouble,' Sho says.

I glance at her in surprise. If we do become friends, I vow to teach her the first rule of dealing with an Organic – never show weakness, especially when it comes to your child.

Misery's eyes widen in delight at this unexpected admission of guilt. If she dared rub her hands together, she would.

'Oh dear,' she says, looking sympathetically fake. 'What have they been up to?'

Sho shoots Milly a regretful look and shakes her head.

'Selling drugs,' she says.

Then she grabs my arm and I tug on Anna's hand and the four of us stride off towards the gates, Sho and I convulsing in laughter.

We don't recover until we're well outside the school.

'I can spot a busybody from a mile off,' Sho says, jerking her thumb towards the school.

Then Anna and Milly discover a bunch of autumn leaves on the grassy verge of the footpath that desperately need crunching, which gives me the opportunity to fill Sho in about Misery and the Organics, their hideous displays of competitive mothering smugness on the Vale Mums Facebook group, and their equally odious texts on the class WhatsApp group. Sho laughs and tells me she has no intention of joining the WhatsApp group, which makes me wonder for the millionth time why I am a member. Then she tells me that she's a freelance tattoo artist and spends portions of the year away tattooing people – music bands mostly – all over the world. She's just spent the last couple of months in New York and LA. Again, far too cool for the likes of me.

'Anyway,' she finishes, 'That's why my partner Ambrose has

been picking up Milly since school started. Typical that the first time I do it, it turns out she's been trashing the joint!'

Milly, clearly sensing that she's being talked about, barrels over to us, pulling Anna behind her.

'Snack!' she says.

Sho reaches into one of her big knitted pockets and brings out two lollipops, and hands one to Anna and one to Milly. They both squeal. The woman is a genius. Anna hands hers back to me almost immediately so I have to wrangle the torturously tight wrapper.

'Are you Milly's mummy?' Anna says, staring up at Sho.

'I am!' says Sho, smiling back at her.

'Why doesn't Milly call you "Mummy"?' she says.

That's a good question, I think, pulling at the wrapper violently. I've been wondering that myself.

'Because Milly prefers not to,' Sho says.

Anna nods as if deep in thought.

'Is that a tattoo?' she says, pointing at the rose tattoo spread across Sho's hand.

Finally, I have the wrapper off.

'Yes!' Sho says brightly.

'My mummy hates tattoos,' Anna says, frowning.

SHIT – she's right, I do hate tattoos. In fact, the only times I allow Anna to use the 'H' word is for tattoos, motorbikes, and for arsehole drivers who don't thank me when I'm pulling in to let them pass.

Sho bursts out laughing and says, 'Tattoos are not for everyone.'

I mumble an apology and quickly pass the lollipop to Anna, praying that it will distract her from mortifying me any further. Anna takes it in an absent-minded way. Judging by the look on her face, she's not finished yet. I brace myself.

'You have peach skin,' she says.

And in an instant, I know where this is going.

'And Milly and her daddy have brown faces,' she continues chattily. 'So, are you weeeeally Milly's mummy?'

Oh, God.

To her credit, Sho doesn't so much as flinch. She just bends down to Anna's level, and says, 'Yes, angel, I am really Milly's mummy.'

Anna gives her a look that says, 'I'm pretty sure you're taking the piss,' but is luckily distracted by Milly who appears to have found a worm to point at.

I turn to Sho, the dread building in my chest. Just when you think you've found a new friendship, your four-year-old craps all over it.

'Listen, I'm sorry about Anna...' I begin. 'She's just a bit...' And I can't really find the right word so I just settle on the one that's the most accurate.

'...racist.'

To my huge relief, Sho bursts out laughing. 'Oh, don't worry, she's not the only child who's curious about mixed race parents.'

'I'll have to give her a stern lecture when I get home,' I say.

Sho just laughs some more.

Desperate to change the subject, I ask her how long she'll be in town for before she goes away for her next tattoo job.

'I'll probably be around for a couple of months. There are some local jobs that need doing. Besides, I need to give Ambrose a break from the school run. It's doing his head in.'

I laugh and tell her I know the feeling.

Just then Milly falls over and the tears start, which is a clear sign that we should all head for our respective homes. To Anna's outrage, Milly's house happens to be in the precise opposite direction of our house and the two little girls spend full minutes embracing each other at the crossroads, with myself and Sho making every effort to prise them apart.

As we walk away, I give Sho a wave and she mouths, 'See you tomorrow,' because there's no point in trying to talk over the din of two best friends who have been cruelly torn apart by their pesky mummies.

By the time I get home I feel a combination of exhausted and exhilarated. Exhausted from dragging a hysterical Anna home with me, but delighted to have made a new friend. It's only when I throw my keys and handbag on the kitchen table and catch a glimpse of the oven clock that I realise what time it is.

Almost 5 p.m.! Bea will have finished her doctor's appointment by now. I fish my phone out of the bag, intending to call Bea, but then my hand pauses. Anna. The last thing I need is for her to pick up on Bea's pregnancy. She'll spill the beans to Harry in two seconds flat. And I can tell by her tear-streaked face that she's not in the mood to do me any favours.

'iPad?' I venture hopefully.

'No,' she growls, folding her arms.

I puff out a sigh of impatience. That's the only negotiating tool I have.

She glares at me for a moment and says, 'Your phone.'

Which is how I end up calling Bea the old-fashioned way: from the landline.

She picks up on the first ring.

'Why are you calling me on the landline?' she says, sounding annoyed.

'Never mind about that,' I say. 'Are you definitely pregnant?'

She lets out a sigh that tells me all I need to know.

'How do you feel?' I say, quietly.

'A bit shell-shocked, I suppose,' she says in a tired voice. 'It hasn't really hit me yet.'

The question, 'What are you going to do?' hangs in the air for a bit, but I don't voice it. She sounds shattered, and I can tell she just needs to talk about something else.

So I ask her how Harry is ('Some little prick at school pissed on his shoes') and then tell her about Anna and Milly's vandalism, and meeting Sho, and the brilliant way she handled that nosy cow Misery, and when I'm finished there is a brief pause before Bea says, 'Do you think you've found "the one"?'

I consider this for a moment. Do I think I have found the school mum whom I can ask about homework, bitch about the Organics and slag off the PTA?

'Yes,' I say quite seriously. 'I think I have.'

'Well, I'm happy for you,' she says, yawning.

Before we hang up, I make her promise that she'll go to bed early, eat some dry crackers to help the nausea when she gets up tomorrow morning, and call me when she wants to talk more.

'All right, Mum,' she says, grumpily.

Then I make Anna some tea and snaffle my phone back in exchange for the iPad and check my emails. As soon as I do, I freeze for a moment, unable to digest what's greeting me on the screen.

I have nine emails from Sebastian Fox.

7

David walks in just as I'm reading the last of the nine emails from Sebastian Fox. I wave my phone at him.

'What's going on?' he says, planting a kiss on the top of Anna's headphones. As usual, she gives him no acknowledgement whatsoever.

'Do you think it's weird for someone to send you nine emails within the space of roughly eight hours?'

He grabs some grapes from the fridge and shovels a couple of them into his mouth.

'I suppose it depends...' he says, chewing slowly.

'Depends on what?' I say, giving him my best eyebrow-raise. I mean, under what circumstances would someone send someone else nine emails in a very short space of time?

'Well, if you've fallen out with someone and you're trying to apologise...' he says.

I take umbrage at this.

'We've fallen out hundreds of times and you've barely sent me a text, let alone nine emails,' I say.

An awkward silence descends. It's probably not the best idea to bring up the topic of falling out given the Ryan/Mr Russell situation.

'So, who's been sending you nine emails?' he says.

I tell him about my call with Harriet that morning and how she'd given my details to Sebastian Fox basically to get him off her back. And then he takes my phone and looks through the emails, hands my phone back to me, and says, 'He's keen.'

'But did you not get any psycho vibes from the emails, then?' I say, because at best I'm a paranoid mess when it comes to meeting new people.

He takes a deep breath and blows out his cheeks.

'To be honest, I didn't,' he says. 'But I do think he comes across as a bit arrogant.'

'YESSSS,' I say, delighted that David has picked up on something negative to satisfy my overly suspicious mind.

'Sounds like a wanker with his highbrow ideas of changing the world with his supposed new top-secret invention...'

And then I stop dead. The word 'wanker' has just reminded me of that idiot dad that Bea puked all over, and I realise that David doesn't know the latest about Bea.

David looks at me.

'What is it?'

My mouth opens to tell him that Bea is pregnant but then I hesitate. Am I allowed to tell anyone? I mean, Bea hasn't told me to keep it a secret and even if she did, she would probably expect me to tell David because he's my husband, and realistically David isn't going to tell anyone, is he?

So I tell him, and his eyes widen and he says, 'No... way...' immediately followed by, 'Who's the father?' When I tell him it's Ryan, his forehead creases and his eyes take on a faraway look, and I know he's thinking about the kiss in the park but there's nothing I can do about it. Then his eyes focus again and he takes a deep breath and says, 'What's she going to do?'

'I'm not sure,' I say, softly, appreciating the effort he has made to move on from the moment. 'It's all so fresh. She needs time to process it.'

He nods for a bit before saying, 'She might end up not having it, do you think?'

I don't say anything because the thought has also crossed my mind. Would I have the baby if I was in her position? Single mum, in her forties, working a full-time job... But deep down I know the answer: I would have the baby. You can take the girl out of Ireland but you can't take the guilt out of the girl.

'Whatever she chooses to do, I'll support her,' I say.

Neither of us say anything for a moment, the silence punctuated only by the background tinniness of whatever Anna is watching – my best guess would be that it's one of those tween pop groups called something that ends in 'sisters'.

As silence is the enemy in my book, I ask David about his day, and he gives his usual, 'Same old,' response, which ends any hope of further conversation. Then David goes off to change out of his work clothes and I sit down at the kitchen table with my phone, looking again at the Sebastian Fox emails. The last few all have the same sort of message, 'You don't want to miss out on being the first to see this amazing new invention in action,' and 'Get back to me quickly if you want to change the world.'

I groan but I know I should at least meet with him. If he turns out to be a nutter in person then I'll bin him off. I type out a quick email thanking him for the nine emails (I can't let it go) and suggest a meeting the following week. I have just pressed the 'send' button when David flops onto the couch beside me, his laptop glued on his knee like it is every night.

'So, what's the verdict?' he says, glancing at my screen. 'Are you going to meet the great Sebastian Fox?'

'I suppose so,' I say, grumpily.

'Don't write him off just yet,' David says, flipping up his screen. 'He might just change the world.'

I stick my tongue out at him and walk into the kitchen to break the catastrophic news to Anna that it is, in fact, her bath-time. However bad Sebastian Fox might be, I think, as I haul a kicking and screaming Anna up the stairs, he can't be any worse than a tantruming four-year-old.

Of course, I am wrong.

8

It's Friday morning and I deliberately resist checking my emails until after I drop Anna at school. Once home, I trudge into the kitchen and glare at my phone for a bit. Part of me is dying to see if Sebastian Fox has emailed me back, while the other part is slightly dreading it. I'm not sure I can handle another deluge of emails. To be honest, I'm feeling a bit deflated. After the high of meeting Sho yesterday, I was looking forward to having a chat today but I didn't spot her in the playground, or Milly for that matter. Perhaps Milly is sick. Instead I spent ten minutes nodding and smiling at Diana's exciting discovery of a knitting circle – 'And right on our doorstep too!' A knitting circle! Jesus, I can't even hold chopsticks the right way.

I tap my fingers on the counter for a bit before biting the bullet and switching on my phone. I ignore the new texts and look immediately at the mailbox icon. To my surprise, there is only one new email. It's from Sebastian. It says that he is DELIGHTED that I got in touch and would LOVE to meet me. Then he suggests Monday at 10 a.m. and gives me the address of his houseboat in Chelsea. I'm not sure about this. I would have preferred to meet him in a public place just in case he really is a psychopath. Still, maybe I am being a bit paranoid. I text back quickly to confirm before I can change my mind and text a quick message to Bea asking how she is today. Just then my phone starts to ping at an alarming rate, which means only one thing. The class WhatsApp group is fired up about something.

Misery:
Mara came home crying last night because another child told her that her mummy was fat.

Oh, bloody hell. I mean, Misery could do with losing a few pounds but it's not something you would say out loud. Cue the inevitable cries from all her Organics cronies, 'OMG! How awful!' and 'That's fat-shaming!'

Grim though it is, what I really want to know is this: why the hell is Misery going on a witch-hunt on a class WhatsApp group rather than going directly to the teacher or even to the parent of the child who has 'fat-shamed' her? Clearly, she already knows who it is – if Mara is anything like Anna, she'll have spilled the beans on the way home from school pick-up. No, the purpose of Misery's text is to 'out' the mother and publicly *shame* her into apologising for her 'wayward' child.

A message from Bea pops up telling me to come over, and I grab my keys and head out the door, grateful for a distraction from all the school pettiness. It suddenly occurs to me that it might have been Anna who called Mara's mummy fat. But I quickly discount the thought. Anna would have been far more likely to use the other 'f' word.

When Bea opens the door I am glad to see her looking less pale than yesterday.

'I only puked once!' she says, giving herself a little sarcastic clap, as we sit down at the kitchen table.

Then she releases a great big sigh. 'I suppose I'm going to have to tell Ryan,' she says, adjusting her glasses towards the tip of her nose. 'Oh, God, I'm going to have to tell my mother too,' she says, putting her head in her hands. 'She's going to be all judgemental and I can't bear it!'

I reach over and pat her shoulder. She stands up suddenly and my hand falls away.

'I mean, I don't even have any BABY stuff any more. I threw everything out after Harry grew out of it,' she says, pacing across the kitchen floor. 'Not to mention the fact that I'm in my bloody forties. I barely have enough energy for Harry, never mind a newborn.'

'Bea...' I say, standing up to join her.

She holds up a firm hand to indicate that her rant is far from over.

'And from a superficial level, am I really ready for no men and no sex for at least another couple of years?' she says, through pursed lips.

Rant or no rant, I have to chime in on that one.

'That's the same for all of us with kids, Bea, whether you have a partner or not!'

She gives me a weak smile and drops back on the kitchen chair. Then she looks up at me and says, 'Do you think I'm doing the right thing keeping the baby?'

I take the time to consider the question before answering it.

'Would you regret it if you didn't keep it?' I say.

She nods immediately.

'Well, there's your answer,' I tell her.

'Okay,' she says, throwing her shoulders back. 'I'm having the baby.'

'You're having a baby!' I say, and the momentousness of it all suddenly hits me and I bend down to give her a big hug.

Then I sit down at the table opposite her where she's looking pensive.

'Oh, fuck!' she says, slapping her hand against her forehead. 'No booze for nine months.'

Oh, God, I forgot about that little nugget, but surely all is not lost? I tell her that she can have at least one glass of red now and then, and didn't doctors used to prescribe Guinness back in the day for pregnant mothers? Sure, it's practically medicine, and so on and so forth. Happy mummy equals happy baby. But then Bea's mood takes an even darker turn when she remembers that mouldy cheese and sushi are also considered pregnancy no-nos. I decide to get out of there before she recalls the restrictions on caffeine.

As we're walking to the door, I give her a brief summary of Sebastian Fox, the enthusiastic prolific emailer.

She looks thoughtful for a moment. 'Nine emails? But you don't get a sense that he's a nutter?'

'Well, I have certainly considered that he might be, but I'll let you know what he's like when I meet him on Monday,' I say.

'Stay on the dock if you don't like the look of him,' she commands. 'He might not be a psychopath but he could be a hashtag-Me-Too.'

'I'll let you know how it goes,' I say, giggling at the 'hashtag'.

I give her a little wave and turn to leave. Just as the door closes, I hear her shout.

'Oh FUCK, NO COFFEE!'

9

It's Monday morning and I wake up feeling shattered. At first, I think it's the result of being with Anna for a straight forty-eight hours over the weekend, but as I get out of bed, other sensations convince me otherwise. I groggily make my way to the bathroom and look at myself in the bathroom mirror. A weird feeling of being slightly outside myself floods over me, like I'm trapped in a glass bubble looking through a blurred image of me. I hang my head and fight the urge to burst into tears for no earthly reason.

Just then David walks into the bathroom, takes one look at me and starts to back out again.

'PMT?' he whispers on the retreat.

'Yes,' I growl. He knows well enough by now that nobody is safe for at least a couple of days before the blessed relief of my period.

'I'll get Anna ready for school,' he says, hurriedly, and I give him my best attempt at a 'thank you' smile, but inwardly I hate him and I hate the world.

I take a long shower, hoping to relax away the blues and try to focus on the day ahead. As terrible timing would have it, I am meeting with Sebastian Fox today. Putting on my game face is going to be a lot harder than normal. I slap on my make-up without paying much attention, drag on my one 'good' pair of black wool trousers and a blue work shirt. Tailored clothes feel uncomfortable and tight after my usual freelance garb of jeans and holey sweaters.

When I get downstairs, Anna is not only dressed but fed, and glued to what appears to be animated slime on the TV in the kitchen. David looks me up and down and does a double take. Then he frowns.

'Is that what you're wearing for your meeting with Sebastian Fox?' he says.

I glare at him shocked that he would dare to comment on my outfit – on today of all days! You're a brave man, I think silently, narrowing my eyes. A brave and stupid man...

Clocking my fury, David holds out a placating hand in my direction, which I studiously ignore.

'I only ask,' he says, hurriedly, 'because you're wearing your pants over your trousers.'

I immediately look down, and there they are – my giant pair of seamless knickers (only ever worn with my good trousers) pulled firmly up around my waist.

'Fine,' I say, stiffly, turning back towards the stairs to change the order of my clothing. One day I'll see the humour in it, but today is not that day.

By the time I change and come down again, David's (wisely) gone to work, and it's almost time for school. I try to persuade Anna to get into her shoes and coat using as few swear words as I possibly can and tread the usual path towards the school gates. We reach the school just as the bell rings, so I give Anna a quick kiss and send her on her way. I glance around for Sho and Milly but I don't see them anywhere.

Just as I am congratulating myself that I've managed to dodge Diana, she walks right into me.

I can't even fake politeness, so I tell her that I'm in a major rush and literally run out of the school gates (no Mr Russell) and leg it up towards the Tube station, where I intend to go straight to Chelsea for my meeting with Sebastian Fox. I am so intent on making my getaway that I run straight into Sho and Milly.

'Oh, sorry!' I say.

'No worries,' Sho says, looking even cooler than she did the other day in ripped jeans, fitted beat-up black leather jacket and the same biker boots.

I wave a little hello to Milly.

'How come you weren't at school on Friday?' I say to Sho. Then I immediately kick myself for how needy it sounds. You've only just met the girl, Saoirse, I chide myself. Play it cool, for God's sake!

To be fair, Sho doesn't look the least bit fazed by the question.

'Yeah, we didn't make it on Friday. Mummy was a bit tired, isn't that right, Milly?' she says, wiggling Milly's hand. Sho makes a drinking gesture with her other hand, and whispers, 'Big night on Thursday – couldn't get up on Friday.'

Wow. I can't imagine ever missing a day of school because I'm hungover. I'm not sure if I'm appalled or impressed.

'Anyway, where are you off to?' Sho says, flicking her hair off her shoulder.

I babble something about a work meeting but then Milly starts to tug at her hand.

'You better get to school,' I say. 'You don't want to get a late pass!'

A late pass? Jesus, what is wrong with me?

Sho gives me a quick, 'Cool, see you later,' and falls into step beside Milly.

I cross the road towards the Tube station, praying that I don't meet anyone else I know. Clearly, I'm not fit to socialise today. I just hope I do better with Sebastian Fox.

* * *

A cold autumn breeze cuts through my only smart, soft, grey coat as I exit Sloane Square Tube station and hurry along Cheyne Walk, pausing every now and then to closely examine the names on each boat floating in the murky River Thames. After several minutes of searching houseboats of all different shapes and sizes, I spot the one I'm looking for: *The Fantastic Fox*. Obviously. It's not the grandest boat by any stretch: long and narrow, coated with what-was-once-white-now-turned-grey, flaky paint, lined with four smudged windows. I hesitate at the end of the pier, half-tempted to bottle it. None of this bodes well. What good can come of a meeting with a man who not only lives in this pile of crap but feels confident enough to name it after himself? But before I can make a run for it, a short, stocky figure leaps up on the pier, his hand outstretched in greeting. I push my shoulders back and try to muster up a smile. Might as well make the best of it.

Sebastian Fox is about five and a half feet tall, probably not much older than me but with prematurely grey hair and a receding hairline. His equally grey beard is in desperate need of a trim and, despite the chill in the air, he is dressed in ragged, beige cargo shorts, loose threads trailing from the edges, and a used-to-be orange, oversized polo shirt. His whole image screams, 'Hey! I might not be the best-looking, but I'm friendly and playful!'

He clasps my hand and pumps it up and down vigorously, beaming all the while.

'Wonderful to meet you,' he says, in an upper crust English accent.

I can't help but smile in return. His enthusiasm is infectious. Still, I'll keep all my spider senses alive just in case he suddenly produces a knife or a thick rope.

He leads me through the small door of the boat, and the inside is about as inviting as the outside. To my left is a tiny kitchen and another door, presumably leading to an equally tiny bedroom. And to my right is a small, narrow bench, which I presume he uses as a kitchen table. Then he guides me towards the back of the boat to a rectangular seating area covered in blue foam and scattered with faded cushions. An uncomfortable-looking, dark, wooden rocking chair sits opposite, slightly tilting with the gentle motion of the boat. There is a small, wooden table covered with a messy pile of paper between the chair and foam-covered seating area.

I choose a spot on the edge of one of the cushions and Sebastian plants himself in the rocking chair opposite me, leaning forward.

'You have NO IDEA how delighted I am that you're here!' he says, running his hand over the bald patch. 'Honestly, I never thought it would happen!'

I smile politely.

'The first thing you need to know is that I have given up everything for my creation and I will do anything to make it work,' he says, his voice suddenly trembling. 'I have left my banking job, and made other huge personal sacrifices, but I have to do this, you know? This is the path I was always supposed to take.'

Then he leans even closer, the rocking chair creaking in protest.

'Saoirse – not only is my invention going to change the world but it's going to make it a better place.'

I look into his shining eyes and instinctively feel the alarm bells going off. Someone who has made this much sacrifice is bound to have very high expectations.

Although Harriet had warned me that he wouldn't tell anyone about the details of the book or the invention, I have a go anyway, and ask him if there is anything at all he can tell me.

'Sadly, no,' he says. 'Not before the confidentiality agreement is signed.'

I nod. There is no way I'm going to get any more out of him.

'Well, will you do it?' he says, his eyes wide with anticipation.

Years of experience has taught me never to make a serious decision or quick judgement when I'm in the throes of PMT and feeling overly emotional and paranoid about everything and everyone. So, I tell him I'll think about it.

His face falls.

'I'll make it worth your while,' he says, nodding frantically.

'Oh, it's not about that,' I say, although, of course, it's a lot about that. 'I just need some time to think it over.'

He stares at me for a moment, then suddenly claps his hands sharply making me jolt a little.

'Can we at least discuss rates?'

'Erm, well it depends...' I say. I'm terrible at quoting rates but I know I should give him some sort of ballpark figure. Then to buy myself some time, I start to babble about how my rates really depend on the length of the book and how long it will take to write it, and he nods along eagerly the whole time.

I need to keep my business head on, but I am horrified at the thought of signing up to a book that I know nothing about. It's a huge risk. What if he's totally delusional and the invention is rubbish?

'Will £50,000 cover it?' he says.

What?

'Yes, £50,000 will be in your bank account once the confidentiality agreement and contract are signed.'

Jesus. My mouth falls open. I probably would have charged him half that figure.

'So you'll do it for £50,000?' he says, his eyes wide.

'Well... I... think it's a fair price,' I stumble.

Then he jumps up and punches the air.

'This is AMAZING!' he says, hopping from one foot to another. 'I KNEW I'd find you!'

The boat starts to rock and my stomach starts to roll.

Then he reaches down and snatches one of the papers off the pile on the table between us and hands it to me.

I take it and the words 'confidentiality agreement' swim before me. My stomach lurches and my whole being is screaming: 'This is all wrong!'. Besides, looking at the state of him and his boat, I'm not sure I believe he has that kind of money. If it looks too good to be true, it generally is. He might be just one of those harmless, but delusional people who thinks he has more to offer than he actually does.

'Oh!' he says, slapping his head with one hand. 'You need a pen!'

Christ.

As he hands me a smart fountain pen, I make my final decision. I have to go with my instincts but, looking at his eager face, I decide to let him down gently over email later. Cowardly, I know, but I just want to get out of there. I tell him that I need to read over the agreement before I sign it (which is bullshit as it's only about two paragraphs) and his face falls.

'Okay,' he says, sighing. 'Well, I will send you the contract along with the agreement to sign, but please don't take too long to make your decision. I am really keen to start straight away.'

I tell him that I will be in touch later today.

Now it's time to make my escape.

I lead the way this time, and he follows close behind me until we are back outside on the dock. He shakes my hand vigorously again and says, 'This is the start of everything.'

I nod, give him a brief smile and thank him politely for his time. On the way back to the Tube station, I fire off a quick text to Bea:

Too intense, most likely delusional.

She comes back soon after with a horror emoji. PMT or no PMT, I'm pretty sure I'm doing the right thing walking away.

10

By the time I get home I'm in a right grump. Between the meeting with the possibly delusional Sebastian Fox, my raging PMT, a bloody signal failure on the Tube five minutes before my stop, and the local shop being out of my favourite jelly sweets (the ones I hide from Anna), I'm ready to spend the rest of the day watching car-crash TV and stuffing my face with biscuits until school pick-up. Technically, I should be working on the motherhood book but that's the beauty of being a freelancer – you can take an afternoon off without anybody knowing. I stick my key in the door and throw it open aggressively enough to create a satisfying bang against the hallway wall. Then I slam it shut, take my shoes off, and chuck my coat on the stairs. It is only then I notice David's black coat hanging off the bannisters which is a bit strange. It's not like him to forget his coat. Then again, who am I to judge? I was in such a mind fog this morning that I had accidentally worn my pants over my trousers.

Desperate for a cup of tea and many biscuits (to make up for the lack of sugar rush from absent jellies), I walk quickly into the kitchen, and let out a huge scream. It turns out I'm not alone.

David is sitting at the kitchen table on his laptop, his fingers moving rapidly across the keyboard. He is so lost in what he is doing that he appears to be entirely oblivious to the scream or the fact that I am even there at all. I approach him gingerly from behind.

'David?' I say, quietly, putting my hand on his shoulder.

His shoulders tense and then drop, and his hands come to a sudden rest on the keyboard.

'It's not even midday,' I say, glancing at my watch. 'Why are you home?'

He shakes his head and breathes roughly out of his nose before turning around slowly in his chair.

'I've lost my job,' he says, looking up at me, his eyes dark with misery.

Oh, God, I think. I knew redundancies were getting more prevalent across the organisation, but David had always assured me that he was safe, that they needed someone like him. But now it seems they don't.

'I'm so sorry, David,' I whisper.

Poor David – he works so bloody hard and now he has to face the stress of being made redundant. For a control freak like him, this is the worst thing that could possibly happen.

He shrugs in a hopeless way and turns back to his screen, which I have just noticed is full of spreadsheets. I pull out a chair and sit beside him. It's never good news when the spreadsheets are out.

'What are you doing?' I say, gesturing towards the screen.

His fingers slide rapidly across the mousepad, clicking from one spreadsheet to the next at a dizzying speed. I close my hand over his to stay the motion and he doesn't protest.

'I'm just trying to figure out,' he begins quietly, 'how we're

GOING TO FUCKING LIVE WITHOUT MY SALARY COMING IN EVERY MONTH.'

The strength of his anger makes me jump a little in my chair. But I don't blame him. Of course, he's angry. Fifteen years with the same company and this is how they treat him? The utter pricks. And although I understand his frustration, I feel completely helpless to comfort him, so I wait until he has recovered from his outburst. Thankfully, it doesn't take long.

'I'm sorry for shouting,' he mumbles, looking like a small boy who has been caught nicking a packet of LEGO cards from the local supermarket.

'It's going to be okay,' I tell him, taking his hand.

He shakes his head miserably.

'Saoirse, we're going to have to cut back on some expenses,' he says, gesturing towards one of the many spreadsheets.

'Of course!' I say, nodding vehemently. But when I think about it, I'm not sure what expenses David is talking about. I mean, neither of us are big shoppers and we're lucky to go away on holiday once a year. What's left?

'Lena will have to go, for starters,' he says.

What? The cleaner? There is no way we're getting rid of Lena – she has practically saved our marriage. And she's way cheaper than a divorce. There has to be another way... And then I have an idea. Why didn't I think of it before? It's the perfect solution.

So I tell David about meeting Sebastian Fox and the amount of money he offered me to do the book, and he listens, mesmerised.

'And did you take the job?' he says, with an unmistakeable tone of urgency.

I hesitate for a second. His face is so full of hope that I can't bear to tell him the truth.

'Well, of course I did!' I lie. 'I'd be a fool to turn down that kind of money.'

'Oh, Saoirse, this is amazing!' he says, wrapping his arms around me. 'This is more than enough to keep us secure until I find a new job.'

A sudden sense of warmth flows all through my body. I have saved the day, and it feels fabulous! There's just one teeny thing I need to clarify first.

'So, we can keep Lena?' I say.

'Of course we can!' he says, smiling. Then he starts to look glum again.

'Listen, Saoirse, this is brilliant news financially, but it might take some time before I find another job. What I do is really niche and there aren't many roles out there.'

I nod along in what I hope looks like a serious way. To this day, I have no idea what David actually does for a living. I know he works in technology for a social media firm, but beyond that... After almost seven years of being together, I can't legitimately ask him now. Then I have another lightbulb idea. Goodness, I'm full of them today!

'There's no rush, David,' I say, authoritatively. 'The money from Sebastian Fox gives us some time now, so take a few months out to just get your head together and get some space from the whole redundancy thing. Maybe you could take a short course or two and explore your options.'

Or do the school run, is what I'm really thinking.

He stares at me for a moment.

'Wow, Saoirse! I never thought of taking actual time out. My first impulse was to talk to head-hunters and tell them I'm on the lookout for a new job, but now...'

'You can do whatever you want,' I say, squeezing his hand warmly.

Gosh, this is brilliant! I feel like Mrs Christmas.

Then, releasing my hand, I grab my phone and tell him that I need to pop to the bathroom and I'll be back in just a minute. As soon as I close the bathroom door, I fight all my better instincts and fire off a quick message to Sebastian Fox telling him I'll take the job. I put my phone down on the side of the sink to do a wee, purely because the mere mention of a toilet makes me want to go whether I need to or not (cheers childbirth!). My phone beeps just as I'm drying my hands. It's Sebastian Fox.

You have made my day! The journey starts here.

My stomach flip flops. There's no going back now.

I walk back into the kitchen to find David, once again, typing furiously on his laptop. Oh no, what now? But when he turns around, there is a big smile on his face. 'I've just booked into a three-month cordon bleu cookery course starting in mid-November!' he says.

'Oh,' is all I can think to say. When I mentioned a course, I sort of meant one that would improve his chances of getting another job, but he looks so happy that I can't bear to disappoint him.

'That's great!' I say with as much enthusiasm as I can muster. Why shouldn't he do something he is so passionate about? Before we had Anna, one of David's favourite things to do was to check out new restaurants and local food markets. Now he has the chance to try cooking the dishes himself, rather than watching other people do it on TV. I sit down beside him and, as he tells me all about the course, I manage to keep my smile firmly plastered on my face the whole time. The course is a full working day five days a week (so no school run duties for him, which stirs up some resentment, but I manage to push my feelings under the surface) and at the end, one of the students is chosen to go and cook in a fancy restaurant somewhere in Europe for a week in the New Year. I study him as he is talking, trying to remember the last time he was this impulsive and animated about something, and failing. This will be good for him, I think. Besides, he needs time off after everything that happened last summer. I shiver as I remember how close I was to losing David when a suicide bomber blew himself up in the street where David works. I'll never forget the paralysing fear followed by crashing waves of relief when I discovered him alive and unscathed. He deserves a break, and honestly it makes me feel good to do this for him.

David tilts the screen towards me to show me some more, and my stomach gives a little lurch because I can't help but notice the enormous cost associated with the course. Thanks to Sebastian, we can afford it, but that's only if I manage to finish the book to his satisfaction – which is never a guarantee in the ghostwriting business, especially when you have no idea what you're going to be writing about. My stomach lurches again.

David gives me a worried look, and says, 'Are you okay with this, Saoirse?'

I tut and wave away his concerns. 'Of course!' I say in an unnaturally squeaky voice. He gives me a strange look but before he can say any more, my phone beeps.

'It's my mum,' I say, reading rapidly. Then I let out a frustrated sigh. 'She wants to know why you're home in the middle of the day.'

'How does she...?' he starts. And then we look at each other and go, 'Ohhhhh.'

How could I forget that she has mine and David's phones tracked? I would never have known if David was dead or alive if she hadn't been able to track his phone to the hospital after the terrorist attack.

'Do you mind if I tell her about the redundancy?' I say.

'Go ahead,' he says, standing up and stretching. 'I'm heading to the bathroom now anyway,' he adds, gripping Anna's iPad.

See you in an hour, I think wryly.

I glance at my watch. I have just about enough time to call her before I pick up Anna from school. Knowing my mother, she'll need more than a text with news this big.

She answers on the first ring.

'Is he sick?' she says.

'Is who sick?' I say, already confused.

She gives a loud I-didn't-bring-you-up-to-be-this-stupid tut.

'David!' she says, impatiently.

'Er, no,' I say.

'Well, what's he doing home in the middle of the day then?'

'He's been made redundant,' I tell her lowering my voice in the hope it will quieten hers.

'WHAT?' she shouts. 'Oh, Jesus, poor David. How will you all live? Without him, you'll be on the breadline!'

I try to tell her not to be so dramatic but she interrupts me in the same panicky voice.

'Do you want money, Saoirse? I don't have much on the teacher's pittance they pay me but the marital miracle boxes are still ticking along and...'

Oh, for goodness' sake. I can't afford to enter into another conversation about the marital miracle boxes that my social media obsessed mother has been selling on eBay – her own invention that aims to resolve marital disagreements with a self-penned haiku and a rock, paper, scissors contest.

'Mother!' I say, firmly. 'Will you stop panicking? We'll be grand!'

So I tell her about my new job with Sebastian Fox and David taking some time off, and finally she calms down.

'Well, it sounds like you've got it all worked out already,' she says, slightly huffily, as if her efforts to swoop in and save the day have been well and truly scuppered.

I attempt to smooth her ruffled feathers by thanking her for the offer of money and she takes a deep breath and sighs.

'It's just that in my day you had a job for life and losing it was one of the worst things that could happen to you.'

I can almost see her shaking her head.

'Well, times are a bit different now. Being made redundant is just a fact of life,' I tell her gently.

Then I tell her that David is going to pursue his love of cookery by doing a gourmet cookery course in November, and this cheers her up immensely.

'I was only looking at some great recipes on Pinterest the other day,' she says, breathlessly. 'Tell him I'll send him the links.'

I glance at my watch – it's almost time to pick up Anna. But my mother's next question gives me pause.

'So, what book are you going to be writing for this Sebastian Fox, then?' she says.

I sit down at the table and rest the side of my head in one hand – I was hoping she wouldn't ask too much about this latest ghostwriting project. The last thing I need is her putting even more doubts in my head when I have no choice but to proceed.

'I don't know yet,' I say lightly.

'What?'

I can just see her scrunching her face up in disbelief; the same way she does when she loses out on an auction on eBay.

'He's created something and it's highly confidential,' I say, attempting to sound more confident than I actually am.

'So he's some sort of mad, eccentric inventor, is he?' she says, thoughtfully.

'I suppose so,' I agree.

Silence.

'Well, just make sure you don't end up with your head in a box,' she says, clearly working the serial killer angle.

'I'll do my best,' I say.

I finish the call and grab my coat and keys and, raising my voice over the podcast chatter, I shout through the bathroom door to David that I'm off to pick up Anna from school. David shouts back, offering to pick up Anna, and I hesitate. Part of me would be delighted to be off the hook from the school run, but I figure that as David hasn't been once to the school since Anna started, it would be more hassle giving him directions to the classroom, let alone describing Anna's teacher. Besides, I would have to call the school and let them know he was picking her up today and the whole thing would become unnecessarily complicated. And then there's Mr Russell... So, I tell him not to worry, and I head out the door.

At the school gates, I tag on to a group of nursery mums and use them as cover to spare Mr Russell more blushes, and head around to the back of the school, intending to take up my usual leaning place against the fence. But to my surprise, my position has already been taken.

'Hi, Sho,' I say casually, determined to avoid coming across as too needy, or indeed nerdy, given our last exchange.

She smiles and gives me a lazy wave. Then her expression changes.

'Incoming,' she hisses, her eyes fixed on a point just over my shoulder.

I turn to find the unwelcome shape of Misery approaching with an even more thunderous expression on her face. My best death stare is wasted on her though, as she makes a beeline for Sho.

'Hi,' Misery says, curtly.

Sho gives her the briefest of nods and crosses her arms over her leather jacket.

'Have you joined the class WhatsApp group?' Misery says. By the accusing way she says it, it's clear that she already knows that Sho is not a member.

'I don't do class WhatsApp groups,' Sho says, stifling a yawn.

Misery narrows her eyes, and says, 'Shame!'

Then she walks away.

Sho turns to me with raised hands.

'What was all that about? Is it a crime not to join the bloody WhatsApp group?'

I laugh.

'Oh, you're better off not joining,' I say. 'In the latest exchange, Misery was on the hunt to find out which child told Mara that her mother was fat.'

Sho looks at me for a moment.

'That was probably Milly,' she says, half-laughing. 'I might have called Misery a fat cow on the way home from school last week.'

My hand flies to my mouth and I make a mental note not to slag off any of the other mums in front of Anna – especially when she doesn't have her headphones on.

Sho clearly noticing my reaction, says, 'What?' in a way that protests her innocence. I look at her closely, her expression of defiance, and to be honest, I envy her don't-give-shit attitude. If I had been caught out like that – which she most surely has been – I would be scrunched up in a ball on the bathroom floor, mortified and wondering how I would ever face the school gates again.

I shake my head, giddy with the possibility of going through life without giving a crap about what other people might think, especially people you don't even like, but before Sho and I can say any more to each other, Milly and Anna barrel their way over to us, and we walk out the school gates together as if we have been doing it all along.

After saying goodbye to Sho, Anna and I walk home together, her full of chat about a beetle she had spotted in the school garden ('He was shiny, Mummy!') and me patting myself on the back once again for swooping in and saving David from the grimness of redundancy.

The front door opens before I have a chance to put the key in the lock and my heart beats a little faster to see David standing there, smiling and looking more relaxed than I've seen him in years. He gives Anna a big hug, and for once she returns it, and then he helps her with her shoes and her coat. He even puts everything away in the cupboard, which never ever happens. Then he gives me a quick kiss. The first intimate contact we've had since the Ryan incident.

'What's that delicious smell?' I say, sniffing the air as I take off my coat.

'Aha!' he says, giving a comic raise of his eyebrows, gesturing for myself and Anna to follow him into the kitchen.

I pause at the entrance, in an effort to take it all in. It's our kitchen all right, but not as I remember it. For a start, the table is laid. Grabbing my hand, he leads me over to the hob where two different earthenware pots (the ones we were given as a wedding gift but have never used) are bubbling away merrily. David hands me a wooden spoon and tells me to have a taste. Frankly, I'm still trying to get my head around the idea of David cooking on a weekday. Usually he's home so late that I end up eating Anna's leftovers and he grabs himself a light bite when he gets in.

I reach into the pot and gingerly taste whatever the hell it is and tell him it is delicious. It's not – it's a mediocre mish-mash of what I'm discerning are red peppers, tomatoes, and a mysterious addition of egg. Usually, all I want when I have PMT is, well, Anna's food (carbs and cheese) followed by salted caramel ice cream. Still, I'm not going to burst his bubble now, especially when he has gone to so much trouble.

I give him a little thank you hug, and he beams at me.

'Thought I better get some practice in before my cookery course starts!' he says.

'Good idea!' I say, just as brightly.

After David makes Anna's tea (I could get used to this!), we finally get a chance to sit down together and talk. It's great to see him so happy but redundancy can hit hard, especially after spending so many years in the same organisation, and I want to make sure he's coping with it.

'It's weird, Saoirse,' he says, running his hand through his thick black hair. 'I mean, I was so devastated when they marched me out of the office this morning, but now all I feel is relief.'

He leans forward and takes my hand.

'The freedom of knowing that I don't have to rush into another job tomorrow is fantastic,' he says, his eyes soft with gratitude.

I squeeze his hand and smile. 'I'm honestly pleased for you. Besides, if today is anything to go by, it will be good to have you under my feet for a few weeks!'

He laughs and shifts to put his arm around me.

'Me too. It's high time we spent more time together,' he says, looking at me in a way that can only mean sex.

And who knows? Maybe this new, relaxed, impulsive David will bring us closer again. Maybe we will turn into one of those couples who swing from the chandeliers before breakfast. Frankly, I would have had sex with him just for making Anna's tea. Then, as if sensing there is a romantic moment to be broken, Anna rushes over, squeezes herself in between us, and shoves her iPad onto David's lap, all the time complaining about the 'wubbish Wi-Fi'. David and I exchange an amused look and our eyes hold for longer than normal. I feel a shiver of anticipation running down my spine. This time together is going to be good for us – I just know it.

After David reads Anna a story and settles her in bed (she actually lets him! No 'I want Mummy'!), we sit down to eat the food he has carefully prepared and I smile through every bite. One day I'll tell him never to make it again, but not today. As he pours me another glass of red wine (wine on a Monday night!), he tells me he'd like to help out with the school run (hallelujah!) until his cookery course starts and asks me if I think that Anna would like that.

I tell him, far too quickly, that Anna would be delighted (it's happening whether she likes it or not) and spend a few glorious minutes filling him in about all the dynamics at the school gates. Of course, he knows Tania Henderson from our baby group years ago, and can just about remember Misery from Rocking Horses nursery, but I haven't filled him in about Sho yet, or Diana the diagonal walker for that matter.

He laughs so much at the WhatsApp group stuff, and Milly repeating what Sho has said about Misery, that some of his wine goes down the wrong way and I have to whack him on the back until he recovers.

'What have I been missing?' he says, chuckling through a sip of water.

Despite all the merriment, there is one area of the school dynamics that I haven't covered and which can't be ignored, so I take a deep slug of wine to prepare.

'About Mr Russell,' I say, placing my glass carefully on the table in an attempt to avoid eye contact.

David puffs his cheeks full of air and blows out slowly.

'So, here's the thing,' he says, swirling his wine around in this glass. 'I would be lying if I said it didn't bother me that you blew the head teacher, and it probably hit harder than it should, especially after the whole Ryan thing.'

'I know,' I say quietly, thinking back to how crazily I behaved when I wrongly concluded fairly recently that he was having an affair with his ex-boss, Jordan.

'But look,' he says, putting his glass down. 'It may not have been the news I wanted to hear, but I appreciate you telling me about Mr Russell. I know I haven't exactly been honest myself in the past...'

True, I think. David had kept his search for his adoptive mother a secret from me but after the terrorist attack everything had come out into the open. Time for a fresh start.

I look at him, properly in the eye, and raise a glass.

'To no more secrets!' I say.

He smiles and echoes my words as we clink glasses.

'So, what shall we do now?' he says, after we have both drained our wine.

I'm feeling a bit pissed and the alcohol has vanquished the PMT so I take a risk.

'Sex?' I say.

'Absolutely!' he says, jumping to his feet.

He takes my hand and makes to move off, but I hesitate.

'What's up?' he frowns.

'What about all the washing-up?' I say, surveying the masses of filthy pots and pans that cover most of our work surfaces.

And then my neat freak husband says four words that make me fall in love with him all over again.

'Fuck the washing-up!'

We run out of the kitchen, giggling, shushing each other (if Anna wakes up, we've had it) and race up to the bedroom. Then we have the type of sex where neither of us is truly satisfied (because it's been so long and we're out of practice) but it's a bloody good start.

11

It's Tuesday morning and I find myself in the most astonishing position of being wrapped up in my duvet at 9 a.m. Why? Because my brilliant, no-job husband has, without being nagged, taken it upon himself to get Anna up, dressed, fed and ready for school before I've so much as opened an eyelid. To be fair, it hasn't all been plain sailing. I found out when Anna came in to say goodbye to me that David had to bribe her with a hot chocolate after breakfast just for the sheer privilege of taking her to school instead of me. Still, they're gone now and I'm enjoying the lovely peace and having the warm covers all to myself. A little ping reminds me that in my haste to get under the sheets with my husband last night, I have forgotten to switch my phone to silent. But that's okay, I think, stretching lazily, because I don't need to check that ping straight way. I drum my fingers on the duvet for a bit. Sighing, I reach over to the bedside table and grab my phone. Who am I kidding?

It's an email from Sebastian Fox, who has sent me the longest, most legally complex contract I have ever seen, with instructions to email a signed copy to him before the next meeting, along with the signed confidentiality agreement. Usually my ghostwriter agreements are only a few pages. This guy better have invented the cure for all terminal diseases, I think grumpily, trying to take in the sheer depth of information. Still, the huge fee makes all the aggravation worth it – *if* it actually materialises in my bank account.

A text flashes up from David, and I immediately click onto it, grateful for the distraction.

Off to check out a new food market in Islington and to pick up some ingredients for our meal tonight!

David – cooking again? I could get used to this. But I need to get one thing straight first. I quickly type back:

PMT = carbs.

He immediately texts back:

Italian it is!

I reply with a thumbs-up and the kissing emoji.

Then I put my phone down and give myself a little hug. I can't remember the last time David and I texted each other so affectionately. My phone pings. It's Jen texting on the WhatsApp group we share with Dee. Unlike the class WhatsApp group, I actually want to belong to this one. The last time I saw Jen – my best friend from school – she had been jilted (as my mother liked to call it) by her long-term boyfriend. He wanted kids – she didn't. Since then she's been jet setting around the world, presenting on popular Irish TV fashion show *Revealed!* and, judging by all the gossipy texts she's been sending me about drunken camera men and models throwing a strop, she's not exactly dwelling on her recent break-up.

As for Dee, she is still struggling with her two kids, Conor and Niamh – not surprising given that Conor is only two and his little sister is six months old. Most of her texts give off a slightly murderous vibe, most directed at her 'incompetent, lazy bastard of a husband', Sean. I recognise the tone well – I thought as little of David when I was sleep-deprived after I had Anna.

Jen:
Jesus, just heard about David losing his job. Is he all right?

I am totally nonplussed.

How do you know?

I type back.

Your mum ran into my mum on the beach.

Jesus Christ – is nothing sacred?
The dots appear again.

Also heard you're working for an eccentric billionaire. (Plus sticky-out tongue dollar sign winky emoji).

For the love of... Not for the first time, I wonder why I tell my mother anything, particularly when less than a third of the information ever hits the accuracy target.

Dee joins.

Listen – send some of that lovely moolah over here, will you Saoirse? I need a bloody holiday from all the feckin neediness and whingeing and that's just Sean!

I quickly send off a few lines explaining the real story but it's too late.

Ah come on Saoirse – you big tightarse!

Jen responds, knowing full well that my version is true.

I'm expecting the Concorde to touch down in my back garden any minute now!

Dee joins in.

I smile and send them the middle finger emoji. After a few happy moments, I decide to shower and get dressed – anything to put some distance between me and that shitty agreement from Sebastian Fox. It's not until after I have had my breakfast that I can face returning to it. But several brain-scrambling minutes in, my phone starts to ring. It's Bea.

'Hey, how are you feeling?' I say.

'Nauseous but not puking since I inhaled half a packet of dry crackers first thing,' she says.

'Crackers are the key,' I say, putting on my wise voice.

Then I tell her all about David's redundancy, and the job with Sebastian Fox, and she listens carefully, but as soon as there's a pause in the chat, the questions start.

'What made you change your mind about working with Mr Super Intense?' she says, in her interrogator's voice.

Damn it, I'd forgotten I'd sent her that text after the first meeting with Sebastian.

'His emotions may be intense, but his pockets are bountiful,' I say, lightly.

'I know you're doing this for David, but are you sure you can work with the guy?' she says. 'You don't even know what you're going to be writing about.'

'Oh, it'll be fine,' I say, casually. 'He's pretty harmless from what I can tell.'

'Hmmmm,' she says, clearly not convinced.

'The contract is only for six months, anyway,' I say, hurriedly. That was one fact I had managed to take in from the agreement. 'It will be worth it just to give David a break.'

'True,' Bea says and then her tone suddenly changes, her voice growing more distant.

'Fuck off, Tom, they're my crackers,' she snaps. I hear a male voice mumbling, and then she's back.

'Another playdate?' I say, through a laugh.

'No, I'm in the office. Honestly, you have to nail stuff down here or idiots like Tom will just come along and nick them,' she sighs.

We say our goodbyes and with huge regret, I turn back to the lengthy contract: weekly interviews at his chosen location (the boat) plus a firm commitment to deliver the full manuscript by the following April or else... the next bit makes me sit up... all monies will be returned to Sebastian Fox.

Well, of course I'll finish his book for him, I think, signing the contract and confidentiality agreement with a flourish before scanning and emailing the documents to him. I have no other choice.

* * *

David comes home around lunchtime, laden with paper bags. Flushed with the cold, he plants a chilly kiss on my mouth and heaves his cargo to the kitchen, where he dumps the bags on the island.

'Have you had lunch yet?' he says, whipping off his coat and scarf and flinging them over a kitchen chair.

I shake my head (I had been thinking about just having biscuits for lunch but I daren't confess that).

'Good!' he says, enthusiastically pulling fresh baguettes, soft cheese and cold meats out of the bags.

I watch him, stunned. Who is this ball of energy and why is he in my kitchen?

He grabs a knife and starts chopping everything up while I whizz around the cupboards getting the plates and cutlery ready. The whole time he's working, David chats about the market and the type of food that was on offer and how he's going to do an Italian extravaganza tonight that I'll never forget. And then, with a flourish, he scrapes everything onto a big chopping board and lays it on the table.

It feels strange sitting down together in the middle of the working week, but I'm already thinking this is the way forward. Through a mouthful of blue cheese, I ask him how dropping off Anna at school had gone.

'Fine,' he says, swigging a mouthful of water.

'Was Anna okay going into her class?' I say.

'Yes, fine,' he says, his fork spearing a large chunk of chorizo.

'Did you meet her teacher? I ask.

'No,' he says, chewing noisily.

'Did you bump into any of the mums?' I say.

'No,' he says, tearing off a chunk of baguette. 'I recognised

Tania Henderson from baby group but I didn't go anywhere near her.'

That's my boy, I think proudly.

'Did you hear the Charity dads say anything about going sober for October?' I say.

'Er, no,' he says, throwing me a look that tells me he is getting fed up with the twenty questions, but I can't help it. I want to know everything about his first experience at the school gates.

'Oh, fine,' I say, grumpily, reaching for the roll of salami. 'I'll leave you alone now.'

'Actually, there's one person I did see,' he says, with a hint of amusement in his voice.

My head shoots up. He has gossip! Finally!

'Who's that?' I say, hoping that maybe Sho has been asking about me like the fan girl I am.

'Mr Russell!' David says, smirking.

Christ.

'He's a lot more robust than I had imagined,' he grins. 'And less hair than I had pictured.'

Now I realise why he's so chuffed, because he clearly no longer sees Mr Russell as a threat. I should be happy that he's coming to terms with the fact that I blew the head teacher in a former life, but I can't help but go on the defensive.

'He was pretty slim when I met him you know,' I say. '*And* he had a lot more hair.'

'Sure he was, Saoirse,' he says, patting my hand in a patronising way.

I grumble a bit, and mutter, 'I bet you had a few exes that were mingers...'

But he just laughs and shakes his head. I'm so relieved that he's finally come to terms with it all that I don't argue any more. We finish eating in contented silence, and both rise to clear away the dishes. I'm halfway to the dishwasher when David says something that stops me in my tracks.

'I've been thinking of meeting my birth mother,' he says, taking my plate and slotting it carefully into the dishwasher.

'Wow!' is all I manage to splutter.

'Yeah,' he says, straightening up. 'I've been giving it a lot of thought over the last few weeks but work sort of got in the way of doing anything about it. Now that I have more free time, I thought it would be good to finally meet her.'

I cross the kitchen towards him and give him a big hug.

'I think that sounds like a great idea,' I say, squeezing him tight.

When we break apart, he tells me that he's going to get in touch with Joss later to arrange it, his cheeks flushing with excitement. And I look at him and smile, thinking about how far we've come since the summer when I discovered that the supposed femme fatale at the other end of his texts, was actually my old hipster flatmate Joss who was helping him to track down his birth mother. I have been in touch with Joss a bit since then, mostly to ask her about her recovery after the terrorist attack where she had sustained some facial burns, but she had told me in her own inimitable way that she was healing nicely ('Yeah, yeah, all good', plus thumbs-up emoji).

'There's just one thing I need to do first,' David says, grimacing.

'What's that?' I say, suddenly worried about how serious he looks.

'I'm going to have to tell Mum,' he says.

I try to keep as neutral an expression on my face as possible, but inside everything is screaming 'Oh no! Rose!' Frankly, it's all been a bit awkward since I screamed abuse at her down the phone during the terrorist attack. I don't regret it. I will never forgive or forget her cold response to the news that her only son was missing and might even be dead. David doesn't know the half of it. It's not necessary to tell him that I had told the woman who raised him to go fuck herself. In fairness, Rose hasn't said a thing to David either, but I'm the only one who seems to notice that the temperature drops from cold to icy whenever we visit.

So, I take a deep breath and tell David that it's the right thing to do and I will be there to support him while he tells Rose (even though it will kill me), and he gives me a quick thank you kiss. And then our eyes meet and we kiss again, and again. A fluttery feeling of panic rushes through me. I grab him by the shoulders and look at him in concern.

'You're not hoping for sex, are you?' I say.

He laughs. 'No way! I'm far too full after lunch.'

A rush of relief floods over me.

'Oh good!' I say. 'Not only did I stuff my face at lunch but I'm about to get my period any second.'

'Fair enough,' he says, rubbing my shoulder. 'And on that note...'

He heads out of the kitchen, clearly on a quest to find something else, *anything else*, to do other than talk about my periods.

I hear my phone pinging just as I'm wiping down the surfaces. Sebastian Fox has received the signed contract and wants the first interview tomorrow morning. I immediately check my bank account and there it is: £50,000. My stomach rolls over: I'm fully committed now, whether I like it or not. Still, it's good news and I am determined to make the most of it. I go in search of David and find him buried in his laptop. He looks up with a happy smile on his face when he sees me.

'I'm checking out the recipes your mum sent over on Pinterest – they're great!'

I shake my head. My mother doesn't mess around. Then I tell

him that the money has arrived from Sebastian Fox and he jumps up and wraps his arms around me and I push all the anxious feelings deep down. I can do this, I tell myself. I am doing the right thing for David and my family.

Then I tell David about the interview with Sebastian tomorrow and he instantly offers to take Anna to school without me even suggesting it.

'I'll collect her today too,' he says. But I tell him that I'll do it. To be honest, I missed taking Anna to school this morning – it's the only time we really get to have a little chat before the headphones go on. I go upstairs to pick out my 'smart' clothes for tomorrow's interview, all the time lamenting my lack of a decent wardrobe. Still, I find a nice, fitted purple sweater and some forgiving black trousers, which should do the job. Frankly, I don't know why I'm bothering making an effort at all, especially for a man who wears shorts and sandals in the middle of cold weather.

My phone pings in my pocket on my way back downstairs. And then again and again. I know without looking that it's the class WhatsApp group. Perhaps they have outed Sho. I pause on the stairs to check. It's not about Sho at all; it's something far, far worse. It's the class bake sale.

Tania Henderson:
It's our class' turn to do the bake sale next month. As it's close enough to Halloween, why don't we make it Halloween-themed?

Oh, for fuck's sake. I just don't know why she has to make such a big deal about it. Besides, it's still only September. Screw her, I'm just going to buy some cupcakes with a few spiders on them when the time comes.

Then another ping from Tania.

Only home-made goodies please!

Shite.

And it goes without saying no nuts, and go easy on the sugar!

Go easy on the sugar? It's a bloody cake sale, you moron.
Then Jane, the full-time working mum, pops up.

Just checked and I'll be in New York for work the week of the cake sale. Our nanny isn't much of a baker so it'll be the shop-bought versions for us I'm afraid! (Plus the obligatory laughing emoji to soften the blow of disagreeing with the queen bee.)

Oh dear, I think gleefully. Tania isn't going to like this! The dots appear and then disappear, and then a message from Tania finally appears.

Hi Jane – so sorry [she's not] but we can only allow home-made organic cakes at our bake sale. Let's all make an effort to save our young children from the amount of preservatives in cakes these days!

Wow. That's a low blow, even for Tania. Not only is she refusing shop-bought cakes but she's also essentially accusing Jane of being a bad mum for letting her children eat them. My heart beats a little faster with indignation. I can't help it – I have to say something.

Actually, I was planning to buy the cakes too. They are so much tastier than my home-made versions! (Plus licking-lips emoji.)

I press send and wait for the fallout. The dots start and then stop – and then nothing. I'm willing to bet my life that Tania has taken a quick break to slag me off to her private Organics crew group. No doubt she will respond in kind later.

David suddenly appears on the stairs.

'Are you still picking up Anna from school?' he says, frowning.

'Yes, why?' I say.

'Well, she gets out of school in ten minutes.'

Shit! I have been so entranced by this stupid bake sale exchange that I have forgotten all about the time. I grab my coat and a packet of cheesy crackers for Anna and start running in the direction of the school gates. I'm moving so fast I barely even have time to register the rumbling sound behind me until I feel something hard graze against my heels. My instincts kick in and I move quickly to the side of the street, only to see Tania speeding past me on her stupid scooter.

That was no accident, I think, angrily picking up my pace. That was pure revenge for defying her organic cakes-only demand. I get to Anna's class just as the door opens and quickly scoop her snack out my pocket, to pre-empt any whingeing. Without so much as a 'Hello, Mummy', Anna snatches the snack and immediately starts to share the crackers with Milly. Not for the first time, I wonder if she eats *any* of her school lunch. She always seems half-starved when I go to pick her up. I look around for Sho and find her with one foot resting casually against the wire fence. Today she is wearing a cropped denim jacket over a tight black dress, fishnet stockings and calf-length silver boots. Her hair is as free and wild as ever. Our eyes meet and she gives me a brief wave. I beckon Milly and Anna to walk with me and make my way over to her, with a mind to fill her in on the latest WhatsApp group rubbish. But just as I reach the fence, I hear a loud whirring noise approaching. I look over my shoulder to find Tania, Misery and a few of their cronies scooting over in my direction. Instinctively I clamp my ankles together. As they get closer, I hear a mumbled, 'What the fuck?' from Sho, but I don't have time to respond.

Tania swings her foot around to the back of the scooter and presses the brake. The others do the same in perfect synchronisation, almost like they have practised it, which they probably have. Judging by their extraordinarily similar, designer black leggings, trainers, and gilets, they look as though they have synchronised their outfits too.

As ever, Tania is the first to speak.

'About the cake sale,' she begins. 'We simply cannot allow shop-bought versions.'

'Why not?' Sho says, taking her foot off the fence and standing up straight.

A little thrill runs through me. Ha! Whatever chance Tania has with me, she has no chance with Sho.

Tania sighs and starts lecturing her about preservatives and all the other crap she was saying on the class WhatsApp group, and all the time Sho just stares at her with a look of sheer disdain on her face. When Tania finally stops for breath, Sho asks her one of the greatest questions I've ever heard.

'Is it against school policy to sell shop-bought cakes?' she says, moving her head to one side as if she already knows the answer.

A crease appears on Tania's forehead and a blush starts to creep up her cheeks.

'Well, no,' she says, shifting the scooter handle back and forth. 'But...'

Before she can carry on, Misery cuts in. 'It may not be school policy, but it's important that we set an example for the rest of the school,' she says, in a voice so sharp it could cut ice.

'I disagree,' Sho says, in an equally chilly voice.

The air is fraught with tension and I am revelling in it. Finally, an ally to put Tania and her judgemental pals, in their places.

Tania tosses her hair about for a bit before repeating, 'Only home-made cakes will be allowed on the stall.'

'Fine,' Sho says, wrinkling her nose in defiance. 'I won't bring any then.'

'Same,' I say, covered in goosebumps from the rebellion of it all. 'I'd rather give the money directly to the school anyway.'

The rest of the Organics spring to life, with choruses of 'school spirit' and 'coming together as a class' but Sho and I stand firm. Then Tania raises her hand and the group falls silent. Jesus, if only that worked for Anna, I think.

'Since you two refuse to contribute cakes to the cake sale, you can both run the stall on the day,' she says in a voice that wants to have myself and Sho whipped immediately. 'Surely selling cakes won't be too much of an imposition?'

What? No way. For starters, I can't count and the thought of working out the right change gives me the willies. Sho gives a firm, 'I've just remembered I'm tattooing the inside of my own nostrils that day,' and I am just thinking of something equally offensive to say, when a little voice pops up from somewhere behind me.

'Mummy, please sell cakes!' Anna says, her eyes as big as I've ever seen them, full of desperate longing.

'I... I,' but I can't get the words out. Shit. I'm trapped by the oldest form of manipulation – puppy dog eyes from a young child.

Tania gives a smile made from a curious mixture of hatred and triumph and claps her hands together sharply.

'Wonderful! That's settled then,' she says. Then she puts one foot on her scooter and sails away towards the school gates, the rest of her crew not far behind.

I let out a load groan just as Sho bursts out laughing.

'Cheers,' I say, sarcastically. 'How come Milly didn't sucker you into it?'

'Milly doesn't give a shit about cakes,' she says. 'She'd rather eat twenty bags of jelly beans, wouldn't you, Mills?'

Milly gives her a serious nod.

Then, as if on cue, Anna and Milly start a joyful 'jelly bean' chant that takes us all the way to the crossroads, where we say goodbye.

Delicious smells greet me and Anna as I push open the front door. That night, David and I spend happy minutes slagging off Tania while enjoying one of the tastiest carb-elicious meals I've had in years. It's actually pretty fun being the breadwinner, I think, going to bed that night, my stomach full of pasta and my head woozy with Italian red wine.

12

It's Wednesday, the day of the first real interview with Sebastian Fox and, to be honest, I'm not feeling all that great. In hindsight I could probably have done without the second bottle of red. Still, that's what being the breadwinner is all about, I think, swinging my legs out of bed and onto the floor: soldiering on in the face of adversity. David is on school duty today, so I give Anna a quick kiss goodbye and head off to the Tube station, trying to fight off the usual symptoms of hysteria and paranoia that always seem to go hand in hand with a hangover.

The walk to Sebastian's boat seems longer than last time, and the chilly, morning wind more blustery. I let out a gigantic yawn just before I step on to the pier and bunch my fist in preparation to knock on the door. It is opened with such enthusiasm that I nearly fall through.

And there's Sebastian, dressed in the same T-shirt and shorts he was wearing the other day, eyes dancing and mouth stretched in a warm smile.

He reaches over and pumps my hand up and down.

'So glad you're here!' he says in his booming voice.

I smile back at him. It could be the huge amount of alcohol I downed last night, but I have butterflies of both anticipation and dread causing havoc in my stomach. Part of me can't wait to find out about his invention, while the other part is absolutely terrified. Still, I am determined to see this project through to the end, no matter what. Unless it's something to do with warfare, adult scooters (a turbo version) or seriously psychotic porn equipment, then I'm in. Who am I kidding? I'm already in no matter what.

He leads me back to the same seating area as last time, while he takes his spot on the old rocking chair. He leans forward with his hands clasped on his knees and stares at me for a bit. Then he jumps to his feet so suddenly that half my arse lifts up from the cushion.

'On your feet, Saoirse!' he commands, beckoning me wildly.

What?

I rise to my feet slowly, trying to ignore the effect of the rocking boat on my carb and wine-fuelled stomach.

'Right!' he says, clapping his hands. 'I want to start every meeting with the following phrase. Ready?'

Unless this phrase is 'Let's all have a nice lie-down' I'm pretty sure I'm not interested. But I nod anyway. For £50,000, I'm ready to get stuck in.

'Okay!' he shouts, punching the air, like a cheerleader who has just made it into the team. 'The phrase is "I am EXCITED"!'

I glance around for the hidden cameras. Surely someone is taking the piss. He looks at me with such expectation that I feel the need to make some kind of effort.

'I am excited,' I say, as enthusiastically as I can under the circumstances. I'm really bad at this motivational stuff – it always makes me feel self-conscious and stupid – kind of like when you're changing a nappy in front of the health visitor for the first time.

He purses his lips and looks at me merrily. 'Come on! You can do better than that.'

Feeling like I'm in the worst version of a Christmas panto, I try again. This time I put a bit more welly into it.

But this doesn't seem to do the trick either. He cups his hand under his chin and says quietly, 'One more.'

So I take a deep breath and think about all that lovely money nestling cosily my account and say it as loudly as I can: 'I AM EXCITED!'

He laughs and stomps his feet and then makes me say it with him three more times.

To my surprise, I do feel a bit more energised and a little less hungover.

I sit down and he stays standing, looking into the distance. Then he drops into the rocking chair quickly and clasps his hands together.

'Before I tell you about my invention, I need to give you a bit of background,' he says.

I nod, although inwardly I'm a bit disappointed. My curiosity has gone into overdrive at this point.

'When I was about five years old,' he begins, 'I rescued a mouse from old Badger the cat. I almost got my hand taken off by Badger for that one!' he laughs.

I smile back encouragingly.

'Anyway, my mother, she did the most extraordinary thing... I'll never forget it...' And honest to God, out of nowhere, his voice starts to break. I start to panic. What if he breaks down in front of me? I've never had a client cry before. Jesus, I don't even think I have any tissues.

'Are you okay?' I say, but he waves a hand at me before taking a few gulps of air.

Then he looks away, and blinks rapidly, taking a deep breath as if to compose himself.

'She passed away recently,' he says, quietly.

'Oh, I'm so sorry,' I begin, but he gently holds up a hand, and I stop. Clearly, it's too soon for sympathy. My heart goes out to him – he's obviously going through a tough time.

'Anyway, my mother took the poor little mouse from my hands and carried it to the airing cupboard. She tried to feed it and keep it warm, but within a few minutes, it had passed away.'

Then he turns to me, misty-eyed, and says, 'Do you know what she did with the body, Saoirse?'

I don't know if it's nerves or tension or what, but I feel a dangerous sense of hysteria bubble up into my throat and I do everything in my power to swallow it back down. What if his invention is something to do with a dead mouse? I shake my head, biting the insides of my cheeks so hard I'm sure there will be white fleshy scars there later.

'She took my hand and brought me out into the garden and dug a hole.'

Fair play to her, I think. That mouse would be buried in a plastic bag and flung into the outside bin if it had been me.

'But!' he says, holding up one finger. 'When she had carefully placed the little mouse into the hole, she sprinkled something on it before she covered it up and patted down the soil.'

He takes a deep breath, raises his hands like a TV evangelist and says, 'My mother, bless her soul, in all her infinite wisdom and kindness, sprinkled...'

And I can't help it. It just comes out.

'Cheese!' I shout.

His hands flop to his sides and his eyebrows wrinkle in disappointment.

Damn it. I mutter a quiet 'sorry' and he gives me an impatient shake of his head. Then he takes another deep breath and announces the answer in a voice that suggests that all the good has been taken out of the moment.

'Seeds,' he says. 'She sprinkled seeds on the mouse.'

Then to my great relief, he rises off his chair and moves off towards the window.

Okay. He's got me. What has a dead mouse laced with seeds by Sebastian's late mother got to do with his life-changing invention?

'Well, time passed, and suddenly shoots started to appear in the spot where she had buried the mouse. Before long, the entire area was covered in a mass of brightly coloured flowers,' he says, softly.

He turns towards me once more.

'As I grew older, every time I looked at that spot, I remembered the mouse and how my mother, by creating this wonderful piece of nature, had brought something cold and dead back to life again.'

His eyes are shining now and for the first time I feel interested in where this is leading. As if sensing my sudden anticipation, he does a slow walk back to the rocking chair, and sinks into it, bit by bit.

'She was an artist, you know, and part of me thinks this beautiful flower patch was one of her greatest creations.'

My adrenaline starts to pump. I love artists – I know nothing about them, but before I had Anna, one of my favourite weekend hobbies was to wander around London's many awe-inspiring galleries. For the first time, I start to feel really excited about this project.

'After my mother died, she left a will,' Sebastian begins. 'She left me this boat and a request that I create something beautiful from her ashes, just like she had done with the dead mouse years before. I couldn't believe she had remembered,' he says, tears prickling his eyes.

I tilt my head in sympathy.

'She always wanted me to be an artist, you see. I'm afraid I failed her on that front – she was so disappointed when I dropped out of art college and went into banking, which she regarded as a soulless profession, but I was really hopeless as an artist!' he says with a bitter laugh. 'So, after the will was read out, I decided there and then that I would do anything to fulfil her dream. The problem was I had no idea where to start. Then I started to ask myself some questions: what if I could ease the pain of losing loved ones? What if I could find a way for people to have the presence of their loved ones forever in their lives? What if I could create something with the ashes of the dead that provided comfort to the ones left behind?'

Listen, I don't know if this is an impulse thing or what, but the words are out before I can control them.

'You're going to grow trees from human ashes,' I say.

He looks at me quizzically and shakes his head.

For the moment, I am nonplussed. It seemed so obvious that's where he was going with the story.

'Jewellery,' I say. I'm pretty sure I've read about people who make ashes into jewellery so you can keep the dead person close to your heart at all times.

After receiving another unimpressed look, I make a conscious decision to stop all the guessing. Besides, after trees and jewellery, I really have nothing else in my back pocket.

He slowly gets to his feet once more and, with one big step, moves to the seating area beside mine. Flinging away the cushions, he opens up the lid to reveal a large storage space underneath. Then he lifts out a small, rectangular, silver, wooden box, cradling it reverently in his hands, and walks slowly back to his rocking chair. Once settled, he stretches out his hands to me and breathes, 'Take it and open it.'

I hesitate. My head is swimming with fearful thoughts. What if there's a dead mouse in the box? Or human body parts? Or something even more sinister? He moves the box a little closer this time. The rocking chair creaks. I take it and weigh it in my hands. It's heavier than I thought – certainly weightier than a dead mouse, I think, with no small measure of relief. But, then again, it might well be the right sort of weight for a human hand or (as my mother helpfully suggested, a human head). I give myself a little shake and tell myself not to be so ridiculous. With renewed conviction, I set the box on my lap and move to take off the wooden lid. When I see what's inside, I almost burst out laughing with relief.

I reach in and take it out and hold it in one hand, all the time wondering if I'm missing something.

'Well?' Sebastian says, his eyes heavy with anticipation.

'It's a smartphone,' I say, dumbly.

'Ah, but it's not just any smartphone,' he says, gently taking it from me. 'The cover of this smartphone is made from recycled materials.'

'Good for the environment,' I say, impressed. And then I have a terrible, terrible thought but he gets there first before I can voice it.

'One of those materials is cremated ashes,' he says, his eyes wide with intensity.

My whole body spontaneously bursts into goosebumps.

'You see, Saoirse?' he says, holding the phone purposefully in front of my face. 'Of course, you can grow a memorial tree or flowers out of ashes, but what if you move house? And you could certainly have the ashes blended with other materials and made into jewellery, but what if you lose it?'

'You could lose a phone too,' I say, thinking of all the times I have left mine in the supermarket trolley or on the bus.

'The thing about a phone is that it is always with us – it is never more than a few feet away. We touch it, hold it, bring it close to us when we're talking. Really, in these modern times, it is the most intimate object that we possess.'

He might be right, but if that's true, it's the most depressing thing I've ever heard.

'Do you know what's so special about this particular phone?' he says, stroking it in the same way you would stroke a small furry animal.

I shake my head.

'You can access an app that's devoted to the deceased loved one. So, you can hear their voice, even have a chat if you want to, and look at photos and videos of them any time you want. No matter what happens, the memories will always be there.'

Apart from when you drop the phone down the toilet, like I have done on many an occasion.

'Can you take me through the app?' I say, suddenly curious, and frankly hopeful that he will hold on to the phone so I won't have to touch it again. The photos and videos are of course standard, but I'd like to see how he captures the dead person's voice, especially if the death has been sudden.

'Oh, this is just a prototype,' he says, giving the phone a little tap. 'I'm just focusing on the phone case for now. The app will come later.'

I'm not exactly in love with his idea but I also don't want to dismiss it out of hand. Technically, all he's creating is an app – sort of like a digital album that you can converse with. It's weird and not really as beautiful as his mother had perhaps intended, but who am I to judge? Maybe it will provide some comfort to people struggling with grief. At least it's not a dead person blow up doll or some sort of human robot. The only part I'm squeamish about is the ashes. Call me fussy, but I just can't cope with the idea of texting or tweeting on a phone that contains a dead person's remains. I'll just have to make sure he gives all the demos next time so I won't have to touch it too much.

'Would you like another look?' he says, handing me the device.

Trying to quell the churning in my stomach, I look at the phone closely, intending to see if there are any differences in design to the usual smartphones. If I'm going to write a book about this, I need to know everything I can about it. As I lean back a little to get a wider perspective, the phone somehow slips from my grasp, and clatters on to the floor.

Sebastian gives a loud groan and snatches it up immediately.

'Careful!' he barks.

I raise my hands in the air, completely confused. What's the big deal? It's only a prototype.

He holds the phone protectively against his chest, hugging it with both hands.

'That's my mother in there,' he says.

13

'It's not funny, Bea,' I say, crossly.

It's Friday and I'm at Bea's house for a cup of tea and a plate of biscuits while she pretends to work from home.

'Oh, it is, Saoirse!' she says, spluttering biscuit crumbs from her mouth. 'The thought of you holding Sebastian's dead mother in your hands is simply priceless!'

I give her my best glare and violently dunk another digestive. Okay, so technically I'm not supposed to divulge any details of the 'amazing' invention – after all, I have signed an overly complex confidentiality agreement, but let's face it, I'll go mad if I can't tell someone.

Bea wipes a tear from her eye with the corner of her sleeve and takes another a sip from her tea.

'Seriously, though,' she says. 'Is he a psychopath?'

'I don't think so,' I tell her.

'A sociopath?'

I shake my head. To be honest, since that interview, I've been asking myself the same questions but I haven't arrived at any of those conclusions. I shouldn't be a stranger to weird inventions;

my own mother used to sell wooden coffins for dead hamsters on eBay, for goodness' sake.

I catch the end of my biscuit and swallow it before it dives straight back into my tea.

'He's hard to describe,' I say. 'I think he means well, and he's very passionate about his invention and he's clearly doing his best to fulfil his late mother's wishes...'

'And he's paying you a shit-ton of cash,' Bea says, adjusting her glasses.

'Well, precisely,' I say.

'Have you told David about the meeting?'

I shake my head. I've been desperate to spill the beans to David, but I am worried that if I tell him the truth, he will also think Sebastian is a weirdo and have concerns about me working for him. And no Sebastian equals no book which equals no money. The last thing I want is for David to go back to work before he's had some time off. More to the point, I love stay-at-home David – the cooking, the taking care of Anna, the lie-ins, the school run... How could I ever give that up? I mean, I know it can't last forever but it's certainly how I want it to be for the next few months.

I tell Bea all this and she arches her eyebrows at me.

'No more secrets, my arse!' she says, attempting an Irish accent, even though she knows full well that nobody outside Ireland should ever try it.

Annoying Irish accent aside, I know she has a point. After everything that happened over the summer, David and I had made a pact to be totally honest with each other.

'Look, if it gets even more morbid, or if he shows any psycho-pathic or sociopathic tendencies, then I'll tell David,' I say.

A slow grin spreads across her face.

'I can't wait until he gets that app working and he starts

having conversations with his dead mother in front of you!' she says, cracking up again.

I give her the finger, which is our usual signal for a change of subject.

'So, how are you feeling?' I say.

'A bit better,' she says, separating the biscuit base from the marshmallow top of a salted caramel teacake. 'Haven't puked in a bin in a few days!'

I give her the thumbs-up.

'When are you going to tell Ryan?' I say, eyeing up one of those pink wafer biscuits I used to have in my school lunchbox as a child.

'I'll wait until after the twelve-week scan at the end of October I think,' she says, sighing. 'No point in him knowing until I'm sure everything is okay with the baby.'

'What about your mum?' I say.

She makes a vomiting sound.

'I'll tell her after the scan too.'

'Well, when the news is out, we'll go on a baby shopping spree!' I say as brightly as I can, although frankly traipsing through baby shops is the last thing I want to spend my time doing.

Bea gives me one of her 'no fucking way' looks and says, 'I have no intention of going on any sort of spree. I did all that with Harry and I ended up buying all sorts of shit I didn't need. This time, I'm going online and buying everything second-hand.'

She's right. Eejit here did the same thing. Even though I could have saved a fortune on nearly-new stuff, I ended up going for the latest buggy (which looked like something out of the Starship Enterprise and was equally as fantastical in practice – it barely fit on the bus for starters) and fell for all the 'make-my-baby-a-genius' toys. Looking back, I wouldn't buy anything new either.

I glance at my watch. It's almost time for pick-up but David is doing the collection today so I don't have to rush home. After cake-sale-gate, I could do with avoiding the Organics for a while. David is also planning a gourmet-style curry tonight, which I'm already looking forward to. I think I might even try to seduce him afterwards. I make a mental note to implement a degree of portion control so we're not too full to have sex.

Still, I should make a move. I need to start transcribing the notes from the interview with Sebastian. I tell Bea I'm off and she gives me a tired wave. Poor Bea, I think, during the walk home. I can't imagine being pregnant again, let alone going through the trauma of the baby and toddler years.

When I get home, I head straight upstairs to my computer to transcribe the interview with Sebastian. And I have to say, even I find myself particularly annoying in this interview. I really need to stop with the interruptions and guesswork. Next time I'll do more listening. About an hour later, Anna bursts into the house. Relieved to have an excuse to take a break, I race downstairs to give her a cuddle.

David gives me a quick kiss and a shifty look.

'What is it?' I say, suspiciously.

'My mum has invited us over on Sunday,' he says, running his hands through his hair. 'I've decided to tell her about looking for my birth mother then.'

14

Sunday arrives far too quickly and, before I know it, we're bundling Anna and our favourite long-distance friend (her iPad) into the back of the car. David is quiet on the drive to Oxfordshire and I turn the radio on to save him from feeling like he needs to make conversation. To be honest, I feel nervous for him. Rose is a formidable force at the best of times. When he reaches for the gear stick, I give his hand a quick squeeze and he shoots me a small smile. Ninety minutes and two unplanned emergency stops on the hard shoulder with the travel potty later ('Mummeee, I need a weeee!' and followed ten minutes after the wee by 'Mummeee, I need a poo!') we finally arrive at Rose's cream, pebble-dashed semi in Oxfordshire. Pulling up outside, David and I exhale at exactly the same time.

'Showtime,' he says grimly, tugging open his door and stepping out into the grey drizzle.

I get out of the car and open Anna's door to let her out. As I'm unbuckling her seatbelt, she looks up at me with wide eyes and says, 'Where are we?'

It's hard to contain my impatience. Frankly, I can't believe this is still breaking news to Anna. Not only did we tell her yesterday we were going to see her gran but also when she got up this morning and when we put her in the car. I tell her that we're at her gran's house and her eyes fill with a 'how could you have betrayed me' look. Mind you, I don't blame her – Gran's house is about as entertaining as a punctured bouncy castle at a funfair. Still, I don't want Anna to kick off and make this whole experience even harder for David, so I tell her that I'll give her extra jellies when we get home if she can make it through the next hour or so. She holds out her little hand and we shake on it. As she wriggles out of her car seat, clutching her iPad, her ears encased in her signature headphones, I breathe a sigh of relief, and say a silent prayer of thanks to the people who invented bribery (and jellies).

As we walk up the narrow garden path, I can't help but notice how stark Rose's garden looks in comparison to next door's carefully planted shrubbery and thriving flower boxes. David rings the bell and we stand there rubbing our hands together, trying to keep out the chilly autumn breeze. I have purposefully dressed for the occasion by wearing a thermal vest, wool sweater and oversized cardigan, but even so, I'm willing to bet the inside of Rose's house is as cold as the outside. She's not fond of putting the heating on at the best of times. Finally, the door opens, but just a chink.

'Who's there?' Rose says, in a wavering voice.

We haven't made it into the house yet and I'm already annoyed. We bloody told her we'd be coming today. David even called her this morning to remind her.

David presses his face to the small gap in the door and says gently, 'Mum, it's us! Open up.'

The door closes very gradually, and there's a clinking sound while she takes off the chain, and then, finally, the door creaks open again and at last we make it into the dark interior of the hallway.

Rose gives David a thin smile and narrows her eyes at me. I think it's fair to say she hasn't quite forgiven me for shouting abuse down the phone at her during the terrorist attack. Anna automatically takes off her coat and shoes at the foot of the wine-carpeted stairs but as soon as she hangs up her coat on the bannister, her eyes take on a haunted look.

'Mummeee!' she wails, running over.

David and I exchange a concerned look.

'What is it, sweetheart?' I say, bending down to her level.

'It's FREEZING in here!' Anna cries, folding herself into me, pressing her headphones tight against her head like earmuffs.

I clasp my hand to my mouth to stop the giggles from spilling out. Anna's right. As I predicted, it is at least five degrees colder in here than it is outside. I can almost make fog rings with my breath. Rose tuts at her only granddaughter.

'Nonsense!' she says, briskly. 'There's no such thing as the cold; only inappropriate clothing.'

Then she gives Anna the once over, shoots a disapproving glare at me, and raises her eyes skyward. Now, much as I'd like to disagree with Rose, I have to say that Anna has surpassed herself in the outfit stakes today. Despite being told repeatedly (a) that we were going to Gran's; (b) that it's a cold day; and (c) that it's always bloody freezing at Gran's, Anna has decided to adorn herself in a black, sleeveless, cotton red-and-white polka-dot dress, sheer pink tights and a pair of yellow neon plastic summer pool shoes. As David whispered to me earlier, 'She looks like a prostitute going to a fancy-dress party.'

As we had agreed that it was far too much hassle to talk her out of the get up, we just bundled her into the car and turned the heating on full. I peel off my cardigan and wrap Anna in it, who is delighted to have hijacked some of Mummy's clothes (there's no way she would have accepted a cardigan that belonged to her. She would have been positively affronted!). David scoops up Anna to save her from stumbling on the overly long cardigan and we start the slow march into the grim looking 'good' sitting room.

As usual, I sit down on the uncomfortable, faded, dusky pink chaise longue underneath the bay window, and David lowers Anna to sit beside me, before seating himself on the brown, rigid-backed 'man's' chair opposite. Instinctively, neither of us sit on the slightly more comfortable-looking sofa next to the 'man's chair', mainly because it is covered in plastic.

Rose stands in the doorway watching us like a prison officer who's waiting for the new inmates to settle, and then offers us a cup of tea. I open my mouth to give her a resounding, 'Yes, please!' A cup of tea is exactly what I need, something to thaw out my ice-cold hands, but to my surprise, David shakes his head.

Instead, he points to the plasticky sofa and gently asks Rose to sit down. Clearly, he wants to break the news as soon as possible. Rose hesitates. I'm not surprised. David is breaking protocol. The tea always comes before any attempt at idle chit-chat. Rose straightens her shoulders and walks over to the sofa, staring at it as if she's never seen it before. It occurs to me that, in all these years, she's probably never sat on that sofa herself.

She lowers herself down and perches on the edge of the sofa, as if fearful of creasing the plastic. David leans forward and takes her hand. A frown flashes across her face – she's not the type of person who appreciates unexpected gestures, particularly affectionate ones. Still, given what he's about to tell her, I think he's doing the right thing. David clears his throat. This is it.

'Mummmeeee!' Anna says, throwing down her headphones on my lap in despair.

Oh, bloody hell.

'What is it, Anna?' I say, trying to keep the irritation out of my voice. Trust Anna to spoil a perfectly decent 'I've found my birth mother' conversation.

'Where's the Wi-Fi?' she demands, giving her iPad a hard shake.

David and I exchange a panicky glance.

'Anna – you know there's no Wi-Fi in this house,' I say, in as calm a voice as possible. 'That's why we downloaded you a new movie for today.'

Anna looks at me as if I am deliberately choosing words to upset her. Honestly, I just don't understand her sometimes. Rose has never had Wi-Fi in the house – in fact, Rose hates anything technology-related as she's always quick to point out whenever we're over. How can this be yet more breaking news for Anna?

'But I want YouTube Kids,' she says, miserably.

David and I just look at each other completely at a loss. Telling her YouTube Kids isn't possible is likely to trigger a full-on meltdown. Rose shakes her head at Anna, slaps her hands on her knees and gets up slowly.

Oh, here comes the judgement, I think as she walks towards Anna. But to my surprise, she holds out her hand to Anna. Anna looks at it suspiciously (as she has every right to, given Rose has barely glanced in her direction over the years, let alone made any attempt to touch her) and then with narrowed eyes, puts her little hand in hers. Then Rose gives her a sharp tug and suddenly Anna is on her feet, the iPad spilling from her lap onto the carpet, her feet tripping over my cardigan.

Rose says, 'Come with me and we'll find you something better than that silly old iPad.'

I raise my eyebrows at David as the pair of them leave the room. He gives me an expression of similar puzzlement.

'Well... that's nice...' I say, scooping up the iPad from the floor.

David nods thoughtfully and then suddenly knits his eyebrows.

'I wonder what she's going to give Anna,' he says. 'I don't think Anna would be too impressed with any of my old toys if they're still around.'

'Battered cars and soldiers?'

'Yep. Not a Disney princess among them,' he says, lightly.

Still, he looks pale and I feel desperately sorry for him. This is a huge moment and we can't afford to have any more interruptions.

'Listen, once Anna is happy again, you can talk to Rose properly,' I say, quietly.

He takes a deep breath and exhales slowly.

Just then, Anna trots back into the room with a wide smile on her face.

'Look what Gran gave me!' she says, thrusting a small wooden box decorated with flowers faded in flaky paint onto my knee.

Rose follows her into the room with something close to a smile, and says, 'It was mine when I was a little girl.'

Good God! What is happening? Has Rose suddenly developed a heart? Maybe she's softening in her old age. Or maybe some of what I shouted at her on the phone that time during the terrorist attack has filtered through.

David crosses the room, smiling. 'Thanks, Mum,' he says, giving her arm a little squeeze. She gives him a 'it's no bother' wave, but I can see by the shine in her eyes that she is pleased with herself.

Anna clambers on to my knee and eagerly opens the lid. My stomach lurches unpleasantly. The last time I opened a box like this, I ended up holding a phone made from Sebastian's mother's ashes.

Anna finally raises the lid and we all peer inside. It's a music box, which would have been a lovely idea, apart from the fact that it's a very broken music box. For starters, the triangular mirror is cracked, and what might once have been a shiny blue velvet background is full of ominous dark spots and large tears. The doll itself is missing her dress and is leaning sideways at an alarming angle. This music box isn't fit for the skip, let alone our daughter. Still, though, it's the thought that...

Anna grips my arm, hissing, 'What is it, Mummy?'

Keeping my voice as neutral as possible, I tell her that it's a music box and she looks at me in disbelief.

'But what does it do?' she says, poking the sideways ballerina.

'Well, it plays music,' I say brightly, turning the box around to find the little lever. Maybe all it needs is a good twist to jump-start it again.

'Aha!' I say, as I locate the small rusted gold mechanism on the back of the box, followed by, 'Oh no!' as it swiftly comes away in my hand.

Anna starts to wail at the injustice of it all and this time there's no bringing her back. I scoop her up into my arms, and shout over my shoulder to David that I'm taking her to the car. Rose gives Anna her best judgemental look, and I'm pretty sure mutters something like, 'Spoiled.'

I march out of the front door, never so grateful for the icy breeze. Then I climb into the back seat with Anna and give her a big cuddle until her wails become silent heaves. She lifts up her tear-stricken face and says, 'That was *not* a nice music box, Mummy.'

I give her a big kiss on her wet cheek and say, 'I totally agree with you, Anna.'

Thought that counts, my arse.

Anna reaches for her headphones and with a few definite finger strokes immerses herself in the movie we downloaded for her earlier – finally accepting the no Wi-Fi situation. To be honest, Anna's meltdown is probably for the best. At least, David can tell Rose his news in peace.

The front door opens so suddenly that I jump a little in my seat. Rose marches down the front path with as much energy as I've ever seen her move. As she approaches the car, I instinctively recoil. She looks absolutely furious.

She raps on the car window and does a 'wind the window down' gesture. I stare at her for a moment and press the button until the glass slides down a couple of inches. With that look on her face I don't want her any closer than she needs to be.

'YOU!' she says, jamming her pointed finger through the gap. 'YOU PUT THE IDEA IN HIS HEAD!'

I am too shocked to do anything but gape and stare.

'That's enough, Mum,' David says gently, his hand gently coaxing hers away from the window.

She shakes him off.

'Well, I'm not your mum, am I?' she shouts, stabbing her bony finger into his chest. 'And don't you like reminding me of it!'

Then she stomps off back up the garden path and slams the front door.

I buckle an oblivious Anna into her car seat and step out to where David is standing. He looks about ten times more ashen than he did before.

'Are you all right?' I say, squeezing his arm.

For a few moments, he looks at me without seeing me, then his eyes come into focus.

'She took that well, didn't she?' he says bitterly, jerking his head towards the front door.

'Well, it's to be expected,' I say. 'Not an easy thing for an adoptive mum to hear.'

He takes one hand and runs it through his hair.

'I'm not sure I can go through with this,' he says.

No way – he's come this far. I'm not letting Rose spook him now.

'David,' I say firmly. 'She's had a shock – she just needs some time to come to terms with it.'

'No, that's not it,' he says, shaking his head rapidly. 'It's what she told me about my birth mother.'

'What about her?' I say, puzzled.

He pauses for a moment, his breath curling in the freezing air.

'Saoirse, she told me that my mother was a whore.'

15

It's after 9 p.m. by the time we get a chance to sit down properly to talk about what happened earlier on in Rose's house. Anna had nodded off at 8 p.m. but had woken half an hour later from a nightmare about an evil 'sideways' ballerina who had just smashed her own mirror. It took me twenty minutes of rubbing Anna's back before she calmed down. That bloody music box has a lot to answer for.

We deliberately didn't talk about what happened at Rose's on the drive home, just in case Anna's earphones had a malfunction. The last thing we need is for her to be dropping the word 'whore' at every given opportunity. Personally, I don't think it's that big a deal that David's mother was a prostitute, but David doesn't seem to agree.

'Look, she's probably not doing that any more,' I say, sitting beside him on the couch in the living room, Anna finally settled. 'That was over forty years ago. She's bound to be doing something different by now.'

David groans and puts his head in his hands.

'How can I take the risk, Saoirse? How can I have her around Anna? "Hey, Anna, this is your grandmother – people pay her for sex".'

'Well, even if she is still a whore...' and then I pause for a moment. I can't stand the word 'whore'. 'I mean, lady of the night...'

David takes his head out of his hands just long enough to raise his eyes skyward at me before dropping his head back again. I ignore him.

'I mean, she could be a high-class escort, or one of those internet sex workers, or just one of those really emancipated women I was reading about who have sex with strangers for the pleasure of it and get paid, sort of like the best of both worlds type of thing...'

His mouth curls into the type of frown that tells me I'm not helping.

Suddenly he sits up.

'What if she's a druggie?' he says, the colour rising to his cheeks. 'What if she comes to our house and asks for money for drugs or tries to steal from us?'

Jesus, I think. Talk about catastrophising.

'Not all sex workers are on drugs,' I say calmly. And I don't say it out loud, but I'm pretty annoyed with him for making such a snap judgement. 'And if she is on drugs or she asks you for money or tries to burgle our house – and I wish her luck on that front because the only thing of real value we have is Anna's iPad and our smartphones – then you never need see her again.'

He shakes his head slowly and leans back against the couch.

'I can't do it,' he says.

'Don't make any decisions now,' I say, but the expression on his face is so hopeless that I decide not to push him any further.

My phone pings. It's my mother, asking us how we got on at Rose's today. Clearly, she has been tracking us again. I have told her that David might be meeting his birth mother but I haven't told her about breaking the news to Rose today.

'It's my mum,' I say.

He waves his hand at me. 'You can tell her about what happened if you like,' he says. 'I'm sick of talking about it.'

Then he leans over and switches on the TV to his favourite cooking channel.

I take my phone and walk into the kitchen.

She answers the phone with a 'Hello,' that echoes through the airwaves.

'Call me when you're out of the toilet,' I say, and immediately hang up.

Only my mother would pick up the phone when she's on the loo.

I grab myself a glass of water and wait for her to call back. A couple of minutes later, my phone starts to vibrate.

'Honestly, Saoirse!' she huffs. 'It was only a wee!'

I don't say anything, mainly because there's absolutely no point.

'Listen,' I say. 'Something happened at Rose's today...'

And then I tell her everything, from the music box of horrors to David's final admission to Rose about looking for his birth mother, to Rose telling him his mother was a prostitute, to David refusing to meet his birth mother because of it. To be fair, she waits until I finish without interruption (which almost never happens) and lets out a slow breath.

'Do you remember Auntie Yvonne?' she says.

Not for the first time I feel myself floating in one of those out-of-body, living-in-a-parallel-universe experiences that only happen when I'm talking to my mother.

'No,' I say in my most dangerous voice.

'Ah, do you not?' she says, wistfully.

'I presume she wasn't my real auntie,' I say, through gritted teeth.

'She was not, Saoirse!' my mother tuts. 'Anyway, your Auntie Yvonne used to babysit you from time to time when I went off to the cinema with the girls. This would have been a few years after your father died.'

'Right,' I say flatly.

There has to be a point to all this.

'So anyway, Yvonne was a prostitute,' she says.

My head snaps up.

'What?'

'Now, she'd only have been very *small-time*,' my mother says thoughtfully. 'She wouldn't be going into the centre of Dublin now. Strictly local stuff.'

I let out a small groan.

'Do you remember Charlie Coughlan?' she says.

Actually, I do. He was our friendly local butcher, very popular with kids as he used to make necklaces out of sausages and hang them around our necks whenever we came into the shop.

'What's Charlie Coughlan got to do with it?' I say.

But before the words leave my mouth, I'm pretty sure I know exactly why she has mentioned Charlie Coughlan.

'He was one of her best clients!' my mother announces triumphantly.

Jesus – no wonder he always had a smile on his face.

'Didn't he have a wife and kids?'

'He had five kids and a wife called Barbara,' she says, practically, as if she's ticking off a list.

'Did Barbara never find out?' I say, wondering how on earth

Yvonne's antics could have stayed private in a small town like ours.

'Ah she *knew*, Saoirse!' she says, clucking impatiently at my naiveté. 'Sure, after five kids, she was thrilled not to have him nagging her in the bedroom.'

'I'm surprised he could afford Auntie Yvonne with that big a family,' I say.

'He paid her in sausages,' she says.

'I bet he did,' I quip, and we giggle.

When she recovers, she says, 'Now, do you remember that odd-looking fella who used to hang around the village green?'

'The one who was always on his bike?' I say.

'Yes, now he was also one of Yvonne's.'

I interrupt her before she 'outs' anyone else and thus ruins every childhood memory I've ever had.

'All this is very entertaining,' I say. 'But what has your pal Yvonne got to do with David's birth mother?'

'The point is,' she says, slowly as if I'm less on the ball than she has ever possibly imagined, 'that Yvonne was a good person. She may have been the town bike, but I trusted her enough to look after you. If you think about it, I trusted her with your life.'

Okay, fine. I get what she's saying and it's nothing I haven't thought or said out loud to David about giving his birth mother a chance, but after all that's happened today, I know he won't want to hear any more about it for the moment.

'Don't be spreading the news of Rose or David's mother when you're down the beach, now,' I warn her, still smarting a bit from her revealing the Sebastian Fox news to Jen's mum the other week.

'Sure, I wouldn't say a word!' she says, in an outraged voice. 'It's none of my business!'

Hmmm.

Then, apropos of absolutely nothing, my mother says, 'So you'll be home for Christmas, will you?'

'It's *still September*!' I say, tiredly. 'Why are we talking about Christmas now?'

'So you'll be home,' she says, as if she's summing up a conversation that never took place.

I sigh.

'Yes, yes. I'll talk to David about booking flights, but I'm sure we will be back in Ireland to spend Christmas with you this year.'

Mind you, I would like to spend Christmas in Ireland this year. It'll be great to catch up properly with Jen and Dee after everything that happened last summer.

Suddenly, my mother lets out a high-pitched shriek.

'What's wrong?' I say, panicky.

'It's HIM. I have to get it, Saoirse!' she says in a voice that's at least ten octaves above what would be considered normal.

'Who's HIM?' I say.

'Miguel! One of the students from my class,' she says, quickly.

And then she hangs up.

I stare at my phone for a moment, totally nonplussed. She's been teaching English to 'foreigners' for a long time and she sometimes mentions her students ('French Simone with the lazy eye' or 'the German fella with the lisp' for instance), but I've never heard of a 'Miguel'. As I walk back into the living room, I make a mental note to ask her about him the next time. He certainly seems to have prompted a bit of hysteria.

'What did your mum say?' David says, through a wide yawn.

I love him too much to put him through the retelling of the 'Yvonne' story, so I just say, 'She thinks you should give your birth mum a chance.'

He nods his head slowly and reaches for the remote.

'I'm off to bed,' he says.

'Good idea,' I say.

He'll be able to think more clearly after a decent night's sleep.

'Are you coming up?' he says, at the foot of the stairs.

'In a minute,' I say. 'Just need to check my email.'

David disappears up the stairs and I sink back down into the couch to read my latest emails.

Two messages from Sebastian: the first one asks if I can come to meet him on his boat tomorrow morning at 9.30 a.m., and the second one asks me to confirm tonight if I can make it tomorrow. I quickly reply and confirm that I will be there.

My eyes start to prickle with tiredness so I start my nightly ritual of plugging my phone into the charger in the kitchen, locking up, and switching off all the lights, before dragging my weary bones upstairs. When I enter the bedroom, David's already in bed, staring wide-eyed at the ceiling.

'I've never seen my mother that angry before,' he says.

I can't disagree with him there. Rose did look absolutely livid.

'She called me ungrateful and disloyal,' he adds.

I walk over to him and perch on the side of the bed. Much as I don't want to take Rose's side over anything, I feel it's important to add some perspective.

'She's just had a massive shock,' I say, putting my hand on his chest. 'Give her some time.'

He turns his head towards me, his eyes full of pain.

'I just don't want to hurt anyone,' he says, looking about five years old.

'I know,' I say soothingly. I stroke his forehead in the same way I did when Anna had her bad dream earlier.

His eyelids start to droop and I rise quietly to my feet.

'I'll take Anna to school tomorrow,' he says, sleepily, and then promptly nods off.

I watch him for a few seconds – the rise and fall of his chest, his long eyelashes, and his relaxed full mouth and, in that moment, I genuinely wonder why we're not having more sex.

Then I change into my pyjamas, brush my teeth, pop my mouthguard in, and switch off the light.

16

I wake up to the sound of Anna crying – and not just the frustrated crying that she does when she loses (a) her favourite doll, (b) her favourite blanky, or (c) Wi-Fi. This is the crying of a child who has been badly wronged. Not even taking the time to put on my slippers, I jump out of bed and run downstairs towards the kitchen, only to find David on one side of the lowered dishwasher door and Anna on the other. David is angrily brandishing a breakfast bowl at Anna who is both crying and screaming at the same time. I rush over to her, lift her up, and hug her close.

'What's going on, David?' I hiss, over the top of her head.

He glares at me, crosses his arms, and juts his chin towards Anna.

'Well, it seems that while I was in the toilet, Anna took it upon herself to put my breakfast bowl in the CLEAN dishwasher, before I had even started eating my porridge,' he says, pointing furiously at the bottom dishwasher rack.

I peer over Anna's shoulder and see quite a lot of globules of cooked porridge laying thickly over the rest of the otherwise gleaming dishes and cutlery.

'Listen, David, I'm sure she was only trying to help,' I say, quietly, trying not to lose my temper in front of Anna.

As if sensing that this is the exact time to pit Mummy and Daddy against each other, Anna pipes up, 'Yeah, Daddy!'

David shakes his head and strides angrily out of the room.

I give Anna another cuddle and when the heaving subsides, I lower her onto the kitchen stool and settle her with her iPad, telling her I'll be back in a minute. Then I go in search of David. The downstairs is empty so I head upstairs, where I find David sitting on our bed, his hands gripping his knees, the same furious look on his face. I sit down beside him.

'Listen, David, I know you're going through a lot right now, but I don't think it's fair to take it out on Anna.'

He blows out some air and looks at the ceiling. Then he suddenly turns to face me.

'Well, Anna isn't the only one who's winding me up. Time and again, I've told you to tidy away all that crap on your desk and you still haven't bothered,' he says, through gritted teeth.

My breath catches in my throat. It's been a while since I've been at the brunt of one of David's petty domestic complaints. I look at his suddenly pale face and his whitened knuckles and my heart sinks. There is no getting through to him when he's like this. This is out-of-control David – the David who I almost walked out on not long after we met, the David I wanted to divorce mere weeks after having Anna, the David who I have been relieved not to see since we hashed everything out about his domestic fussiness after the terror attack.

I take a deep breath and try to remain calm – this isn't my first rodeo. It is obvious why David is behaving like this. He is upset because of Rose's reaction to finding his birth mother and telling him that his birth mother was a prostitute. I need to handle this calmly. So instead of rising to his nit-picking and escalating the matter into a full-blown argument, as I normally would, I make a conscious grown-up decision to give him the time and space to calm down.

So, without saying another word, I leave the room and go downstairs to talk to Anna, feeling very proud of my sudden maturity. Anna's exactly where I left her, glued to her propped-up iPad with both elbows on the kitchen island, her chin resting on her little hands. I bend down so my face is level with hers and say, 'Anna, sweetheart, I'd like to talk to you for a minute.'

Not even an eyelash flickers. I repeat myself again, slightly louder this time, taking the volume of the headphones into account. Still nothing.

'ANNA!' I say, impatiently.

Her head whips up.

'WHAT?' she says, her cheeks stained with dried tears from earlier.

I explain to her as best I can that Daddy didn't mean to shout and that he's very sorry and it won't happen again.

'He needs to say sowwy to me,' she says, her bottom lip well and truly out.

'Don't worry, he will on the way to school,' I say, hoping that David will have calmed down enough in the next hour or so to make things right with Anna.

'WHAT?' Anna says, scrunching up her face. 'YOU'RE taking me to school.'

The emergency sirens go off in my head. If I don't do something now, I'll never persuade her to let David take her. First, I try to appeal to her better side: 'But Daddy loves you!' – that one earns me an unshakeable, 'No he doesn't!'

Next, I try tugging on her heartstrings, 'But Mummy will miss her Monday work meeting if she has to bring you to school.' I know as soon as the words fly out of my mouth that that approach is going to fall on deaf ears.

She shakes her head vigorously.

I can tell by her high colour and scarily enlarged pupils that I'm one step away from a full-on tantrum. My eyes dart to the oven clock. Anna needs to leave for school in less than an hour and she's not even dressed yet. I can't miss this meeting. There's only one thing for it. Bribery. I desperately search my mind for something that will fend off any further rebellion so I can get to my meeting on time. And then suddenly I have the perfect plan.

'If you get dressed now, like a good girl, then Daddy will get you a pink doughnut on the way to school,' I say, giving her my best smile. Doughnuts are Anna's Achilles heel and she's never had one for breakfast before.

A hint of a smile plays on her lips.

'Weeally?' she says, throwing her arms around me.

'Absolutely!' I say, giving her a little hug back.

I pop her gently on her feet and lead her to her bedroom, where we only have minor disagreements about her clothing choice (to my shock she agrees that it might just be a tad too cold to go bare-legged under her gold-sequinned, pink tutu and lets me put on a pair of tights). While Anna runs water over her toothbrush for no earthly reason, I take a deep breath and head back to our bedroom to find David. A rush of running water tells me he is in the bathroom. I knock on the door.

'Are you doing a dump?' I call.

'No,' he says, gruffly.

I open the door to find him standing at the sink, half his face covered in shaving foam.

'Anna's ready for school,' I say, evenly.

He picks up the razor from the edge of the sink and stares grimly into the mirror.

'Can you take her?' he says, his voice hard and unyielding.

That does it. I'm only human and this whole understanding wife thing only goes so far.

'No, I can't, David!' I hiss. 'I have a meeting at 9.30 a.m. and I haven't even had a shower yet.'

He smiles grimly and shakes his head in disbelief, as if I am the unreasonable one. I'm not having it.

'So, here's what's going to happen,' I say, folding my arms. 'You're going to get your shit together, apologise to your daughter for being an arsehole to her earlier, take her to school, and buy her the pinkest doughnut you can find on the way.'

Then I turn around, grab the door, and slam it behind me.

I stamp downstairs again to find Anna playing with the keychain on the front door. For the first time in four years, she has voluntarily found and put on her own coat and shoes. She's even put her schoolbag on her back, rather than making the poor sod who walks her to school carry it. My heart swells. I see more pink doughnuts in her future.

She huffs a bit when I explain to her that Daddy's not *quite* ready yet (although he'd bloody well better hurry up) but then cheers up when I tell her she can use my phone until Daddy comes down. I leave her sitting on the bottom stair stroking my phone tenderly and head into the kitchen to have a bowl of cereal. When I finish, I automatically go to put my breakfast bowl into the dishwasher but the big vomity-looking blobs of porridge (which I had completely forgotten about) put me off, so I hand-wash it instead. Part of me thinks I should probably attempt to clear up the mess but another, more forceful part shouts at me to leave it to David as punishment for shouting at Anna before.

As I'm walking out of the kitchen, I hear the stairs creak and look up to see David walking slowly down them. I hang back a bit – if he does intend to apologise to Anna I want to make sure it doesn't look like I'm lording it over him. Sure enough, he sits beside her on the bottom step and gives her a little hug.

'I'm sorry Daddy shouted at you,' he says, softly.

Anna pushes him away, looks him in the eye, and says, 'Doughnut!'

Confident that all has been forgiven, I walk over to Anna to rescue my phone and give her a goodbye kiss.

David pulls on his shoes and grabs his coat from our unofficial coat rack, the bannister, before turning around to face me.

'Sorry,' he mouths, his eyes soft.

'It's okay,' I mouth back.

Because we both know why he's behaving like this, it makes it a lot easier to forgive him.

I wave them off from the doorstep, and then race upstairs to shower and dress for my meeting, which is in less than an hour. Because of this morning's drama with David, I don't have time to wash and blow-dry my hair so I spray a load of dry shampoo on it, hurriedly massaging it into my scalp before the 'greying old lady' look has a chance to set in. Then I throw on a smartish sweater and beige, chino-type trousers and head out the door.

* * *

Thanks to a 'passenger incident', the Tube crawls all the way to Sloane Square. By the time I spill out of the carriage with several hundred other frustrated passengers, I am already ten minutes late. I am never late.

Heart thumping and pulse racing, I run as fast as I can to Cheyne Walk, not stopping until Sebastian's mouldy-looking boat comes into view. He opens the door before I have a chance to knock.

'I'm so sorry I'm late,' I say, trying to catch my breath. 'Passenger incident...'

'Hey, no problem!' he says, with his usual enthusiasm. 'Just glad you're here!'

I take off my coat to stem the inevitable sweating from an unusual burst of energy and follow him to the seating area. He takes his usual seat on the rocking chair and waits until I have settled myself on the bench. Then he suddenly jumps up off his seat and starts doing star jumps.

'Remember?' he says, panting. 'We are excited!'

Slightly breathless after our star jumps, I get out my Dictaphone and lay it on the little table between us, before sitting back down on the hard bench. I begin the interview by asking him to tell me more about his early life, intending to use the material to build a picture of the man behind the invention: stories that might instantly capture the attention of an audience. But I am struggling to find anything about Sebastian's upbringing that would even encourage the reader to flick the page, never mind read the whole thing.

I try to interject from time to time to try to find out if there are juicier elements to his early life – perhaps a mother who once drove off leaving him on the car roof in his Moses basket, or an evil nanny who used to whip him across the legs, or maybe a time where he was caught stealing sweets from the local shop – but despite gentle questioning, the man seems to remember nothing but sunshine and rainbows. About half an hour in, my mind starts to wander. This happens to me sometimes when the conversation isn't exactly scintillating which is why I am so grateful for my trusty Dictaphone. I start to think about David and if he'll decide to meet his birth mother after all and if Rose will come around and...

'Saoirse!'

I jump a little in my seat.

Sebastian raises his eyebrows.

Determined to look professional, I throw back my shoulders before coolly answering. 'Yes, Sebastian?'

'I was just saying that we should probably finish there.'

I nod emphatically but inwardly I'm feeling a little panicky. I remind myself that it's still early days – there is plenty of time to get the information I need.

The rocking chair creaks as he slowly rises and stretches.

'You know,' he says, thoughtfully. 'This has been really thera-peutic. I never thought it would happen, but some of the stuff I've told you, I've never told anyone before. Thank you for listening.'

I give him a slow, serious nod. I haven't the faintest idea what he's talking about.

Then he tells me he's off to 'the little boy's room' and I start to tell him that I'll see myself out but before I can get the whole sentence out, he disappears into a little door on the left.

I cover my ears with both hands in an effort to block out the stopping and starting of a middle-aged man having a pee. Then I pull on my coat and bag and reach for my Dictaphone, keen for a quick exit. I let out a hysterical giggle when I realise that I haven't stopped the recording yet, which means that it has probably picked up on the sound of Sebastian peeing. Grinning, I push the 'stop' button. Except that the stop button doesn't make its trade-mark little beep. Puzzled, I look at the device more closely. There is no sign of the tell-tale recording red light. My hand flies to my mouth. I have forgotten to turn the Dictaphone on.

17

Somehow, I manage to say a sensible goodbye to Sebastian and make it home without bursting into tears of shame and mortification. Jesus, how could I have been so stupid? I've never forgotten to press the record button before. I flop down on the stool by the kitchen island and scream into my hands. I'm just glad I'm the only one in the house. David texted earlier to say that Anna had gone to school 'high as a kite' thanks to the pink doughnut sugar rush, and that he was off to some Food Expo in East London. I pick up the phone and call the one person who will understand.

'What's up?' Bea says, sounding even more brusque than usual.

'Oh, sorry, are you busy with work?' I say.

'Oh, no, it's not that,' she laughs. 'I was just on my way out to stock up on more cream crackers. They have become an addiction, thanks to you.'

I tell her to go and I'll call her later but she refuses.

'What's going on with you anyway, Saoirse? You sound all squeaky,' she says.

So I tell her all about the Dictaphone catastrophe and, to her credit, she doesn't laugh.

'Hmmm, tricky...' she says, thoughtfully.

'What am I going to do?' I say, trying and failing to stop my voice wobbling. 'He's going to fire me.'

Bea tuts.

'He's not going to fire you for forgetting to switch on the Dictaphone,' she says.

'You don't know him,' I say with a sigh. 'He's emotional at the best of times and apparently he has confessed something to me that he has never told anyone about before.'

'Perhaps you can claim narcolepsy,' she says.

I don't respond, hoping my silence speaks volumes. Then she says something that makes my heart lift a little.

'Or how about next time you go in there with some leading questions? Tell him you've been giving everything he said a lot of thought and you'd like him to expand on various aspects.'

Hmm, not bad, I think. I could try and steer him back to the subject without giving away the fact that I have made a massive cock-up. It's a big risk but it's worth a shot.

'Actually, that might work,' I say slowly.

'What does David think?' she says.

'I'm not telling him,' I say quickly. 'If I give him any impression that there's trouble with Sebastian, he'll only start to panic about the finances again.'

'And more importantly, if he's back to work, you'll be back on the school run and cooking duties full-time,' Bea says.

Damn it – she knows me too well.

'Yes, well, that's beside the point,' I say, stiffly.

'Oh, come on, Saoirse,' she says, laughing. 'You love being the breadwinner.'

And for the first time that day, I laugh along with her. It does feel good to be the one earning the finances for a change.

Then she tells me she has to go and get the crackers before she murders someone, and we hang up.

As I am feeling a bit better about the Dictaphone situation, I decide to reward myself with a teacake. I literally have my hand in the biscuit jar when I hear the key in the lock. Thinking it's David, I rush over to the sink to splash water on my face. I don't want him to notice that I've been crying.

'Hello!' A woman's voice rings out.

It's not David. It's Lena, our cleaner. I have completely forgotten she is coming today. Shit. I'm pretty sure I haven't any cash on me to pay her.

I hurriedly dry my face with the tea towel and walk out of the kitchen to greet her.

'Hi, Lena,' I say, warmly. You are the reason my husband and I are still married, I add silently. Seeing her reinforces my resolve to make things right with Sebastian. I need the money. I can't lose Lena.

I found Lena through Vale Mums Facebook Group (which is pretty much the only value I've ever managed to wring out of it) and I love her. I love her mainly because I'm convinced she once told David to fuck off in her native language (Polish) when he was following her around the house, monitoring her cleaning on the first day she started working for us.

Although David hadn't picked up on the actual swearing, he had certainly picked up on the tone, and hadn't bothered her since. Which is just as well, as she's about sixty years old, with bleached blonde hair, and built like a brick shithouse.

She flings her enormous padded coat across the bannister, and pops on a pair of worn-looking, close-toed slippers.

'Now,' she says, putting her hands on her waist. 'I start with the kitchen first.'

Then she shoos me out of the way with her giant hand, and I decide to use the opportunity to head out to the cash machine to get her some money. Just as I have my hand on the front door, I hear a loud groan.

My first thought is that it's another bloody mouse, but then again, Lena would make mincemeat out of any rodent. I rush back into the kitchen to find Lena bending over the dishwasher. When she sees me, she straightens up and glares at me.

'Someone has been sick, no?' she says, pointing at the porridge splatters.

Oh, God, I'd forgotten all about Anna's overly energetic 'help-fulness' with David's bowl of porridge this morning. I apologise to Lena and explain about what happened with Anna (leaving out the fact that her dad shouted at her unnecessarily) but her expression doesn't change.

A couple of moments go by where we just stare at each other – it's a cleaning standoff. She raises one eyebrow and I instantly cave.

'I'll sort it out, Lena! Don't worry, Lena!' I say, hurriedly closing the dishwasher drawer.

She gives me a brusque nod and then jerks her head towards the kitchen door. I leave with another apology.

Crap, I think, on my way out the door. Now I'm going to have to clean it up when I get back. Making a mental note to tell David he owes me, I brace the chilly breeze and head off to the bank. When I get back, I clean the dishwasher, give Lena her money, and spend the rest of the time hiding in the spare room pretending to work so Lena doesn't judge me for being too lazy to clean my own house. Instead, I click into Vale Mums only to find

Rosalind, one of Woodvale's most vulnerable mums, being lacerated by the Organics for the millionth time.

Rosalind:
Can anyone recommend some leak-proof night nappies? My five-year-old boy wakes up drenched every night!

Tania:
Oh no! Maybe you should try him without the nappies (plus thinking emoji) given that he is quite old to be still bedwetting.

Yes Tania, I think, enraged. Why not whip the nappies off him and let him piss the bed several times a night? Just what Rosalind needs when she's trying to cope with three boys under the age of six.

As if that isn't bad enough, Caroline, one of Tania's henchmen, piles in.

We haven't had to deal with bedwetting because Fenella caught on so quickly at the age of two, but I wish you luck with it all!

If it's possible, I'm actually more annoyed with Caroline than I am with Tania, particularly as Caroline has obviously spotted an opportunity to boast about her 'clever' non-bedwetting child and chosen to publicise it to 800 other Vale Mums members.

I watch the screen for a bit but there's nothing more from Rosalind. I feel a twinge of guilt. Despite all my good intentions for another meet-up, I haven't caught up with Rosalind since we met for coffee over the summer not long after the terror attack. We have sent each other the odd text since about how annoying our kids are, but neither of us has suggested catching up in person. Anyway, meet-up or no meet-up, the least I can do is show her a bit of solidarity. So this is what I write, including a link:

These are the ones I use for Anna. They're great! In fact, she can use them until her wedding night as far as I'm concerned.

Then I log out and get ready for the school run.

I get to the school gates just as they're being unlocked by Mr Russell so I stand in the black spot against the side wall so he doesn't see me.

'Hi, Saoirse!'

Oh, God. I've been outed.

'Hi, Diana,' I say, stepping out from my hiding place.

Mr Russell opens the gates and I dip my head as Diana gives him a cheery wave as we walk through.

'Do you think he's okay?' Diana whispers, nudging against my hip.

'What do you mean?' I say.

'Well, it's just that he is as red as a beetroot. Could be high blood pressure.'

'Hmmm,' is about all I can manage.

As we walk to our usual standing spot round the back of the school, I am surprised to see Sho already there.

'How did you get in so early?' I say.

'Jumped the fence,' she says, casually.

I'm not sure if she's joking or not. Then I introduce Sho and Diana, while wondering if there are any other women on this earth quite as opposite as these two.

Diana starts off by excitedly telling us about her broken boiler and how freezing the house is and how she can't find anyone to fix it. Sho folds her arms and looks at her feet throughout. Diana finally finishes and there's a pause in the conversation. I can't bear pauses.

'We had a broken boiler last year,' I say in desperation.

'Oh! What a coincidence!' Diana says.

Jesus, I walked into that one.

Sho looks slowly from me to Diana, takes out her phone, and starts texting. I watch her in awe, wishing I had the nerve to do that during inane small talk. Okay, it's rude, but at least it's honest. Diana wrinkles her nose for a bit and tells me she must 'dash off' to pick up Jonty, even though it's at least another five minutes before school finishes.

Sho puts away her phone as soon as Diana leaves.

'What was that?' she says, through a yawn. 'Zero chat.'

'Oh, she's harmless,' I say, suddenly feeling sorry for Diana. She might have no chat but there's no malice in her.

'Listen, would you be able to take Milly to yours for a bit after school today?' Sho says, running her hand through her tousled hair.

Although I have been desperate to get Milly and Anna together for an after-school play, I don't agree straight away. Firstly, the 'English' side of me can't help but baulk at the short notice. A playdate arranged on the same day? Unheard of. Surely there must be at least one week's notice given. Secondly, I'm a bit all over the place after this morning's Dictaphone fail and I'm not sure I have the energy to cope with two boisterous four-year-olds. But then again, Anna will be thrilled so...

'Cool,' she says, when I tell her.

'Any dietary requirements?' I say.

'Milly only eats carbs and cheese,' she says.

Just like Anna! What a coincidence!

Just then, Anna and Milly come running out of school. I tell Anna that Milly is coming home with us and I bask in the temporary popularity. Sho walks as far as the school gate with us and then gives Milly's hair a quick goodbye ruffle.

'You working this afternoon?' I say, suddenly wondering the reason for the impulsive playdate.

'Nah,' she says, scratching the back of her head. 'Off to a gig.'

Then she gives us a quick wave goodbye and heads off in the opposite direction.

I grab Milly and Anna by the hand and turn for home. It is only then I realise that she hasn't told me what time she's going to pick up Milly. Nor has she given me her phone number.

The next few hours pass in a flurry of doll-bathing, LEGO and drawing. The girls beg to do a spot of painting but I put my foot down – you have to draw the line somewhere. Before I know it, it's teatime so I settle them down in front of the telly with a plastic bowl of pasta and grated cheese, while I tackle the inevitable destruction that comes from having two small kids in the house. By the time David walks in the door at 6.30 p.m., I'm exhausted.

'The fucking Tube was down,' he announces at the top of his voice, his arms laden with paper bags.

'Shhhhhhh!' I tell him, pointing furiously towards the kitchen. 'Milly's here!'

I may forgive him for dropping the 'F-bomb' when Anna is around, but we can't afford to do the same in front of someone else's child.

David dumps all his bags on the floor.

'Bit late, isn't it?' he says, glancing at his watch. 'When is she being picked up?'

I shake my head. I've been wondering the same thing myself.

At 7 p.m., Milly and Anna decide to run another bath for their dolls. Fine. Then, without saying anything, they sneak my hairdryer out of my bedside table, bring it into Anna's bedroom and attempt to give the dolls a blow-dry. David catches them in the act and confiscates the hairdryer. Cue inevitable meltdown from Anna. In the middle of this 'crisis', Milly wees on Anna's purple fluffy rug, which is when I hear David bellowing my name down the stairs. By the time I clean up the wee (David has been ordered to get the pair of them some jellies to shut them up) and scrub the rug, it's not far off 8 p.m.

As I walk downstairs, I start feeling a bit panicky. Have I just been shafted with Anna's first sleepover? Then there's a loud knock on the door. My heart leaps.

I run down the rest of the stairs and open the door with a flourish.

Ambrose stands on the doorstep, clad in a brown leather jacket, his head almost buried in the same gigantic headphones he wears at school.

'Hi!' I say, brightly, and then I start to babble passive-aggressive commentary about not having his number, and how I was getting concerned because the evening was marching on (hahaha) and how Anna's usually in the bath by now, and so on.

Just as I run out of words, Milly comes tearing down the stairs.

'Daddy!' she says.

His face brightens and he picks her up and swings her around. Then he says his first, and what I will soon find out to be his only, words that evening.

'Her stuff?'

Fuming, I beckon him to come in while I run around the house collecting Milly's schoolbag, coat and wet clothes. I hand him the plastic bag and tell him that Milly had an accident. He takes it and gives another brief nod. I'm pretty sure it hasn't occurred to him that she's wearing Anna's clothes. Then Anna comes running out and they hug like two people forced to separate by a cruel world, and then finally, they are gone. And I'm livid.

'Did you see that?' I hiss to David, who's strolling out of the kitchen eating from a tub of ice cream with a small spoon.

'That Ambrose!' I explode. 'The CHEEK of him.'

I spend the next few minutes ranting about Ambrose, and the lack of apologies, never mind thank yous.

David walks over to me and hands me the tub of ice cream.

'You don't like it when you don't get the credit, do you?' he says, folding my hand over the spoon.

'I really don't,' I say, feeling a bit tearful.

David points to the couch.

'I'll put Anna to bed,' he says.

I shoot him a grateful smile and settle down on the couch to eat my ice cream. It takes a while for the sense of injustice to subside. I mean, who just dumps their child on someone they barely know and then gets her partner to pick them up far too late without so much as a by-your-leave? Talk about taking the piss! Well, whether she's 'the one' or not, I'm going to have a few words for Sho next time I see her at the school gates. Just you wait.

I wake up on Tuesday with my passive-aggressive side firmly switched on. David offers to take Anna to school, but I wave him away. I need to face Sho head on. An overly late playdate without an ounce of contrition from her or her mute husband just isn't good enough. My heart beats faster as Anna and I approach the school gates. I don't like confrontation, but this time it's personal. She better have a bloody good excuse, I think. I round the corner to the playground, my eyes fixed on the back fence. But this time it's Ambrose who leans casually there, not Sho. I sigh in frustration. A whole night of tossing and turning and rehearsing imaginary passionate dialogue, all gone to waste. My heartbeat slows along with my adrenalin. No use confronting Ambrose, especially when he's still wearing those stupid headphones. Although, to be honest, I wouldn't bother even if he was headphone-free. Men don't get passive aggression. Anna lets go of my hand and flies off to find Milly, and I resume my Billy-no-mates stance against the fence, deliberately leaving a larger gap than normal between myself and Ambrose, in the vain hope that he'll notice and report back to Sho. I don't know who I'm kidding – he probably hasn't even realised I'm there.

I spend the next few minutes earwigging on the Charity dads' conversation about going sober for October. Apparently, it's a daunting prospect ('I mean realistically, how are you supposed to stay sober for your best mate's vows renewal?' to which the other responds, 'Oh, I know! There's no way I will be able to get through the twins' bathtime without at least half a bottle of whisky,' and so on and so forth).

Just before the bell goes, Diana joins me to fill me in on the latest with her broken boiler, and despite my dark mood, I smile and nod along, resigned to the inevitability of this morning's small talk.

Finally, the blessed bell rings and we are all released back into the world. I trudge home umbrella-less in the pissing rain, feeling oddly deflated. Despite my frustration with Sho, deep down, I really wanted to see her, to give her a chance to apologise or at least make up some reasonable sounding excuse about the late pick-up. I mean, maybe I'm making too big a deal of it. If that was me, I would have been absolutely mortified, but, as David says, I can't expect everyone to react the same way I would. Still, I can't help feeling sad that I've lost my only ally against the Organics.

Oh, well, maybe she'll be there tomorrow, I think as I let myself back into the house.

Glumly, I throw off my wet coat and fling my sodden shoes and socks on the bottom of the stairs. David calls to me from the kitchen so I walk barefoot across the hallway, intending to have a good rant about the Sho no-show. But something else stops me in my tracks. David's cooking again. I know this because the kitchen island is covered in white flour, and every other available surface is occupied by a toppling arrangement of pots and pans of all sizes.

'What's all this?' I say, trying to absorb the sheer amount of cleaning that it will take to get our kitchen back to normal again.

David waves a floury rolling pin in my direction, and says, 'I'm making quiche – from scratch!'

My mood suddenly brightens. I love quiche.

'So, you're making the pastry yourself and everything?' I say in awe. I envy people who make their own pastry rather than buying a lump of it and leaving it in the freezer for months on end like I do.

He nods and starts rolling the pastry out, letting out a little whistle of contentment as he does so. I don't think I have ever seen him this happy.

'Amazing!' I tell him. 'What's the occasion?'

He stops rolling and gives me a serious look.

'I was a dick to you and Anna yesterday and I want to make it up to you both. Anna got her pink doughnut, and now you get a home-made quiche!'

I walk over to him and kiss him tenderly on the cheek.

'This is lovely – thank you,' I say.

He smiles and returns to his rolling.

'Besides,' he says. 'I thought quiche was the perfect food choice for brunch sex.'

What?

I stare at him.

'What the hell is brunch sex?'

He stops rolling again and brushes the flour off his hands.

'Well, I've been giving our sex life, or lack thereof, some thought lately, and I think I've figured out why we're not doing it very much.'

I watch him, open-mouthed.

'I mean, think about it – night-time is crap because we're both usually knackered, and, let's face it, you're not a morning person.'

To be fair, I can't argue with that one. He's barely allowed to make eye contact with me in the morning, let alone touch me.

'So, I've concluded that the only time we're both relatively energised and child-free is late morning, hence the reason for brunch sex.'

Then he starts throwing the pastry dough up into the air and sort of flinging it around.

Brunch sex, I think, trying to get my head around it.

'So how does it all work?' I say.

'Well, we have sex before we eat,' he says, slamming the dough onto the worktop, 'and then we will have worked up a decent appetite for some fabulous home-made quiche!'

He kneads the dough for a bit and then looks at me sideways.

'Sound good?' he says, almost shyly.

'It sounds fucking fabulous!' I tell him, kissing him full on his floury mouth.

And later that morning we experience our first session of brunch sex, and for the first time in months we finally get our mojo back. Afterwards, we eat David's delicious home-made quiche in our underwear and giggle at absolutely nothing. Sex and food. You can't beat it.

18

And that's how the rest of the week carries on. I take Anna to school in the morning, still hoping to have it out with Sho, who I will soon find out doesn't make an appearance for the rest of the week, followed by warm and tingly brunch sex with the added bonus of David's scrumptious cooking afterwards. Neither of us mention anything about the fallout with Rose or David's birth mum. It's almost like we've both made an unconscious decision to ignore stressful situations and indulge in pure fun for a change.

I am so caught up in this exciting new routine of sex and food that I almost forget about Sebastian Fox and the Dictaphone drama. That is until he emails me on Friday night while David and I are watching something subtitled and sinister on Netflix, asking me to come in for another interview that Monday. I go to enter the date into my phone calendar only to find an entry that gives me serious pause.

'David!' I say in such a horrified voice that he immediately switches off the TV.

'What is it?' he says, his brown eyes wide and full of concern.

'It's bloody inset day on Monday!' I say.

How could I have forgotten about inset day? Is this what the joys of brunch sex has done to me?

David gives an automatic groan.

'What are we going to do with Anna?' he says.

I shake my head.

'I have a meeting on Monday morning with Sebastian Fox,' I say. 'So, you're on duty then.'

'Oh, that's fine,' he says. 'I'll take her to the cinema.'

Right, so that's three hours sorted. But then he says something that makes my heart leap.

'Well, maybe since we're both pretty free agents for the rest of the week, we can go somewhere on the Tuesday for a couple of days?' he says.

A mini family holiday! I can't remember the last time we went away together. But then I remember something fairly important.

'Anna is in school for the rest of the week, though,' I say.

'So why don't we take her out for a few days? She's four. What's she going to miss? Advanced finger painting and colouring?'

Feck it.

We immediately abandon the overly dark and scary Netflix thriller and start hunting for accommodation in the Great British Countryside. Two hours later and we still haven't found anything. I even call up a few places, hoping for cancellations, and then stop mostly due to the laughter at the other end.

'It's hopeless,' I say to David, flinging down the phone. 'We've left it too late.'

'Hang on...' he says slowly, his eyes fixated on his screen. 'I may have found something.'

He shows me an image of a perfectly reasonable looking

cottage handily located in the New Forest, a beautiful part of the countryside about two hours' drive away.

'What's wrong with it?' I say instantly, because it is impossible for something this good to be available at such short notice.

'It's about a forty-minute drive from the nearest shop, but apart from that, nothing...' he says.

Then he taps his fingers rapidly on the keyboard.

'Right, all booked,' he says, smiling at me.

I smile back at him, once again marvelling at how happy and relaxed he has become since he was made redundant. No more worrying about promotions and deadlines, and, thanks to my new job with Sebastian Fox, no more fights about finances. I know this situation can't last forever – David will have to go back to work at some stage – but I am determined to enjoy every moment while it does.

The weekend passes by in a whirlwind of Anna and our combined efforts to entertain her, which inevitably end in total failure. Still, she is suspiciously excited when we tell her on Sunday morning that we're off on a family trip to the New Forest next week.

'I love the New Forest!' she says, clapping her hands excitedly.

David and I exchange an amused glance. What does she know about the New Forest?

'Danny Dare lives there!' she says, jumping up and down.

'Who's Danny Dare?' I say, puzzled.

She tuts at me for a bit and puts her hands on her hips.

'He's an influencer!' she says.

Later on, when she's having her tea, David checks out Danny Dare. It turns out he is indeed a popular children's influencer with his own YouTube channel who carries out dares posted on his wall by young kids. Danny Dare made an appearance at some festival in the New Forest but it was weeks ago. We break the news to Anna that she won't be seeing Danny Dare because he doesn't actually live there, and she bursts into tears.

'Not going to New Forest then,' she says, folding her arms across her chest.

David and I make an unspoken decision to ignore her and focus on getting through the rest of Sunday without losing our minds.

On Monday, I wake up with a feeling of dread buried in the pit of my stomach. Today is the day I need to get Sebastian to repeat whatever the hell he told me last week. I can't afford to screw this one up – brunch sex is at stake, for goodness' sake! Over breakfast, David, obviously picking up on my pensive mood, asks me if I'm all right, and I tell him yes, with as much enthusiasm as I can muster. Then I kiss him and Anna goodbye and with a heavy heart trudge to the Tube station. I can't afford to mess this interview up.

* * *

The boat rocks more than usual when I make my way inside which, to be honest, does very little for the butterflies in my stomach. After a rousing series of 'I am exciteds!' we both sit down, and I calmly tell Sebastian that I would like to go over a few things from the last interview and then very deliberately press record on the Dictaphone, waiting a moment before speaking to make sure the red light is on.

'Okay, what do you need to know?' he says, leaning forward with his hands clasped.

I mirror his body language, and also clutch my own, sweaty-nervous palms. I take a deep breath and look into his eyes.

'Firstly, I just wanted to thank you for sharing your story with me last week,' I say. 'It was a real privilege.'

He gives me a meaningful nod.

'I just need to know a few more details about what happened,' I say.

He leans back for a moment and frowns.

'I thought I was pretty clear,' he says.

Shit.

'Well, it's just that your story was so powerful that I really feel the need to find out more to give it the justice it deserves,' I say.

He bites his lip for a bit, and I hold my breath.

'Maybe I didn't tell you enough about how I felt after Phillipa seduced me.'

'Yes!' I say, my heart singing. 'You hit the nail on the head.'

And then with a bit of prompting and a few more carefully worded questions, I find out exactly what I failed to record last week: Sebastian had been seduced at seventeen by one of his mother's friends, a fifty-year-old woman called Phillipa, from the local tennis club. At last something interesting, I think. This whole *The Graduate* stuff will look great in the memoir side of the book – it will really liven things up. I wonder what other scandalous tales he has in his back pocket.

'You know,' he says thoughtfully. 'Now that I think about it, my first real sexual awakening has everything to do with my new invention. The connection between sex and death is so powerful.'

I nod seriously, although inside I am cringing. I'm not great with people who use the words 'sexual awakening.' Nevertheless, when the interview ends, my mood is buoyant. Not only have I managed to get away with last week's Dictaphone disaster, but I have uncovered a great bit of scandal for the book.

I put my coat on and turn around and smile at Sebastian, with the intention of thanking him again for sharing something so intimate with me. But the serious expression on his face gives me pause.

'Now that I've gone through it all again, I don't think I want this story in the book. I just don't think it's fair to my mother's memory,' he says, his eyes filling with tears. 'She never knew about Phillipa, you know.'

You have got to be fucking kidding me.

* * *

I call Bea at work during my angry stomp back down Cheyne Walk.

'Well, at least he didn't catch you out on the recording fail,' she says.

'That's true,' I concede, albeit huffily. 'All that worry over nothing, though...'

I hear the sound of tapping and ask her if I have caught her in the middle of something important.

'Well, only if you count doing an online shop as important,' she says, briskly.

I shake my head. Honestly, does Bea ever do any real work?

Then I ask her how she's feeling and she tells me she's booked in her twelve-week scan for the end of October. I ask her if she wants me to go with her and she responds with an immediate, 'No.'

'Are you sure you don't want me to come along?' I say, thinking back to the way David and I were at our twelve-week scan when I was pregnant with Anna. I can't imagine seeing something so wondrous and not having anyone to share the sheer emotional enormity of it.

'Saoirse,' she says, sucking in her breath. 'I gave birth to Harry by myself. I am perfectly capable of going to a twelve-week scan on my own.'

I know by her tone that there's no point in persisting, so

instead I make her promise that she'll text me the second the scan is over and show me the images. She sighs an impatient, 'Fine'.

'How are you going to break the news to Ryan?' I say.

'Over email,' she says, instantly.

'Ah, Bea! You can't tell him over email!' I say. 'It's far too impersonal.'

'Okay, fine,' she says with a groan. 'I'll tell him over FaceTime but he's probably going to cry. Honestly, he's become far too emotional since he moved to America.'

I smile. Bea doesn't 'do' overly emotional people.

Just before I end the call, Bea asks me for news and I tell her we're whipping Anna out of school for a few days to go on a spontaneous holiday to the New Forest.

'Good for you!' she says. 'Anna excited?'

'She is – but not for the right reasons,' I say, tapping my Oyster and pushing through the Tube turnstile. 'She seems to think that some influencer called Danny Dare will be there to personally make all her wishes come true.'

'Oh, God,' Bea sighs. 'Harry is obsessed with him too,' she says. Then she suddenly snaps, 'Fuck off, Tom!'

'The cream cracker thief again?' I giggle.

'He can't keep his hands off them,' she huffs, 'It's bloody harassment at this point.'

I hang up, full of admiration for the man. He must have some sort of death wish to take on such a fierce opponent as Bea.

Just as I hang up, my phone pings and I'm relieved to find that it's not the class WhatsApp group; it's the group I share with Dee and Jen. Jen tells us that since I'm coming home for Christmas (it appears my mother's been sharing all my news again) she has booked a table in the local pub for New Year's Eve and she can't wait to see us both. Dee sums it all up with a gif of a group of pissed people cheers-ing with a 'Happy New Year' message blinking in the background. I respond with three drunk emojis. Despite everything going on with Sebastian, it's a great feeling to know that I have something to look forward to at the end of the year.

19

Anna and I wait patiently in the car as David flings the bags into the boot with unnecessary force. Between trying to pack for our mini break in the New Forest and Anna still wailing about missing Danny Dare, it's been a rough morning.

Anna suddenly tugs at my hand.

'What is it?' I say, impatiently.

'That lady is weird,' she says, stabbing her little finger against the car window.

I tut, ready to tell her off for pointing and calling people weird. But then my eyes follow her finger and I see an elegantly dressed older woman who looks to be in her sixties, her naturally white hair falling in soft curly waves on to her shoulders, just standing there, staring at David. David walks purposefully towards our front door, presumably to lock up, when I notice the woman slowly crossing the road towards him, her smart, dark navy coat swaying slightly against her low-heeled, black ankle-boots. Curious, I quickly step out of the car. There's something about her that looks familiar.

She stops in front of David and looks at him closely.

'I'm so sorry,' she says, in a soft Scottish accent, her hand cupping her mouth. 'It's just that...'

David looks back at her and the bags he is holding fall heavily to the ground.

'It's you,' he says.

* * *

And it is her. I can't believe she is sitting in our living room like any other guest, with her handbag resting on the floor between her smart boots. I also can't remember the last time David let anyone into the house with their shoes on. But the woman with smart boots is not just anyone. She is David's birth mother, Bonnie.

'How did you find me?' David says, sitting on the couch opposite her, his face ashen.

I stand at the entrance of the doorway, not knowing where to put myself. There's a whole part of my brain that thinks this is some kind of weird dream: that David hasn't just recognised his birth mother and instantly ushered her into the house as if it's the most natural thing to do. I had stayed behind to bring in the bags and settle a curious Anna ('She's a friend of Daddy's, sweetheart') in the kitchen with her iPad. I've also broken the news to her that we might not be going to the New Forest after all, and her little eyes light up. To her four-year-old brain, the New Forest does not exist without the infamous Danny Dare. Now I've come back, intending to offer Bonnie a cup of tea, but the words stick in my throat and all I can do is watch.

'A few months ago, a woman called Joss from the Missing Persons Bureau contacted me and told me you were trying to find me. I was so pleased to finally get the chance to meet you, but then nothing happened. I thought you might have changed your mind. All I had was the area where you lived, but that was it. Then today I had an appointment close by and I thought I'd just take a walk around and then I saw you get out of the car and I just knew it was you.'

Her eyes fill with tears and she looks away.

David takes a deep breath and catches my eye. I cross the room to sit beside him and squeeze his hand. The room is thick with silence. So many questions, but nobody knows where to begin.

David's hand tenses over mine.

'Why did you give me up?'

His words come out in a rush and his hand squeezes mine harder.

Bonnie's eyes fill again.

'I never wanted to give you up...' she begins in a faltering Scottish lilt and she tells us her story.

Bonnie left school at seventeen and went to work in a care home for the elderly just outside her home city of Edinburgh. She liked taking care of people and enjoyed her work. When she was twenty, the home was taken over by a new manager, Frank. He was in his forties, married with no kids of his own, and very well thought of in the local community. Bonnie fell in love with him and ended up getting pregnant at twenty-one. When she told him the news, he accused her of trapping him and trying to ruin his reputation. He told her that if she didn't get rid of the baby, he would get rid of it for her.

'What did that mean?' I break in, too caught up in the story not to interrupt.

Bonnie hesitates for a moment.

'I was a stubborn sort of girl,' she says, allowing herself a sad smile, 'So I told him that he could do his worst but I still wouldn't give up my child.'

'So, what happened?' David says, his voice cracking.

God, this must be so hard for him to hear. His birth father sounds like a right arsehole.

'He told me that next time he saw me he'd kill me and then you,' she says, tears running freely down her face now. 'I swore then that I would never put you in danger again.'

David leans forward, his elbows in his knees, head towards the floor.

'What about your parents?' he says. 'Did they not support you?'

Bonnie shakes her head.

'My mother died when I was little.'

'And your dad?' I say, gently.

'A vicar,' she says.

Jesus, say no more.

'So where did you go?' David says, sitting up straighter now.

'I drove as far away from Edinburgh as I could and ended up in Cornwall. As you can imagine, I had very little money but I got a job in a care home there all the same and they allowed me to rent a small room on the premises. When I began to show, they tried to persuade me to keep you but I was so terrified that Frank would somehow find me and then hurt you, that I did the only thing I felt I could do to keep you safe. And that was to give you up.'

'Where is Frank now?' I say.

'Dead,' she says, simply.

I glance at David, but his eyes are dazed.

Her hands shake a little as she reaches down to her handbag to fish out a packet of tissues. I look at David but his eyes are focused firmly on Bonnie. He frowns a little.

'I'm not judging you or anything...' he starts. 'But how did you end up becoming a prostitute?'

Oh, bloody hell.

'He means lady of the night!' I rush in hurriedly.

Bonnie pauses like a statue, her mouth open in a perfect 'O', a single tissue suspended in the air.

David, uncharacteristically picking up on the fact that he has made some waves, starts to apologise, but she suddenly comes to life again.

'I was never a prostitute!' she says, her hands falling firmly onto her knees. 'Wherever did you get that idea?'

David and I exchange a look and I know he is thinking exactly the same as I am.

Bloody Rose.

Then David mumbles some nonsense about an article he had read about 'fallen women' giving up their babies and apologises again.

She cocks her head to one side and smiles for the first time.

'Och, don't worry, son. There were plenty of fallen women in my day but I wasn't one of them.'

The word 'son', said so casually, hangs in the air.

Desperately trying to rescue the situation, I ask Bonnie what she does for a living.

'I'm a rent-a-friend,' she says, matter-of-factly.

I have no idea how to respond to this. Judging by the expression on David's face, he doesn't either.

Bonnie gives us both a patient smile.

'Don't worry – I get that reaction all the time.'

'But what does it involve?' I say.

'It's a service for lonely people who want a friend to talk to,' she says.

I think about this for a second. How sad is it that people are so desperate for company that they will pay a stranger just to talk them?

'There's a strict no-touching rule,' she says, hastily, looking at David, clearly trying to remove any more implications of prostitution.

David goes bright red.

'So is that why you were in the area today?' I say.

'Yes, I was visiting a lonely young mum who needs a friend.'

Of course, now I'm dying to find out who it is. I mean, there's less than two degrees of separation in this little suburb, but I don't want to appear like the gossip I am, so I don't dig for any more details. Yet.

'How did you get into the er... rent-a-friend... business?' David says, clearly struggling with the concept as much as I am.

'I suppose it came out of all those years I spent working with the elderly. Many of them had family who struggled to visit regularly, so they would ask me to spend some extra time chatting to them. In return, they would give me little gifts, which was lovely of course, but the real privilege was hearing all their stories, of guilt, of happiness, of sadness, and of fear. The feelings and emotions we all experience. And it occurred to me that you don't have to be elderly to feel lonely or want someone to talk to, which is why I became a rent-a-friend.'

Wow. This is fascinating! I could listen to her all day.

'So what kind of experiences have you had?' I say, leaning forward.

'Well, I've been contacted by people who are new to the area and need a friend to show them around, or are looking for some company over dinner, or are searching for someone to confide in when they're feeling a bit lonely – like the mum I saw today.'

Gosh, she makes it sound so simple.

I look at David to see if he has anything else to say about this, but I can tell from his dazed expression that he's probably had enough conversation for today.

For the sake of something to do, I offer Bonnie a cup of tea, but she says a kind no, glances at her watch and gets to her feet. David and I automatically follow suit.

'I'd love to stay and talk more, but I'll miss my train back to Cornwall if I'm any longer,' she says, picking up her bag.

David swallows.

'Can I see you again?' he says, sounding like a small boy.

'I'd like that,' she says, swinging her handbag onto her shoulder.

Then they exchange numbers and promise to text and, before I know it, Bonnie's gone, leaving a mild scent of flowery perfume in her wake, and a man who has just found his birth mother after over forty years.

David shuts the door behind her and looks at me in a way that doesn't really see me.

'I never asked her to take off her shoes,' he says, faintly.

Then he bursts into tears.

20

Needless to say, we don't make it to the New Forest. For the next few days, David goes through a whole rollercoaster of emotions, from relief ('I'm so glad I met her,' to anger, 'Why was my real dad such a horrible bastard?' to regret, 'Why didn't I ask her more questions?' to mortification, 'I can't believe I accused her of being a prostitute'). I weather these changes as best I can while trying to keep Anna at bay. It's only right that David has some space to digest everything he's heard, but I'm exhausted juggling the pair of them by the time the week comes to an end. As usual, Sebastian has emailed me on Sunday evening to schedule a meeting the following day, so that night in bed, I tell David to take Anna to school. He nods absentmindedly, and says, 'Do you think I should text Bonnie tomorrow? Or do you think it's a bit soon?'

I tell him he should definitely text her and that there's no such thing as the 'three-day rule' when it comes to newly formed mother and son relationships. But my attempt at humour falls on deaf ears and he just lets out a low contemplative 'hmmm'. Then he switches off the light and starts to snore within minutes.

The next morning, David does a few things that are distinctly un-David-like. For starters, he leaves the tap running in the bathroom, the bed unmade and uses the wrong towel to dry the dishes. It's like living with someone who's either in love or who has major PMT (I should know). As I step onto the Tube, I worry that in his distracted state, he'll have forgotten that Anna needs her PE kit packed in her schoolbag, even though I've reminded him close to a dozen times. I call his mobile but nobody answers, so I call the landline. Anna picks up.

'Hello?'

She sounds very far away.

'Anna! Hold the phone to your ear!' I say loudly, trying to ignore all the hard stares from my fellow passengers.

But instead I'm treated to the sound of energetic tapping, followed by an anguished, 'Why can't I see you?'

'Sweetheart, there's no camera on the landline...' I say hurriedly as we approach a tunnel. Smartphones and iPads have ruined her for life. 'Get your dad for me?'

There's a clatter and then the phone goes dead.

When I'm out of the tunnel, I dial again. The phone is now engaged. I'm pretty sure Anna has lost interest, dropped the phone, and wandered off in search of more sophisticated technology. Gritting my teeth, I try David on his mobile again. This time he answers on the first ring.

'Can I call you back?' he says, sounding flustered. 'I'm getting Anna ready for school.'

I tell him about the PE kit and, as predicted, he acts like it's breaking news. Then I spend the next five minutes guiding him to the whereabouts of said PE kit ('No – not the wardrobe – the top drawer!') all the while trying to stifle a new wave of frustration – I can't cope with two Annas.

Coming out of the tube station, I nearly get blown sideways by the freezing river breeze and I have to say, by the time I get to the boat, I'm finding it difficult to muster up any enthusiasm for my next interview with Sebastian Fox. My head is too full of Bonnie and David. But there he is anyway – this time dressed in a different pair of shorts, long woollen socks, the same sandals and a fisherman's jumper. He starts the 'I am exciteds' before I even have a chance to take my coat off, which really does nothing for my mood, but I do my best to join in.

I start the interview. 'Can you think of a memory in your early life that you think might interest your readers?' I say, hoping he'll come up with another Mrs Robinson-like juicy anecdote.

He takes a breath through his nose and blows it out slowly.

'Well, I think my biggest childhood memory is the one I already told you – when my mother buried the dead mouse in the back garden,' he says.

I take a deep breath and shout down the rising butterflies of panic. Realistically, all I have is the dead mouse story, which really isn't enough to fill a couple of pages, never mind a daunting 60,000 words. Still, it's early in the writing process and I am determined to get something of substance out of Sebastian yet. Besides, knowing that there is a large sum nestling in my bank account is incentive enough to keep trying.

'Maybe you could tell me more about your mother?' I say, softly. 'It must have been fascinating to have an artist for a mother.'

His eyes suddenly fill and he shakes his head slowly. I get it – it's too soon.

So I change tack. The backstory can wait. Maybe he will feel more comfortable talking about the business side of the ash case.

'At the moment, you have a prototype for the ash case. How are you going to develop it into the real thing?'

His eyes suddenly light up. 'I'm flying out to China to discuss the design of the real product over the Christmas break. The testing will be done out there.'

Okay, this is good.

'And when it's tested and ready to go, how are people going to hear about it?'

'Oh, they'll know about it, Saoirse!' he says, as if it's the obvious thing in the world.

For a moment, I am stumped.

'Right – well, *how* will they know about it? Are you going to advertise it?'

He looks at me in horror. 'Absolutely not! The whole process will be very organic, Saoirse.'

This means nothing to me and only makes me think about the Organics at school.

I try again. 'What about investment? It's going to take a lot of money to get something like this off the ground.'

He shakes his head and bites his lip. 'There's no way I'm letting investors near my invention. Why should I give up a percentage of my business when I am the one who created it?'

I attempt a bit of the old 'Well, it's better to have a small slice of a big pie than no pie at all' approach but he looks at me as if I've just suddenly switched to a different language. That day, I leave the boat with the sinking feeling that so far, I have nothing for this book. Nothing at all.

* * *

Later on, I get home to find David sitting at the kitchen table staring at his phone. He doesn't look up. I feel a selfish pang of pity – I have been so used to walking into the delicious smells of David cooking and the prospect of brunch sex.

'I texted Bonnie,' he says, running a shaky hand through his hair. 'Do you think she'll text back?'

'I'm sure she will,' I say, pulling out a chair opposite him.

I wonder if he was like this after he texted me for the first time – anxious, pale, worried, full of anticipation. I decide to share this thought with him and, for the first time since Bonnie's visit, he bursts out laughing.

'No way!' he says. 'I knew I had you in the bag! The biggest surprise would have been if you hadn't texted me back.'

The arrogant bastard! But it's good to see him smile, all the same. For the millionth time, I tell myself that although it has been slow going so far, it will work out with Sebastian Fox. It has to.

Then his phone pings, and he snatches it up before it stops vibrating. A slow smile spreads across his face.

'Bonnie?' I say.

He nods.

'She's back in the area on Friday.'

'Great!' I tell him.

'Do you mind if I see her by myself this time?' he says, reaching for my hand.

'Of course not,' I tell him, making a mental note to keep Anna out of his way.

He puts his phone down gently on the table, his brow suddenly furrowed.

'What's the matter?' I say.

'What am I going to do about Mum?' he says.

This is the first time he has mentioned Rose since meeting Bonnie, and I imagine his head is all over the place trying to make sense of everything. Much as I can't stand Rose and hate the way she lied to David about Bonnie being a prostitute, I do understand her reasons for behaving the way she did. To be honest, I feel desperately sorry for her. Maybe her coldness towards David all these years was a way of protecting herself in the event of this very thing happening. Or maybe I'm giving her too much credit.

'Your mum will come round, David,' I say, squeezing his fingers. 'She's upset and she's afraid of losing you.'

He sighs and rubs his eyes. 'Maybe you're right.'

Then he looks around the kitchen as if seeing it for the first time, and says, 'God, sorry. I totally forgot to cook today. I've been so preoccupied...'

I nod sympathetically as my stomach gives a slow rumble.

'How are you feeling about your father having passed away already?' I say.

He hasn't mentioned a word since Bonnie broke the news and I haven't wanted to push him on it.

He folds his arms and looks at the ground.

'It's hard to know how to feel,' he says. 'How do you grieve for someone you've never even met?'

I can't even imagine what he's going through – how he must feel about a man he never knew, and a life he never had.

Then David raises his head and looks at me.

'It's a bit of a sliding doors thing, isn't it? What would my life have been like if Bonnie had kept me? Constantly living under the threat of my father? Things could have turned out very differently for me.'

'Bonnie did the right thing,' I say, softly.

He nods, his eyes filling up.

'Besides, your father sounded like a right wanker,' I say, in an effort to lighten the mood.

David bursts out laughing.

'That he did,' he says, running a hand roughly across his eyes.

I don't want to push him any further, so I pat him on the shoulder and start rummaging through the cupboards to find something to eat.

David gets up mumbling something about checking the bins, even though it's not bin day, so I use the opportunity to grab my phone, intending to add a reminder about David's meeting with Bonnie on Friday. My heart sinks: it's also the day of the sodding cake sale at school.

There's no getting out of that one.

I spend the next few days working on my motherhood book, desperately thinking of angles for Sebastian's book, and trying to cope with David's continuing erratic behaviour. When I find the car keys in the fridge for the third time in a row, I know he needs a change of scene. So, I go online and book him a ticket to a cookery demo in Hammersmith. Thankfully, he seems pleased and sets off on Friday morning after dropping Anna to school, with his shoelaces untied. I'm not going to lie – the second that front door closes, I heave a huge sigh of relief. Between dealing with Sebastian's book and David's unpredictable behaviour, I could do with some space. I spend a happy few hours writing the motherhood book, just grateful that at least one project seems to be flowing well, followed by head-in-hands moments of despair when I realise how little I have for Sebastian's book, despite my efforts so far. Then my reminder pings. It's almost time for the school cake sale.

That afternoon, I arrive before pick-up to set up for the cake sale. I haven't a clue what to do, of course, and I am loathe to ask Tania or any of her Organics crew for advice, so instead I badger Jackie-in-the-school-office for help. She points me towards a folded table resting against the office wall and brings out several boxes of cupcakes that have clearly been delivered by parents far more organised than me. I drag the heavy table outside, huffing and puffing, set it up through a veil of muttered swearwords, and start arranging all the baked goods in what I hope will turn out to be a fairly attractive display. I reach the final box, open the lid and freeze. Some fucking prick has made a big chocolate sponge cake covered in little white ghosts. Why would anyone do that? Not only is it going to take up valuable space on the table, but I'm going to need a knife to slice it up, not to mention napkins to wrap up all the pieces.

I stomp back into the office again. Before I open my mouth, Jackie gives me a look that says, 'Whatever it is, the answer is no.' But I have to ask, and so she tells me, through a heaving sigh, to go to the school kitchen and borrow a knife and napkins. Then I ask her where the kitchen is and she looks at me as if she's mentally flogging me. As I make my way through the green-carpeted corridors, I make a mental note not to ask her anything ever again.

I finally make it back outside, armed with the knife and napkins, but I'm not the only one there. Mr Russell is behind the table, looking intently at the cupcakes. Suddenly, he reaches out and grabs one.

'I hope you're going to pay for that,' I say.

I can't resist.

He looks at me as if I've just caught him weeing in the nursery sandpit, and I start to feel sorry for him. I mean, it's bad enough that he's been rumbled trying to steal a cupcake, but it's even worse that it's me who has caught him.

'Oh, yes, of course!' he says, stiffly, blushing and rummaging around in his suit trouser pocket.

He drops fifty pence into the collection box just as the school bell rings. Then he walks briskly towards the school gates, the cupcake dangling by his side. I take my place behind the table and take a few deep breaths to calm the nerves. Even though I'm cross with her, part of me had hoped that Sho would suddenly turn up and redeem herself by giving me a hand on the stall. My internal dialogue tells me to stop being so ridiculous – it's just a school cake sale. There is really nothing to worry about. I can do this!

Then the school gates open and my stomach plummets. I don't think I have ever seen that many people headed in my direction at one time. This is what *Game of Thrones*' Jon Snow and his pals must have felt when the White Walkers started to stampede the castle – except Snow had his mates to help him, and a couple of dragons. I'm on my own.

The kids are bad enough.

'I want that cupcake!'

'No – I want that one!

'It was my turn next!'

'He skipped me!'

But the adults are worse:

'Do you have change for £10?'

'I believe my daughter was next.'

'We have been waiting here for three minutes!'

I'm trying to hand out cupcakes as fast as I can, while smiling, apologising, being polite, and giving the right change, when all I want to do is drop a few 'grown-up' words and sink into a bottle of gin. A voice behind me says, 'Need a hand?' and my knees buckle in relief. I turn around, ready to lavish thanks on my saviour, but stop dead. It's Tania.

'No, thanks,' I say, stiffly. 'I'm absolutely fine.'

She gives me a smug smile.

'In that case, Heath would like a slice of that delicious looking cake,' she says, pointing to the chocolate cake beast I had been swearing at earlier.

In a flash, I know that she's responsible for that monstrosity and I want to do more with that knife than cut cake with it. I quickly cut off a slice, wrap it in a napkin, and hand it to Heath. Tania smiles and hands me a twenty-pound note, the absolute bitch. I root around for her change, all the time trying to ignore the dozens of impatient glares boring into my soul. Then I pick out all the brown coins I can and give her back a huge pile of change. Her smile falters and she stomps off.

Good.

'Mummmmeeee.'

Oh, Christ, I have completely forgotten to pick up Anna. I thank her teacher for bringing her over, too busy to acknowledge the judgement in her eyes, and turn back to sell cupcakes to an ever-growing angry mob. Anna stays quiet for about two minutes, and then announces that she wants to help, so I grab a few slices of Tania's cake and give them to her. I can't afford any more 'helpers' right now. Just when I think things can't get any worse, the senior part of the school comes out, pushing and shoving each other to compete for the final couple of dozen cupcakes (why are there so many?). One hilarious joker from Year Six decides to make a grab for the collection box and spills the coins all over the ground. Him and his oversized pals start to shovel the money into their pockets. I look desperately around for help, but given those kids tend to walk to school and back by themselves, there aren't any of their parents in sight. Jesus, at this stage, I'd even welcome Mr Russell, although I'll bet any money that he's off stuffing his face with that cupcake I spotted him thieving. I take a deep breath, aware that the next few seconds could well determine whether I'm going to cry or use the cake knife. I walk purposefully towards the group of thieves, even though I know that the rest of the crowd is taking full advantage of the unattended table of treats, intending to tell them to empty their pockets like a headmaster from the 1930s. But then a loud 'Oi!' stops me in my tracks. I look around only to see a small but determined figure march through the gates and straight over to the gang of delinquents. It's Sho.

'Give it,' she says, punctuating each word with a stamp of her boot.

The boys, who suddenly look very young indeed, start to turn out their pockets, hurriedly placing the money back into her cupped hands.

'Now get lost,' she says, jerking her thumb towards the school gate.

An overwhelming feeling of adoration runs over me. I feel like the class nerd who has been saved by the coolest kid in school, and it feels great.

'Thanks, Sho,' I say, grinning at her.

'Little dicks,' she says, dismissively, spilling the coins from her hands into mine.

Then she glances at her watch and starts to walk off towards the back of the school. 'Have to pick up Milly.'

'Can I go too?' Anna says, standing up, her face covered in chocolate icing from Tania's cake.

Sho raises her eyebrows at me and I say, 'Sure!' Then Anna slips her hand in Sho's and I watch them walk away, doing everything to keep my facial expression cool and neutral. I've just started to wipe down the table when Sho appears with Milly and Anna.

'Did you get in trouble for being late?' I say, hating myself for being such a geek.

Sho just shrugs.

'Teacher gave me a lecture, but that's about it,' she says.

God, I'd be mortified if Anna's teacher had to tell me off for being so late for pick-up. It's bad enough I forgot to pick up Anna today, but it doesn't appear to bother Sho at all. She's probably right not to worry about it, I think, as I continue wiping down the table – with her relaxed attitude, she's bound to live longer than a stress-head like me anyway.

'Mummmeee – can we help tidy up?' Anna says, swinging Milly's hand impatiently.

I scan the site quickly, trying to find them something to do that won't make the situation even worse, but Sho gets there before me.

'Sure!' she says, brightly, kneeling down in front of the pair. 'How about you pick up all those smashed cupcakes off the ground and put them in that bin over there?' She points at the big frog bin outside the office reception nursery that all the kids love. Milly and Anna squeal in excitement and start to scrape all the cupcake debris off the ground with their bare hands. Then Sho upturns the collection box and starts to count the money at enviable speed. When she's finished, she goes into the school office, and comes out again empty-handed.

'She's a grumpy old cow, isn't she?' Sho says, jerking her head towards the direction of the school reception.

I laugh, thrilled that I'm not the only one that finds Jackie-in-the-office unhelpful to say the least.

'So, where have you been over the last couple of weeks?' I say, trying to keep the neediness out of my voice. Because despite the whole late pick-up, playdate incident, I realise that I have missed her.

'Remember that gig I went to? Well, I ended up doing tattoos for the band, and then went on tour with them for a bit,' she says, scuffing away some cupcake crumbs with her boot.

I nod nonchalantly, in a way that looks like this sort of stuff happens all the time, but inwardly, I'm screaming, 'Oh, my God! Who just takes off with a band for days on end? That's so cool!'

'Milly okay about it?' I say, thinking back to my stay in Ireland over the summer. It was hard enough to leave Anna for just over a week, never mind a whole month.

'Ah, she's used to it,' she says, looking at Milly, who must be on her twentieth trip to the bin at this stage. 'At least she has Ambrose to look after her. It's a good thing he works from home.'

'What does he do?' I say, curious about the man with low-slung worn jeans and the gigantic noise-cancelling headphones. I'm guessing DJ, music producer, or some other kind of cool artist.

'He's a coder,' she says.

'Is that why he wears noise-cancelling headphones?' I say.

She crosses her arms and says, 'Yeah, he doesn't like distractions. He wears those things all the time, even when he's not working.'

I don't tell her that I've more than noticed. Mind you, I have to admit, it's a great way of blocking out all the idle chit-chat that goes on at the school gates.

Hearing her mention Ambrose reminds me of the playdate and the late pick-up and I am momentarily annoyed. I open my mouth but then shut it again. It occurs to me that Ambrose might not have told her. Still, I can't resist a little passive aggression – I'm only human, after all.

'Coders are usually great time-keepers!' I say, in an unnaturally high-pitched voice. This is also bullshit because I have no idea if keeping time is something that coders do, but I'm willing to take a punt anyway.

But she doesn't pick up on it. Instead, she calls to Milly and Anna and tells them it's time to go. She's right. It's getting dark and cold and we are all gloveless and scarfless. We gather up all the schoolbags and paraphernalia and make our way out of the school gate, with two hyped-up, sugar-infused children in tow. Sho walks beside me and I try to think of something cool to say.

'What band did you go on tour with, anyway?' I say. Frankly, I don't know why I'm bothering to ask. There's no way I'll have heard of them. Music stopped as soon as Anna came along and the only songs I know now are from Anna's Disney musical obsession. But then something miraculous happens.

'Oh, it was an old-school band called Pirana,' she says, through a yawn. 'They're on a reunion tour.'

I stop dead and let out a loud screech. Milly and Anna jump at this unexpected noise, but I can't help myself. Pirana. God, me and Jen practically stalked them in the mid-nineties. The drummer was an Irish, twenty-something called Eamonn with light brown hair, shaved up the back, and falling in adorable, dead-straight strands (my mother always said he had the type of hair that would fall out in his thirties) over his beautiful, lightly stubbled cheeks. It was constantly rumoured that Eamonn hung around the grunge venues in Dublin's Temple Bar. This was all the incentive Jen and I needed to find him. We would pretend that we were staying over in each other's houses and get the bus into Dublin city centre, wandering around Temple Bar all night, praying for even the smallest glimpse of our hero. Of course, we never saw him, but we never lost hope. And now here I am, standing beside someone who has just spent whole days with Eamonn and the rest of the band.

Sho cocks her head to one side and says, 'So you've heard of them, then.'

As there is no room for nonchalance in this conversation, I say in a breaking voice, 'Heard of them? I LOVE them!' Then I tell Sho about Jen and me and how we used to spend all our pocket money on the bus in our efforts to find Eamonn.

Sho grimaces and gives a low whistle, clearly unimpressed by my fan-girldom. Then she taps her foot on the pavement a bit.

'Listen, if you're that much of a fan, I might be able to do something for you,' she says.

Then she asks me to stop clutching her arm. I look down and it seems as though I have grabbed her arm in excitement, although I have no recollection of doing so. I say a quick sorry and quickly remove my hand. No doubt I'll be mortified later, but I'm too excited to hear about what she's going to say next to care too much.

'So, I might be able to get you a backstage pass at their next gig in a couple of weeks,' she says, taking a big step back, presumably for fear that I will grab her again.

She was wise to take caution but realistically she should have retreated further because, before I know it, I am embracing her like I have never embraced someone before. It is only when my head starts to clear that I realise that her arms are hanging loosely by her sides. I step back again and apologise many times, but try as I might I can't wipe the silly grin from my face.

Sho sighs and looks away.

'Seriously, Saoirse, if you're going backstage, you need to keep it together,' she says, frowning.

'I will! I promise!' I say.

'Pinky pwomise?' Anna adds.

'Er, yes,' I say, ruffling her hair.

'Do it then!' Milly says, grabbing Sho's hand and tugging it towards mine.

So Sho and I end up locking our little fingers and then doing it a second time (because according to Milly and Anna, moving the fingers up and down in the same motion renders the promise obsolete) before breaking free again.

As if sensing the party is over, Milly and Anna skip ahead

again, leaving Sho and I to catch up with them. Much as I'm trying to contain my enthusiasm, I can't resist asking about Eamonn.

'So, what's Eamonn like now?' I say.

'Bald,' Sho says, shooting me a sideways glance.

Damn it – my mother was right. I make my mind up never to tell her. Well, I don't mind if Eamonn's balding or fat or plain unrecognisable. It'll be enough just to meet him and then gloat to Jen about it.

I give myself a little shake – if I'm really going to meet Pirana, I'm going to have to get prepared. So I take out my phone and tap until I've accessed my calendar.

'Now, what date is the gig?' I say, trying to sound a bit more together, although deep inside I feel self-conscious about even using the word 'gig'. Is it something women in their forties are allowed to say?

Sho fixes me with another look.

'I don't know yet. I need to check,' she says.

Okay, so she doesn't know the date of the gig yet, I tell myself. I can live with that.

'When will you know?' The words shoot out before I can stop them.

'I'll check tonight, okay?' she says, running her hand impatiently through her hair.

I know I'm pissing her off and I should stop asking her questions, but there's something I really need to know.

'Do you think Eamonn will take a selfie with me?' I say, quietly, because if I'm going to do this I'll need proof that it happened, especially if I'm going to surprise Jen with it.

'If you don't behave like a total psycho, then possibly!' she says.

I give myself a little hug. After all the stress of the last few weeks, this is exactly the thing I need to lift my spirits. As usual we say goodbye at the top of the road. Judging by the dismissive wave of her hand, I'm pretty sure Sho regrets mentioning anything about the backstage passes to me, but it's too late now.

As we round the corner to our house, Anna says out of nowhere, 'Who cares?' and throws her hands up in the air.

'What do you mean?' I say, puzzled.

'About Eamonn!' she says, squeezing my hand hard.

Look, I know she's only four but I can't help but take a bit of umbrage at this completely unprovoked attack. So, trying to keep my voice as level as I can, I explain to her that Eamonn was one of my favourite people growing up and that Milly's mummy might be able to find a way that I can meet him.

She thinks about this for a second.

'But he only sells fish,' she says, wrinkling her nose.

I stare at her for a second, trying to figure out what on earth she is talking about. Then it suddenly dawns on me. Our fishmonger in the village is called Amman. Jesus, has she been thinking this whole time that I've been squealing about the local fishmonger? I am still giggling when David opens the door.

'What's so funny?' he says, smiling.

'Oh, nothing. I'm just excited because I have backstage passes to see Amman down the local fishmonger,' I say, laughing hysterically. 'Maybe he'll give me free fish and chips!'

I am so caught up in my own hilarity that I don't notice Bonnie standing in the hallway, wearing the same smart bag and coat. With all the chaos of the cake sale and the excitement of the Pirana gig, I have completely forgotten that David is meeting her today. I give her a big wave.

'I'm just on my way out,' she says.

'How was your appointment?' I say, hoping she'll let something slip about who has been hiring her as a rent-a-friend.

I mean, the chances are I don't know this person, but still, I can't help but be desperate to find out. If this was some drama on TV, it would be someone you would least expect, like Tania Henderson, but I just know it's not her because she is too shallow for proper friendship.

'It went well, thanks,' Bonnie says, tightening her scarf around her neck.

'Did you have to walk a long way to get from her house to ours?' I say.

She purses her lips at me in a way that tells me she knows what I'm up to.

'Not too far,' she says, walking towards the door.

Damn it. I'll have to find another way to make her crack.

I move to let her pass, but she pauses for a moment to smile at Anna.

'Hello, Anna!' she says, smiling.

Anna, who is not known for her tolerance for greeting new people, just stares at her. Bonnie gives her head a quick pat and says goodbye. As she lets herself out of the front gate, Anna turns to me and says, 'She looks like Daddy.'

I look at David and he raises his eyebrows. Anna's no eejit. We might have to tell her sooner than we thought. Still, she might be smart but she's no stranger to the classic distraction techniques.

'Where's your iPad?' I say, in the same voice you might use when you're asking a dog to find a ball. As predicted, she throws off her coat and races into the kitchen to find it.

David closes the door behind me, and says, 'I don't want to tell Anna yet. I'm still struggling to get my head around it myself.'

I nod. He's right – it's best he comes to terms with it all and gets to know Bonnie a bit more before we introduce her formally to Anna.

'How was it with Bonnie today, anyway?' I say.

'It was good,' he says, his eyes lighting up. 'Turns out she watches all the same cooking programmes as me. She's also a big fan of the chef who was doing the cooking demo today.'

He leans over and kisses me lightly on the lips. 'Thanks for that, Saoirse – it really helped to take my mind off things.'

I smile back at him. It's great to see him a bit more back to his old self.

'Is Bonnie a neat freak as well?' I say, although I'm pretty sure David got his obsessive tidiness from Rose, but maybe it's also in the genes. Who knows?

'I didn't ask her,' David says, giving me a look.

Then Anna starts to shout about the whereabouts of her pasta-with-cheese-on-top and that's the end of all adult conversation until we put her to bed. That evening, instead of heading to the living room to binge-watch Netflix like we always do on a Friday night (not to mention every other night of the week since David has been off work), we sit in the kitchen with a bottle of wine between us and just chat. David fills me in about Bonnie. 'Do you know she wanted to call me Magnus, but the girls in the care home talked her out of it?'

I burst out laughing.

'I would never have married you if you were called Magnus!'

'Well, I guess I would have dodged a bullet there!' he jokes.

He takes a sip of wine and looks thoughtful.

'I still can't get my head around it all,' he says. 'I mean, of course, I've thought about her over the years – what she might have looked like, why she gave me up, if I had any half-brothers or half-sisters out there... but she was never real. Almost like a fantasy that could never come true. And now, after all these years, she's here: I can talk to her, touch her, ask her questions, find out more about her life, what we have in common. I'm her son but she is a complete stranger, you know? Talk about a mindfuck!' he finishes with a bitter laugh.

'I know, it's a lot to take in,' I say. 'But you will get there in time.'

He reaches over and grabs my hand.

'Look, I'm sorry I have been all over the place,' he says. 'Can't be easy on you.'

I wave him away in a 'Sure, you're GRAND' sort of way, but he knows me too well. He looks deep into my eyes, and says, 'Thanks for putting up with me.'

I punch him playfully on the arm and he leans over and gives me a kiss.

'Go on – tell me about your day,' he says.

So, I tell him all about the cake sale and that bitch, Tania Henderson leaving me with the deliberately large cake, and being set upon by the feral, thieving Year Sixes, and being rescued by Sho, which is where he interrupts me.

'Did you mention anything about Ambrose coming very late to pick up Milly from the playdate at our house?'

'No, no,' I say, waving my wine glass-free hand at him dismissively. 'People make mistakes, David, you should really let that one go.'

He raises his eyes skyward.

Then I tell him about Sho offering me backstage passes to Pirana the following week and how I can't wait to tell Jen but I can't tell her yet because I don't want to jinx it, and he just folds his arms and shakes his head.

'You've become all teenagery,' he says, laughing.

I blow a raspberry at him.

'It's going to be the best night of my life,' I say, cupping both my hands around the glass and staring dreamily into the red liquid inside.

David mutters a quick, 'Jesus,' and downs the rest of his wine in one gulp.

Then he leans back in his chair and says something that will guarantee that I get no sleep that night.

'What are you going to wear to this gig?'

21

It's 10 a.m. on Saturday and I've managed to duck out of swimming duty with Anna even though it's my turn. David is not happy about it, but I've promised him I'll tidy up my work desk in return (which is never going to happen but he doesn't know that yet). Instead I'm on a panic visit to Bea, who is sure to know what the hell forty-somethings are supposed to wear to a gig (and if, in fact, we're allowed to say the word 'gig'). Bea opens the door, make-up-less, and dressed in pink fleecy pyjamas. Harry shoots out from behind her.

'Where's Anna?' he shouts, fists bunched.

'Swimming,' I say.

He sighs and kicks the wall.

'Go and watch your iPad,' Bea says, sternly.

'Oh, fine,' he says, in the manner of sulky student who's just been told to study for his exams.

He slopes off upstairs and Bea beckons me to follow her into the kitchen.

'I can't wait to have another one of him,' she says, wryly, patting her stomach. 'So, what's the big clothing emergency?'

She flicks the switch on the kettle.

I had texted her last night telling her I needed some urgent fashion advice. The only other person who might have a clue is Jen, but judging by her Instagram she is in Dubai reporting on a fashion shoot and I don't want to bother her. Besides, I want to surprise her with my selfie with Eamonn.

I fill Bea in on Sho and the tickets to Pirana and how much I love Eamonn and how I don't want to look a state in front of my biggest teen crush, and so on.

'Firstly, women over forty are allowed to use the word gig,' she says, pouring the hot water into each cup.

'Secondly, I doubt very much that Eamonn will care what you're wearing.'

'But...' I say, but she holds up her hand and I close my mouth again.

Then she brings over the cups to the table and passes me a teabag and a little spoon.

'And, yes, I know that you will care what you're wearing, even if Eamonn doesn't,' she says.

I smile. That's exactly what I was going to say.

'Especially if there's going to be a selfie. So, do you have any tips?' I say, swooshing the teabag around with the spoon.

'I might have something that will work,' she says, standing up.

I follow her into her bedroom, and she reaches into the wardrobe and pulls out a black leather jacket. She passes it to me and tells me to try it on. The leather is so soft that I feel like stroking my face with it, but nevertheless, I hesitate.

'I don't think I can get away with a leather jacket at my age,' I say.

'Nonsense!' she says, folding her arms. 'A leather jacket is a classic choice for all ages. Now try it on!'

Oh, fine.

She waves me over to the full-length mirror on the opposite wall and I put my arm into one sleeve and then the other. I risk a glance in the mirror, poised to take off the jacket at any second, but I'm surprised to see, it's not half bad. It's fitted and slightly cropped, which shows off my usually non-existent waist, and adds a bit of depth to my narrow shoulders.

'Looks good!' Bea says, nodding her head.

'Are you sure I can borrow it?' I say, running the soft leather between my fingertips. 'It seems very expensive.'

'Oh, sure. It's not going to fit me for a while, is it?' she says, sticking out her still enviably flat stomach.

I thank her and take off the jacket, folding it carefully over my arm. Then something occurs to me.

'What will I wear with it?'

Bea sighs and throws me a look that says, 'Surely you can't be that hopeless,' but she replies anyway.

'Plain white T-shirt, jeans, and boots,' she says, as if she's rhyming off a shopping list.

Okay, I think I can manage that.

When we go back downstairs to the kitchen, I hang the jacket carefully over the back of my chair, giving it a fond stroke just before I sit down. Bea shakes her head.

'So, how's David getting on with Bonnie?' she says, splitting open a packet of strawberry teacakes.

I had filled her in on meeting Bonnie on the street and a bit about her background, but I hadn't really updated her since.

'Really well, I think,' I say, crunching into the delicious chocolate, marshmallow and biscuit combination. 'She seems very nice, but it will take a while.'

Bea chews her biscuit thoughtfully.

'I can't get my head around the rent-a-friend stuff,' she says.

'Who around here would hire her? All the mums in this neigh-
bourhood are so cocksure of themselves.'

'Well, that's what I've been dying to find out,' I say, leaning
forward, delighted to engage in the gossip. 'I wonder if it's anyone
on Vale Mums.'

'Hmmm,' Bea says. 'Well, the only person I can think of who
uses Vale Mums as a cry for help is Rosalind.'

I spit out my crumbs at her. Jesus! Maybe it's Rosalind.

* * *

I swap my big, padded, winter coat for Bea's leather jacket on the
walk home, but it doesn't make me feel any better. Why haven't I
been in touch with Rosalind when I knew how lonely she was? I
think back to our first and only meeting at the coffee shop not
long after the terrorist attack and think about how fragile she was
– three young kids with a husband working overseas, for Christ's
sake. I should have followed up with her after the bedwetting
posts on Vale Mums, but to be honest I just plain forgot. God, I
am a shit friend.

I pause at the front gate and fire off a quick text to Rosalind,
asking her if she wants to meet for a coffee. Poor Rosalind – so
lonely that she has to pay someone to talk to her. David pulls up
beside the kerb just as I'm slipping my phone back into my bag. I
can hear Anna crying before he shuts off the engine.

Oh, God, what now? The usual panicky sensation I feel when
Anna's upset rushes over me, and I hurry to open the door. I
unlock her seatbelt and reach in to give her a hug, before asking
her what's wrong a million times, even though she's too upset to
answer. David sticks his head in and tries to calm her down, but
every word he says she takes as an insult ('Stop Daddy!'). Eventu-

ally, he beckons me outside and says quietly, 'She's been moved up a level in her swimming.'

I frown. 'But that's good news, surely?'

'It would be, but Amy isn't going to be joining her.'

'Oh, shit.'

Amy is Anna's best 'swimming friend' and pretty much the only reason she gets into the pool. I stick my head back into the car and try and offer some words of comfort, but the wailing drowns out anything I have attempted to say. Then I hear a familiar voice behind me.

'Oh, dear! What's wrong with Anna?'

I sigh and back slowly out of the car.

Just as I thought, it's one of Tania's little Organic soldiers, Caroline. But before I get to say anything, David pipes up.

'She's upset because she's moved to a different swimming class to her best friend.'

I glare at him, desperately wanting to give him a hard nudge. Why would he say something like that? Now Caroline will only go back to the Organics and tell them that Anna has problems with emotional regulation or some bullshit. I have to save this.

'In a way it's good news!' I say brightly. 'Because she's been moved up a level.'

David shoots me a strange look, but I don't care.

'Oh, that's wonderful!' Caroline says, smiling. 'What level will she be in?'

Shite. I walked into that one. Suddenly, I have a vague memory of a Facebook post showing her daughter Fenella in a swimsuit with a gold medal around her neck. Fuck it – I'm going to make something up, but just before I open my mouth, David once again rushes in with his stupid, ill-timed honesty.

'Level two,' he says.

She gives me a smug smile before telling us she has rush off to pick up her older son Benjamin from advanced chess club.

Fuming, I wedge myself into the back of the car, eventually coaxing Anna out with heartfelt promises of hot chocolate. As we finally close the door, David drops Anna's swimming bag down on the bottom stair and says, 'Who was that?'

'Caroline,' I say, grumpily, still annoyed with him for saying all the wrong things.

'She seems nice,' he says, walking into the kitchen.

I give his retreating back the silent two fingers, and then bend down to help Anna take off her shoes.

That night, Caroline sends a photo to the class WhatsApp group of Fenella wearing a 'junior champion' sash and dripping in gold medals. The caption is:

So proud of our daughter for winning the latest swimming gala – can't believe she's only just turned five!

22

'Mummy – slow down!' Anna says on Monday morning, as I propel her along the path to school. So keen am I to see if Sho has managed to acquire the Pirana tickets I have batted away David's offer to take over the school run. To my relief, Sebastian Fox has emailed a request to meet on Wednesday instead of our usual Monday interviews, which means I have a bit of free time.

The unmistakeable sound of an adult scooter causes me to slow my pace and move into the walled side of the pavement, tucking Anna protectively beside me. I give a quick glance over my shoulder, expecting to see the lycra-attired Tania Henderson with Heath balancing in the front, but instead I see the similarly lycra-attired Caroline from yesterday. And she's scooting in my direction.

After her smugness yesterday over the swimming, not to mention sending that boasty and irrelevant photo of Fenella to the class WhatsApp group, I refuse to acknowledge her, and so continue walking with Anna at as brisk a pace as I can manage with a reluctant four-year-old. Caroline scoots alongside us with a cheery, 'Morning!' before skidding to a stop. I take a deep breath and turn to face her. Clearly, there's no outrunning her.

She leans her scooter carefully against the wall, and then walks over to me with her arms outstretched. I look at her completely horrified. What is she doing? Before I can figure out how to react, her arms are wrapped around me in a tight embrace. I freeze.

Then she lets me go and says, 'Oh, you poor love. I felt so sorry for you yesterday.'

And honest to God I haven't a clue what she's talking about.

'What do you mean?' I say.

She gives Anna a sideways look and whispers, 'Well, Anna was creating quite a fuss.'

The hairs on my neck start to bristle. Yes, my four-year-old was throwing a temper tantrum. Why is this something out of the ordinary? Before I can say anything, she looks at Anna and sighs in a sort of regretful manner.

'I just don't know what I would do if Fenella behaved like that.'

The bitch. As if Fenella has never thrown a shit fit in her five years.

'Where is Fenella?' Anna pipes up.

'Her daddy is taking her to school today,' Caroline says, smiling at Anna.

I am raging that I have nothing on Fenella. In fact, this is the only time Anna has mentioned her since she started school. There is nothing I can do – I am impotent and helpless with rage.

Anna tugs my hand.

'I know, Anna, we have to go,' I say, glaring at Caroline.

But then Anna tugs my hand again, beckoning me with her other hand to come closer. I bend down to her and she presses her mouth closely against my ear.

'Fenella bit me the other day,' she says.

A feeling of pure joy rushes through me.

'What was that, Anna?' I say in a loud voice, in the fervent hope that she will project this golden nugget far enough to reach Caroline's ears. And the child doesn't disappoint.

Caroline stiffens.

'Well, I'm not sure if that's true,' she huffs, crossing her arms and narrowing her eyes at Anna.

Oh, we're on the home stretch now, I think gleefully.

'Anna doesn't lie,' I say, folding my arms right back at her. This is total bullshit, of course. Anna lies all the time – she lies about brushing her teeth (she simply wets the top of her toothbrush); she lies about finishing her tea (she tips it into the bin as soon as my back is turned); and she lies about her age (apparently, she's already five or six, depending on what mood she's in). Frankly, she's also a bit of a thief, but that's a story for another time.

'Well, I'm sure even if Fenella did bite you, she didn't mean it,' Caroline says, attempting a cutesy-pie voice with Anna.

And in that moment, I know that Fenella has bitten before. Why else would Caroline entertain it further if it wasn't true?

'She didn't even say sowwy,' Anna says, her little face screwed up in indignation.

'Perhaps it might be worth having a word with Fenella,' I say in my most patronising voice.

Caroline's mouth twists into an ugly shape. Then she grabs her scooter roughly and rides off.

I lean down to give Anna a little hug.

'Did Fenella really bite you?' I say, just to make sure, because you never really know what's going on inside her head.

She nods sadly.

God, I don't think I have ever loved her this much. Not only

has she got me out of a sticky situation, but she's given me
enough ammo against Caroline to take us all the way through to
the end of primary school.

I give Anna a little kiss before straightening up again.

About five steps later Anna says thoughtfully, 'Or was it
Freya?'

We walk the rest of the way to school in silence.

Mr Russell gives me a half-wave without blushing as I go
through the gates, which I count as significant progress, although
I'm not sure if he's making an effort because he wants to move
past the blowjob incident or because I caught him stealing a
cupcake. Whatever the reason, I'm grateful that the awkwardness
between us seems to be on the decline. As I walk past the Organics, I see Caroline muttering furiously to Tania. Presuming she's
bitching about me, I strain my ears as much as I can, but all I can
pick up is, 'AND her daughter is still in nappies at night!' which of
course is a dig at the comment I had added to Rosalind's Facebook post. That reminds me – I haven't heard from Rosalind since
I sent her a message on Saturday. Maybe she's so lonely and
depressed that she's too far gone for company. I vow to call her on
the way home. Then Diana sidles over, raving about the new
made-of-wood children's adventure playground that's just opened
in the local park, and I try my best to look interested (although
give me a few swings and a splinter-free plastic slide any day of
the week). Although I hate when other people do this, I break eye
contact with Diana while she's still talking to see if I can spot Sho.
My stomach jumps a little when I see her walking around the
corner with Milly a few steps behind. Sho catches my eye and
gives Diana a sideways glance, before coming to a stop a little
distance away. Diana reflexively looks over her shoulder, and
then back again. God, I really don't want to offend her, but I know
that Sho isn't going to come over as long as Diana is around to

bore the shit out of her. Just then, Anna's teacher appears, which is a sign that the bell is going to go soon.

As politely as I can, I tell Diana that I just need to talk to Anna's teacher about something and she smiles and wanders off. I stroll over in the direction of the teacher until Diana's out of sight, and then make a hard swerve to the right towards Sho.

'Did you get the tickets?' I ask, breathlessly.

'Good morning to you too,' she says, wryly.

'Sorry,' I say, blushing.

Honestly, what is wrong with me? I'm like a hormonal adolescent. Is this what a mid-life crisis looks like?

'And yes, I did get them,' she says, sighing.

My fists clench with the effort of not hugging her.

'That's amazing!' I squeak. 'When is it?'

'Tomorrow night,' she says.

So soon? Normally the short notice would have sent me into a panic spiral: who's going to look after Anna if David doesn't make it back in time? What the hell am I going to wear? But thanks to David being off work, and my stellar idea to borrow clothes from Bea, I feel totally prepared for this moment. So chilled about it, in fact, that I feel genuinely cool.

'Where's the gig on?' I say, feeling not in the least bit self-conscious.

To my relief, her head doesn't explode with disgust.

'The O2 in Greenwich,' she says.

Then she tells me to meet her outside the venue at 7 p.m. tomorrow and she will give me the tickets. I wonder why we can't travel in together but I don't want to sound too needy, so I smile and agree, and thank her again. Then the bell goes and I lose her in the flurry of last-minute hugs and goodbyes.

When I round the corner of my street, I am greeted by a lovely aroma of pastry and spices and herbs and all things nice. I feel a bit of a twinge; all this deliciousness reminds me of brunch sex, something that David and I haven't enjoyed since Bonnie came into our lives. Still, I can't blame him – his head's been all over the place since being reunited with Bonnie.

But then I open the gate to our house and the smell gets stronger. My heart lifts as I throw back the front door. David comes springing out of the kitchen wearing a splattered green-and-white-striped apron and a playful smile.

'Brunch sex?' he says, grabbing my bottom and pulling me towards him.

I smile back at him, desperately wanting to say something sexy like, 'Why wait until brunch?' But the truth is that I am pretty behind on my transcribing from the Sebastian Fox interviews. Also, my hair needs a wash and my legs could do with a shave, so I just say, 'Absolutely – see you in a couple of hours!'

When the time comes, I am so thrilled at the thought of going to see Pirana tomorrow and meeting Eamonn, my teen crush, and another scrummy brunch to look forward to that I throw an uncharacteristic amount of energy into sex with David. After he collapses on top of me, he raises himself on both arms and looks deeply into my eyes.

'That was phenomenal,' he says, his eyes twinkling.

'I know,' I giggle happily. He's not wrong – my head is still spinning.

'Bet you were thinking of Eamonn the whole time,' he says playfully.

'Haha,' I say sarcastically, but inwardly I'm thinking: 'Not the *whole* time...'

23

I wake up on Tuesday with a feeling that could only be described as 'wired'. Tonight's the night of the big gig and I can't wait to come face to face with my teen idol.

I skip out of bed, crossing the room quickly to the wardrobe. I open it and take out the leather jacket I'm going to be wearing that night and hold it close, luxuriating in the softness and deliciously addictive leathery smell. I'm looking forward to at least pretending I'm cool at the age of forty.

Humming a Pirana tune, I dance merrily downstairs in my pyjamas to kiss Anna goodbye. Her eyes are full of resentment.

'I want you to take me to school,' she pouts at me.

'Pink doughnut!' David says, taking her little hand.

Anna lets out a whoop of joy and immediately turns towards the front door.

'After I drop Anna to school, I'm thinking of heading into town to check out a food museum,' David says, his hand on the latch. 'Is that all right?'

'After yesterday afternoon, you can do whatever you like,' I say, in what I hope is a sexy voice.

He picks up on it and laughs.

I watch the pair of them as they walk peacefully hand in hand out of the front door. As David opens the front gate, I hear Anna saying, 'What happened yesterday afternoon, Daddeeee?'

Then I close the front door.

After a rare uninterrupted breakfast, I go back upstairs, throw on my comfy jeans and my favourite squashy red jumper and head towards the spare room to do some work.

Technically, I should be preparing questions for the Sebastian Fox interview the following day, but instead I spend the time googling Pirana, checking out facts about Eamonn (letting out a little squeak of excitement after I find out he's still not married, and then feeling ridiculous) and brushing up on my Pirana lyrics for the night ahead.

Just as I'm taking my third biscuit break, I get a text. It's from Rosalind. She would love to meet for a coffee. Hurrah! Saved from work guilt for the moment. I quickly text back and we agree to meet in the same coffee shop as last time.

Half an hour later I arrive at the coffee shop, eagerly scanning the throngs of mums and cranky babies for Rosalind, but she doesn't seem to have arrived yet. So I push my way through the maze of tangled buggies towards the stools by the window, plonk myself down and stare at my smartphone to look as if I'm far too busy to be alone.

Not two minutes later, I hear a large 'Oooh' in my ear and I whip around with a big smile on my face. Then I do a double take.

'Holy God!' I say, before I can stop myself.

Because Rosalind is not the same Rosalind I remember from a few months ago. That Rosalind had mountains of black curly hair piled up on top of her head and big, round black-framed glasses.

This Rosalind has neatly styled soft curls sweeping her shoulders and no glasses. She looks absolutely fantastic.

'Do you like it?' Rosalind says, shyly, twisting a strand of hair. 'I'm still getting used it.'

'I love it!' I say.

'Also got my eyes lasered,' she says, sitting down on the stool beside me.

'I noticed you were glasses-free!' I say.

But to be honest, it's not just the hair and the glasses, she just seems so calm and contented since the last time I saw her. The waiter comes over and takes our orders and we smile at each other. I am desperate to know how this change has happened to her but I'm not sure how to phrase it ('So Rosalind, remember you used to be a big bag of nerves who relied on those bitches from Vale Mums for child-rearing advice?'). But before I say anything, she starts talking.

'So, I got a new full-time nanny!' she says, giving herself a little clap.

'Jesus, no wonder you look so amazing!' I blurt out.

For a moment I'm worried she might be offended, but she just laughs.

'Honestly, Saoirse, she is fantastic.'

Just as I'm having one of those out-of-body 'where's my friend Rosalind and what have you done with her' moments, the waiter arrives with two steaming cups of coffee.

'Tell me more,' I say, taking a deep sip.

God, if anyone deserves a nanny, it's Rosalind.

She spends the next half an hour filling me in about Elsa the nanny, and by the end of it, even though I don't need a nanny, I want an Elsa too. From the sounds of it, nothing is too much for Elsa – not the three boys under the age of six, the housework, or even making a quick nip to the shops (with the three kids) where necessary.

'She sounds like a powerhouse!' I say, shaking my head in awe.

'Ooooh, she is!' Rosalind smiles, clutching both hands around her cup.

'And do the boys like her?'

Her brow creases.

'Actually, not really, but they have no choice, do they? Because Mummy is finally getting her life back!'

Then she raises her cup and we 'cheers' so vigorously that some of my coffee sloshes out.

'Well, I'm happy for you,' I say, running a napkin against my cup to stop the dripping.

'Thanks,' she smiles. 'Oh, and thanks for sticking up for me on Vale Mums.'

For a moment I'm confused, and then I remember her bedwetting post.

'It's no problem,' I say. 'How's the bedwetting now?'

'Worse than ever,' she says. 'But at least I know if I'm up in the night, I have Elsa to take over during the day.'

I nod. It must be wonderful to have all the extra support, especially with her husband working so far away.

'Mind you, a full-time nanny isn't cheap, so I'm going to start looking for a job,' she says, sipping her coffee. 'Although she's more useful around the house than my husband and much cheaper than a divorce!' she adds, but she says it in such an offhand way that I don't know if she's joking or not.

I don't really know her well enough to find out more, but by nature I'm fairly nosy so I ask her about her husband and if he's still working abroad. She blows out some air and swishes her coffee around slowly.

'We're giving each other some space at the moment,' she says, staring into her coffee.

'Oh!' is all I can think of to say.

'Listen – it's fine,' she says, but her eyes tell a different story. 'It's not like he's ever around very much anyway.'

'Still, though...' I say. 'If you need anything...'

God, I'm bloody useless in these situations.

'I don't need anything – I have Elsa the supernanny, remember?' she says, lightly.

Then she asks about David and Anna and, curious as I am, I can sense a subject change when I hear it.

So I tell her about David and throw Bonnie's name into the conversation, but her face doesn't betray even the tiniest flicker of recognition. I'm not surprised – Rosalind may be having some marriage problems but she seems the picture of strength. The only time she reacts to any of my news is when I casually tell her about the Pirana gig that night. She practically jumps off her stool with excitement.

'I LOVED that band when I was younger,' she says, her face flushed.

'Eamonn?'

'Well, who else?' she laughs. 'You have to send me the selfies!'

We exchange Pirana stories, squealing like schoolgirls, until Rosalind checks her watch and gasps. Apparently she has a massage booked, the lucky thing.

As we are saying goodbye, she says, 'Enjoy the Pirana gig!'

'I will!' I say.

Then she leans in closer and whispers, 'Are we allowed to say gig in our forties?'

And I look her straight in the eye and say, 'Too right we are, Rosalind. Too fucking right.'

* * *

I spend the rest of the day trying to think of 'leading' questions for Sebastian Fox, in the vague hope he will divulge something more interesting about his life, but to be honest, I don't get very far. The day drags on and, by the time I pick up Anna, I'm jittery with impatience.

'Ready for tonight?' Sho says, briefly looking me up and down.

'Yes, but I'm not wearing this!' I say, hurriedly, mortified that she thinks that I might be going to such a cool event in my battered mum jeans and ancient brown duffle coat.

She gives me a vague nod.

Out of the corner of my eye, I see the familiar lycra-shaped form of an Organic striding towards us. Caroline. Again.

She gives Sho a haughty sniff before turning to me.

'I've had a chat with Fenella, and she tells me that she didn't bite Anna,' she says.

I look at her indignant face for a moment, at a loss for something to say. There's really nowhere to go from here, yet I don't want to lose all the ground I have gained by admitting that Anna may have accused the wrong child. Every part of me just wants to style it out, but how?

'Fenella bit Milly, too,' Sho says, folding her arms.

What?

Caroline whips around.

'She did not!' she says, glaring at Sho.

'Are you calling Milly a liar?' she says, her head cocked on one side.

Caroline pulls her fleece tightly around her and storms off to her fellow Organics, no doubt ready to rage about us to whoever can be bothered to listen. When she is out of hearing distance, I elbow Sho in the arm and say, 'Did Fenella really bite Milly?'

She looks me straight in the eye and says, 'Nope.'

24

That evening, I walk out of North Greenwich Tube station breathless with excitement. I am a few minutes early for Sho, so I stand against a side wall, taking in the crowds of fellow Pirana lovers. To my huge relief, nobody seems to be dressed in anything cooler than me. As Bea predicted, there are more fans of my age than there are younger ones and most people seem to have gone for classic leather with either a white or black T-shirt underneath – apart from the guy who is actually dressed as a piranha, but he seems to be in the minority.

Minutes go by and I try not to panic. Sho isn't a time-freak like me, I remind myself over and over. Besides, if she's anything like her partner Ambrose, she probably won't turn up for a while yet. I wriggle my toes in my hard leather boots. They are the only cool ones I have, but I never normally wear them because they are so bloody uncomfortable. Then I notice that most of the other fans are wearing white trainers, which makes me cross that I didn't do the same. The doors open and the crowd piles in. Still no sign of Sho. A terrible thought crosses my mind. Why didn't I get her number? What if she's stood me up? What if this is like the movie *Carrie*, when the popular boy invites her to prom only to dump a bucket of pig's blood on her head? What if...

'Hey there!'

I have been catastrophising to such a degree that it takes me a moment to register that Sho is actually standing in front of me. A rush of relief floods over me. I'm not Carrie after all.

I find my voice and say, 'Hi,' and she leans towards me, arms outstretched. For a brief moment, I think she's leaning in for a hug, but then I feel a light weight against my chest. I look down and see a metal badge emblazoned with the Pirana logo, with the words, 'Backstage pass' on it.

I clutch it close to me, and take a quick look around, for fear that some other superfan is going to clock it and wrestle it from me.

Sho shakes her head slowly and says, 'Shall we go in then?'

I follow her into the cavernous entrance hall, my ears already humming with the buzz of an excited, growing crowd. With a sinking heart, I spot the mammoth queue at security, but Sho doesn't even pause. When we reach the top of the line, she holds up her backstage pass to the security guard and then nudges me to do the same. This is easy for me to do, given that I haven't actually stopped clutching it since she gave it to me. The security guard gives us a brief nod, quickly searches our bags and then we're through. As we walk towards the escalators to the stadium, I feel the weight of a thousand envious glares from the fans who have been forced to wait boring into my back, but I don't care. This is the first time I've gone VIP on anything, and I'm determined to enjoy it as long as it lasts.

After a walk that reminds you exactly how big the O2 is, we finally reach the arena itself. The last time I was here, it was to see

Frozen on Ice with Anna, but the place couldn't be any more different now. For starters, the stage is covered in sweeping blue and green lights, with a lit-up black background showcasing the four faces of the band in black and white. As Sho leads me closer to the stage, I have a terrible feeling she's bringing me to the mosh pit. Much as I can't wait to get up close and personal with my favourite band, I can't face being squashed against hundreds of sweaty strangers crowd-surfing and throwing their heads around in impossible-looking patterns. I'm not great in crowds at the best of times. To my relief, she takes a sharp right, climbs up about a dozen steps, and finally reaches our row. Thankfully, we're right on the end so we are saved from forcing people to their feet and doing the whole 'Sorry, excuse me' thing. I settle down on the seat and beam at my good fortune. Not only are these excellent seats (even better than the *Frozen on Ice* ones), but being at the end means that I am closer to the toilets. Nothing makes me happier than having complete access to toilets when I'm out of the house – the trigger-nature of my post-Anna bladder makes this an essential requirement at all times. Sho springs up as soon as we have sat down.

'Toilet?' I say.

'Drink!' she says. 'What do you fancy?'

'I'll have a glass of Pinot Noir,' I say.

She gives me a look.

What have I said wrong? Maybe red wine isn't cool enough for a gig but I don't care. If I hit the beers I'll be running to the toilets more often than usual.

'A large one!' I say.

She sighs.

'And if they don't have Pinot Noir?' she says, raising her eyebrows at me.

'Oh, any red wine will do,' I say, strongly getting the impression that she thinks I'm being fussy.

I step out into the aisle, offering to give her money for the drinks, but she waves me away and tells me I can get the next round in.

As I watch her disappear into a side entrance, I start to worry. Pinot Noir is the only wine I can drink without it staining my lips into a weird crooked line. I can't be dealing with that during the meet and greet with Eamonn. I would have got white wine, but it's too cold to drink in the chilly weather... Then I tell myself to stop being such a massive arsehole.

I spend a happy few minutes people-watching – the row below ours is clearly on a hen do. Most of the party is wearing black Pirana T-shirts, apart from the bride-to-be, who's wearing a white T-shirt emblazoned with the words, 'Fourth time lucky'. Everybody in that row seems to be my age or older. In fact, looking around, the only youngsters I can see are teenagers, with their mums or dads, who wear the sort of furious expressions you might have when you're forced into doing something you don't want to do.

Ten minutes later, I spot Sho climbing the steps holding a bottle of wine in one hand and two wine glasses in the other. The hen party gasps.

'You're not allowed to bring glass bottles in here, love,' the bride-to-be calls in a strong Liverpudlian accent.

Sho just ignores her and squeezes past my knees to sit down. She hands me the wine glasses and holds the bottle close to my face. It's a Pinot Noir.

I grin at her.

'How did you manage that?'

'I tattooed Dave the barman during that last tour,' she says, setting the bottle between her legs and deftly opening the screw top. 'I didn't charge him so he's giving me a few freebies.'

I smile at her in admiration, but before I can say anything else, the lights start to dim. She sloshes some wine into my glass and we clink. The sound of the bass guitar strikes up and I lean forward in my seat, sipping wine, my heart beating with the anticipation of seeing my favourite band.

Except of course it's not Pirana who leap on stage waving their guitars around like they have taken on a life of their own. It's the support band. I'm no music expert but even I know they're dreadful. Lots of frenzied bouncing around the stage, with lyrics that seem to go nowhere. I lean in closer to Sho with the intention of slagging them off, but stop short when I see her transfixed expression. So I slide back in my seat and take a large glug of my wine. Maybe this is the sort of thing the cool kids are into, but it's not my cup of tea at all.

Twenty minutes of appallingness later, the support band finally call it a night by breaking into a fight on stage, and everyone cheers and claps (perhaps, some of them like me, cheering that it's all over).

The lights come on again.

Sho looks at me, her eyes shining. I've never seen her look so alive.

'They were awesome, weren't they?' she says, throwing her arms up into the air.

I don't have the heart to tell her what I really think so I just say, 'Let's have more wine!'

To be honest, I'm not sure if it's the wine or the buzzy environment, but Sho suddenly starts to become uncharacteristically chatty. She talks about the school run and how much she dislikes the Organics, and how the whole school thing just really isn't her kind of 'vibe'. Then I ask her what is her vibe, and she says, 'This!'

making a circular movement with her hand. 'Being here in a crowd watching music, and hopefully tattooing the artists afterwards, is exactly where I belong.'

I feel a flash of envy. I don't fit into the whole school thing either, and I envy Sho for knowing exactly where she wants to be.

'Since I had Anna, I don't really do this sort of thing,' I say.

'You mean go to gigs?' she says.

The look of horror in her face is enough to give me the giggles.

'Well, what do you do for fun then?' she says, her eyes wide.

I have to think about that one for a moment. Sit in with David, and watch Netflix? Too boring to share with someone so cool. Finally, I say, 'Well, if I'm having a girls' night, I'll go around to my friend Bea's house and drink wine.'

'Oh, that's cool,' she says, taking a large swallow of wine.

'But I have to admit that since Bea got pregnant, those drinking sessions have come to an end.'

She nods thoughtfully and looks into her glass.

'Did you ever think the school gates would be your thing?' she says suddenly.

'Definitely not. Although perhaps school would be more bearable if it wasn't for the bloody Organics giving me evils every time I walk into the playground.'

'They're not the only ones staring at you,' Sho says with a giggle.

'What do you mean?'

'You've certainly caught the eye of Mr Russell!'

I burst out laughing and maybe it's the second glass of wine going to my head, but I suddenly feel all confessional, and so I tell her about Mr Russell and the blowjob.

She laughs until the tears roll down her cheeks.

'I can't believe you gave the head teacher a blowjob,' she says, wiping her eyes with the palm of her free hand.

'You're not allowed tell anyone!' I say, wagging a warning finger at her.

She giggles again and makes a zipping motion across her lips.

Then she goes off to get another bottle of wine from her pal at the bar which gives me a chance to think about everything. I never thought I'd get to the point where I could have a decent chat with Sho, let alone confide in her about Mr Russell. A momentary feeling of doubt passes over me. Should I have told her about it? Can I trust her? But I bat it away – she doesn't seem like the type to share other people's secrets.

Then she's back, more wine is poured, the Liverpudlians grumble again ('It's not right, you know') and are ignored, and then the lights go down. This is it. The big moment. It's Pirana! The crowd rises to its feet with a collective roar. By the time the interval comes, I am lathered in sweat from the dancing, my throat is raw from screaming along to the lyrics, and my neck is sore from all the headbanging. Still, it's all worth it. Eamonn may be middle-aged but his voice is as powerful is ever. I am having the time of my life. When the lights go on, Sho heads off to the bar while I go to relieve my seriously over-full bladder. I am one bottle of wine down and my head is swimming between that happy feeling of loving everybody and getting the spins. Instead of heading back to my seat, I go to the bar to find Sho. I push myself through the crowds and eventually spot her leaning over the bar, chatting to a tall man with straggly long hair in a fitted black T-shirt. I make my way over and Sho squeals and introduces me to Dave, the poor man who has been giving us free drinks all night, and because I am quite drunk I thank him about a million times. He laughs and calls us both pissheads, before discreetly sliding bottle number three over the counter. We are just about to wave goodbye when his mouth drops open.

'Oh. My. God,' he says, throwing his hand against mouth.

My first thought is Eamonn. Eamonn the drummer is here. I am going to meet my idol. My heart races and I'm not sure I have the courage to look, but then I hear Sho squeal and I can't bear it any longer. But when I whip around it's not Eamonn at all.

It's Ryan.

25

Somewhere in the distance I hear Dave the barman saying, 'Ah, for fuck's sake, it's not him.' In the mist of my drunken haze, I try to register the fact that Ryan – Bea's ex who kissed me in the park a few months ago – is now standing in front of me wearing a fitted white T-shirt and, objectively speaking, looking like the real Ryan Gosling more than ever before. I'm sure he does it on purpose. Judging by the size of his pupils, he is as shocked to see me as I him. He runs his hand through his hair and says, 'What are you doing here?'

But I don't have a chance to answer because Sho cuts in.

'Saoirse, you know this guy?' she says, peering closely at Ryan.

I open my mouth to respond but she cuts me off.

'Do you know who you look like?' she says, placing the flat of her hand flirtatiously against Ryan's chest. It is just then I realise how drunk she is. I, on the other hand, feel like I've been thrown into a bucket of ice. My stomach flip flops dangerously and I try to tell myself it's just the effects of all the drink, but God, seeing him again after everything that happened brings back some memories I would prefer to remain buried.

Ryan smiles politely at Sho before looking at me again. I find my voice and introduce them.

Ryan gives Sho a warm, 'Hi,' and Sho responds by slurring that he is the absolute image of Ryan Gosling, and that she can't believe his name is also Ryan, and I can see this train of conversation dragging on for longer than either of us wants. I put an end to it.

'What are you doing in London?' I say.

Ryan bites his lip softly and says, 'I'm visiting my girlfriend.'

'Who's your girlfriend?' Sho says, giving Ryan an unnecessary poke in the arm.

He looks at her evenly and says, 'Adriana Santos.'

Sho lets out a squeal that makes me wish I'd downed that third bottle of wine and starts to punch Ryan in the arm.

'I KNOW Adriana!' she says. 'She does the make-up for Pirana!'

Then she abruptly stops her assault on Ryan and whips around to face me.

'Adriana is HOT! I mean she is Brazilian but Gisele has nothing on her.'

I feel my cheeks grow warm. It wasn't too long ago that Ryan confessed he had feelings for me, and now he's fecking off with some Brazilian hottie, probably in her twenties. Honestly, does he have to be so transparent? What a cliché.

'Any plans on seeing Bea and Harry?' I say, my voice deliberately accusatory.

I wonder what your new girlfriend is going to think when she finds out that you're going to be a father again? I think. Bet she won't want to hang around you too much then. Then I stop myself from thinking such ugly thoughts because I sound like a jealous cow even though I'm not. I actually couldn't care less who he ends up with. More power to her. Adriana is probably a perfectly nice girl.

Before Ryan can answer, Sho says, 'Adriana went out with Eamonn for a bit.'

I hate Adriana.

Ryan gives Sho an impatient shake of his head and turns to me.

'Yes, I have texted Bea and I am seeing her tomorrow,' he says, giving me a look that tells me he has picked up on my disapproval.

I am just about to reply with a falsely bright 'Good!' when Sho cuts in yet again.

'Wait a minute,' she says, slowly, waving her finger between myself and Ryan. 'Is this the same Bea you were telling me about earlier?'

I nod at her impatiently. God, she is really drunk.

'Your pregnant friend Bea,' she says, swaying a little.

'Yes, yes, it's the same Bea,' I say, giving her a little push towards the bar and telling her to get us both some water.

Thankfully she wanders off to accost Dave the barman and I breathe a sigh of relief that I have a few minutes peace.

And then I freeze.

Oh, shit.

I feel the weight of Ryan's stare bearing down on me but I can't meet his eyes.

'Wait – Bea's pregnant?' he says, his voice loud.

Fuuuuuuuuckkk!

My mind whirs with 'What I have just done?' and the wine starts to rise back into my throat.

'Saoirse, looks at me,' he says, in a dangerous voice.

I blow out a tortured sigh and do my best to meet his glittering stare.

'Is it mine?' he says.

I hold his stare as evenly as I can but suddenly I don't know what to say. My silence clearly speaks volumes because he suddenly jerks into action.

'I have to call her,' he says, brandishing his phone.

Bea is going to KILL me. I have to warn her before he calls her.

With shaking hands, I open my bag and reach for my phone.

'Fuck, no signal!' we both say at the same time.

We give each other an 'It's on' glare and run in opposite directions. I need to find the exit so I can call Bea. There is no way he's getting there before me. An announcement is made that the intermission is over and a wall of people start rushing in my direction. I refuse to be carried along with the crowd; there has to be a quicker way out of here. Suddenly, I spot an unmarked brown door and push my way through it only to find myself in a long, dark corridor smelling suspiciously like piss. I check my phone. Still no signal. I race to the end of the corridor and almost keel over in relief to see an exit sign. I fling myself through it into the freezing cold air (dimly aware that I've left Bea's beautiful leather jacket on my seat) and punch the call button.

She answers on the first ring.

'Saoirse, what's up?'

She sounds tired and her voice is echoey.

I take a deep breath and tell her that I've just bumped into Ryan and I've totally stuck my foot in it and that I'm so, so sorry, and to please, please don't answer any calls from him.

'I've already spoken to him,' she says, her voice sounding more weary than cross.

'Oh, God, I'm so sorry,' I say tearfully. 'Honestly, it was a stupid mistake...'

'It doesn't matter now anyway, Saoirse,' she says, her voice wobbling.

'Yes, it does, Bea!' I say. 'I am the WORST friend. I don't know how I'm going to make it up to you but I will – I promise.'

'Saoirse, shut the fuck up,' she snaps.

My stomach lurches at the sharpness of the voice.

'Saoirse – I'm losing the baby.'

* * *

I keep her on the phone for the entire time it takes for the taxi to get from southeast to southwest London. It turns out she's been in the bathroom bleeding for a couple of hours. She refuses to go to the hospital.

'I can't leave Harry,' she says.

'Wake him up and bring him with you!' I say.

'I can't have him see all this blood, Saoirse. It's like a crime scene in here.'

'Maybe it's not as bad as you think,' I say, hopefully. 'I had a bit of bleeding with Anna but it all turned out well in the end.'

But even as I'm saying the words, I know in my heart that it doesn't sound good.

'I mean, I can't understand why there's so much blood,' she says, her voice full of genuine wonder. 'I'm only ten weeks gone.'

I don't know what to say about this, but I promise her that I will be there as soon as I can and that the roads are pretty clear and I should only be another thirty minutes or so. She sniffs in reply and then sighs.

'Realistically speaking, we can't fill the next thirty minutes talking about my miscarriage...' she says, finally.

It's true, but I'm struggling to find the courage to ask the question I really want to know the answer to.

'What did Ryan say when he called?' I say, finally.

'Well, he was hysterical and emotional, accusing me of hiding things from him and so on,' she says, in a bored voice.

'Oh, God, sorry Bea,' I say for the millionth time.

The poor woman has been sitting on the toilet bleeding for hours – the last thing she needed was an angry call from her ex.

'So, what did you say?'

'Well, given his state of mind, I had to make a judgement call. I knew if I told him I was miscarrying, he would be over here like a shot, and I'm just not in the mood for his histrionics.'

I see her point.

'So in the end, I told him that I thought I was pregnant but it had been a false alarm,' she says.

Wow.

I blow out some air. That's some judgement call. As if sensing my disapproval, she says, 'Oh, Saoirse, what was the point in telling him the truth? He'd only torture himself over it and annoy me in the process. What could he do, anyway?'

'I don't know, Bea – maybe he could have provided some support? Taken Harry for you? Brought you to hospital?'

'Saoirse, Ryan hasn't provided me with an ounce of support since he left me five years ago. I don't need it now,' she says, sharply.

That's me told.

'Besides,' she says more softly, 'I have you.'

And my heart fills.

'Now how far away are you from my house?' she says, sounding more like her usual demanding self.

I look out the window and I am surprised to see the bright lights of busy Earlsfield high street.

'Less than ten minutes,' I tell her.

'Oh, good. I'll do my best to get off the toilet by the time you get here.'

Then she hangs up.

It's just gone 10 p.m. by the time the taxi pulls up outside her house. I fumble in my bag, praying that I have enough cash to pay for the massive bill that comes with crossing London from one end to the other. Bea opens the door before I have a chance to knock. She is dressed in oversized black tracksuit bottoms and a zip up hoodie and looks utterly drained.

'You're very pale,' I tell her as she closes the door behind me.

She looks me up and down and says, 'Where's my leather jacket?'

Shite.

I tell her that I've left it in the stadium but I'm sure Sho will pick it up and bring it back.

She'd better pick it up.

Suddenly, Bea buries her head in her hands, all the fight gone out of her. I don't like how pale she looks.

'I'm taking you to hospital.'

'What about Harry?'

'I'll get David over to sit in the house while we're out.'

'What about Anna?'

Shite, Anna.

I may be sobering up but my head is still all over the place. Then I have a brainwave.

'I'll ask Rosalind to sit in the house,' I say. 'She has a live-in nanny so hopefully she can duck out for a couple of hours.'

Normally I wouldn't dream of asking Rosalind for a favour but, seeing as she lives the closest, it makes sense to try her first.

I hold the phone to my ear and point Bea towards the living room, mouthing, 'Sit down.' Honestly, she must be feeling really weak after all that blood loss.

Rosalind answers on the fourth ring.

'Ooooh, Saoirse!' she says, by way of greeting.

I fill her in quickly and she tells me she'll be around my house in a 'jiffy'. I smile as I end the call. I've only met her a couple of times, yet she is willing to drop everything to help me out. Then I call David who is very concerned to hear about Bea and tells me he will be over to keep an eye on Harry as soon as Rosalind reaches our house. Just before I hang up, he says, nervously 'I've never met Rosalind. Are you sure it's okay to leave her with Anna?'

'She's lovely, kind, and has three kids of her own,' I say quickly. Honestly, as if I would leave our only daughter in the hands of a serial killer. Then something else occurs to me.

'Are you worried she won't take her shoes off when she comes into the house?' I say.

David says nothing. I knew it. He feels awkward telling people he doesn't know to take their shoes off, but not awkward enough to just let it go. Once a neat freak, always a neat freak.

'I'll tell you what, David,' I say quickly, because let's face it, there are more pressing matters to deal with. 'I'll text her and tell her about the no-shoes policy, ok?'

He breathes a sigh of relief.

I walk into the living room to find Bea on the couch, propped up against some cushions.

'All sorted,' I tell her.

She looks at me, eyebrows raised, and says, 'Are you really going to tell Rosalind about the no-shoes policy?'

'Am I fuck.'

She bursts out laughing. It's a relief to see her smile.

'I'll order a taxi for the hospital when David gets here,' I say.

She nods rubs her forehead in exhaustion. Frankly I feel like

doing the same thing – my head is thumping from an early hangover. Bea grimaces and shifts position.

'Do you have something for the bleeding?' I say. And I'm
kicking myself because I should have asked David to go into my
supplies and bring over a few packets of sanitary towels.

'Bleeding is ongoing but I'm well stacked,' she says.

'Are you sure? Because I can get David to...'

'It's fine, Saoirse,' she says, sounding irritated. 'Honestly, I
have that many layers in my pants I'm like the bed from the
Princess and the Bloody Pea.'

* * *

I can't help but give a little shiver as the taxi approaches St
George's hospital. The last time I was in a hospital I was looking
for David, desperately hoping that he had survived the terrorist
attack. As the taxi pulls in outside A&E, I squeeze Bea's hand. She
has been quiet during the short journey. She returns the squeeze
and then drops my hand to open the door. We queue in silence to
check in at reception before eventually being directed to the early
pregnancy unit. To my huge relief, the waiting room is empty. I
grab a paper cup and fill it with water and give it to Bea. Then I go
back and fill several more cups, one at a time, trying to quench
the dreadful thirst so typical of a hangover. Just as I down the fifth
cup, a nurse enters and calls Bea's name. I quickly throw the cup
in the bin and walk back to Bea. She stands and shakes her head.

'I'll be fine on my own,' she says, her neck rigid.

A wave of frustration rushes over me. Why does she have to
be so bloody stubborn? But I know from her grim expression that
I have no chance of dissuading her, so I wait and watch her walk
away with the nurse.

While I'm waiting, I text David to let him know that Bea's

being seen. To be honest, I've been feeling a bit guilty about biting his head off for knocking too loudly on Bea's door earlier, but it would have been a nightmare if Harry had woken up during all of this. Mind you, David took my hissing at him on the chin – probably because, as he told me triumphantly shortly afterwards, Rosalind had taken off her shoes without being asked. David texts back telling me that there hasn't been a sound from Harry's room, but he will check on him anyway. Cue a list of instructions from me to NOT step on the third stair because it creaks, and for the love of God, NOT to flush the toilet, OR be tempted to turn off any of the lights (David likes to save electricity) because Harry finds the brightness comforting – as Bea puts it: 'Harry needs the whole fucking house lit up like a Christmas tree before he closes his eyes.' He gives me a thumbs-up in reply. Then I fire off a quick text to Rosalind to thank her again for staying in the house with Anna. She replies as quickly as David and tells me all is quiet. I glance at my watch, not quite believing it's only 11 p.m. It feels like days since I set off to the O2 to see Pirana. I flop back against the hard, plastic chair, the energy suddenly draining out of me. What a night.

Then I hear footsteps and I turn to find Bea walking slowly towards me, the nurse following closely behind her. I get to my feet, hoping with every fibre of my being that it's not bad news.

'That was quick!' I blurt nervously, because honestly, I have no idea what to say to someone in her situation.

'Look after her, now,' the nurse says to me. Then she pats Bea kindly on the arm and walks away.

'I will!' I say to her retreating back.

I motion to Bea to sit down but she stays standing.

'I've lost it,' she says, her face devoid of any expression.

'Oh, Bea, I'm so sorry,' I say, and lean over to give her a hug. She takes a step back. 'Let's get you out of here.'

We walk in silence outside to the waiting taxis. I'm shivering but Bea stays stock still. I desperately want to say something, anything that will offer her some words of comfort, but I am completely lost. I still haven't thought of anything by the time the taxi arrives or indeed during the short journey home. I snatch glances at her whenever I can, but her face is turned towards the window. By the time we pull into her road I'm beside myself. She is my best friend. I have to say something!

'What happens now?' I say, taking a risk. 'Do you have to go back to hospital again?'

She moves her head slowly towards me as if the effort is almost too much, and then sighs.

'They scanned me and the sac is on its way out. Because it's an early miscarriage, I don't need to go through any surgical procedures. I just have to let nature take its course.' Then she adds, sounding brittle, 'Lots of painkillers and brisk walks!'

I blink away the tears. Anyone else would think that Bea is taking all of this in her stride but I know her well enough to know she is hurting.

The taxi comes to a stop outside Bea's house and we get out in silence. This time David opens the door, looking expectant. I think, like me, he had been hoping for good news. I shake my head quickly at him and his face falls. The warmth of the house is a welcome respite from the cold, but I still feel shivery. I tell David to put the kettle on for Bea, but she holds up a firm hand.

'I'm going to bed now,' she says. 'Thank you for everything.'

Then she turns quickly and hurries up the stairs.

David and I look at each other.

'Poor Bea,' he whispers, his eyes full of sympathy.

'I know,' I say, pulling open the front door.

I wait until we're safely outside her front gate before I start crying.

26

Pressure on my shoulder wakes me up on Wednesday morning. I force my eyes open and see David sitting beside me on the bed.

'I thought you could do with a lie-in,' he says.

I give him a thank you nod and stretch. My mind feels foggy, probably from the wine I had with Sho, and it takes a moment for yesterday's events to sink in. I heave myself up into a sitting position, think of poor Bea, and sigh. I know I need to check in with her but something tells me a 'How are you feeling after losing your baby?' text just isn't going to cut it.

'What time is it?' I say.

David checks his watch and tells me it's just gone 11 a.m. Eleven in the morning! I haven't got up that late since before we had Anna.

'Thanks for taking Anna to school today,' I say, stroking his hand.

In fairness, he was up pretty late too, and it's good of him to get up early with Anna.

'No worries,' he says. 'I'll do pick-up too if you want.'

But I tell him I'll do it. I need to see if Sho had picked up Bea's leather jacket from the stadium. At least if I manage to get it back and give it to Bea, I'll be doing something rather than sitting around feeling useless.

I give David a quick hug, and just as he's leaving the room, he turns around quickly.

'I keep meaning to ask. How was Pirana last night? I know it was cut short, but you must have seen some of the band in action.'

Flashes of Ryan rush into my mind and I can feel my cheeks redden. I haven't mentioned anything to David about bumping into Ryan, nor have I told David that Ryan was part of the reason I left the concert early. As far as he knows, Bea called me to let me know she was bleeding and I went straight over to her house to bring her to hospital. I look at David's warm, slightly enquiring expression and I say, 'Pirana were phenomenal – everything I thought they would be!' There's no point in telling him about Ryan – we have come too far to let it come between us again.

David smiles. 'I'm glad you finally saw your hero in action! No selfies, though,' he jokes, on the way out the door.

I shake my head. Despite everything that happened last night, I am still disappointed that I have missed out on a selfie with my biggest teen crush. I won't be able to gloat to Jen now. No reason to mention it at all. I tell myself to cop on. There are far more important things to focus on – like getting my best friend Bea's fabulous leather jacket back, for instance. I hop into the shower, feeling better now that I have something productive to focus on. Then I quickly pull on a pair of jeans, my thermal vest, throw a fleece on and head to the kitchen to find my phone. When I press the white button on my smartphone my screen looks much busier than normal. There's a text from Rosalind asking me how I am – bless her. She was so lovely when me and David got back to the house last night. I can still feel the warmth of her embrace after seeing me in tears. I fire a quick text back to thank her again, making a mental note to drop a bottle of wine over to her for looking after Anna. Then I spot a text from Bea:

Don't fuss – I'm fine. Bleeding better. I'll call later.

I get the message loud and clear – she needs space.

'Any news from Bea?' David says, walking into the kitchen.

I show him the text and he nods.

'Makes sense,' he says.

Then he announces he's off to some cookery demonstration in Notting Hill, and I wave him out the door.

It's only when the screen returns to its normal state that I notice my mailbox has over twenty-six messages. Given that my agent, Harriet Wood is pretty much the only person to email me these days, I find this is a bit surprising. In fact, the last time I got that many emails, it was... Sebastian Fox!

My hand flies to my mouth. Jesus Christ – I have forgotten about our meeting this morning. FUCK!

With mounting dread (please let it just be spam), I open my mailbox, and there they are – twenty-six emails from Sebastian. My stomach lurches as I read through them quickly. They start out politely enough:

Think you might be running late? If so, drop me a line.

...To slightly more impatient:

You're half an hour late now Saoirse – let me know what time you're going to be here.

...To downright pissed off:

Saoirse – as a paying client I expect you to show up to pre-arranged meetings – get in touch please.

I can't blame him. Granted, he didn't mind when I was a few minutes late before, but forgetting about a meeting is a whole different ballgame.

It takes longer to type with shaking hands, but I try and send as grovelling an email as I can. I apologise profusely and tell him it won't happen again. Then I press send and collapse onto the kitchen stool. If he bins me off after this, I only have myself to blame.

My phone pings.

It's Sebastian.

I'll expect you at the same time tomorrow.

I let out a cry of relief. He's given me one more chance. Thank Christ. I race upstairs and review the interview preparation I had started yesterday. Then I spend a couple of hours going over all the transcripts, making notes of anything I need to ask him about. I stop at 1.30 p.m. to grab a sandwich and then go back to work, trying to blame the sinking feeling in my stomach on the stress of the previous day. The truth is that Sebastian Fox is a difficult interviewee, but I have to find a way of shaping what he tells me into a book. I have to.

The hangover munchies kick in just before 3 p.m., so I grab a packet of heavily salted crisps and a handful of fizzy sweets from the cupboard before heading out to pick up Anna – and to find Sho.

Mr Russell gives me a blush-free brief nod at the gates, but I am too intent on finding Sho to return the gesture. I walk quickly round to the playground but to my disappointment, she's not there. Only Diana.

Diana walks to meet me and says, 'Hi,' in her cheery, sparkly voice, and God help me but I'm not in the mood for her.

'What's been happening?' she says, full of moonbeams and cheery skies.

I'm just about to say, 'Not much,' but the words don't come out. Suddenly, I'm sick of this small talk.

'Well, Diana, last night my best friend had a miscarriage, and to be honest I haven't a fucking clue how to deal with it. I don't know what to say to her, and I don't know how to help. All in all, I feel absolutely useless. *That's* what's been happening.'

Throughout this little speech, Diana's eyes have been getting wider and wider. Then she blows some air out and says, 'That's a coincidence.'

Bloody hell. Is that all she has to say for herself? No wonder we've been trapped in small talk hell for the last few weeks. What is the point of this? This isn't friendship – this is just a bloody waste of time. I'm just about to make my excuses and walk away when she says, 'I also had a miscarriage recently.'

God, I'm a dick.

'Oh, Diana – I'm so sorry,' I say, and I reach out and give her a hug. Unlike Bea, she allows me to.

'I was only eight weeks,' she says, shrugging sadly, 'It could have been worse.'

I'm not having that.

'A loss is a loss, no matter what way you look at it,' I say, fiercely.

Then she starts throwing out the miscarriage stats, how one in eight pregnancies end in miscarriage and how common it is, and I stop her again.

'Listen, Diana – it doesn't matter how common miscarriage is.

It was a terrible thing to happen to you and you need to give yourself time to grieve.'

Her eyes fill with tears and she squeezes my arm. 'Thanks, Saoirse – that really helps.'

And it occurs to me that Bea is the one I should be saying all this stuff too, and I say this to Diana but then she says something that makes me think.

'Listen, those first few days after the miscarriage, I just felt numb. I didn't want to speak to anyone or hear from anyone. I just wanted to hide away for a bit. It sounds like your friend wants to do the same thing. By all means, check in on her every day to see how she is – but don't expect her to be crying in your arms. Not yet, anyway.'

I smile at her, marvelling that, of all people, Diana is the one I've been able to confide in.

'Having said all that, it is always nice to be pampered when you're feeling shit,' she says, with a wink.

'Go on,' I say, because I need some insights into how to make Bea feel better.

'It probably sounds a bit boring, but since I was spending so much time in my pyjamas, my husband went out and bought me a fresh new pair – the ones that feel like clouds on your skin – and a gorgeous matching robe. It was only something small, but it really was a comfort, you know?'

'I don't think that's boring at all,' I tell her.

My mind starts to whir with all the things I might get for Bea to give her some sense of comfort but, before I have a chance to decide, a flash of neon catches my eye. It's Sho, dressed in a neon-pink fluffy jumper, and denim shorts with thick black tights underneath. For once I am reluctant to break away from Diana, but I have to see if Sho has Bea's leather jacket. I make my apologies and Diana waves a 'no worries' gesture.

'Hey,' Sho says.

My words come out in a rush.

'Do you have the leather jacket I left on the seat last night?' I say.

'Nah,' she says, with a violent sniff.

I can feel my blood start to boil. The least I could do for Bea was to return her bloody jacket but it seems I've failed in that quarter too.

'Why didn't you pick it up?' I say, trying to keep my voice steady.

'Thought you were coming back, didn't I?' she says, with a shrug.

I can't face filling her in on all the details, so I just tell her that I had to leave because my best friend had a miscarriage. Her one-word response sends me over the edge.

'Shit,' she says, blowing her messy fringe out of her face. It's like I've just told her that my washing machine is broken.

'SHIT?' I shout, furious now. 'Is that all you have to say?'

She gives her maddening shrug again and I just want to shake her until her defiant little face falls off. But instead I start screaming and swearing at her – about how she thinks she's so bloody cool but really she's just a selfish little bitch who doesn't give a shit about anyone but herself. Then I end with, 'No wonder you have no fucking friends.'

She flinches at that last bit and I'm glad. Finally, I've found something to penetrate that 'Don't give a shit' exterior. It's only when I turn to walk away that I notice a wide circle has formed around Sho and me. A circle full of open-mouthed Organics, people I've never seen before – and Mr Russell.

Mr Russell is the first to approach us.

'Ladies, this is highly inappropriate language for the school playground,' he says, sternly.

Sho raises her eyes skyward like the sulky teenager she is, and I just shake my head. I'm too het up to eat humble pie right now.

'Listen,' he says quietly, leaning over to me, 'I overheard some of it and I'm sorry about your friend, but this behaviour is unacceptable.'

My shoulders slump and I mumble a quick sorry. He thanks me and then turns to Sho. She looks from myself to Mr Russell and back again. Her eyes are blazing.

'Oh sure, take her side,' she spits, 'That must be some blowjob she gave you.'

Then the class doors open and the kids spill out.

* * *

It's two hours since Sho outed me and Mr Russell and I'm trying not to cry with the mortification. David has just come back from the food market and we're sitting at the kitchen table trying to have an adult discussion about two grown women having a fight in the school playground.

'So, let me get this straight,' David says. 'You lost it with Sho because she didn't pick up Bea's jacket, and then she told the whole school you blew Mr Russell.'

I nod, my hands over my eyes, every part of me fighting against reliving the whole mortifying experience. David sighs and runs his hands through his hair. Don't get me wrong, I spent long minutes wondering if I should tell him or not, but knowing Tania, Caroline, Misery and the rest of the bitchy Organics, I knew that somebody would make a snide comment to David anyway. It's best he hears it from me, but it's no less humiliating.

'I'm sorry,' I say, reddening.

'I just don't know why you told Sho in the first place,' he says, drumming his fingers on the table in frustration.

'I was pissed at the gig and I thought we were bonding...' I say, uncovering my eyes. 'It was a mistake, David.'

He nods slowly.

'So, what happens now?'

I don't know how to answer this because I can't see a way out. It's no use trying to set the record straight – that the blowjob was years ago, way before I even met David – because the Organics will believe whatever they want to believe and gossip anyway. And, angry as I am with Sho, I can't go around calling her a liar because, much as I'd love to deny it, she was telling the truth. The only option is to pretend the whole sorry incident didn't happen, but it will take me a while to face the school gates again.

'I don't want to go to school any more,' I groan.

'And you think I do?' David shoots back.

'I can't, David,' I say, my eyes pleading.

David shakes his head.

I know this can't be easy for him – the whole school (and knowing the Organics, the whole of the Woodvale community) will soon think that his wife has been up to no good with the head teacher but one of us has to bring Anna to school, and it can't be me. Not yet.

'You'll have to face the playground sometime,' he says, crossing his arms.

'Just do the school run until the end of the week. Then I'll take over,' I say, quickly.

That will give me the time I need to work up the courage to put my game face on for when the moment arrives. He raises his eyes skyward but agrees all the same. I've never loved the man more.

'I owe you big time,' I say.

'Blowjob?' he says.

'Haha,' I say drily, although judging by the glint in his eye, I'm not quite sure he is joking.

Feeling slightly better after the chat with David, I go in search of Anna. She's very cross with me. After the class doors had opened, she and Milly had run towards me and Sho, begging for a playdate. The timing couldn't have been worse. Sho had grabbed Milly by the hand and simply marched out of the playground, leaving a confused and wailing Anna behind. It had taken me minutes to calm her down, but in a way I had been grateful for the distraction. After Anna eventually agreed to swap her meltdown for a bag of fizzy sweets, I grabbed her hand, trying to walk out of those gates with as much dignity as I could muster, feeling the eyes of the other mums on my back, the atmosphere already charged with gossip.

I sigh as I trudge up the stairs to Anna's room – I will be the subject of 'did you hears' until someone else takes the heat off me by performing a similarly mortifying indiscretion.

I peep into Anna's room. She's lying on her front, chin in both hands, watching her iPad.

'ANNA,' I shout.

She glares at me and moves her headphones down to her neck.

'What is it?' she says, furiously.

I sit on the edge of her bed.

'I'm sorry that Milly couldn't come over today,' I say.

Her bottom lip trembles.

'But when will she come over, Mummy?'

This is the question I have been dreading.

'I don't know, Anna,' I say, stroking her hair.

And that's as honest as I can be with her.

She glares at me and puts her headphones back on.

Conversation over – for now. Frankly, I think I've got off lightly.

I make my way downstairs to find my phone. I want to tell Bea everything that happened at school but then I stop dead. I'm supposed to be giving her space. The last thing she needs is to hear about playground dramas when she's in the middle of a miscarriage. I flop down heavily on the couch in the sitting room, suddenly feeling ridiculous. Why am I moping around when my best friend is going through something so much worse? Then I think about Diana and what she said about the small things giving her a sense of comfort, and suddenly I have an idea.

I grab my bag, tell David I'm off to the shops, get in the car and drive to a supermarket in the next borough, purely so I don't run the risk of bumping into any of the school mums. I can't face their inevitable stares and raised eyebrows after everything that happened today. Parking the car in the underground car park, I make my way towards the supermarket. Once inside, I trudge up and down the aisles, gripping the trolley tightly, determined to find everything I need. Then I pay at the till before loading everything into the boot and driving home again. David comes to greet me as I'm parking the car on our street. I'm relieved to see him. I'll need a hand lugging this stuff in.

'What have you got there?' he says, looking at the array of shopping bags.

'Stuff for Bea,' I say, heaving three bags at once.

He does the same.

After all the shopping has been brought in, we set about emptying the bags and laying everything on the kitchen island. It's quite a lot.

Anna wanders into the kitchen, unusually iPad-free, and announces she's bored.

A shiver rushes down my spine. I don't have time to sit with her and play dolls or any of the other mind-numbing stuff she has me do when she's in this mood. Then I notice her eyeing the mass of items suspiciously.

'Did you get me anything?' she says, a hopeful glint in her eye.

Okay, so my focus might have been on Bea, but I'm not stupid. Going to the shops and not picking up something for Anna is the very definition of shooting oneself in the foot.

I hand her a bag of crisps, and she runs off into the living room.

My mind whirs as I examine our cluttered kitchen island. I don't want to just dump a load of bags on Bea's doorstep. A gift needs to be presented in the right way. Then I have an idea. I run upstairs and fling open the wardrobe in our bedroom. Years ago, one of David's friends gave us a huge impractical picnic basket as a wedding gift. As David and I place picnicking on the same low level as camping (we never want to do either), we had scoffed all the goodies and tucked the basket away on the top of the wardrobe never to be seen again. Until today. Balancing on the edge of the bed, I lug the basket out from its resting place with two hands and throw it behind me onto the bed. Then I pick it up and carry it down into the kitchen, making a 'ta da' sound to David upon entry.

He looks at it with an expression that can only be described as sceptical.

'It's filthy,' he says.

Jesus, only David would notice the odd bit of dust.

'It's grand,' I say, defensively, giving it a bit of a shake.

Dust flies out in all directions, making us both cough.

'Oh, fine!' I say, grumpily, grabbing a sponge from the sink. 'Let's give it a clean, then.'

Ten minutes later, the basket is looking presentable enough for us to start packing everything into it.

When we're finished, we step back to admire our handiwork. David goes to lift it off the kitchen island but a little voice says, 'Wait!'

We turn around to see Anna standing in the doorway, with an empty packet of crisps scrunched up in one hand. She glares at me, throws her hands up in the air and says, 'It needs a WIBBON!'

David looks at her completely nonplussed, but before I can translate, he stupidly asks her to repeat herself. Above all, Anna hates being asked to say something twice.

She lets out the sort of frustrated groan that could wake up a sleeping sloth, stamps her foot, and says, 'A WIBBON – a WED WIBBON.'

David cocks his head. He still hasn't understood her.

Jesus.

'She's saying that the basket needs a red ribbon,' I hiss at him quickly.

The last thing we need is to set off another meltdown.

I don't wait around to hear the inevitable, 'Ohhhhhh.' Instead, I take Anna's hand and tell her that she's going to help me find a red ribbon. She skips along beside me – happy now that she has my full attention. We locate a piece of ribbon in the spare room in a box I have reserved for gift wrappings (so messy I actively hide it from David in the corner between the wall and sofa bed) and then we head back into the kitchen, where I spend several frustrated minutes trying to teach Anna (at her insistence) to tie a bow. She can't do it and the meltdown happens anyway, so I decide to abandon the hamper until she's in bed.

Later that evening, after an exhausted round of, 'Just one more story,' David and I return to the kitchen to put the final touches on the hamper. Thanks to Anna's suggestion, it looks a lot better now. David lifts it off the kitchen island and lowers it gently by the front door.

'It's pretty heavy,' he says, straightening up. 'How are you going to transport it to Bea's?'

I grab the handle to try it out and manage to lift it a mere couple of inches off the floor before dropping it again.

Oh, bloody hell, I don't want to have to make two trips. I rub my eyes. Suddenly, I'm exhausted. David rubs my shoulder.

'Leave it until tomorrow. I'll give you a hand bringing it round,' he says.

'I have bloody Sebastian Fox in the morning,' I say.

'Afternoon then,' he says.

'Listen,' he says, moving closer so his body is pressing against mine. 'Everything is going to be okay with Sebastian. He made it clear he's giving you another chance, so try not to worry about it too much.'

'Thanks,' I say, giving him a quick peck on the lips. I know he's probably right but I'm still dreading the inevitable amount of humble pie I'm going to have to eat tomorrow to make it up to him.

He kisses me back, then again, and once more before breaking off and looking at me searchingly.

'I suppose you're not in the mood for...'

Jesus, what is it with men? Besides, it's way past brunch.

'No, David!' I snap.

His shoulders slump.

'Netflix?' he says.

'Perfect.'

27

I wake up on Thursday morning exhausted. Despite the stress of the previous day, I haven't been able to get much sleep. Instead, I spent the night tossing and turning, replaying the argument with Sho, worrying about Bea, and dreading the meeting with Sebastian.

As I thought, the class WhatsApp group is alight with the gossip about 'blowjob-gate' and the row with Sho. Scrolling back up to the original text, it all seems to have started fairly innocently.

Tania:
Can we please have some volunteers for blowing up the balloons on the morning of the Christmas Fair?
Caroline:
I can think of one mum in particular who would be an excellent 'blower'. (Plus winky face.)
Misery:
Oh yes! A professional blower is exactly what we need in this situation. (Plus crying laughing emoji.)

Then the pile on begins as the Organics swap comments back and forth – each more 'hilarious' than the next, all of them clearly directed at me. I scroll down quickly, barely scanning the messages, desperately wanting them to stop. Then the final message catches my eye.

Jane the full-time working mum:
I'm happy to volunteer to blow up balloons at the Christmas Fair if this WhatsApp group becomes less childish and more relevant to important school matters!

Woah! BURN!

'Thanks, Jane,' I mutter. Then I click into group info, scroll down and press Exit Group. A feeling of relief rushes over me. Why haven't I done this before? There is no law in place to say that anyone has to participate in this school bun fight. I'm done with the class WhatsApp group. I jump out of bed. It's time to deal with more pressing matters.

I shower, dress and take extra care with my appearance in an effort to look as professional as possible for my meeting. I need Sebastian to trust me again, otherwise I'll never be able to get anything useful out of him. I go downstairs to say goodbye to David and Anna, who are just about to leave for school.

When I reach the hallway, Anna stares at me.

'You're wearing make-up!' she says, her face lighting up.

'I am!' I say, brightly. 'What do you think?'

She shakes her head a bit and then says, 'Too much eye shadow.'

Everyone's a critic.

'You look great, Saoirse,' David says, pecking me on the lips. 'Good luck with the meeting – let me know how it goes.'

After a quick breakfast of toast (I am too nervous for anything else), I gather my Dictaphone and my notes and go to put on my coat, glancing at my reflection in the mirror in the hallway.

Damn it – Anna's right. I am wearing too much eye shadow. I grab a baby wipe and try and dab some of it off without smearing it halfway down my face. Finally, I'm ready to go. I'm going to fix everything with Sebastian and get his bloody book done if it's the last thing I do.

* * *

'I am excited! I am excited! I am excited!' I say, jumping up and down with so much enthusiasm that the boat begins to rock in an alarming way. Even Sebastian looks taken aback.

I don't care – after missing the last meeting, I'll do anything to get back into his good books. So here I am, shouting like a maniac and doing the sorts of jumping jacks that are most certainly going to have a negative impact on my pelvic floor.

When I've finished, I sit down primly on my chair, balance my notepad on my knee, press the record button on the Dictaphone, and hold my pen steadily in my right hand. Today, I am the very picture of professionalism.

Sebastian sits down on the rocking chair with what I hope sounds like a grunt of approval.

'Now, I have been making some notes, and there are some questions I would like to ask you during today's session,' I say, in my most efficient-sounding voice.

'Actually, I want to go through some other stuff today,' he says, giving me a firm look.

I try my best to look accommodating, but I'm inwardly disappointed. All that time spent preparing for the interview and he doesn't want to know. Still, he is the client and he is paying a huge sum for this book, so I don't have much choice but to play along.

He jumps up purposefully and strides to the front of the boat before returning with a small box. Then he sits down again and starts to open it reverently. I hold my breath, praying it's not another phone with ashes in it, but to my enormous relief, the box seems to be full of leaflets. Then he hands me one and says, 'Marketing leaflets for the ashes phone case,' he says, smiling. 'I made them myself.'

My mouth falls open in surprise. 'I thought you weren't going to do any advertising?'

'No – I said that the type of advertising I was going to do would be organic,' he says with a hint of impatience.

This still means nothing to me.

I nod and try to focus on the leaflet in my hand, trying to work my mouth into a way that masks my revulsion. The black background is peppered with ghostlike faces, women, children, even babies with speech bubbles saying things like, 'You'll always be with me' and 'Carry me forever'. These floating heads encircle the ash phone, which is headed with the tagline: 'The Ash Phone Case – may it always be with you.'

'Well, what do you think?' he says, sounding impatient.

Creepy, weird, smacks of psychopathic tendencies, I think. But instead I just say, 'Very impactful,' because I can't afford to piss him off.

Up until this leaflet, I don't think it hit me about how grim his whole business idea really was. I have been too focused on the money to really give it much serious thought. But now with this grotesque leaflet in my hands, the reality strikes hard. He starts drivelling on about the font he chose for the leaflet, and, despite my best efforts, my mind starts to wander. I think about the interviews I have done with him so far and how little material I have. A panicky feeling shoots through me and the voice that I have been silencing over the last few weeks finally breaks through. You don't want to do this book. There is no material for a book. This is a project that's going nowhere.

'Are you all right, Saoirse?' he says, crisply.

'Sorry, yes!' I say, sitting up, pressing my pen against my blank notepad.

Come on, Saoirse! I tell myself. You cannot afford to lose this job. Plenty of people have to do jobs they hate – some of them for years and lifetimes! You only have to last another few months. I take a deep breath and, for the rest of the interview, hang off his every word as if it's the most interesting thing I've heard in years. By the time our meeting comes to an end, I can tell by his enthusiasm that I have him back onside again. As I stand up, I feel the crampy dullness of a full bladder that definitely won't make it home before bursting. I've clearly overdone it with the jumping earlier. Sebastian points me to the door to the toilet, and I squeeze myself into the tiny space and reluctantly sit down, flushed with the embarrassment of knowing that he can hear the sound of me weeing. I wash my hands quickly, keen to get out of such a claustrophobic space. I am just about to unlock the door when I hear the unmistakeable beep of a text. I frown – I'm pretty sure I've put my phone on silent, which I usually do for work meetings.

Then the beeping sound happens again. I look around the tiny space and, apart from a hand towel and a sink, there is really nowhere anybody could hide a phone. A small cubby hole just above the toilet catches my eye. I tentatively reach my hand inside and my hand touches on something cool and smooth – it's a phone. Most likely Sebastian's – if he's anything like David, he probably brings it in with him when he is doing a dump. The thought of it makes me shiver and I decide to pop it back into its cubby hole where it belongs. As I am easing back into its place, my thumb accidentally presses the little white 'on' button. The screen saver flashes up, and I can't resist taking a little peek. I draw the phone towards me to get a better view. The first thing I see is a grinning Sebastian, with his arms around three small boys. A tall, dark-haired woman stands just behind them, her face pointing away from the camera to focus on the scene before her. Even though I don't see her full features, I would know that dark mass of curly hair anywhere.

It's Rosalind.

* * *

I make my way home in a haze of confusion. I haven't said anything to Sebastian – I'm too stunned. Besides, I don't want him to think I've been prying. A million questions race through my head. How have I ended up working for Rosalind's husband? Sweet, kooky, kind Rosalind who stepped in at no notice to babysit Anna the other night while my best friend Bea was going through a miscarriage. Does she know I'm working with her husband, writing a book about his mad, morbid invention? If so, she's an incredibly good actor; and, if for some reason she doesn't know, should I feel guilty about it? I'm desperate to talk it over with Bea, but not after everything she's just been through.

When I finally get home, David places a bowl of home-made soup in front of me that looks delicious, but I can only manage a small bit of it. The truth is I feel low. Low about Bea, low about the row with Sho, and even more low about having to work with a man who turns out to be married to a friend of mine. Worst still, a friend who seems to be going through some marital troubles.

David wants to know what's wrong, but he's so pleased that I've managed to get Sebastian onside again that I tell him I'm only feeling down because of the level of crawling I had to do (which to be fair is also true). I don't have the heart to tell him about

Rosalind yet. If he senses the slightest hitch in this project, it will send him into a panic spiral again. I need to figure this one out for myself.

After lunch, I throw a couple of blue and red gingham tea towels over the hamper to complete the picnicky look and tell David I'm off to Bea's. He helps me load it into the boot, and I give him a quick kiss before I drive away. At the end of the road, I can see two women waiting to cross. Tania and Caroline. Great. Two Organics for the price of one. I peer to the side of the road, looking for potential puddles to splash them with, but sadly, today is dry and sunny. Instead, I slow down and let them cross, ducking down slightly in my seat to avoid any chance of contact. When they are safely on the other side of the road, I pop up again, grateful that they haven't spotted me. Then I hear a knock on the passenger window.

It's Tania with a grinning Caroline beside her. Tania calls to me to lower the window, and I go to press the button and then stop. What good will it do? They're only going to bring up the playground incident. So, instead I lean over towards the passenger window as far as my seatbelt will let me, look Tania straight in the eye, and give her the two fingers. One each. I don't wait around for the reaction – instead I press my foot on the gas and take the turn onto Bea's road. It may not have been the most mature thing to do, but it has made me feel a lot better.

I credit my dark mood for the ability to lift the insanely heavy basket from the car boot to Bea's doorstep without stumbling once. Suddenly, I feel a bit nervous. What if she doesn't like the hamper? What if she thinks this is a really insensitive thing to do? What if...?

Then the door opens.

'Oh, hello, Saoirse.'

It's Maria, Harry's nanny.

'Bea's not here,' she says, looking curiously at the mountainous hamper on the doorstep.

'Oh,' I say, feeling both relieved and disappointed. Nervous as I am about Bea's reaction to the hamper, I had hoped to at least see how she was doing.

'She won't be long,' Maria says, kindly, clearly registering the disappointment on my face. 'She's just gone for a walk.'

Lots of painkillers and brisk walks, I think, remembering what Bea had said in the hospital.

'Come in!' she says, grabbing both handles of the hamper.

'No, no! It's too heavy!' I tell her.

But she gives it a heave anyway and carries it into the house without so much as a sigh. I follow her down the hallway into the kitchen and watch her effortlessly place the basket on the kitchen table.

'Now!' she says, clapping her hands smartly together. 'I was just about to put the kettle on. What can I get you?'

I thank her but tell her I'm fine. It occurs to me that I could ask her how Bea is doing, but I'm not sure if Bea has mentioned the miscarriage, and I don't want to stick my foot in it again. I watch her fill up the kettle, waiting for a suitable point to make my excuses to leave, but then I hear a key in the door.

My stomach plummets as the footsteps grow closer. I will find out in a matter of seconds if Bea thinks the hamper is the act of a kind, caring friend, or the sign of a tactless imbecile.

Bea walks into the kitchen, wearing grey joggers and a sky-blue hoodie. She looks tired. She stops short when she sees me standing awkwardly by the kitchen table.

'I didn't expect to see you today,' she says, walking over to give me a little hug.

I hug her back, comforted that she is at least happy to see me. Maria offers her a cup of tea and she refuses with a casual wave.

Then Maria grabs her own cup and tells us she is off to drink it in the living room.

Bea points to the hamper, and says, 'What's all this?'

My stomach flutters again and suddenly I am lost for words. How am I supposed to explain this monstrosity? 'Hey Bea, I wasn't sure what the correct etiquette was for somebody who has just had a miscarriage so I made you up a hamper instead!'

Jesus, what was I thinking? This is a terrible idea. She shoots me a bemused look before carefully removing the tea towels, taking out the items one by one, and placing them gently on the table.

'Erm,' is about all I can get out. Mortification has struck me dumb.

When the hamper is empty, she lifts it off the table and drops it on the kitchen floor underneath the window. Then she surveys the whole display of champagne, wine, sushi, mouldy cheeses, tins of gourmet coffee, different types of shellfish, and a gigantic tiramisu.

She folds her arms and stares at me.

'You madwoman!' she says. 'What have you done?'

Jesus, I knew this was a bad idea.

'This is everything I couldn't eat or drink when I was pregnant, isn't it?' she says, matter-of-factly.

'Erm, yes.'

I want the ground to swallow me up right now.

'Saoirse Daly,' she says. 'You really are...'

A fucking eejit? I fill in silently.

'An absolute genius!' she says, with a wide smile.

I hang on to the edge of the table to stop my knees from shaking.

'Seriously?' I croak, unable to fathom that the hamper has been a good idea after all.

'Honestly,' she says, grabbing a bottle of white wine. 'Do you have any idea how much I have missed having my daily glass of wine in the evening? I don't know how I have managed to get through Harry's bathtime without it.'

She moves swiftly around the kitchen, grabbing two wine glasses from the cupboard and a corkscrew from the kitchen drawer.

'Now, sit down and join me,' she says sternly, moving a couple of packets of blue cheese out of the way to make room for the glasses.

Relieved though I am to see her back to her bossy old self, I am a bit concerned that she seems almost too well. I'm no expert, but doesn't miscarriage take a bit longer than a couple of days to get over?

She sloshes the wine into each glass, before raising hers and taking a large sip. I do the same, grateful to feel that instant heady sense of relaxation that tends to accompany a relatively empty stomach. Although I can feel the nerves slipping away, I'm still not sure how to bring up the miscarriage or even if I should mention it. She seems in good form, but I don't want to be too invasive, especially since she sent me that text telling me not to fuss over her. But at the same time, I don't have it in me to ignore the elephant in the room. I take another glug of wine and open my mouth. Then I close it again and take another deep swallow.

Bea shakes her head at me, adjusting her glasses with one hand.

'For goodness' sake, Saoirse, spit it out!'

I take a deep breath.

'I was just wondering how you're feeling,' I say, quietly.

'Oh, I'm fine,' she says, like someone who is just getting over a mild cold. 'The sac came out this morning when I was on the toilet, which was handy. I'm bleeding but brisk walks do seem to help with the cramping and the flow.'

I feel my forehead crease in concern.

'Honestly, I'm fine!' she says. 'Just as well, actually, because Harry would have murdered me if I hadn't been able to take him to Mathias' fancy-dress party in Surrey this Sunday.'

I resign myself to the fact that I'm not going to get much more out of her, so I go along with the subject change.

'Jesus – have you seen Mathias' dad since you puked on his designer shoes?' I say.

Instantly I feel terrible. Bea was pregnant at the time. How could I have stuck my foot in it so badly? I open my mouth to apologise but she doesn't seem to notice.

'Nope, I haven't been up at the school, but I'm hoping he'll stay away from me because of it!' she says, cheersing me with her glass.

I can't help giggling. Anyone else would have been mortified to face someone whose shoes they'd vomited on, but not Bea. I envy her resilience. I'm convinced that, if she'd been the one humiliated by Sho in the playground, she wouldn't have been hiding away from the school gates like I am.

'Now,' she says, rapping the table smartly. 'Tell me your news.'

So I tell her all about Sho and how she hadn't the decency to pick up Bea's leather jacket (I apologise profusely at this point and tell her I'm going to pay her back every penny, but she tells me to fuck off and continue my story) and how I had a massive row with her in the playground. Then I pause to drain the rest of my wine, because I need to steel my nerves for the next part.

'Anyway, things got heated and she announced to all the Organics and everyone else who happened to be within hearing distance that I had given Mr Russell a blowjob.'

Apart from memes, I have never seen anyone spit out their wine in real life, but that's exactly what Bea does. Then she breaks into such deep-bellied laughter that I have to grip the table to stop it from shaking. Even though I'm not at the 'you'll laugh about it one day' stage yet, I can't help but smile at the sight of her in convulsions. The only problem is that she doesn't seem to be stopping. Figuring that I might as well make myself useful until she does recover, I grab the bottle of wine and refill both glasses to brimming. Then I bring the glass to my lips, sipping steadily, and glaring at her.

'Honestly, Bea, it's not that funny!' I say as sternly as I can.

She covers her mouth with both hands and takes a few deep breaths. Then she raises her head, looks at me and giggles before going through the same motions again. Eventually, she gives a decisive cough and arranges her mouth into a firm line. Then she picks up her glass, takes a large sip of wine and swallows quickly.

'Oh, God, Saoirse,' she says. 'I needed that. I can't remember the last time I laughed that much.'

I do.

'It was last summer when I thought David was having an affair,' I say.

And it's true. Bea had found the idea of David having an affair so remote that she had gone into paroxysms of laughter.

She starts laughing again, sees my expression and stops.

'Oh, sorry, Saoirse,' she says, wiping her eyes with the corner of her hoodie. She sits up straight and throws back her shoulders. 'I'll be good now.'

'The thing is, I just don't know what to do about it. I mean, thanks to the Organics, the whole school will know by now. David is doing the school run, so at least I can hide out for the moment, but I can't avoid the school gates forever.'

Then I sigh. 'There's really nothing I can do.'

She wags her finger at me.

'Not true. Firstly, you cut Sho out of your life. Whatever you said to her in the playground does not justify breaking a confidence. She clearly doesn't know the meaning of girl code. Secondly, you are well within your rights to stay away from the school gates for a bit – let the dust settle. Finally, hold your head high when you're around the Organics. If they mention it again, tell them you've blown all their husbands – that will shut them up.'

I don't know if it's her advice or the wine, but suddenly I feel better.

'Anything else to report?' she says, folding her arms.

I think again about telling her about Sebastian Fox and Rosalind, but I decide not to. For starters, I don't want her to think it's her fault that I missed the meeting, and also, in light of her miscarriage, I really don't feel it's appropriate to be discussing death and ashes, despite her seemingly unshakeable mood. So I just shake my head and say, 'Nope, being outed as the school blowjobber is as far as my news goes today, I'm afraid.' Which, of course, sets her off again.

When the first bottle of wine is finished, we open another. Then we decide we're feeling peckish and break into the sushi.

I'm just eyeing up the tiramisu when she says, 'Ryan's coming over tomorrow to see Harry.'

Oh, God. Ryan. I feel another twinge of guilt. If it wasn't for my blabbing, he wouldn't have been giving Bea an earful the other night on the phone.

'Have you heard much from him since you spoke to him on Wednesday?'

She sighs and fiddles with the edge of the plastic containers left over from the sushi.

'Only every few hours,' she says. 'Just wanting to know how

Harry is, what he's been doing, why he hasn't been able to see him sooner... that sort of thing.'

'What did you say?'

'I just told him that I was working crazy hours and I didn't have time to set something up with Harry.'

I can't believe Ryan bought that excuse – the thought of Bea working any more hours than she legally has to is beyond outlandish. Still, it can't be easy for her. Seeing Ryan after all that's happened; he was the father of her baby, and now he'll never know.

'Will you be all right seeing him after... everything?' I say.

'I'll be fine,' she says, quickly. 'Now, is it too decadent to crack open the tiramisu?'

* * *

If Harry hadn't crashed through the door from school, we would most certainly have opened a third bottle. After staring at the car for whole seconds, wondering how it got there, the realisation strikes that I will have to walk home. I slur goodbye to Bea and she slurs what I think is a, 'Thank you for coming over,' back. Then I walk unsteadily in the direction of my house. When I am about three doors away from home, I hear the unmistakeable scream of a child having an absolute hissy fit. As I draw closer, I realise that child is mine. I decide to hang around the front gate for a bit until the screaming at least reduces in volume. There's nothing like one of Anna's legendary tantrums for killing a lovely alcoholic buzz.

'Good afternoon, Saoirse.'

I jump about a foot in the air. It's Joseph, our elderly and fussy neighbour, holding a large jug of water. Christ knows how long he's been standing in his front garden. I do my best to arrange my features into a sober state, but it's not easy when your head seems to want to sway to one side. He puts the jug down beside one of the window boxes and squints at me.

'Are you quite all right?'

My attempt to say 'absolutely' comes out with an unnecessary 'sh' sound, so I just give up and give him the biggest smile I can muster. He frowns.

'Lot of noise coming from your house,' he says, reprovingly.

I nod vigorously. Can't argue with that.

'Shouldn't you be making your way in?' he says, pointing his head in the direction of my front door.

I look at the front door and then look back at him.

'Would you go in there?' I slur.

But before he can answer, the front door opens to reveal a very frazzled David on the doorstep. He looks less than impressed to see me.

'Saoirse!' he says, crossly. 'Anna's going fucking mental and...'

'Hello David,' Joseph pipes up in an even more disapproving voice.

David jumps a little. Clearly, he hadn't clocked Joseph either.

He gathers himself and says a polite hello back. In the meantime, Anna's wails are getting louder. The jig is up – I'm going to have to face the music. I shamble up the path towards David, giving Joseph a big wave on the way. As soon as David closes the front door, I burst into giggles. Honestly, what must Joseph have thought? Screaming child, pissed-up mother, angry father – we must seem like the world's most dysfunctional family.

David grips me by the shoulders. I try to focus on his face. I am dimly aware that he is not laughing.

'Jesus, Saoirse, how much did you drink at Bea's?' he says.

'Only one bottle each!' I say, aggressively holding up one finger too close to his face.

He purses his lips.

'You know you're a rubbish daytime drinker,' he says.

I nod obediently because he is right. I AM a terrible daytime drinker. Look at that time I started drinking in the day with Dee in Ireland over the summer. I had been so hammered, I thought I had slept with Ryan. Ssshhhh, I hear an internal voice say. Mustn't mention Ryan.

David creases his eyebrows.

'Why are you saying ssshhhh?' he says.

Whoops! I must have said it out loud after all. Before I can explain, Anna appears at the top of the stairs: red cheeks, swollen eyes. I shrug David's hands off my shoulders and stumble up the stairs to greet her. When I reach the top, I swivel around to sit on the top step. Then I pat the space beside me. She lets out a huge sigh and plonks herself down.

'What's wrong, sweetheart?' I gush in the same voice I used to use for her when she was a baby.

'I'm saaaad,' she says sniffing.

'Why are you sad, baba?' I say to her, stroking her lovely silky hair.

I don't know why I think she's hard work – I mean, look how beautiful she is.

'Daddy was being mean,' she says, folding her arms.

I look at David, who is still standing at the bottom of the stairs, and he raises his eyes skyward.

Then I tut at him. Honestly, he really has no idea how to handle Anna's meltdowns. I mean, I have only been in the door two minutes and I have already calmed her down.

'And why was Daddy mean?' I say.

Seriously, David needs to have more patience.

'Because he took away the basket with the wed wibbon,' she says, tears spilling down her cheeks.

Oh, shit.

'I tried to explain that it was a gift for Harry's mum,' David says, throwing his hands out helplessly. 'But she wasn't having any of it.'

I grab her little hand and say, 'Daddy's right – it was a gift for someone else...' But I don't get to finish because the screaming drowns out any hope of further conversation. My head starts to thump mercilessly, and I stand up, the sudden movement forcing me to clutch the wall to balance. Suddenly I don't feel very well. I mumble something to David and then turn around forcing my legs to walk towards the bedroom. The last thing I remember before I pass out is Anna, who seems to have been shocked out of her tantrum by my sudden exit.

'Daddy, what are the spins?'

28

It's 4 a.m. on Friday and I feel like death. Because I ended up going to bed earlier even than Anna, I have woken up too early and I am now in the full throes of alcohol-induced horrors. I look at David snoring peacefully beside me and feel a sharp stab of guilt. Regardless of the stress of the last couple of days, I shouldn't have got myself into that state, especially in front of Anna. God knows how he managed to calm her down. I close my eyes and try and go back to sleep, but it's no use. My thumping heart and severe dehydration won't allow it. So I get up and feel my way through the darkness and quietly open the door, grateful that I appear to be over the spins. I peep into Anna's room, admire her peaceful little face (how did David even get her to bed after such a show of temper?) and make my way down the stairs into the kitchen. It's too soon for bright lights, so I cross the kitchen in the dark, and feel for the fridge door. Then I grab a can of 7Up and crack it open in one smooth move. I let the sweet fizzy liquid down my throat and instantly feel a bit better.

When I have drained every delicious drop, I turn around to close the fridge when something catches my eye. There seems to be something large and bulky on the kitchen table. I walk closer and let out a small giggle. Now I know exactly how David had managed to calm Anna down. For there in front of me is the basket I gave to Bea with the red ribbon neatly tied in a bow. David must have ducked out with Anna to get it while I was out cold. I really didn't expect to see it again, but I know Bea would have understood why David needed it back. The fridge starts making an annoying beeping sound, so I go back and shut it quickly. I stand in the dark kitchen for a bit at somewhat of a loss. No point in going back to bed because I won't be able to sleep and I feel too foggy headed to even attempt any work. Instead I grab my phone and text Jen and Dee on our WhatsApp Group to let them know the urgent news about my hangover. I doubt if either of them is up, but it's something to do anyway. To my surprise, Jen instantly replies with a vomit emoji. Then I realise that she's still in Dubai and it's around 9 a.m. over there. A couple of seconds later, Dee sends a gif of a woman holding a wine glass to her mouth and spilling it all over her dress. I ask her what she's doing up at such an ungodly hour and she replies with another gif – this time it's a cartoon baby crying violently in its cot.

God, poor girl. Those hideous nights pacing back and forth praying desperately for sleep. I remember them well.

On impulse, I press the video call button.

Jen picks up first.

'The state of you, Saoirse!' she says, presumably taking in my bloodshot eyes and wild hair.

'Don't...' I groan. Of course, she looks immaculate in an ivory robe, make-up carefully applied, with just the right amount of blush on her creamy skin.

'What brought this binge-fest on?' she giggles.

And I don't know if it's the after effects of the alcohol but something bursts inside me and I realise then and there that I need to talk to her about Sebastian Fox. In a rush I tell her everything that's happened, his madcap ideas, and finding out that he's Rosalind's husband. When I'm finished, she pauses for a moment before saying, 'So you're working for this man who is clearly bananaramas but he's got a few quid. And you're hanging on by the skin of your teeth because David's been made redundant and you need the money, and you can't be going back to the school run full-time?'

Well, in a nutshell.

'And this Rosalind is a friend of yours but doesn't know you're working with her husband who she seems to be in a pisser with. Is that it?'

'Well, I don't know her very well, but she's a really kind person, and...' I stop there. I was going to tell Jen how Rosalind did me a massive favour by babysitting Anna the other night, but I don't want to let it slip about Bea's miscarriage. It's not gossip.

'Listen, Saoirse. Business is business, you know? You don't know what's happening in their marriage. It might not be anything to do with his grotesque—' (she gives an exaggerated shiver here) '—invention. The real issue is if you think you can get the book done and hang on to the fifty thou.'

Hang on a second.

'Did you just say fifty thou?' I say, utterly gobsmacked.

'Jesus, did I?' she says, immediately slapping her hand to her mouth.

I shake my head at her.

'I must be hanging around with the media lot too much,' she says, the blood rushing to her peaches and cream complexion. 'They're always coming out with shite like that.'

I tell her not to do it again and she apologises once more.

Then a look of horror flashes across her face. 'Jesus! I have to go. I'm due to present at a photo shoot in an hour and I don't even have my knickers on!'

I smile as we hang up. Fifty thou or no fifty thou, she's still the same Jen.

A couple of minutes later, Dee texts.

Sorry I missed your call! Fucker still won't settle and her DAD is living his best life SNORING in our bed.

I send her back a quick 'men are pricks' text to show her some solidarity, and decide to head back to bed, where I fall into a semi-doze until Anna jumps on me with unnecessary force at 7 a.m.

I spend the rest of Friday feeling rough, my mind still racing with thoughts of Rosalind. Despite what Jen has said, it doesn't feel right that I'm working with Sebastian without Rosalind knowing. Still, I can't afford to walk away, either. With David out of work, I have to put my family first. David doesn't make any of this better by being all judgemental about my daytime drunkenness. He's in a bad mood because he's been getting 'looks' at the school gate from the Organics about blowjob-gate. He won't admit it, but he's also cross because Bonnie has postponed their Friday meeting until Monday. The rest of Friday and most of Saturday are mostly spent sniping at each other through clenched teeth; ('Did you collect that parcel from the post office?' 'No – I thought you were doing it!'). By the time Sunday comes around we're ready to murder each other. We spend the morning arguing over whose turn it is to take Anna to the park – I win that one by a mile, given I have been shafted with park outings for the last four years.

My phone pings around midday, just as I'm shutting the door on David's frowning face and Anna's delighted one. It's Bea, sending me a photo of Harry in a Captain America outfit:

Ryan gave it to him yesterday and he's insisting on wearing it to Mathias' party.

Then, a few seconds later:

Why is he giving Harry a Captain America outfit? Ryan is SOUTH AFRICAN.

Although I was in touch with Bea yesterday to thank her for the return of the picnic basket, I have completely forgotten about Ryan's visit to see Harry. What is wrong with me? The alcohol must have damaged more than a few brain cells. I text her back quickly to ask her how the visit went. She pings back a few seconds later, saying that it was fine but she's glad that Ryan is heading back to the US tomorrow. Before I can ask her anything else, she tells me she's just about to leave for Mathias' party and she'll fill me in later.

Not long afterwards, I get a couple of passive-aggressive emails from Sebastian Fox 'politely confirming/reminding' me of our meeting tomorrow. How could I forget? I think miserably. I've only been dreading it all bloody weekend.

The day gets worse when David returns with a bawling Anna a mere half an hour after they left the house.

'She wanted to take her shoes off in the sandpit!' he says, outraged, as if Anna had told him she wanted to go squatting in a drug den.

'So what if she did?' I say crossly, throwing my arms protectively around her heaving little body.

I know that David can't stand sand (beach holidays are out of the question) and can't cope with it in the house (in the same way I have a slime ban), but given his grumpiness over the last couple of days, I'm not in the mood to be tolerant. David looks from me to Anna and throws his hands up in a 'I'm sick of being ganged up on' way, and thumps off towards the living room, presumably to tune in to some vitally important food podcast. I sigh and take off Anna's coat and shoes.

'I'LL go and sort her lunch out then!' I shout into the living room as I'm leading Anna into the kitchen. Then I mutter a few 'fuck's sakes' to myself while I prepare toasted cheese sandwiches for myself and Anna. David can make his own bloody lunch.

After a few tense words with Anna about how much more of the sandwich she has to eat before she's allowed a biscuit – I say 'all of it!' She says 'none of it!' – we compromise on two bites. After that, I hide out in Anna's room for a bit of peace (David will never go into Anna's room because it's too cluttered for his taste) and read my book. If Anna needs anything, David can bloody well sort her out, especially after his poor performance at the park. After about an hour, I start to feel guilty about neglecting the chores, so I stomp grumpily to our bedroom to get the laundry basket and spend the next couple of hours buried in domestic hell. My phone rings in my back pocket. It's Bea.

Grateful for the distraction, I greet her with, 'Party over already?'

She doesn't say anything.

'Bea?'

'Listen, something's happened.'

Her voice sounds wobbly and unBea-like.

'What's going on?' I say, immediately concerned.

'I'm at a police station in Surrey. I need you to pick me up.'

Jesus Christ.

I immediately think car accident.

'Are you okay? Is Harry okay?' I say, envisioning cars in ditches or flipped over on their roofs.

'We're both fine, I promise,' she whispers, sounding exhausted. 'Harry's with me... I'll explain everything when I see you.'

Then she tells me the name of the police station and I tell her I'll be there as soon as I can.

I rush down the stairs to find my bag and coat. Then I hurry into the living room to find the car keys.

'David, I have to go,' I say.

He glares at me and looks away. I've forgotten we're in the middle of a row. Well, this is more important. I tell him about the call from Bea and he immediately jumps up.

'What can I do? Do you want me to come with you?' he says, his face full of concern.

I thank him and tell him to look after Anna and I'll let him know what's happening as soon as I see Bea. Then I run into the kitchen to tell her I'm off out for a little bit and she wails until David promises to download a new movie on her iPad.

He walks me to the front door and gives me a little hug.

'Let me know how you get on,' he says.

I squeeze his arm and promise I will.

Panicky though this situation has left me, I'm grateful that David and I can switch from the urge to kill each other to mature adults when it really matters. Then I get in the car, Google the police station, and punch the postcode into the SatNav as quickly as I can. Thanks to quiet Sunday afternoon roads, I reach the police station just before 3 p.m., just under the estimated forty minutes, and I pull into a parking space alongside three police cars. I park very, very carefully just in case a policeman happens to be looking out of the window. Then I get out of the car and lock it, taking a moment to absorb exactly where I am. I've never actually been to a police station before, but I've driven passed plenty, and this one is particularly grim, with its dreary brown outdated eight-floor building and tinted green windows. I take a deep breath and walk towards the station and enter the glass doors to the reception area. Faded purple lino covers the floors that sit beneath walls painted in yellow-beige faded paint. A refuse bin labelled 'Knife Bank' sits against the wall opposite me, underneath a poster urging people to surrender their knives. I immediately feel guilty, without knowing why.

I shiver. What the hell has Bea done to end up in a place like this? A voice from the left makes me jump.

'Can I help you?'

I look over to see a woman in her fifties sitting behind a large L-shaped desk wearing a black police uniform, her grey-streaked blonde hair in a loose bun. By the downturned corners of her mouth, I'm guessing it's already been a long day. My heart beats quickly as I move towards her. Not only have I never been to a police station before, I'm pretty sure I've never talked to a police officer before either. Reasoning that it's probably the same as talking to the grim customs officers at passport control, I use the same strategy I always do: too friendly and over compensating.

'Hiiiiiiii,' I shrill as I reach the desk.

She stares at me, unimpressed.

'I'm looking for my friend Bea and her son Harry,' I say, wringing my hands.

She nods slowly and shuffles a few papers around. The silence makes me nervous.

'I don't have any knives!' I say, for absolutely no reason whatsoever.

Her eyes widen.

'What?' she says.

'I mean for the bin,' I babble. 'Otherwise I would have put them in.'

Jesus Christ, what is wrong with me? If I'm not careful she's going to lock me up for being mentally unstable.

'Right,' she says, in a long, drawn-out sarcastic way.

Then she gets up and stretches.

'I'll go and get your friend Bea.'

I thank her and watch her retreat through a side door, hoping she won't be too long. I can't bear for Bea and Harry to be stuck here any longer than they have to. But within two minutes she is back again – without them.

'I will pay the bail!' I shout.

She shakes her head at me as if she has never come across such a hopeless case, which in her line of work is pretty offensive, if you think about it.

'Your friend is in the bathroom with her little boy and she'll be out shortly,' she says, taking the seat behind her desk once more.

I pace nervously for a few more minutes. On the one hand, I'm relieved that bail doesn't seem to be necessary, but I am still apprehensive about what the hell they are doing here. A familiar and very welcome shout permeates my thoughts. Harry bursts into the room in a slightly-too-big Captain America outfit, runs at full force past the desk, and stops dead when he sees me. His hair is all sweaty and his face is covered in chocolate – the hallmarks of a kids' party.

'Where's Anna?' he says, putting both hands on his hips, Captain America-style.

'She's not here,' I tell him, ruffling his already messed up hair. I am delighted to see him so happy.

'Oh,' he says, looking downcast for a moment. Then his face lights up. 'It was the best party!'

A figure steps out of the door behind him. It's Bea, looking pale and drawn – probably the worst I've seen her since her miscarriage five days ago.

'Are you okay?' I mouth.

She smiles in a resigned sort of way. Then she turns to the policewoman.

'Do I need to sign anything?' she says.

The policewoman waves her away and tells her that she's free to go. Bea thanks her quietly and makes her way over to Harry, who has turned his attention to rattling the bin full of knives to an alarming degree.

'Come on, Harry,' she says, tiredly. 'Let's go home.'

Then Harry starts to wail.

'But I want to go in the police car again!'

I see Bea's shoulders slump. She is too exhausted to be coping with a tantruming child.

'Right, Harry!' I say, cheerily. 'Let's go and see what treats Anna has left behind in the car.'

He looks at me suspiciously, probably wondering if it's some sort of ruse, but he allows me to take his little hand all the same. To be honest, I'm more nervous walking out of the station than I was walking in. I hope to Christ I still have a stash of emergency sweets in the glove compartment.

Thankfully I do, and Harry spends the drive back gobbling down several different types of jellies while sporadically breaking into tuneless songs with indecipherable lyrics. I know better than to ask Bea what happened while Harry is in the car. Besides, judging by her blank stare out the window, I can tell she is as unreachable as she was on the way back from hospital a few days ago. So I keep driving, throwing in the odd compliment here and there to Harry for his enthusiastic (if overly loud) singing.

It's only when I finish parking outside her house that Bea addresses me directly.

'Will you come in for a bit?' she says, lightly enough but her eyes tell a different story.

'Of course,' I say.

When we're inside the door, Bea sends Harry upstairs to find his iPad, and I send a quick text to David to let him know where I am with a promise to fill him in when I get home. I put the kettle on as soon as we're in the kitchen and wave a mug at her.

'Tea, coffee... or something stronger?' I say.

'Coffee is fine,' she says, dropping heavily down on the kitchen chair.

I busy myself with making two cups of coffee and set both mugs carefully on the kitchen table. Then I pull out the chair opposite her, sit down, and bring the lovely warm liquid to my lips. It feels comforting after the strange events of today. Bea leans over folded arms, staring into her coffee. Then she gives a little cough, looks at me with tired eyes, and finally tells me the story.

Apparently, everything had gone well at first. Mathias' party was 'lavish to the point of ridiculous' as Bea put it, with whole acres of garden devoted to a funfair theme, including a full-size carousel, bumper cars, and gigantic bouncy castle. The kids were swept off by professional childminders so the adults could enjoy the towers of champagne and endless trays of canapés in the grand hallway of a house that 'looked like a country hotel'. Having being unaware of the black-tie dress code for the party, Bea had rocked up in a pair of smart jeans and a fine knitted jumper, which led to a couple of tense conversations with a couple of expensively dressed mums (one asked her if she was Harry's nanny, and another told her to 'be a dear and hurry into the kitchen to grab more canapés'). Given that it was a kids' party,

Bea restrained herself from tapping into her bank of wide and varied swearwords and decided to simply walk away instead.

'Very grown up,' I say, impressed.

I don't think I would have been able to manage the same restraint under the circumstances.

Bea holds up her customary one finger.

'Wait,' she says.

Then Bea tells me that she felt the onset of more bleeding and had gone in search of a bathroom to put in a fresh sanitary towel. When she came out of the bathroom, Jonathan, Mathias' dad, was standing right outside.

'The creep!' I say.

She sighs and nods.

'So he started joking about the fact that I owed him a new pair of shoes because I had puked all over them, you know?'

'What a dick! What did you say?'

'I didn't say anything, just moved to get past him, but then he blocked me.'

Jesus, he must have some nerve to take on Bea.

'Then he moves in really closely – like the way he did here last time – and he says, "Was it a stomach bug?"'

I give a little shiver. Only a man like Jonathan could make an innocent question so smarmy.

Bea lifts the coffee mug halfway to her mouth before putting it down again.

'Then he moved in even closer, put his hand on my stomach and said, "Does it still hurt?" in this voice that I'm guessing he thought was sexy.'

I am covered in goosebumps. What a sleazy, sleazy bastard.

'So, what did you do?' I say, taking a quick, nervous sip of coffee.

'I'm not sure what came over me,' she says, fiddling with the mug handle. 'But I ended up kneeing him in the nuts.'

I can't help it – the coffee comes spraying out of my mouth and hits the table, just shy of Bea's folded arms. My hand flies to my mouth. Bea's expression is blank.

'Well, good on you,' I say, firmly.

I'm not a big fan of violence, but the man got what was coming to him.

'He lets out a roar and, before I know it, I am surrounded by a sea of sequinned bolero jackets and Jimmy Choos. Then he points at me, looks down at his crotch, and sort of gasps: "She did this!"'

'I hope you explained what happened!' I say, but as soon as the words fly out of my mouth, I know that she probably hasn't – just like I never told my side of the blowjob story. People will believe what they want to, especially when you're not exactly flavour of the month.

She shakes her head and raises her hands in a 'what would be the point?' sort of way.

'Anyway, I reasoned it was time to go home, so I just pushed through the circle, and went outside to find Harry. The grounds were so bloody big that I ended up tramping over miles of muddy grass. Eventually I found him on the bouncy castle, having the time of his life.'

Oh, God – that's the worst. Trying to coax a child off a bouncy castle is as bad as trying to persuade them not to eat an ice cream after it's landed headfirst in dog poo.

'Of course, he had no intention of listening to me, so I took my shoes off and got on it myself,' she says.

I stifle a giggle. The thought of no-nonsense, Amazonian Bea on a bouncy castle is almost too much to bear.

'The second he saw me he started throwing a meltdown, so I

had to physically carry him off, wrestle his feet into his shoes, grab my own shoes, and tramp back the way we came – with Harry screaming the whole way.'

'Nightmare,' I say.

She nods grimly.

'Anyway, I decide to go round the side, rather than back through the house, to get to the car park and avoid the lynch mob, but the minute I go round the corner, I see a bigger crowd than before surrounding my car. It's only when I get a bit closer that I notice the policeman.'

I inhale sharply.

'Hang on – you're trying to tell me they called the police because you kneed that prick in the nuts?'

She takes a mouthful of coffee and says, 'Mmm hmm.'

'I mean, talk about over the top!' I say, angrily.

'Oh, that's not the half of it,' she says, wearily. 'There were shouts of GBH, drunken behaviour... one woman even said she was going to start a petition to get Harry and me removed from school.'

God. This is worse than I thought. And all in front of Harry too. I feel sick.

'So, what the hell did you do?'

'I ignored them, and pushed my way towards the car, intending to get in it as fast as possible, but the policeman – turned out his name was Jim – told me very gently that because of the "drunk" accusations, he couldn't let me drive until I took a breathalyser test back at the station.'

'And had you been drinking?' I say, because I would have been very tempted to have a small glass of champagne if it had been freely available.

'No – not a thing,' she says. 'I told Jim but he said it would be better if I went with him anyway. At that point I just wanted to get out of there, especially as Harry was still hysterical.'

I nod sympathetically. I would have done the same.

'Anyway, I needed to access my car to grab Harry's car seat and move it to the police car, but Harry was still wailing and wiggling. Then Jim started chatting to Harry about superheroes and Captain America and Harry immediately stopped crying. It was like some sort of miracle.'

Wow – I love Jim already.

'He ended up taking Harry from me while I rushed to get the car seat. At this stage, a few of the kids have started to wander over, thinking this is all part of the birthday party entertainment.'

'Who needs bumper cars when you have a real police car on the premises?'

'Precisely,' she says, adjusting her glasses.

'Then the birthday boy himself appears, marches straight up to Jim and says, "I want a ride in your police car" – real Verruca Salt stuff.'

'The little brat,' I say.

'So Jim, who still has Harry in his arms, peers down at Mathias and says, "Sorry, son, Harry's the only one who gets into my car."'

'Jim is a legend,' I breathe.

'Then Mathias starts screaming that he should be going in the car as he's the birthday boy, and then all the other kids start kicking off, and the parents are going mad, and champagne starts spilling, and it's just total mayhem.'

'Serves them right,' I say.

'At this point, Jim tells me it's time to go, and he carries Harry over to the car and straps him into his car seat, and I sit in the back beside him. As soon as we're settled, he turns around, gives

Harry a little grin, then switches on the sirens and the flashing lights, and speeds up the driveway.'

'Wow. This is the best day of Harry's life,' I say.

'I have never seen him so much in awe,' she says. 'The only problem is the station is less than ten minutes from Mathias' house, so the car journey was a lot shorter than I think he expected.'

'Oh, God, not another meltdown!' I say.

'It was touch and go when we pulled up outside the station, but as we were getting out of the car, Jim announced that he was going to take Harry on a grand tour of the police station.'

I love Jim. I need a Jim in my house.

'Anyway, he took us into the reception area...'

'The one with the knife bin,' I say.

'The very one,' she says.

'...disappeared through a side door by reception and reappeared with a mini police van for Harry to play with. Then he signalled to me to follow him to the seating area.'

'Doesn't sound like he was going to arrest you!'

'Far from it,' she says. 'He told me that Jonathan and his wife Matilda are total time-wasters who call the police if a dog so much as looks at their lawn, never mind pisses on it, and that he knows that I'm not a threat, and will be happy to let me and Harry go as long as I promise to get a friend to pick me up.'

'So he didn't even breathalyse you?'

'Nope. He told me I looked pale and shaken and didn't want me to drive after going through such a horrible incident.'

'Is Jim fit?' I say, probably an inappropriate question given the circumstances, but he sounds so lovely and caring, and so great with Harry, that I think he could be the perfect match for Bea.

She gives me a look that would wither the sturdiest of flowers, and says, 'He's in his sixties, full white beard, married for forty years, has three kids, and nine grandkids of his own.'

Damn it.

'So then I called you, and Harry got a tour of the station while we were waiting, and you know the rest.'

I lean back, suddenly exhausted. What a shitty, shitty thing to happen.

She puts her head in her hands and says, 'I don't know what's going on with me. Ever since I saw Ryan yesterday, I've felt really, really angry, and I don't know why.'

She looks at me, her eyes anguished.

'Listen,' I say, reaching over to stroke her arm. 'You've just had a miscarriage – give yourself a break!'

She shakes her head slowly.

'I thought I was fine about it, but seeing Ryan, I just started feeling so resentful that he wasn't going through the same thing. Part of me wanted to tell him so he could hurt as much as I was, but it was my choice not to tell him and I couldn't bring myself to, especially when he started banging on about his new Brazilian girlfriend.'

Shit. I had totally forgotten that the whole reason Ryan was at the O2 was because of the new love of his life.

'So you didn't say anything to Ryan in the end?'

'No,' she sighs. 'It would have been unfair.'

'Well, it's not fair on you either,' I say.

She sighs heavily.

'Anyway, when I got up today, I still felt angry. And I feel so stupid for feeling angry that I lost the baby because it was only ten weeks.'

'There's no such thing as "only" when it comes to loss,' I say, quietly.

Then her eyes fill with tears.

'The thing is, I had already started making plans – how I was going to fit a baby in a two-bedroom house, how Harry would react to a little brother or sister, how much maternity leave I would take, how Maria would cope with two kids instead of one. I had so many thoughts running around my head, and now my head just feels empty...'

She pauses to brush tears away from her eyes and I blink away mine.

'And then when that loser Jonathan put his hand on my stomach, it unleashed something in me, a fury that I couldn't contain.'

'He deserved it, Bea!' I say.

'But that's not like me. I could have handled it differently if I was myself. But I don't feel like myself, Saoirse,' she says, her voice breaking.

'I'm so sorry, Bea,' I say, squeezing her hand.

She looks at me blankly and says, 'This is my fault.'

'No way,' I say, sternly. 'You did nothing to cause this.'

'I don't know, Saoirse,' she says, in a trembling voice. 'Remember, I wasn't exactly thrilled to be pregnant in the first place, and I broke the no-coffee rule more than I should have...'

'That's nothing to do with it!' I say, thinking of the odd glass of wine I had when I was carrying Anna, not to mention the pint of Guinness ('It's good for you!') on St Patrick's Day. 'If that was the case, nobody would have babies at all!'

She smiles weakly.

'Listen to me,' I say, leaning towards her. 'You've had a big shock. Your hormones are all over the place. You need to give yourself time to grieve and recover.'

She lets out a big sigh.

'Everything will be okay,' I say.

Her forehead suddenly creases.

'What about work, and... oh, God, how is Maria going to get

Harry to school tomorrow without the car? It's still at bloody Mathias' house.'

She buries her head in her hands.

'You will call work in the morning and tell them what happened,' I say.

She opens her mouth to protest but I cut her off.

'Listen – you've had a miscarriage. I don't give a shite what week it was. It's serious and you have every right to take more time off.'

She closes her mouth again and nods wearily.

'As for your car – give me the address of that McMansion you went to today, and I'll get David to pick it up for you tomorrow morning after he drops Anna to school. I'd do it myself but I have a meeting at 9 a.m.,' I say, heart sinking at facing Sebastian yet again.

Bea waves her hands and protests a bit, but I'm not having it.

'Maria can take Harry to school in a taxi. David will definitely have the car to her before pick-up anyway.'

Bea mutters a quiet thank you and then we fall silent for a bit.

My phone pings – it's a text from David asking me if I'll be home for dinner. I glance at my watch, surprised to see that it is already close to 6 p.m.

'David?' Bea guesses.

'Yes,' I say.

Bea gets up wearily and stretches.

'I suppose I'd better feed Harry,' she says. 'Although given the amount of rubbish he has eaten today, I'm sure he'll take two bites of whatever I give him, regardless.'

I look at her reddened eyes and drawn complexion and immediately feel bad about leaving her by herself.

'Let me stay with you tonight,' I say. 'We can eat shite and watch a stupid movie and take the piss out of the bad acting and wobbly sets.'

Bea shakes her head gently.

'Thanks, Saoirse, but I have great plans to take a long, hot bath after Harry goes to bed and get an early night.'

'Are you sure?' I say, standing up to face her.

She nods.

'Besides, I don't want you scoffing any more of that hamper you got me. Honestly, it's my gift and I have no intention of sharing it!'

I laugh, glad to hear a bit of her old commanding voice coming back.

Then she links my arm with hers and walks me towards the front door.

'Now,' she says, dropping my arm. 'Go home to your husband and daughter and stop worrying about me.'

I nod reluctantly and step out into the freezing cold air. I start worrying about her the second the door shuts behind me.

29

I wake up on Monday morning with a hollow feeling in my stomach. Having spent a restless night tossing and turning over what happened to Bea, I am in no mood for Sebastian Fox and his morbid invention. I shower and dress quickly, resenting the fact that I have to make an effort when all I want to do is stay in my pyjamas and crawl back into bed.

David hands me a cup of coffee the second I walk into the kitchen. I shoot him a grateful look, and then go and give Anna a quick kiss on her headphones. She grunts and stuffs a big piece of toast into her mouth. Last night, after I had filled David in about what happened with Bea at the party, we had made up properly (not sex but a good chat, which is even better) and exchanged a number of apologies – me for getting hammered with Bea on Friday – and him for overreacting about me getting hammered with Bea on Friday.

'Will you be okay dropping Anna to school today?' I say, because I do feel bad for him that he is suffering the consequences of my past blowjob history with Mr Russell.

He gives a good-natured sigh, and says, 'I can handle it.'

'Thanks, David,' I say, my heart filling with warmth. 'And Bea's car?'

'Yes, I'll grab a taxi after I drop Anna to school and pick it up then.'

'If anyone accuses you of trespassing, take a leaf out of Bea's book, and give them a kick in the nuts,' I say.

'I will indeed!' he says, lightly.

Then we give each other a little kiss, and Anna goes, 'Urrggggh,' so we stop.

'Oh, before I forget, I've invited Bonnie over for lunch today,' David says, looking at me searchingly. 'Is that okay with you?'

'I think that's a wonderful idea,' I say.

And I do – it'll be great to get to know Bonnie a bit better.

'It'll be early, though, probably just after 11.30 a.m., as she has her client meeting at 1 p.m. I should be back in time with Bea's car by then.'

'Ah, so it will be brunch then,' I say, and catching his eye we both say at the exact same time, 'but without the sex.'

Then we smile at each other, delighted to be in synchronisation again.

I call Bea on the way to the Tube station and she tells me briskly that she has called into work and intends to take the rest of the week off. Then she tells me (kindly) to piss off as she has a hamper to work through. I smile as I hang up, relieved that she seems to be in better form than yesterday. Still, I can't shake the sadness I feel for her, for having to go through something so terrible in the first place. None of it is fair. I am so lost in thought that I almost miss my Tube stop, but manage to push my way out onto the platform just in time. The chilly air hits me as soon as I leave the station, and I curse inwardly at the drops of rain that have started to fall on my uncovered head. I have no umbrella. A few minutes later, the heavens open and I start to run towards the boat, blinded by the pelting rain. I'm making good progress until my shoulder makes contact with something which forces me into a half-spin.

'Ooooh! I'm so sorry!' a woman's voice says, gently gripping my arm, helping me to regain my balance. Winded, I look up to wave her away, but when I see her face, I do a double take.

'Saoirse!' she says. 'So sorry! Talk about literally bumping into you!'

Her voice is light-hearted enough, but her eyes are red and swollen. She looks as though she has been crying.

I try to calm my breathing but inwardly my heart is thumping.

'Hi, Rosalind,' I say, attempting a smile.

Just your disloyal sort-of-friend here who's helping your crackpot husband bring his creepy invention into the world, for the princely sum of £50,000, and you probably know nothing about it.

Suddenly she bursts into tears. 'I'm so sorry,' she sobs. 'It's just that something horrible has happened and I...'

Immediately, I wrap my arms around her, holding her shaking body, while the rain tumbles down on us both.

'Come on,' I say, eventually. 'Let's get some shelter and you can tell me all about it.'

I can't leave her like this. I'll just have to risk Sebastian's wrath later.

She takes a great big breath and attempts a watery smile. I lead her to the first coffee shop I see and settle her in a corner booth to give her a chance to recover, while I go and queue for our coffee. Feeling like a complete cow, given his wife is sitting so close by, I text Sebastian to let him know that I'm stuck on the

Tube and will get to him as soon as I can. This is a perfectly valid excuse as the Tube rarely runs smoothly in bad weather. He texts back immediately with a curt, 'Fine.'

By the time I bring back the coffees, Rosalind seems much calmer. She still looks pale but her eyes are dry.

'Oooh, thank you,' she says, quietly, cupping her hands around the warm coffee mug.

I rest my coffee on the wooden table between us and pull off my sodden, blue padded jacket and sit down opposite her, my heart beating quickly. I'm not sure what's happened to make her so upset, but given how close we are to Sebastian's boat, I can definitely take an educated guess.

Rosalind takes a sip of her coffee and then looks at me over the rim of her mug.

'I'm so sorry, Saoirse. What must you think of me, creating such a fuss? I'm so embarrassed.'

I wave her away immediately.

'Don't be mad! Everyone gets upset. Please don't feel bad about it.'

She places her mug back on the table, and folds her arms tightly against her chest, chewing her bottom lip all the while.

'Listen, Rosalind. Whatever it is, you can talk to me, okay?' I say, gently. Although I'm half-terrified of what she is about to tell me.

She nods slowly and takes a deep breath.

'Remember the last time we met, I mentioned that my husband and I were giving each other some space?'

I nod.

'Well, I just had huge fight with him and I'm not sure if we'll ever get back together,' she says, her eyes watering.

I wrinkle my eyes in sympathy but inwardly I'm thinking,

please may this argument have nothing to do with this ghost-writing project.

'It all started when his mother died a few months ago,' she says, staring down at her hands.

I murmur a token, 'I'm sorry to hear that,' as if it's breaking news, and her head shoots up.

'Well, I'm not!' she says, indignantly. And this is such an unexpectedly strong reaction from fragile, kind Rosalind that I am momentarily taken aback. All I can come out with is, 'Oh!'

'She made my life hell,' Rosalind says, her eyes taking on flinty look.

Jeepers, this woman must have been a real piece of work if she had this much impact on her.

'Er, what did she do?' I say.

Given that Sebastian has only talked about the artistic, loving, dead-mouse-burying side of his mother, I'm desperate to hear Rosalind's side of the story.

'Well, I liked her at first. I knew Sebastian's mum, Maggie, from her coming into the art gallery where I worked. She was a local artist and we displayed some of her pieces and she liked to pop in now and then to see how sales were going.'

I nod encouragingly.

'Anyway, one day this man in his thirties wandered in asking to see some of her paintings. He was a lot shorter than I am, not exactly great-looking, but there was something about him,' she says, her eyes taking on a faraway look. 'Everything he said was so full of passion and enthusiasm,' she says almost smiling at the memory. 'He was so honest – he told me that his mother was an artist and that he had not inherited her skills. Instead, as she saw it, he had sold his soul by going into the corporate world. But, for him, banking was all just a stopgap before he saved up enough money to travel the world.'

Frustrating though I find Sebastian, I can just see him bouncing into that art gallery sharing his hopes and dreams with somebody he's just met.

'Anyway, he asked me to dinner there and then, and that was it. We saw each other whenever we could and when we both realised it was getting serious, he introduced me to his Maggie as his girlfriend.'

She pauses and takes a deep breath.

'I can't even describe her reaction now. It was like her face collapsed in on itself. For some reason, I thought she'd be glad that we knew each other already, but she was clearly not happy. I tried to pretend I was just imagining it but, whenever she came into the gallery after that, she was really terse with me, accusing me of not promoting her paintings enough. I couldn't figure out what I'd done wrong, but when Sebastian announced our engagement, that was when she showed her true colours.'

Jesus, she sounds like the future mother-in-law from hell.

'A few weeks before the wedding, Maggie stormed into the gallery, shouting at me for "hoodwinking" her son into marrying me. Apparently, she never wanted a conventional life for her boy and, because of me, he was entering into a lifetime of boredom, domesticity and apathy.'

'And did you tell Sebastian all this?' I say.

'Yes, I told Sebastian, but he defended her to the last. Told me she was bound to feel upset that her only child was getting married as it had just been the two of them for so long. His father was never in his life, largely because she had no idea who his father actually was! He told me repeatedly that his mother would eventually come around. To be honest, he was so convincing that I actually believed him,' she says, with a bitter laugh. 'But then the boys came along and she only got worse.'

She starts to twirl her mug of coffee in slow circles.

'Everything I did was wrong,' she says. 'The way I fed them, clothed them, the fact that I had help. Apparently, she did all the child-raising by herself – a single mother on an artist's salary. What the hell did I need help for? Of course, she made all these little digs out of earshot of Sebastian and he never fully grasped her antagonism towards me – he would just tell me that she meant well and I was being too sensitive.'

Jesus – no wonder Rosalind was such a regular on Vale Mums. Clearly Maggie had done such a number on her that she had started to second-guess everything she did.

'Then, a couple of years ago, Sebastian was offered a job abroad. The salary was too good to turn down. It was just a few months after I had my third child, and I just couldn't face the upheaval of moving to a new country. So we agreed that Sebastian would relocate for a couple of years and we would use the extra money to top up our dream fund.'

'Your dream fund?' I say.

She shoots me a sad smile.

'We went to New Zealand on our honeymoon and fell in love with this little town on the South Island. Sebastian decided that we should start a dream fund so we could afford to eventually move there when he finished his stint abroad. Besides, even back then I thought the move would put some distance between me and Maggie.'

'So we saved and saved, and when Maggie died, we had pretty much reached our goal. And then the other day, I was checking our bank accounts to see how much longer I could pay for Elsa until I was earning again, and the money had just disappeared.'

Oh, God.

'The worst thing was that Maggie had left an inheritance – a boat which she had typically named after herself – and had specified in the will that Sebastian should leave his corporate job and go spend the money she left him doing something creative. The bitch – she knew that whatever she said Sebastian would do it.'

I take a deep swallow.

'I knew he was grieving so I tried to be supportive. I agreed that he should give up his banking job to fulfil his mother's wishes and spend the money she left him – it was his, after all. Then I told him to come home.'

She releases a shuddery breath.

'But he never came home, Saoirse. He told me he needed the space to create and moved into that bloody boat. At that point I decided to give him the time to grieve, hoping he would recover enough to move home.'

'And did Sebastian tell you what he was going to do with the inheritance?'

'No,' she sighs. 'Said he was working on a top-secret invention and there would be a big reveal in time.'

I breathe a sigh of relief. Rosalind knows nothing about the invention or my involvement in it.

'So that's when you decided to make some changes,' I say, thinking of her new look, the full-time nanny, and her determination to go back to work.

She nods and brushes her damp curls away from her eyes.

'I know it sounds stupid, but I was so cross with Sebastian for not coming home to his family, that I started to spend more money on myself, kind of like a "fuck you!" you know? Like if you're going to do your own thing, then so am I. But as time went on, and he still showed no sign of coming home, I started to get really worried about the finances. Sebastian had given up his job to go on this crazy mission and I had no income. I needed to make a plan to make sure that our boys were taken care of.'

My stomach starts to churn unpleasantly and I'm pretty sure it has nothing to do with the coffee.

'So then this morning, I checked the dream fund to see how much was there in case I needed to dip into it to tide us over if I had trouble finding a job and the money wasn't there.'

She buries her head in her hands and looks at me through parted fingers.

I have a really bad feeling about the dream fund.

'When I went to see him on the boat just now, he told me that he had already spent the inheritance *and* had emptied the dream fund to invest in his invention,' she groans. 'It was £50,000, Saoirse.'

I feel the acidity of the coffee rise rapidly into my throat.

Before I can say anything, my phone rings. I mumble an apology to Rosalind, too ashamed to make eye contact, and dig my phone out of my bag.

It's Sebastian.

* * *

Sebastian frowns when he sees me.

'I'm so sorry I'm late,' I say, half-drenched for the second time that day.

'Let's try to make up the time, then,' he says, in a clipped voice.

Unhappy as I am to be here, I rush in quickly, grateful for the blast of warm air that hits me. It's only when I take my coat off that I realise how rocky the boat is. Immediately, I start to feel dizzy and I wobble a bit as I ease myself onto my usual seat.

Sebastian arches his eyebrows.

'I think I need to find my sea-legs,' I say, shakily.

He puts his hands on his hips and says impatiently, 'Well, no "I am exciteds" for you today, that's for sure!'

Then he sits down opposite me and leans over, his hands on his knees.

'You don't seem yourself, Saoirse,' he says, frowning. 'Is it just the rocking motion or is something else wrong?'

Understatement of the year, I think. Christ knows what Rosalind must have thought of me rushing out of the café like that. I had told her that I was late for a meeting and called Sebastian back on the walk to his boat. Understandably, he'd been a little terse. I'm over an hour late. Now I'm here and I haven't the first clue how to sort out this mess, but I know I have to do something.

It's just then that I notice that the creepy marketing leaflets are still on the small wooden table between us, and I try and not look at them directly. My mind is whirring. I know that I can't afford to lose this job, but knowing what I know now, how can I accept the £50,000 that Sebastian has taken away from his own family, without seeking permission from his wife first?

'So I thought that today, we could discuss...' Sebastian begins. And then there is a sound of loud buzzing coming from the windowsill.

Sebastian grimaces and springs up from his rocking chair in one swift movement.

'Apologies. I'm just going to get this,' he says, grabbing his phone and heading towards what is probably the bedroom.

Grateful for the brief reprieve, I try to organise my thoughts, but then I hear Sebastian shouting. Desperate to find out why he is so angry, I will my legs to behave and edge closer to the bedroom door, but I only make it a few steps before the violent swaying forces me back to my seat again.

The shouting continues and then stops. Then a red-faced Sebastian flings open the door, and stomps down the middle of the boat as if his steps alone can calm the churning water below.

'Sorry about that!' he says, fists bunched. 'Family problems.'

My head shoots up. I'm willing to bet anything that he's been arguing with Rosalind.

Clearly noticing my reaction, he just raises his hands in a 'what are you going to do' sort of way.

'Not everyone realises the commitment it takes to create something that will change the world,' he says, with a great big sigh.

A dreamy look washes over his face and as I look into his eyes, I suddenly understand what the expression 'blinded by ambition' means. This man is willing to risk his whole family and their future for this perverse invention. And even more to the point, how dare he speak to Rosalind like that? Something snaps inside me.

'There is no book,' I say quietly.

He looks at me puzzled and leans forward. The rocking chair creaks gently.

'What was that, Saoirse?'

'There is no book,' I repeat.

'I don't under—'

'What you have created… I can't be a part of it. I can't write about an invention I don't believe in, especially when it seems to be causing problems with your close relationships.'

He looks at me closely and his mouth drops open and he jumps up out of his rocking chair.

'You've been talking to Rosalind!' he shouts, pointing a stubby finger at me.

I'm pretty sure my jaw and my stomach drop at the same time. What does he know about my relationship with Rosalind?

'How do you know?' I ask, kicking myself for being so obvious.

'Saoirse – how do you think I found you?' he says, flinging both his hands up in the air.

My head is spinning.

'But she never said anything to me...' I say, totally confused.

'That's because she doesn't know I hired you! She probably doesn't even remember telling me how you contacted her over Vale Mums a couple of months ago. I Googled you out of curiosity, went into your website, spotted that you were a ghostwriter, and called up your agent, Harriet Green to find out more.'

'But how did you know that I wasn't going to tell her about the book?' I say.

'Because you signed an iron-tight contract and confidentiality agreement,' he says, folding his arms.

Fair point, although I'm impressed that he thinks I'm that good at keeping a secret, considering I've already spilled the beans to Bea, Jen and Dee.

'Besides, I felt that she might need a bit of convincing from a friend when I eventually told her about my idea,' he says, lowering himself into the rocking chair once more. 'She can be a little short-sighted at times.'

I feel sick. Is this the reason he hired me then? So I would persuade a wavering Rosalind that emptying their bank account and destroying their future was a worthy thing to do?

A slow bubble of anger makes its way from my stomach, and into my throat. Between David's redundancy, Bea's miscarriage and the school gates fiasco I have had enough. The red mist descends and before I know it I am on my feet, yelling, swearing and telling him to shove his creepy book up his arse and that he must be DELUDED if he thinks his ash case is going to make the tiniest dent in the world, never mind changing it. And how he's BLOODY lucky he has someone as wonderful as Rosalind in his life. But the whole time he just sits there staring up at me, shaking his head slowly as if I've absolutely lost it (which of course I have). I can't cope with even looking at him any more, so I grab my coat, and walk at speed towards the door. Then he says the words that are expected under the circumstances, but no less chilling.

'I want my money back.'

30

The implications of what I have done hit me as soon as the adrenaline wears off – which is approximately five minutes after I storm out of Sebastian's boat.

Oh, Jesus – I have lost my job, I think, my initially angry walking pace slowing to a heavy tread. The words become a mantra all the way home – I have lost my job... I have lost my job. I have lost £50,000. I fight tears all the way home. What the hell am I going to tell David?

The panicky feelings escalate the closer I get to home, and when I reach our front gate, I'm not sure if I have the courage to go in. Then I feel a hand on my shoulder.

'Ah, Saoirse, what are you doing standing outside in the freezing cold?'

I turn around and fall straight into Bonnie's soft cloud of hair, and promptly burst into tears.

'Oh, my poor dear,' she says, holding me close.

Her soothing Scottish lilt only makes me cry more.

After a moment, she takes me by the shoulders gently and says, 'Come on – let's get you inside.'

My hands are shaking too much to even attempt to find my keys, so I knock on the door instead.

David opens it with a wide smile. 'Bonnie! You're early.'

Then he spots my tear-streaked face and his eyes cloud over with concern. The thought of what I have to tell him throws me into a fresh bout of sobbing.

'Saoirse! What is it? Are you okay?'

He throws Bonnie a questioning look, but she gives a little shake of her head.

David takes my hand and leads me into the house, leaving Bonnie to close the door behind us. He sits me down at the kitchen table, keeping hold of my hand. I am still shaking and I can't seem to stop.

I hear Bonnie's voice saying that she'll leave us to it, but I wave her in. Why not? She's going to find out sooner or later. I hear the sound of the tap running and then Bonnie appears with a glass of water.

'Take a sip of that,' she says, setting the glass down on the table in front of me.

I manage a feeble smile of thanks and gesture for her to sit down beside me. Then I take a few sips of water and finally begin to get some control over my breathing.

David wrinkles his forehead.

'Please tell me what's wrong,' he says.

I take a deep breath and tell him all about Sebastian Fox and how much I hated him and his morbid invention and how it was impossible for me to write his book, but I felt I had to make the effort because he had paid me such a lot of money. Then I take a breath and tell him what Sebastian has done to Rosalind and how I just couldn't keep my frustrations in any more and lost it completely.

'And now I'm fired,' I finish, miserably.

David looks at me and exhales.

'Saoirse!' he says, impatiently. 'WHY didn't you tell me all this before?'

'Because you had lost your job and I wanted you to have some time off and not to worry about money,' I say, through fresh tears.

'Do you think if I had known what he was like that I would have wanted you to work with a nutcase like him?'

He shakes his head incredulously.

'But I wanted to be the breadwinner!' I say, aware that my voice is becoming more childish than Anna's, yet I'm powerless to stop it.

David runs his hand impatiently through his hair.

'He wants his money back, David,' I say in a small voice.

David nods but for the first time his eyes shift away from mine. I know exactly what he's thinking – it's a real shock going from five figures to zero in the space of a few minutes.

'Can he do that?' Bonnie says, softly.

I turn to look at her.

'With the contract I signed he can do anything he likes,' I say, miserably.

Then I turn around to David and say, 'I am so sorry.'

He squeezes my hand and says, 'Saoirse, don't beat yourself up about this. I was honestly going to look for a job anyway after the cookery course finished.'

My free hand flies to my mouth. Oh, God – the cookery course. The majorly expensive gourmet cookery course. There's no way we can afford that now. I don't even want to know what we have spent on food and drink living like kings over the last few weeks.

'It's okay, Saoirse. I'll cancel the course and look for a job straight away. I was getting bored of hanging round the house anyway!' he says, smiling. But we both know that's not true.

Then he stands up abruptly, mumbles something about finding his laptop and heads out of the kitchen, his shoulders slumped.

'I feel so bad, Bonnie,' I say.

She rubs my arm and says, 'Listen – breadwinner or no bread-winner – do you think he would want you working for someone like that?'

I shake my head.

'Would you want him to do the same?'

I shake my head again. No way – I would never want that for David under any circumstances.

'That's because you're a team and you love each other. This project didn't work out, but a better one will come along, you'll see!'

Suddenly I feel a little better. Bonnie's right. This isn't the end. I'll get another job with a sane person and hopefully David will find something less pressurised than his last job.

'You give good advice,' I say, with a watery smile. 'I can see why you'd be a good rent-a-friend.'

She laughs, her lovely white cloud of hair falling lightly on her shoulders.

'I try my best,' she says, her eyes twinkling.

A warm feeling rushes over me. I'm so pleased that Bonnie has come into our lives.

'I'll leave you in peace for a moment,' she says, rising to her feet and walking towards the living room.

I take a deep breath, pick up my phone, and scroll down my contacts quickly.

Rosalind takes it a lot better than I would have. The worst part is confessing to her that I had decided to continue working with Sebastian even when I found out he was her husband. She goes a bit quiet then and I don't blame her. Then I tell her that I plan to give all the money back to her, and she actually protests. She says that it's not my fault that I got dragged into all this, and surely I should be paid for the work I have done so far. That one is easy to argue – barely any material equals no book, which equals zero reward. After a bit of back and forth, I finally persuade her to send over her bank details.

Then I call Bea.

As soon as she picks up, I start to cry, and immediately she thinks I've been attacked.

'What is it, Saoirse? Have you been hurt?'

Through great big sobs, I tell her all about Sebastian, Rosalind and losing the money. When I've finished, she says quietly, 'He's the ratbag. You've done the right thing.'

'I know, but I feel like such a shit friend – I knew the connection between him and Rosalind and I still went ahead with it,' I say, miserably.

'Why didn't you tell me all this before?' Bea says.

'Because these are trivial problems compared to what you've just been through,' I say, sniffing.

'Saoirse! Just because I've had a miscarriage doesn't mean you can't talk to me any more. Frankly, I need stuff like this to take my mind of it!'

'I'm sorry,' I mumble.

Then she tells me to piss off and she sounds like her old self, and it makes me feel better.

'Look, clearly Rosalind and Sebastian have their own problems to work out. You have done the right thing getting out of that project. Losing the money is shit, but David will get a new job and something will come along for you, too. Now it's time to move on.'

She sounds so definite about everything that I can't help but let out a watery laugh.

'Thanks, Bea,' I say, sniffling.

'Any time, Saoirse. And for God's sake, get a tissue!'

When I finally hang up, I rest my head in my hands for a bit. I am absolutely exhausted.

Then my phone pings. I check it immediately relieved to find that Rosalind has emailed over her bank details. Then a text flashes up: it's Sebastian. Just a one-liner demanding that I refund him his money immediately. Well, no time like the present. I access my account and add Rosalind's details to transfer the money – and with a whooshing sound, £50,000 suddenly disappears from my account into hers, leaving very little in its wake.

31

David spends the next few weeks meeting head-hunters and going to endless interviews. By the time the Christmas holidays come round, he still doesn't have a job. As for me, I use the time to complete the first draft of the motherhood book, but I feel flat when I email it off to the publisher. After everything that has happened, I really don't feel like celebrating this milestone. It also doesn't help that I am back on the school run and on full Anna-duty, pretending to ignore the whispers and derisory glances from the Organics. On the positive side, nobody has hassled me about manning a stand at the school Christmas Fair, so every cloud... Sho hasn't made an appearance in the playground since our fallout. Instead, Ambrose stands in his usual spot, noise-cancelling headphones glued to his ears. The school playground is a lonely place when you have nobody to talk to. I don't even have Diana, the diagonal walker any more – she told me on my first day back on the school run that she was moving out of London for good. I miss her. Once we got past all the small talk, she turned out to be a good friend.

Still, at least I still have Bea, who isn't having an easy time of it

at school either. True to her word, Jonathan's wife, Matilda, has
started a petition to get Harry removed from school because of
his 'violent and abusive' mother, and most of the mums have
signed it. Bea has completely ignored it all, of course, but I know
it must get to her, especially when Harry comes home upset
because Mathias and some of the other boys won't play with him
any more. Still, there is light at the end of the tunnel. She has
decided to 'get Ryan off my back' by agreeing to take Harry to
South Africa for Christmas and New Year to meet Ryan's parents
for the first time. The break will be good for her.

Bonnie has been coming to see us every week after her client
visit and has really bonded with Anna, who calls her 'the cloud
fairy'. One day, when she is a bit older, we will tell her who
Bonnie really is.

David and I, on the other hand, have been forced to travel
across to Ireland on Christmas Eve for our Christmas holidays on
the Irish Ferry – significantly cheaper than flying – important
when your husband hasn't found a new job yet. The ferry is
cheaper for good reason. Factoring in the six-hour drive to Holy-
head in Wales, it will take a mere twelve hours to get to my mum's
house by the coast in north County Dublin. Worse still, crossings
are notoriously rough at that time of year. The last time we got
the ferry, the waves were so angry that I filled several beer glasses
with my own vomit and couldn't move my legs until we reached
smoother waters. Anna was only two at the time but still
managed to tell everyone we met that 'Mummy was sick in a cup'.
So, all told, I'm not looking forward to the journey and I'll be
ladling in the seasickness tablets when the time comes.

* * *

It is the day before Christmas Eve. Anna is off school, of course, and I'm trying to pack all her presents from Santa on the sly. This is frustratingly difficult, especially as she has taken it upon herself to shadow me all over the house. David has just left to get the car cleaned inside and out in preparation for the drive over to Ireland tomorrow. He does this every time we're about to go on a long car journey and, quite frankly, I've never understood it. To my mind, there's very little point in cleaning it beforehand, given that Anna is bound to litter it with endless crumbs from the inevitable bags of sweets and crisps we will have to bribe her with to keep the peace in the back seat. I glance at my watch, almost midday, and my heart leaps. Bonnie will be here soon to give Anna her Christmas present, which will hopefully distract her enough for me to do the rest of my packing.

Just as I am trying to persuade Anna that she won't need her entire stuffed bear collection in Ireland, there is a welcome knock on the door. I rush downstairs, a sulky Anna trailing behind me, and swing it open with a big smile on my face.

It's Bonnie, looking equally as cheerful, holding a giant rectangular box wrapped in unicorn-patterned paper. Anna switches from grump to elated in a nanosecond and rushes at Bonnie immediately. Bonnie laughs and hands the box over to her.

'Happy Christmas, Anna!' she says.

Anna gives her the briefest of thank yous and rushes off into the living room, ripping off paper as she goes.

She comes back before Bonnie has had time to take her coat off. The shoes still stay on, though (but only for Bonnie, as David has warned me about a million times).

The gift is a beautiful ballerina doll, with shiny brown hair tied up in the sort of complicated bun Caroline would favour. By the look on her face, Anna is already besotted. Then she throws her little arms round Bonnie before heading straight upstairs, presumably to introduce the doll to all her other toys.

'Thanks, Bonnie,' I say, smiling. 'It's the perfect gift.'

I think about what a breath of fresh air she is compared to Rose. Rose, who still won't take David's calls, even after all this time. He doesn't say much about it, but I know he's still hurting, especially at this time of year when families come together.

Bonnie goes upstairs to find Anna, which gives me a chance to pack with freedom, and by the time lunchtime comes round, I'm feeling a little more organised.

I find Anna and Bonnie in the bathroom washing her new doll's hair in the sink. I knew that complicated ballet bun wasn't going to last too long.

'Go away, Mummy!' Anna says, ferociously, terrified that her killjoy of a mother is about to ruin her fun.

'It's lunchtime, Anna!' I say, shaking my head.

Bonnie shakes the water from her hands and grabs a towel to dry them.

'Anna, how would you like to join me for pizza today in Joe's Italian?' she says, smiling.

Anna squeals and throws her arms around Bonnie's legs.

'I think that's a yes!' I say, laughing.

Anna loves Joe's Italian – our local pizza restaurant. We rarely go there because it's significantly more expensive than any of the other pizza places.

'Are you sure?' I mouth to Bonnie.

'Aye,' she says, smiling. 'My treat!'

I'm just about to thank her when something occurs to me.

'Are you not seeing your client today?' I say, puzzled, because this is the usual time she goes to her meetings.

She shakes her head.

'No, I haven't seen her in weeks. She travels quite a bit.'

'So you came all this way from Cornwall just to see us?' I say, astounded at her level of generosity.

'Well, I couldn't let this wee bairn go to Ireland without a Christmas present, could I?' she says, using the towel to gently dry Anna's hands.

I squeeze her shoulder.

'Thanks, Bonnie,' I say. 'And for taking her for pizza, too.'

'It's no bother,' she says.

We rush downstairs following Anna, who I've never seen so keen to get out of the house. I wave them off and head back upstairs to throw a few more items into the cases before wandering into the kitchen for some lunch, where I see Bonnie's smart, navy, leather handbag resting on the countertop. She must have forgotten it in the rush to leave. I grab it and head out the door. There's still plenty of time to return it to her before she pays the bill.

Five minutes later, I am at the restaurant, scanning the busy room for Anna and Bonnie. I see Bonnie sitting at a corner table chatting animatedly to a woman, Anna busily drawing with the usual broken crayons the waiters are told to give to small children. They haven't spotted me yet, which is just as well. I back out carefully until I'm outside the door and out of sight. I take a deep breath, trying to calm my racing mind and process what I have just seen. The woman Bonnie is talking to is Sho.

I hide in the pretentious gift shop next door for a good ten minutes to avoid running into Sho, and end up bankrupting myself by buying 'artisan, hand-woven, organic' cards that supposedly turn into Christmas trees if you plant them. Then I step back out onto the pavement, and tentatively peep in the glass door of Joe's. I breathe a sigh of relief – no sign of Sho. Feeling more confident now, I swing open the door and approach Anna and Bonnie. Anna immediately drops her slice of pizza, holds up one hand and says 'No!' Jesus Christ, can I not even enter a room any more? Mind you, it's great that she's so fond of Bonnie – it bodes well for future babysitting opportunities.

Bonnie looks up at me and smiles – a little tomato sauce from the pizza staining the corner of her mouth.

'You forgot your handbag,' I say, handing it to her across the table.

'Oh, goodness! I didn't even miss it!' she says, taking it from me and resting it on the floor beside her feet.

'We saw Milly's mum!' Anna says.

'Really?' I say, feigning surprise.

Bonnie gives me a neutral look and says, 'That's right.'

And I know immediately that my assumptions are correct.

'Is she your client?' I say, quietly.

Bonnie nods.

I don't know what to say, because of all the people in the world, I can't believe someone like Sho would hire a rent-a-friend.

'But she's always been so confident!' I blurt out. 'She doesn't care about what anyone else thinks!'

Bonnie sighs, 'Sometimes the most confident people are the loneliest.'

Suddenly I feel sad. To have to put on that front all this time must be exhausting. I don't think Sho and I will ever be friends again but knowing this about her makes me a bit less angry and a little more forgiving.

Then it hits me that Bonnie must know everything that happened between Sho and me – the Mr Russell blowjob incident included. I feel the colour rushing to my face. Clearly picking up on my discomfort, Bonnie stands up, takes a couple of steps towards me, leans over and whispers, 'Listen, love, you thought I was a prostitute. Nothing shocks me any more.'

I walk slowly back home, my head full of Sho. Much as I sympathise with her, I can't find it in my heart to forgive her for breaking a confidence, even if it was in the heat of the moment. I am so lost in thought that it takes me a moment to notice that a familiar figure is standing just outside our front gate. She turns her head, her mouth set in hard line, arms folded across her bony chest. My heart races. I take a deep breath and attempt a smile.

'Hello, Rose.'

32

'Cup of tea?' I say, shrilly as I close the front door behind us.

Her surprise visit has caught me off guard. I have no idea what to do.

'No, thank you,' Rose says stiffly.

'Can I take your coat?' I say, reaching out a tentative hand towards her but she shrinks backwards and hugs her coat more tightly around her.

'No, thank you,' she says again but this time her tone is more indignant as if I have somehow offended her.

In a moment of hysteria, I consider asking her to take her shoes off to comply with David's no-shoes rule, but even I'm not that brave or stupid. The few times she has been to our house, she has taken off her shoes, but that's for David, not for me. To be honest, after the tea and coat offers, I have nowhere to go from here, but David's not home yet so I'm going to have to deal with her whether I like it or not.

'Well, why don't you come through to the living room anyway?' I say, trying to sound chatty and welcoming. Despite her antagonism towards me, I know how difficult it must have been to come here.

'David's just off getting the car cleaned but he'll be back soon.'

She eyes me suspiciously as if I'm trying to hoodwink her into something she doesn't want to do, but eventually she follows me into the living room and lowers herself slowly onto the couch, legs crossed, one hand covering the other.

I stay standing, trying to fight the feeling of panic of a supremely awkward social situation.

'Do you need the toilet?' I blurt out.

Jesus, where did that come from?

She raises her eyebrows and shakes her head slowly.

I nod seriously as if treating my mother-in-law like a child by asking her if she needs the toilet is the most normal thing in the world to do. Inwardly, I'm screaming, 'Save me!'

Another long, unbearable pause follows. Just as I'm about to pretend that *I* need the toilet as an excuse to get away from this dire situation, I hear the blessed sound of a knock on the door. 'That must be David!' I say, brightly, although inwardly I'm wondering why he hasn't used his keys. Maybe he left them at home.

Rose nods, but I notice her hands twist together. Whatever she has to say after months of ignoring David, she is clearly nervous about it. I just hope with all my heart that she has come to make peace.

I rush to the front door to greet David and warn him about the surprise guest, but my stomach turns over when I open the door to find Bonnie and Anna there instead. They both shout cheery greetings and bustle into the hallway, Anna full of chat about her pizza, brandishing the picture she coloured in at the restaurant and how it was her best one ever.

I open my mouth and close it again. Somehow, I can't find the words to tell Bonnie that Rose is sitting several feet away in the living room. I watch Anna race upstairs, barely registering her excited shouts about showing her picture to her new doll.

Then I feel a warm hand on my shoulder.

'Is everything okay, Saoirse?' Bonnie says, her eyes kind with concern.

I take a deep breath in an effort to settle the nerves, but before I can fill her in, I hear the sharp thud of heels approaching. I watch in horror as Rose's tall frame fills the doorway.

A warm smile crosses Bonnie's face.

'Saoirse, you never told me you had a visitor!' she says, nudging me in a mock scolding sort of way.

I freeze.

'Hello, I'm Bonnie,' she says, reaching her hand out towards Rose.

Rose stares at her hand for a moment and then takes it, giving it a brief squeeze, before letting it go.

All this seems to happen in slow motion and I am helpless to stop it.

'I'm Rose, David's mother,' she says,

Bonnie's eyes widen as her fingertips fly to her mouth. She stares at Rose for a bit and lets her hand drop to her side again.

'Oh, Rose – I've been wanting to meet you for such a long time,' she says, her eyes soft.

Rose frowns and narrows her eyes, before glancing at me as if to say, 'Who the hell is this lunatic?'

Grateful as I am that she hasn't twigged who Bonnie is yet, I know that I can't stop this from happening. It's time I found my voice.

'Rose – this is Bonnie, David's birth mother,' I say, as gently as I can.

Rose instantly turns white as her eyes dart between Bonnie

and me. I notice her fists clench and unclench and for a moment I'm worried she's going to lash out. To her credit, Bonnie stays perfectly still, the same kind expression on her face. Then Rose's face twists and she does something I never thought I'd ever see her do: she bursts into tears.

Bonnie immediately springs into action and throws her arms around Rose's heaving frame.

'Oh, my poor love,' she says over and over again.

Rose initially tries to fight her off, but she has no chance against Bonnie's determination and overwhelming empathy. Eventually, Rose starts to sink into Bonnie's embrace and they rock back and forth for whole minutes, while I stare at them dumbly, still trying to get my head around the fact that David's adoptive mother and birth mother are sharing this intimate moment together.

They probably would have been there for longer, if it wasn't for David walking in the door.

'What the...?' he says, as he takes in the scene in front of him.

I can't imagine what must be going through his head.

Rose immediately springs away from Bonnie as if she has been caught doing something she shouldn't.

I'm desperate to fill him in.

'Rose stopped by and Bonnie took Anna for pizza and then brought her back to the house, and then Rose was here, so they sort of met and...' I stop then because I'm babbling. Maybe this isn't the time to find my voice.

Bonnie takes Rose's hand and I notice that Rose doesn't pull it away.

'David – I have just had the honour of meeting the woman who did such a magnificent job of raising you,' Bonnie says, smiling.

Then she turns to Rose.

'I want to thank you from the bottom of my heart,' she says, her eyes welling up.

Rose's head drops to her chest.

'I haven't been... it's not always been easy...' she says, the tears starting to flow again. 'I wanted a child of my own so much but, when things didn't work out, I felt like I had failed. Adopting David was a reminder of that failure.' Rose raises her head and looks at David. 'I kept you at a distance all these years,' she says through great heaves. 'But I need to tell you that my biggest fear is losing you, which is why I was so upset when you told me you wanted to find your birth mother.'

David's eyes water and he swallows deeply.

'Mum – you will never lose me,' he says, his voice trembling. 'I'm so sorry – I never wanted to hurt you. I just felt a part of me was missing – an emptiness that's hard to describe – and I felt that finding my birth mother might help to fill that space.'

Rose nods and brushes her tears away. Then she takes a deep breath and says, 'I understand.'

Bonnie lets go of Rose's hand and subtly nudges her towards David, but David doesn't wait for Rose to approach. In two quick steps, he has his arms round her and for the second time that afternoon, I watch as two people who I never thought would come together share this emotional moment. Now it's my turn to well up – but from happiness. Because, at long last, David has found what he's always wanted: his birth mother and, hopefully, a closer relationship with Rose.

There's just one more thing left to do. Quietly, I leave the hallway and make my way up the stairs towards Anna's bedroom. I can hear her chatting merrily to her new doll and my heart fills with love for her innocence – so caught up in her imaginative play that she is oblivious to the dramatic scene downstairs.

I sit on her bed and pull her on to my knee, her new doll

firmly clasped in her arms. Then I explain to her about Rose and Bonnie in the most child-friendly way I can, and she uncharacteristically doesn't interrupt me once. When I finish, she addresses the doll and says, 'So Daddy has two mummies?' And I tell her yes. Then she says, 'So now I have THREE grandmothers?' And I give her a little cuddle and whisper another yes into her soft brown, slightly-smells-of-pizza hair. She pauses for a moment, and then quickly twists around on my knee to look me in the eye.

'I already have Brenda Bear,' she says, frowning.

That's true. She has a bear teddy named after my mother, which never fails to give me the giggles, especially as it's falling to pieces. Every time my mother sees it, she says, 'Jesus, Saoirse, that bear is in desperate need of a wash!'

Anna's face suddenly lights up.

'Can I call my new doll Rose-Bonnie?'

'I think that's a lovely thought,' I say, kissing her on her silky-smooth forehead, breathing in the little-girl scent of her.

Then she frowns and mutters, 'OR should I call her Bonnie-Rose?'

'You can call her whatever you like,' I say, although inwardly I'm hoping she chooses Rose-Bonnie as I know that it will please Rose no end to be higher in the pecking order.

Anna turns back round to face the doll again.

'I will call you Rose-Bonnie!' she says, hugging the doll tightly. 'Because I met Rose first.' Then she mumbles, 'Even though Bonnie gives me better presents.'

33

It's a punishingly early Christmas Eve morning, and David and I are ready to murder each other. We stayed up late last night talking through everything that happened with Rose and Bonnie, and even though we both went to sleep happy and content, now we're both tired and cranky. Yesterday, after I had told Anna about Bonnie, I ushered David, Rose and Bonnie into the living room and made everyone a cup of tea and left them to it while I continued packing for our trip. David told me afterwards that Rose asked Bonnie a lot of questions about herself and Bonnie responded in her usual easy way. When Rose finally decided to make the journey back home, she gave Bonnie a quick hug good-bye. I was there with Anna for that bit and was glad to see the two women part on such good terms. Before Rose left, Anna announced the new name for her doll and Rose patted her on the head, cheeks puffed out, clearly pleased to have been awarded top billing. Bonnie left shortly afterwards with hugs and promises that we would get together after we arrived back from Ireland.

Last night David was so elated about how everything had worked out, how he felt that a huge weight had been lifted, and how grateful he was that I had told Anna the truth about Bonnie. Yet all that intimacy between me and David has been stripped away during this storm-ridden, treacherous drive to Wales, not to mention the extremely unkind ferry crossing (although no puking incidents this time for any of us, thank Christ). Worst of all, Anna, clutching her new doll in the back seat, has reached a new low on the whingeing stakes, her constant cries of 'I'm bored' followed by 'Rose-Bonnie is ALSO bored' cutting into our frayed nerves like glass. By the time we turn into my mother's housing estate at 8 p.m., none of us are speaking to each other.

A small grey-haired figure in a red padded coat runs down the path of my childhood home – a smart semi-detached affair with cheerful window boxes filled with snowdrops. In spite of the tense journey, a feeling of warmth runs through me. It's good to be home.

My mum raps at the window and I open the door, almost shutting it again, such is the strength of the freezing Irish Sea breeze.

'Jesus, will you get into the house!' she says, swinging the door open. 'It's feckin' freezing!'

We all troop inside and immediately get ready for bed. David complains that he's not feeling great and my heart sinks, although I'm not surprised. After all the stress of the interviews and rejections, not to mention everything that's happened with Rose and Bonnie, he's probably a bit run down. Still, he mentioned this morning that he is waiting to hear the outcome of a recent interview so hopefully he'll have some good news soon. I tell him to go to bed and settle Anna in the toddler bed my mum has made up for her in the little box room next to ours. Then I say goodnight to my mother and fall into bed, exhausted.

* * *

Thanks to Anna and her cries of 'Santa's been!' we have all been up since 6 a.m., helping her open her many, many gifts from Santa, and my mother. The small living room is littered with wrapping paper and cast-aside pieces of tiny plastic (my mother has learned the hard way not to buy Anna LEGO). David, who has been irritatingly snuffily and unnaturally flushed, has been given a box of tissues and ordered back to bed. He's not allowed to come anywhere near me, Mum or Anna. The last thing we all want is to be dying of a cold over the Christmas break.

After the mayhem of the present opening, my mother announces she's off to get ready for Mass, so I head into the kitchen to peel spuds for the roast potatoes later, yawning every few seconds. It's going to be a long day. Suddenly my mum appears in the door and I drop the peeler in shock. Not only is she dressed in a fancy-looking red woollen coat, with a grey fur collar, but she is wearing a face full of make-up – heavy grey eye shadow, bright-red lipstick, Aunt Sally blusher... My mother never wears bright colours, and the last time I saw her with make-up on was at our wedding, and even then you'd barely know it was on her. Then Anna appears beside her with a mischievous look on her face, and the penny drops.

'Anna,' I tut. 'Did you do Nana's make-up today?'

My mum folds her arms and glares at me.

'She did not!' she says. 'I did it myself!'

Shite.

'Well, it looks good,' I say, trying to sound positive.

Anna looks up at her critically and says, 'Too much lipstick.'

'Oh,' Mum says, her fingers flying to her mouth.

Anna disappears and before I have a chance to overcompensate for my daughter's directness, she reappears with a few tissues and hands one to my mum.

'Now blot it,' she commands, holding the tissue to her own mouth and smacking her lips up and down.

Her earnestness makes me smile. On the rare occasions I've worn make-up, she has been an avid audience. Clearly, she has picked up a few tips.

So my mother blots her lips, bends down, and then says to Anna, 'Better?'

Anna puts her hands on her hips and says, 'Too much eye shadow.'

My mother bursts out laughing and straightens up.

'Saoirse, can you give me a hand?' she says, quietly, suddenly looking uncharacteristically vulnerable.

I give my hands a quick wash in the kitchen sink until they no longer smell like potatoes and then follow her into her bedroom. She sits down on her little stool in front of her dressing table and vanity mirror. Then I grab a few pieces of cotton wool and gently remove the worst of the blusher and eye shadow to give her more of a natural look. Anna hangs around for a bit, and then announces she's off to find her iPad. Clearly her Christmas presents have lost their novelty already. Just as I'm finishing up, I hear a phone ping. Mum jumps up and looks wildly around the bedroom.

'Where did I put my phone!' she says, waving her hands frantically.

'It's here, Mum!' I say, picking it up off the bed.

She grabs it off me and clicks into her messages.

'Is it the Queen texting?' I joke.

'No, no,' she says, sounding distracted. 'A friend is giving me a lift to Mass. He'll be here in five minutes.'

In all the years I've been alive, I've never known my mother to get a lift to Mass. She has always walked the ten minutes, in every type of weather imaginable.

'And who's this friend?'

'It's just a student from one of my classes,' she says, not looking me in the eye.

Then I remember her frantic state from one of our calls a few weeks ago.

'It's not Miguel, is it?' I say, chancing a guess.

Her head snaps up.

'And what of it?' she says, sharply.

I hold my hands up in defence.

'Nothing, nothing!' I say, astounded by her reaction.

Clearly this Miguel is someone she cares about.

Then she races to the window like a teenager and says, 'He's here!'

'You look lovely,' I say, fondly, following her to the front door.

She takes a quick look at herself in the hall mirror and turns her head this way and that.

'I'll do,' she says, matter-of-factly, but I can tell by the proud angle of her head that she is pleased with the way she looks.

I open the door and give her a gentle push.

'Have fun!' I tell her, giving her a wink.

She tuts, and says, 'Saoirse. It's Mass. It's not supposed to be fun.'

I smile and close the door behind her. My mother has been on her own for so long, I'm delighted she has a bit of male company at last. Then I run into the living room and shove the lace curtains aside, desperate to get a glimpse of this Miguel, but I'm too late. All I see is the back of a car driving away. I fix the curtains, feeling disappointed.

'Where's Nana gone?' Anna says, wandering over.

'Nana has gone on a date!' I say.

'What's a date?'

'I'll tell you when you're older,' I say, ruffling her hair.

Much older.

* * *

The rest of the day passes with no more mentions of Miguel, but my mum has returned from Mass in a very good mood. We all sit down for Christmas dinner at 4 p.m., and tuck into roast potatoes, assorted veg, and the usual turkey crown. As my mum always says, 'Sure, what would be the point of getting a whole turkey when there's only four of us!' David manages to hang around long enough to help with the washing-up and then, waving away dessert (trifle and Christmas pudding) goes straight to bed, his face full of fever.

As soon as he leaves the room, my mum shakes her head and says, 'Ah, God, that's the real flu.'

I sigh in frustration. It's not like David and I had any real plans for the Christmas break, but I feel for him all the same. After the dramatic reconciliation with Rose, he could have done with a few days to relax and let off some steam. My mother puts a Christmas movie on for Anna and then tucks her into bed. We spend the rest of the evening cuddled up on the squashy blue sofa, my mother and I dipping into the Baileys at leisure while I fill her in about Rose and Bonnie finally meeting. After several interruptions, ranging from, 'Isn't that gas!' and 'Would you credit it!' and an emphatic 'Jesus, Mary, and Holy Saint Joseph!' she finally settles back into the couch, looking thoughtful.

'Do you think Rose and Bonnie will ever be friends?'

I look at my mother and swish the ice around in my glass.

'I'm not sure. It's still early days. For now, I'm just glad that everybody is getting along.'

My mother nods thoughtfully.

'I'm looking forward to meeting Bonnie,' she says, taking a sip of her drink.

'You'll definitely like her,' I say.

And she will. Bonnie and my mother share that level of warmth and empathy that will be sure to bond them from the get-go.

Then my mother gives a heavy sigh.

'It's just a shame Bonnie isn't a prostitute after all,' she says, shaking her head.

What?

'She'd have had a great number of stories to tell us.'

I raise my eyes skyward. My mother loves nothing but a good gossip.

'Great to see a change in Rose, too,' she says thoughtfully. 'Do you think she'll have less of a poker up her arse when I see her next?'

I can't help but giggle.

'Let's hope so,' I say, and we clink our glasses together.

By the way the Baileys almost sloshes out of her glass, I'm pretty sure my mother is a little tipsy.

'What a year!' she says, slightly slurring.

I knew it.

Then she jerks her head towards me and says out of nowhere.

'Money or not, Saoirse, it's never worth it working for someone like that Fox fella, especially when he treats his wife like that. The cheek of him STEALING the money out their bank account without even telling her!'

I nod as if I haven't already heard this a million times. My mother has been dining out on the story of Sebastian and Rosalind ever since I told her I had lost the job. What my mother doesn't know is that I ran into Rosalind about a week after I returned the money and she is considering a reconciliation with

Sebastian, on the proviso that he drops the invention and attends couples' therapy. She's a better woman than I am for giving him another chance, and I just hope he isn't stupid enough to blow it this time. Still, I know I won't be able to bear my mother's outraged reaction if I tell her the latest – 'WELL! Isn't she a FOOLISH girl to be taking that EEJIT back?' – so I've decided not to mention it at all.

Then she leans over and asks me yet again if David and I need money.

'I can't have you on the breadline, Saoirse!' she says, her eyes suddenly watery.

I reassure her that we will be fine, that David will get a job, and a new writing project will come my way, but all the while I know I'm struggling to convince myself. The truth is I don't know what the future holds for David and me.

Then she suddenly puts her glass down on the table with a resounding smack.

'I've got it!' she says, her eyes glinting with mischief. 'Sure Saoirse, you can all RETIRE when your motherhood book becomes a bestseller!' Then she cracks up, doubling over with the 'hilarity' of her joke because my mother, along with mostly everyone on the planet knows that, unless you're J. K. Rowling or Stephen King, there is very little money to be made in being an author.

I raise my glass, intending to do a sarcastic 'cheers', when we both jump at the thunderous sound of one of David's enormous sneezes.

'Jesus, Saoirse. Would you ever make David another hot lemon drink before he wakes up the whole feckin' street?' she says, slurring heavily and frantically waving me towards the kitchen.

I get up and lean over and kiss her on the cheek.

'You always were a bloody lightweight,' I grin at her.

Then I think this might be a good time to try and get some more out of her about Miguel.

'So... does Miguel like the odd Baileys then?' I say casually.

She looks at me with slightly glazed eyes and mumbles something which suspiciously sounds like, 'Ah, feck off with yourself.'

I laugh as I make my way to the kitchen. She might be tipsy but she's clearly not drunk enough to confess all about her new fancy man! David's poor health notwithstanding, it's been a pretty relaxing Christmas Day all round.

34

It's 8 p.m. on New Year's Eve and the pub is buzzing. After spending the last six days playing nurse to David (if I have to make another hot lemon drink for him, I am going to kill myself) and trying to entertain Anna in prohibitively grim weather conditions, I am more than ready for a girls' night out. Even so, I feel guilty about not ringing in the New Year with David. I know my mum doesn't give a shite – she'll be in bed by 10 p.m. with a hot mug of cocoa – but I have told David to come out for the countdown if he feels up to it. At least my mum is there to babysit Anna. But he has told me, still red-nosed and pale-faced, that he's not making any promises.

The queue for the bar is four people deep, but I'm not worried because everybody knows that Irish barmen are the most efficient in the world. I push my way through the throng towards the seating booths on the right-hand side in search of the table Jen reserved for us specifically for tonight. At first glance, all the tables seem to be occupied, but then I spy a 'reserved' sign on a corner table. My heart sinks when I see that it's not empty. I'm not great at kicking people off tables or indeed anywhere else they're not supposed to be. I approach the table and three young lads with buzz-cut hairdos and different coloured shiny tracksuits (we used to call these 'youths' STVs when we were kids – silk tracksuit victims) look up and glare at me.

'Excuse me,' I say. 'But I think this is my table.'

The one in the shiny blue tracksuit picks up his pint of cheap cider (I can smell it even from this distance) and takes a casual sip.

'Your table, is it?' he says. 'Buy it yourself, didja?'

Oh great. A trio of smartarses – just what I need.

'It has a "reserved" sign on it,' I say, primly, all too aware of how pathetic this sounds.

'Wha'? This one?' shiny green tracksuit says, picking up the paper sign and slowly ripping it in half.

The other two burst out laughing, high-fiving each other in triumph.

Then yellow tracksuit leans over, clearly determined to have his say.

'Look, love, we were here first, so feck off and get another table.'

Defeated, I turn to go, when a familiar voice stops me in my tracks.

'Jesus Christ – would you get the FUCK off our table or I'll call the guards!'

It's Dee, sporting a new short, pixie haircut, looking every bit as angry as she was last summer in Wexford when she ran her buggy over my foot.

The three youths take one look at her rage-filled eyes, grab their pints and move off quickly towards the bar.

'That was amazing!' I say, throwing my arms around Dee.

She grimaces.

'Listen, with the day I've had, they had no chance,' she says, sitting down at the corner of the leather booth behind the wooden table.

I grab the stool opposite and ask her if she's all right, but, before she can respond, Jen arrives with a big, 'Howerya bitches,' looking as fabulous as ever in a gold sparkly bat-winged top paired with black leather trousers.

I jump up immediately and throw my arms around her.

'Look at the colour on you,' I say, taking a step back to look at her properly. She is gorgeous and tanned from Dubai and looking as stunning as ever.

Dee remains seated but smiles and gives her a little wave.

Jen throws her bag on the table and tells Dee how much she loves her new haircut.

'Well, I have no time to be washing and drying long hair and the baby was pulling the shite out of it anyway, so I decided to get it all chopped off.'

'Right!' Jen says, clearly not knowing what to do with Dee's dark mood.

Then there's a few moments of tense silence, which I decide to break with the usual time-honoured tradition.

'Shots!' I say, grabbing my handbag.

Dee immediately perks up.

I take a step towards the bar, but Jen clutches my arm.

'It's table service, Saoirse.'

I feel my eyes prickle with tears. Even Dee looks a bit emotional. Table service. On New Year's Eve. How the hell has she managed it?

Then Jen stands up in all her magnificence, and waves to one of the hassled-looking barmen wearing a wine waistcoat and he gives her a quick nod. I notice a few heads turning in her direction, which isn't unusual given her sheer beauty, but this time even the girls are taking notice, falling into deep whispers. It suddenly occurs to me that Jen has become recognisable from her fashion reporting on Ireland's most popular TV show. Maybe that's why she's getting table service. Either way, I am never falling out with her. How brilliant is it to have a celeb as your best friend!

It doesn't take any more than one shot for Dee to tell us the reason for her bad mood.

'I'm going to kill Sean,' she says.

Husband troubles – I should have known.

Jen takes one look at Dee, rises to her feet and waves to the barman, oblivious to the stares she is attracting. Then she cups her hands to her mouth and shouts, 'Listen, just bring the bottle.'

The barman gives her another quick nod, and before we know it, we have a full bottle of vodka sitting in the middle of the table. Jen fills the glasses quickly and tells Dee to go on.

Dee downs her shot like water and shakes her head.

'He can be such a bastard,' she says, slamming her glass down on the table.

'What's he done?' Jen says.

'So I haven't been on a night out since the summer with you guys, right? And he's known about me coming up to Dublin for New Year's for feckin' weeks, okay?'

Jen and I nod. She's right – no doubt about it.

'So what does he do?'

Whatever it is, it's not good.

'As he's "hamstrung", as he likes to call it, by the kids, and he can't go out, he decides to invite the lads over.'

'Ah, Jesus,' I sigh.

'Exactly. Which means that they're all going to get shitfaced; they'll wake up the kids, and I'll have to deal with crankiness tomorrow because he'll be dying of a hangover.'

That's not good. If David did that I'd kill him too.

'I mean, what a prick,' she mutters, pouring another drop of vodka into her glass.

Then she looks at our still brimming glasses and says crossly, 'Are you drinking those or what?'

Jen and I knock them back quickly, and she fills our glasses again.

'So, what are you going to do?' I say.

'I don't know, Saoirse. What do you do with a selfish—'

And then she drops the c-word.

'Ah, now,' Jen cuts in immediately.

'There's no need for that,' I add, because despite my fondness for swearing, the c-word is firmly out of bounds.

Dee's face reddens.

'Ah sorry, I know... it's just been a shitty few days. So stressful... I nearly put my head in the oven with the turkey on Christmas Day.'

This sets off a whole range of stories about Christmas Day and all its woes. I tell them all about Mass and Miguel, Mum's mystery man, and they both love the idea of old people finding love, and then Jen proposes a toast to Brenda and Miguel, and we clink glasses and do another shot, and the room becomes fuzzier around the edges and suddenly everyone is in flying form.

Then it's Jen's turn to tell us about her Christmas Day, which she spent with her parents, and she has Dee and myself in stitches telling us how her mother had got so tipsy, she'd forgotten to turn on the oven, and they'd ended up eating the turkey at midnight. Then we all decide we need to take a break from the shots in case we peak too soon, and Jen, slightly more unsteadily this time, rises to her feet, and shouts 'Water!' at the barman.

When we're all settled again, Dee asks me how Anna is getting on at school.

'Fine,' I say. I could have stopped there. After all, Jen has no kids and zero interest in having any, and Dee's two aren't old enough for school yet. But before I know it, I'm telling them all about Mr Russell and Sho, and needless to say I am drowned out by the raucous laughter that follows.

'Ah, Jesus,' Dee says, wiping a tear from her eye. 'That's fantastic.'

Jen, equally as mirthful, turns to me and says, 'Of all the places to discover an ex. That's just unlucky, Saoirse.'

'And how's David?' Jen says. 'Will we see him tonight?'

'I'm not sure,' I say. 'He's smothered in cold. I'd say it's all the stress of losing his job, and then the whole drama with Bonnie and Rose.'

I've already filled them in over text about Rose's surprise emotional outburst at our house just over a week ago.

'Any jobs on the horizon for David?' Dee says, pouring another round of shots for us all.

'No, not yet. Things haven't been easy since I lost the job with Sebastian Fox,' I say, knocking my shot back quickly.

'Sounds like you were dead right to give the money back to Rosalind,' Jen says.

'I know,' I say, 'It's not easy financially but hopefully something will pop up soon, I—'

I am interrupted by piercing microphone static.

'Sorry we're late, folks!'

We crane our necks and see a traditional Irish band, setting up at the back of the pub.

Jen groans and says, 'I hope they're not too loud.'

Dee and I nod sombrely because we're at the age where we want a conversation over loud music any day of the week. I glance at my watch.

'Jesus! It's almost 10 p.m.!' I say, jumping up so fast the table wobbles.

'What?' Dee says, with an incredulous look on her face.

I grab my bag and dig out my phone.

'It's almost the New Year in South Africa! I promised Bea I'd call her!'

Pressing WhatsApp audio, I hold the phone to my ear, just as the band strikes up its first – very loud – diddle-aye tune. I can't hear a bloody thing. So I press the end button, and signal to Dee and Jen that I'm going outside and they both give me a thumbs-up. I push through crowds of merry faces singing along to familiar tunes, until I finally reach fresh air. Freezing air, that is – in my haste, I have forgotten to bring my coat with me. Shivering, I try Bea again this time trying a video call and she picks up.

The first thing I notice is that she is wearing a light peach T-shirt. Of course – it's lovely and warm over there. I'm jealous rotten.

'Happy New Year!' I say.

She laughs and puts a finger over her mouth.

'I have to be quiet – Harry's fallen asleep beside me,' she says, moving the camera over to show me Harry nestled against her waist.

'Where are you?' I say, quieter now.

'I'm in our back garden on the swing chair. My mother is having a New Year's party where she is serving only plant-based options. Harry was, of course, outraged by the lack of party food, so I brought him out here to calm him down. Then he fell asleep, probably out of hunger.'

I giggle.

'Poor Harry.'

'Poor Harry, my eye,' she says dryly. 'He's been ruined by

Ryan's parents. Honestly, even I had to put a stop to all the crap they've been feeding him.'

'So everyone is getting on well, then?'

'Actually, it's been good,' Bea smiles. 'Ryan's parents were always so lovely to me – it's not their fault their son turned out to be a ratbag. They are also brilliant at taking the piss out of Ryan's American accent.'

'How are you getting on with Ryan?'

'It's fine – we'll never be best friends but we're keeping it civil for Harry's sake.'

Then she asks me about Christmas and we chat for a bit until she cocks her head to one side and says, 'Saoirse, your lips are turning blue.'

She's right – if I stay out here any longer, I'll turn into a block of ice. I open my mouth to say my goodbyes, but she puts up one finger.

'Before you go, I have some good news,' she says, smiling.

'Oh, yes?' I say, intrigued.

'So a few days ago I got a voicemail from the council. Apparently, a space has come up for Harry at Woodvale Primary starting next term.'

'Oh, my God!' I squeal. 'Tell me you took it!'

'I bit their hand right off!' she says, laughing.

'This is the best news!' I say, delighted to finally have an ally at Anna's school.

'I know!' she says, her eyes bright. 'Maria won't have to do that stupid drive to Surrey any more and I'll be able to do some of the drop offs and pick-ups when I'm working from home.'

Gosh – Bea at the school gates. Watch out Organics!

'I can't believe you never told me you were applying to other schools!' I say, wagging a finger at her.

'To be honest, I wasn't sure if he'd get in anywhere.'

Then she pulls a face.

'I haven't told my mum yet,' she whispers. 'She's going to kill me for taking Harry out.'

'Maybe she'll be happy that you're saving her a ton of cash!' I say.

Bea shakes her head. 'I doubt it!'

Then something else occurs to me.

'Did you tell her anything about the miscarriage?' I say, softly.

'No, I decided not to,' she says, thoughtfully. 'Besides, she'd only devise some miscarriage recovery diet based on blended beetroot or some shit.'

I smile. It's good to hear her make jokes after everything she has been through.

'Now go back inside!' she says. 'And Happy New Year yourself!'

I blow her kisses and then end the call.

The noise hits me as soon as I pull open the heavy pub door. A particularly popular Irish song is being played by the band, and people are singing, stamping, drinks in hand – beer flying everywhere. I make my way back to Jen and Dee, who are busy shouting at each other across the table. By the dazed looks in their eyes, and the disproportionate greeting ('Way-haaay Saoirse!') many more shots have been consumed since I've been gone. It's time to play catch up. I pour a bit of fiery liquid into the glass and take a moment to feel the warmth through my body, enjoying the feeling of finally thawing out.

'We're talking about sex!' Dee shouts.

'Not that I'd remember what that is,' Jen says, wryly.

I haven't wanted to ask, but clearly she hasn't met anyone since she was 'jilted' over the summer.

'You're gorgeous!' I say, blowing her a kiss.

'Jesus, I'LL shag you!' Dee says, stroking Jen's hair.

Oh, Christ. Things are getting messy. I grab the bottle again and do another shot.

Jen moves her head gently away from Dee and says, 'Dee told Sean to leave her alone and feck off with a sex robot instead.'

We all break into fits of laughter.

'Honestly, I'm done with him in the bedroom. Done!' Dee slurs, swaying in her seat.

I feel the alcohol kick in.

'Do you know what you need to do?' I shout across the table to Dee.

Dee shakes her head.

'Brunch sex!' I shout, just as the music stops.

I ignore the laughter from a few people around us. I have no time to be embarrassed – the loud music might start up again at any minute and then my theory will have no chance of landing. Everybody with young children needs to know about brunch sex. But the conversation doesn't go well, and I quickly realise that brunch sex is completely impractical unless you have school-age kids and a husband who's out of work. The band strikes up again and suddenly I don't have the energy to shout any more. Looking at Jen's drooping eyes, I can see she feels the same. What is wrong with us? It's not even II o'clock. At this rate, we'll all be in bed before midnight. In the end, it's Dee who saves the day.

'Did I tell you that Sean is a night farter?'

That sets us all off and suddenly we're fighting each other to tell stories of men and their bad habits, and before we know it the music has stopped and the countdown to New Year has begun.

I stand up and strain my neck to see if I can spot David. He's probably fast asleep by now, but suddenly I really want to bring in the New Year with him. The countdown ends, and the band strikes up its own warbly version of 'Auld Lang Syne', and Dee, Jen and me tearfully hug and link arms and sing along at the top of our voices. Then I feel an arm slip through mine, and I flip around to see David grinning at me, red snotty nose and all.

'Hey, you made it!' I say, kissing him full on the mouth.

Pissed as I am, I'm going to regret that in the morning when I wake up full of flu.

He laughs and waves at Jen and Dee who give ecstatic squeals in return.

'I have some news,' he says, his voice close to my ear.

'What is it, David?' I shout impatiently.

'I've just been offered a brilliant job,' he says, proudly.

I pull my arms free and throw them around his neck.

'That's fantastic news!' I say.

Wow! Between Bea starting Woodvale Primary and David's fabulous new job, this is shaping up to be the best New Year's ever!

Then he gently takes my hands from around his neck, holds them tightly, and looks deep into my eyes.

'It's in New York.'

ACKNOWLEDGMENTS

It turns out that writing the second novel is even harder than writing the first one, especially when it's a series. Tying up all those loose ends and creating subplots that actually make sense wasn't easy, so it's a good thing we writers are not doing this all by ourselves.

There is NO WAY *The Juggle* would have made it anywhere near publication without the talented eye of my editor, Sarah Ritherdon, whose excellent insights encouraged me to go deeper. A big thank you also goes to Ellie, Nia, Megan and everyone else on the Boldwood team who work so tirelessly to champion their authors.

I also owe my agent, Bea Corlett, a debt of gratitude for her calmness, patience, and fortitude, especially when I'm in '*Why am I doing this? I must be out of mind!*' mode.

A special mention also goes to international bestselling Irish author and all-round *legend* Cathy Kelly, for her generosity, wisdom, and unconditional support. She is one of the most talented and hilarious people I have ever come across, and I feel so privileged to count her as a mentor and friend.

To my friends and family, thank you for spreading the word. My mother is still valiantly flying the flag in Ireland for my first novel, *Time Out*, and no doubt she will be as tenacious with *The Juggle*. I am forever grateful for her support.

And finally, thank you to all you fabulous readers for buying, reviewing, and blogging about my books. It is your wonderful words that chase the doubts away and keep me going.

BOOK CLUB QUESTIONS

1. What do you think are Bea's true feelings towards Ryan?

2. What do you make of the power dynamic between Saoirse and David when she takes over the role of breadwinner?

3. Who is your favourite character in THE JUGGLE?

4. When it comes to parenting styles, who do you relate to more? Saoirse or the Organics?

5. What do you think of the relationship between David and Rose? What do you think Rose's perspective on the relationship would be?

6. In THE JUGGLE, Saoirse takes a dubious ghostwriting job mostly for the money - does this make Saoirse's character more likeable or less?

7. If you have read TIME OUT, do you think the author's writing has developed in THE JUGGLE?

8. Was there anything in particular that surprised you about Saoirse's actions in THE JUGGLE?

9. How does David's relationship develop with Bea in THE JUGGLE?

10. TIME OUT ends on a cliff hanger. Does THE JUGGLE deal well with tying up all the loose ends?

MORE FROM EMMA MURRAY

We hope you enjoyed reading *The Juggle*. If you did, please leave a review.

If you'd like to gift a copy, this book is also available as an ebook, digital audio download and audiobook CD.

Sign up to Emma Murray's mailing list for news, competitions and updates on future books.

http://bit.ly/EmmaMurrayNewsletter

Have you read *Time Out*? Discover the first laugh-out-loud instalment of Saoirse's story.

ABOUT THE AUTHOR

Emma Murray is originally from Co. Dublin and moved to London in her early twenties. After a successful career as a ghost-writer, she felt it was high time she fulfilled her childhood dream to write fiction.

Visit Emma's website: http://www.emmamurray.net/

Follow Emma on social media:

 facebook.com/EmmaMurrayAuthor

twitter.com/murrayemma

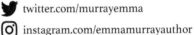 instagram.com/emmamurrayauthor

bookbub.com/authors/emma-murray

ABOUT BOLDWOOD BOOKS

Boldwood Books is a fiction publishing company seeking out the best stories from around the world.

Find out more at www.boldwoodbooks.com

Sign up to the Book and Tonic newsletter for news, offers and competitions from Boldwood Books!

http://www.bit.ly/bookandtonic

We'd love to hear from you, follow us on social media:

facebook.com/BookandTonic

twitter.com/BoldwoodBooks

instagram.com/BookandTonic

Printed in Great Britain
by Amazon